Jordan and Darrel found the room where Althea was being held.

D1601402

Darrel's hand tu[...]
times before he caught the string to release the
latch. He gave the door a little shove—it swung
open easily.

Inside they found the Inquisitor and Ivo
right beside him brandishing a knife long enough
to be called a sword. The Inquisitor raised his
arms. Ivo lunged. Darrel couldn't move a muscle;
confusion or magic, he didn't know which.
Jordan surged forward. Darrel managed to find
his legs and started for the bed.

"Thea—come on. Let's get out of here!"

Althea saw him. He'd swear she saw him
and recognized him, then she made a horrible
face and began to scream—a single unwavering
note that hurt his ears. Jordan was on the floor
wrestling Ivo for the knife; and the Inquisitor
was three unfamiliar syllables into a magic spell.

Darrel dove for the door as a singularly foul
odor filled the room behind him. Too frightened,
he scrambled to his feet and up the column to the
roof without once glancing back to see what had
become of Jordan.

Althea kept on screaming. She hadn't paused
for a breath . . .

ALSO BY LYNN ABBEY

THE FORGE OF VIRTUE

Published by
WARNER BOOKS

LYNN ABBEY

THE TEMPER OF WISDOM

WARNER BOOKS

A Time Warner Company

WARNER BOOKS EDITION

Questar® is a registered trademark of Warner Books, Inc.

Cover design by Don Puckey
Cover illustration by Janny Wurts

Warner Books, Inc.
666 Fifth Avenue
New York, N.Y. 10103

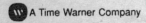 A Time Warner Company

Printed in the United States of America

First Printing: January, 1992

10 9 8 7 6 5 4 3 2 1

Dramatis Personae

The Lead Characters: Five young people bound together by kinship, custom, and most of all by destiny.

Balthan Wanderson: The emancipated ward of Lord Iron-hawk and elder brother of Althea, Balthan is a precocious magician whose talent and ambition are both much larger than the Second Circle mysteries into which he has been initiated. He makes enemies more easily than friends, but none so powerful as the nightmare wraiths who haunted and hunted him across Britannia. In desperation, he sealed himself in a tiny, isolated cave behind a curtain of magic. He'd hoped to be rescued by the Avatar; he got his sister and her friends instead.

Jordan Hawson; Jordie: The eldest son and heir of Lord Ironhawk. His education has prepared him for the responsibilities and privileges of Britannian lordship, but his greatest aptitude dwells in his swordarm. When Althea told him that Balthan had vanished, he set out alone with notions of quest-adventure and glory swirling in his head. He got all the adventure he wanted, and more, but his hopes for glory died when he touched Balthan's curtain of magic and was blinded by it.

Darrel Hawson; Squirt: Younger son of Lord Ironhawk. Prone to mischief and his own worst enemy. His nickname, Squirt, refers not to his size, but to his ability to wiggle out of trouble. Ignored and neglected except when he's done something wrong, he idolizes his brother Jordan who is, in almost every respect, his opposite. No one invited him to join the search for

Balthan. He needed uncanny luck to catch up with the
others—but Darrel has always had uncanny luck.

Althea; Thea: Balthan's younger sister. With her brother,
she became Lord Ironhawk's ward after the disappearance of their ne'er-do-well father, Simon. The quiet,
constrained, yet comfortable life behind the walls of
Ironhawk's estate suits her temperament—or it did until she examined her brother's talisman and realized
something terrible had happened to him. When Jordan
would not agree to rescue Balthan *her* way, she sought
the help of another. She meant to leave Jordan behind,
but he'd had exactly the same notion and they wound
up traveling across Britannia together.

Drumon the Farrier; Drum: A journeyman smith living
with his family on Ironhawk's estate. Though he's
grown up with the others, Drum sees himself as part
of a different world, the world of honest working folk
who have no use for adventure or glory. He has little
use for his landlord's sons, and less for the magician
they rescued, but they're Althea's family, and important to her. Drum would not have left his forge for
himself or for any member of his own family, but
because it was Althea who asked for help, he was ready
to leave everything on a moment's notice.

Hawksnest: The home these young people left behind and
to which they return. A large, self-sufficient estate several
days travel southwest of Britannia's capital, Britain City.
Most of Hawksnest's residents live in isolated cottages and
hamlets scattered across the vast estate, but the undisputed
heart of Hawksnest is the fortified villa where the landlord's
family lives with their privileged guests, hired retainers,
and menial servants. Clustered against the villa walls, the
foregate artisan community is an integral part of estate life
although its residents lease the land beneath their houses

and give their oaths to Britannia's various guilds rather than to their landlord neighbor.

Erwald, Lord Ironhawk: The landlord of Hawksnest, the father of Jordan and Darrel, and the guardian of Althea, he is himself a younger son of a wealthy, mercantile clan. Although he had an appetite for reckless adventure and glory in his youth, he's matured into a responsible landlord who cherishes tradition and dislikes surprises, especially from the younger generation. Before marrying and taking possession of Hawksnest, Erwald received enlightenment at four Shrines of Virtue, an accomplishment which places him high in the supposedly unstructured ranks of Britannia's Peers of Virtue.

Barbara, Lady Ironhawk: Erwald's wife and mother of his sons. A Peer in her own right although she received enlightenment at only one of the eight shrines before abandoning her quest. The only child of aging parents and the last of a proud, ancient, but impoverished lineage, Barbara inherited the estate and its debts. She married Erwald, and his family's money, willingly and has never regretted her decision.

Britannia: An island continent where magic is part of the natural world. For more than a hundred years it has been united under the enlightened rule of a singular and remarkable man, Lord British, from whom it has taken its current name.

Lord British: Born in another, much different world. He came to Britannia—then known as Sosaria—as a young man and although he has aged somewhat in the intervening centuries, he remains a vigorous man in the prime of his life. Lord British's authority has become largely symbolic as his *Great Council* has taken over the daily governance of the land. Thus freed from ordinary responsibility, Lord British has largely devoted himself to arcane pursuits not the least of which was his exploratory expedition into the vast Maelstrom caverns, an expedition from which he has yet to return.

The Companions of Lord British: From time to time Lord British has sought kindred spirits from his own world. Some of these invited folk remained with him as his near-ageless *Companions* while others came as heroes, completing a monumental quest before returning to their otherworldly homes. No hero left a greater legacy to Britannia than the *Avatar* who personified the eight virtues of humanity and whose life and quest remains an example for all Britannia.

Lord Blackthorn: One of Lord British's Companions and a man whose genius lies in orderly administration. When Lord British left his castle to explore the underworld, he asked his trusted friend, Blackthorn, to act as his regent while he was away. As the days of Lord British's absence lengthened into weeks, then months, a change came over Lord Blackthorn. Perhaps it was the all-too-human realization that a temporary honor might well become a permanent responsibility, although others have hinted that darker powers and deep-hidden flaws in Blackthorn's character might be the true cause. Whatever the reason, Lord Blackthorn holds Britannia in a tight fist and has lost all tolerance for those who disagree with him. He has disbanded the *Great Council* and outlawed its former members. In the Council's place he's established the *Inquisition* whose many members are pledged to see that everyone obeys the regent and are empowered to interrogate and punish any citizen who does not.

One

"*I* will count to three, Jordan. Then open your eyes, and look upon the glyph. Name the runes within it as quickly as you can. Now . . . *one* . . ."

Annon of Britain whispered two syllables and released a bitter-smelling substance into the air. A shimmering golden coil rose above a rough-hewn table.

". . . *Two*. . . ."

Among Annon's five visitors, only Balthan Wanderson watched the magician's hands weaving in the candlelight rather than the emerging glyph. Balthan was himself a magician, a novice of the Second Circle. He could cast an identical In Lor light spell—it was First Circle spellcraft—and he knew how to capture a glyph on parchment—he'd been amanuensis for Annon's counterpart, Felespar of Yew. Not long ago he'd spent the better part of each day doing just that. Annon, Felespar, and other master magicians earned a good living fabricating magic scrolls for ordinary people to buy and use. Balthan had not yet been instructed in the thaumaturgical art of transmuting spells into glyphs; that was not a trick taught to Second Circle novices. Balthan Wanderson was a precocious—some said *dangerously* precocious—novice. By the time Annon lowered his arms, he knew the thaumaturgical secret of glyph-making.

". . . *Three!*"

Jordan's eyes opened; Balthan inverted an hourglass. The dark, musty loft was silent as Jordan stared at the slowly rotating glyph. Annon; Balthan; Balthan's sister, Althea; Jordan's brother, Squirt; and Drumon the Farrier looked between their companion and the magic.

Three weeks had passed since they rescued Balthan from a harpy-guarded cave in the northern wilderness. The first was a week of frustration in Yew where luck and fortune ignored them. The second two were spent on the road between Yew and Britain. With food and sleep, Balthan's health had restored itself. But Jordan remained intractably, miserably blind, although not, he insisted, midnight blind. When his eyes were open he saw brilliant, exploding spheres. From time to time these explosions released a frozen image: a clumsy portrait of something that had already happened, something his blind eyes had seen and his memory retained.

Althea consoled Jordan in his misery. She guided him through the tasks that were suddenly mysterious or impossible, but she couldn't understand why he kept a blindfold knotted tightly over his eyes. Any vision, even exploding spheres or still-life memories, should be better than the midnight blindness Jordan fabricated with the blindfold—until she watched him staring at the glyph.

Jordan's pupils swelled until they consumed the golden hazel iris. Then they began to pulse each in different, meaningless rhythms. Althea whimpered, and ran away. The sound drew Jordan's attention.

"Watch the glyph!" Annon reprimanded.

Jordan blinked and obeyed.

"C'mon, Jordan. Can't you see it yet?" Squirt's eyes were as wide as his brother's and focused on the glyph, as if they could, together, overcome malingering magic. "Please?"

Annon quashed the boy with a scowl. The glyph shivered. Magic decayed quickly; In Lor light could no longer be kindled from the rippling glyph. Balthan glanced at the sand in the lower bulb and worried that Jordan would not see the runes before the glyph faded completely. He looked at Annon, hoping to read the Councillor's thoughts on his face.

Would Annon blame *him* for Jordan's affliction? Sleep-starved and hounded by wraith-shadows, he had not been sane when he invoked the potent scrolls he'd taken from Felespar's workroom in his escape. He'd expected to hide behind their magic for years, perhaps centuries; he had certainly not expected the companions of a childhood he routinely denied to come and rescue him. Even if his wraith-shadow persecutors were not bound to Regent Blackthorn, and were not the root cause of Blackthorn's quarrel with the Council of Magicians, it would be unjust for Annon to blame him for something he could not have foreseen. Justice, as Balthan understood it, should bring congratulations. After all, his desperate commingling of light, annihilation, and the negation of time had created an effective defense Annon himself might find useful if Blackthorn's minions got too close. —

There was, however, Jordan—whose bulging, pulsing eyes seemed ready to pop from his skull. With undeniably virtuous intentions, Jordan had breached Balthan's defenses and by that act lost everything he cherished: his sword mastery and his Virtue Quest.

As the furrows above Annon's wire-bound spectacles deepened, Balthan made a silent orison: *Destiny—bring back Jordan Hawson's sight . . . please.*

"I see it!" Jordan exalted. "Ih-n . . . T-ih-m!" The glyph vanished, so did Jordan's joy. He knew the names of all the common spells. He looked across the table, where he remembered hearing Balthan's voice. "Create time—is that possible?"

Balthan didn't answer. He stood beside Annon with the hourglass now. In another few moments Jordan might remember that he'd questioned empty air, not Balthan Wanderson. Years of martial training had hardened Jordan against physical pain; the blindness had made him brittle. His embarrassment would resolve into rage or despair. Balthan could bear the abuse of his foster-brother's rage, it was the other that unnerved him. He held his breath.

In the unnatural silence, Jordan did not need to wait for memory. His face darkened. He pounded the table with his fist. "Hythloth take you all!"

Althea scurried to Jordan's side. "In Lor: Create Light," she whispered. "The runes were poorly formed. I could hardly read them myself." She tried to pull his fist away from the table. It might have been the Hawksnest tower for the success she had. "Don't get so angry," she pleaded. "There's nothing to be gained by anger."

"There's nothing to be gained anywhere! Nothing!" Jordan surged to his feet. "Damn magicians and all their magic."

"We'll leave." Althea put her hands around Jordan's waist to guide him. She touched him freely now that he was less than whole. Less of a threat to her virtue. "You don't need someone telling you what you already know—"

"A moment, my dear lady." Annon's voice was soft, polite, and powerful. "I would like to tell Jordan what I've learned—even if he does already know it."

Althea hid her hands in the frayed sleeves of her gown. Jordan confronted Annon's voice. His eyes no longer pulsed.

"You're not blind, Jordan Hawson. There is nothing wrong with your eyes, nor your mind. Your affliction rises solely from miscast magic. You understand that a healer might leave an arrowhead in the wound rather than cause more harm removing it—?''

"Magic's not like an arrowhead!" Squirt interjected. "Magic's not *real*, it's just spells. Can't you say something to make it go away?"

Annon shook his head sadly. He liked the boy; he liked and pitied all of them. "Once cast, a spell is as real as an arrowhead, Darrel." Removing his spectacles, the magician massaged the bridge of his nose. "Imagine I have wine and water. After I pour the wine into the water, is there any way I can get the wine back again?"

The boy's jaw dropped; Balthan took up the argument for him: "Distill the mixture. The elements will separate—"

"I did not ask how to get *water* back," Annon chided. "The merchants of Trinsic might pay you well for your brandy but the *wine* would remain lost."

Balthan grimaced. "The question remains: can a spell be withdrawn? and the answer is yes."

"It's quibbling, I know, but you did not release *a* spell from the scrolls you filched. I distinguished three by name, and others I could not decipher—"

"Dust-be-gone and stir-the-pot to raise the barrier." Balthan's pride was evident.

A bemused smile ghosted across Annon's face. "You mixed linear magic with Eighth Circle scrollcraft?" It was replaced by a sterner expression. "A mage who knew what he was doing when he did that, that mage might be Anabarces reborn, but you are merely a fortunate fool and a danger to those around you. You overreach yourself, Balthan Wanderson. You'll lose it all," the Councillor warned.

Annon opened one of the countless drawers in his sandalwood box—the signature possession of a mage of the Sixth or higher Circle. The contents of the drawer glowed. Balthan could not guess what spell it was, though he could be certain there was nothing in his novice's sack to counter it. He wanted everything magic had to offer and he wanted it badly enough to swallow his pride.

"I was wrong," he said thickly. "I am a fool. I'm sorry. I accept your judgment, your pun—"

"Don't plead or apologize," Jordan interrupted. "It wasn't your fault. I don't blame you for my destiny. You were desperate; you were justified. You told me he could help, so we came. That, and only that, was your mistake. He's no help. He says I'm not blind. He's a fine one to call you a fool. Let's go."

Jordan took a long step in the wrong direction. Althea led him back to the stool.

The wooden spindles of the hourglass snapped in Balthan's hands. "No, there's more. The magic's inside you, like poison. I can't withdraw it, and neither can Annon, but magic doesn't last forever. It can't. It fades and nothing makes magic fade faster than more magic." Balthan dared to look at Annon. "When he stared at the glyph, and his eyes pulsed—that was magic against magic, wasn't it?"

Annon dropped a panel over the glowing drawer. Everyone blinked at the sound. Those who could see when they reopened their eyes, saw that the sandalwood box was half its former size.

"Well, wasn't it?" Balthan demanded.

"I've never thought about it—but, yes, probably. Although I should think that Jordan himself, with his will to see the glyph, ground them against each other. Spells do not of themselves oppose each other—or how could you have wrought your barrier?"

Squirt grasped the significance of Annon's words. "Jordie—*you* can make it go away. You can wear it down until you can see again. All you have to do is *try*!"

"Is that true?" Jordan looked at Balthan; Balthan looked at Annon.

"Yes, that is true," Annon poured a wealth of reservations into the words.

"There's more," Jordan guessed. "It's true, but not true enough. That's magic for you: a thousand ways to slay a man, but only one to bring him back . . . and no one dares to use it." He did not see Annon's scowl and was not quieted by it.

"Balthan admits he used an An Tym scroll to negate time. An Tym is an illusion—the power of time cannot be negated—but, as Anabarces meant it to be cast, An Tym surrounds the spellcaster with an anomaly in which time—perceived as movement—stands still. The illusion does not last long but, as I'm sure your swordmasters taught you, a single moment can be the difference between life and death—"

"This *illusion*'s lasted three weeks."

"Our clever friend has found a way to make An Tym last longer by reducing the anomaly to the size of a dust mote.—That is what you did, isn't it?"

Balthan moistened his lips. "Smaller."

"How much longer?" Jordan demanded.

Annon rephrased his question: "How much smaller?"

Balthan stared at his feet. "I don't know."

"Anabarces!" Annon gestured at the ceiling. "How can you not know?"

Balthan was saved from further humiliation when Jordan's fist struck the table. "What are you talking about? Answer me, either of you! Am I going to be restored tomorrow? Or am I going to be flash-blind the rest of my life?"

"That seems to be exactly what your foster-brother doesn't know," Annon said.

"You have to fight it, Jordan." Balthan found his voice and conviction. "It won't last as long as it could, if you fight it tooth and nail."

Jordan's exploding spheres revealed the magicians as they had been moments ago: confronting each other above the glowing sandalwood box. His self-pity was transformed into fury. "The world would be a better place without your

kind," he snarled as he searched for the blindfold. "None
of this could have happened without magicians. Balthan
couldn't make a talisman to lure us on a wild quest. By the
Eight, the Three, and the One-All-Around—Annon, you
wouldn't be outlawed and hiding, because there'd be no
Words of Power for the regent to demand from you. Britannia would be ruled by its peers, not master magicians and
strangers from another world." He uprooted a tuft of hair
knotting the blindfold; everyone but him flinched. "No
moon gates, no Avatar telling us how to live—"

"That's enough!" Annon clapped his hands. The sound
was louder than it should have been, reminding them that
magic did exist and the Councillor was among its foremost
practitioners. "You've every reason to be angry, but no
excuse for sedition—not now, not in Britain City, nor anywhere else. Balthan's told you the truth. Put your anger into
fighting the magic within you. No one can tell you how long
it will take, but it *will* take longer if you act like a fool. Go
home. Your life isn't over—don't throw it away."

The stool tipped when Jordan stood up. He stumbled over
its legs, then kicked it across the loft, narrowly missing
Squirt.

"Be careful, you'll hurt yourself," Althea soothed.

Jordan allowed her to guide him to the ladder.

Annon frowned. There was magic in Britannia, but no
clairvoyance. The only sense of the future Annon had was
an altogether human foreboding that these five young people
had gotten themselves enmeshed in the chaos sweeping the
realm in the wake of Lord British's disappearance. For their
sakes, he hoped they returned safely to Hawksnest. Belatedly, he noticed they were gaunt as well as travel-weary.
Their clothes were not merely stained, but threadbare.
"You've chosen to go hungry rather than let Lord Ironhawk
know where you are, or what has happened to you," he
concluded aloud. "You're penniless."

"I've got a year's savings in Yanno Goldsmith's vault in

Yew," Balthan snarled. "And when I went in to claim it, he swore I was an imposter. When I *proved* myself, he threatened to turn me in—"

"Yanno's loyal," Annon interrupted with unchallenge-able certainty. "*I* told him to keep an eye out for you. *You're* the one we doubted. You disappeared under suspi-cious circumstances."

Balthan ground his lower lip between his teeth. Would anyone ever believe his story that shadowed evil accompa-nied Blackthorn that fateful night when the regent came to take the Word of Power from Felespar? Balthan recognized Blackthorn's shadows as the wraiths who haunted his dreams. He hadn't mentioned the dreams to Annon and—judging from the edge in the Councillor's voice—that decision had been wise. But wise or not, silence and meek-ness galled Balthan to the core.

"I told you what happened. Felespar trusted me. Be-sides—the silver belongs to me."

Annon raised his hand. "Felespar's a prisoner of the Inquisition; you're not. It raised questions."

The loft was filled with dazzling light. When everyone recovered, the sandalwood box was opened up like a count-ing board. Annon extracted and divided a small pile of coins. "I cannot see you all horsed, but coaches still travel the Old Paladin's Road. This should buy an inside seat for your lady, roof passage for the rest of you, and a daily meal at the charterhouses."

Annon gave the larger division to Balthan who clutched the coins and meant to stash them in the leather pocket beneath his shirt without shaming himself by counting them, but Drum, who'd said nothing at all since they'd arrived, foiled the young magician's plans.

"If the Councillor has no objections, I'll take my share. I've no mind to sit on a coach roof when my feet will serve and I'm indebted to my guild." He plucked two silver coins off Balthan's palm and was reaching for a third when the magician closed his fist. "I owe one and a half crowns . . ." the smith muttered.

Jordan reached for Balthan, missing him by an arm's length. "Give him what he needs to settle his debts; we'll walk partway. I thank you for your generosity, Lord Councillor, but we're in no hurry. The more time before I meet my lord father, the better my chances of seeing him—isn't that right?"

All of the coins in Balthan's fist didn't make one gold crown. Jordan was the only one who hadn't seen that, but for his sake no one said anything. Althea led Jordan to the ladder. Squirt hooked his fingers in the corners of his mouth. He made a demon's face at Drum before scampering to the ladder.

The farrier was genuinely puzzled: "My guild debt is one and a half crowns," he repeated. "Nothing changes that."

"No, nothing changes that," Annon agreed mildly.

Feeling vindicated, Drum headed for the ladder, leaving Balthan alone with the Councillor.

"Try to persuade your friends to take the coach—"

"I'm not going. I'm staying here . . . with you."

Annon closed and reclosed his box, shrinking it and re-shaping it until it could be hung from a belthook. "I have no need for an amanuensis. Your place is at Hawksnest."

"I didn't mean grinding reagents or illuminating scrolls. You're not alone against the Inquisition. Perhaps I was wrong about Yanno—but I know we were spied on in Yew. We hadn't been in Britain City an hour before we were spotted. There's a resistance forming, and you're near its head. I want to join. I saw wraiths with Blackthorn that night, I swear that I did. I can recognize them. I've felt them overhead when miasma blankets the cities with madness. The wraiths *are* miasma: you didn't know that before. You know you need me; there's no one else who knows what I know."

"Lord Blackthorn does," Annon said simply. "Lord

British trusted Lord Blackthorn enough to leave him regent. If Lord British could not sniff out corruption in a Companion—If a Companion of Lord British could not *resist* the corruption, how did you manage it?''

Balthan had no answer. He folded his hands in supplication. "My lord, I need to clear my name. Set guards around me; charm away my will—but give me a chance—"

"If you want to clear your name, do what you're told: go to Hawksnest. Stay out of sight. Stay out of trouble." He lifted Balthan's chin; their eyes met. "I believe you. I'll be your advocate. Anabarces' restless ghost, Balthan: you say you know what these wraiths can do to a man's will. Try to understand my caution. Patience and obedience will win your cause."

Balthan slung his sack over his shoulder and pulled a feathered hat down to his eyebrows. "Don't make me wait forever." It was a plea, not a threat.

"I won't make you wait one moment more than is necessary—no longer than Jordan Hawson waits for his vision to return."

"If he keeps that damn rag tied over his eyes, he'll never get it back."

"Then persuade him to untie it."

The loft was silent. The sounds of the young people had completely faded.

"Another false trail. Another false hope."

The voice came from the rafters. Annon spun around, startled, but not frightened.

"Shamino, my friend . . . When did you arrive?"

Lean, pale, and ageless, Lord British's Companion and mentor leapt lightly to the floor. "Before your other guests. So, you believe Balthan Wanderson?" The ranger was plainly skeptical.

"I never believed he betrayed Felespar. As for the rest, it tallies with all we've learned these months since Lord

British vanished. Blackthorn is possessed; whatever possesses him cannot manifest itself physically, though by Destiny and Virtue, it is trying.''

"Can you believe that overreaching whelp resisted it?''

"I believe he sought, and received, Felespar's help. I suspect Balthan Wanderson will be forever ambitious, arrogant, and overreaching—that barrier he made was sheer genius—but evil? I think not. He's stood in the Flame of Virtue, remember, and survived.''

"Then why send him away?''

"I know he's been tempered in the Flame, but he doesn't. Nothing will strengthen him like a few seasons with the foster-brother his genius blinded.''

"Jordan Hawson? It's too bad—he had promise.''

"*Has* promise, my friend, Jordan Hawson has promise so long as he doesn't lose heart. Once he's back at Hawksnest and reconciled with his father, he'll come around.'' Annon watched Shamino frown. "Tell me—could a Companion be corrupted?''

Shamino's frown deepened. "We're ordinary people, Councillor. That we age so slowly is a quirk, an accident—sometimes a curse. One of us could be very corruptible and very skilled at concealing that corruption. If Blackthorn's embraced manifest evil, we're in for a long ordeal. He's already recruited enough derelict humanity to make an army of Inquisitors.''

"Our Resistance will grow by itself . . .'' Annon—ever the optimist—countered.

"It should. It may. But evil is attractive and uncertainty feeds oppression. I don't think we'll turn Blackthorn's flank. Innocent folk embrace his cause, Annon, they embrace his uncompromising laws. They welcome the Inquisitors.''

"We're lucky, then, that so many live on peerage estates beyond the crown's reach and grasp.''

Shamino shook his head. "By harvest every estate will play the host to Blackthorn's guests, will they or nil they.

The largest find themselves harboring one already—including Hawksnest.''

''Ironhawk's a doughty plodder for Virtue. One miscreant Inquisitor won't push him off course.''

''I saw the man they sent: his name is Lohgrin. He worked in the chancellory, before that he came from Verity Isle. He's a piece of work, born to wear black robes.''

The Councillor's shield of optimism slipped. ''Lohgrin? I knew a Lohgrin when I was on Verity Isle at the Lyceum. Brilliant in a way. A bit like young Wanderson, but deviant, cruel. He would not be purged of his vices. The masters turned him out. That was twenty years ago.'' Annon quenched his doubts with one of the Avatar's maxims: ''Only Virtue endures.''

Shamino had heard the Avatar speak those confident, reassuring words more than a hundred years earlier. Britannia needed no gods because Britannia had Virtue. Evil ravaged, evil destroyed, and evil might shine with a fearsome light, but in the end, evil consumed itself. Only Virtue nurtured, sustained, and endured. The ranger assured himself his faith in the power of Virtue was unshaken; but doubts were finding fertile soil. Hadn't he just told Annon that the Companions were not immune to corruption? Hadn't he known that all along? Lord British's belief in Virtue was pure and adamant; it had created the Avatar. Shamino believed in Lord British's Virtue.

Lord British had vanished without a trace six months ago.

A gloomy pall permeated the loft. The air did truly thicken and turn malignant in Britain City and elsewhere. Miasma, it was called, and it stoked humanity's basest instincts, but this was not miasma.

''Still no sign of our Lord British?'' the Councillor asked, already knowing the answer.

Shamino shook his head slowly. He had followed Lord British's trail through Spiritwood and into the Maelstrom river caverns until it became unreadable. He tracked through stench and mist to the bottom of a cataract where the trail disappeared on unyielding stone. "All I know for certain is they did not, could not, return the way they went in," he muttered. "There are other ways out—dozens, maybe hundreds. I'll cover them all, if I have to—"

Annon clapped a comradely arm around the ranger's shoulders. "What else can we do?"

Two
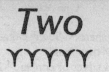

*T*he young people were in the weedy courtyard of what had been, until recently, a wealthy merchant's residence. It was abandoned now, like so many others, because of the miasma, the black fog that maddened the citizens of Britain City, then left them ashamed.

Drum took another coin from Balthan's palm. "I'm off to pay my debts—the lesser part of them. I'll return within the hour unless someone offers me wagework. Two days wages would see me clear. I'll take it if I can." The farrier shrugged in Jordan's direction. "Start without me. I'll catch up." He took off for the smithguild's freehold.

Before Althea could say anything, Balthan removed his portion and spilled the twice-reduced remnant into her hands.

"I'm not leaving without restocking my reagents." His tone allowed no argument. "I'll find an apothecary. You'll be safe enough here," he added quickly. "You're out of sight and this place has already been looted of everything worth having."

"It's *you* I'm worried about—" But Althea was already speaking to her brother's back.

"Can I have my share?" Squirt begged. "Can I? Please? Can I *hold* it in my own hand?"

"You don't need silver or copper," Jordan snarled from the low stone wall where he sat with the blindfold over his eyes.

Althea shot him a glower he would never perceive. "There's no harm letting him hold his share," she said, dealing the coins into the boy's palm. "There aren't enough left to squabble over."

Jordan stiffened. "What do you mean 'aren't enough left'? How much did Drum take? Balthan? Let him sell his clothes first, especially that damned hat." He scuffed toward them. "There's no such thing as a poor magician." His tongue made the adage into a curse.

"There is since the regent outlawed the Council," Althea reminded him. She hung the lightened purse over her belt. "Councillor Annon *was* generous. I'm sure he—"

The sounds of scattering dirt and gravel stopped her. Squirt ran away as fast as his legs could carry him.

"I won't be long!" the boy shouted. "I promise." He was gone.

"Squirt! Damn you—get back here!" Jordan ran a few steps before stumbling and crashing to the ground. Althea was beside him before he dusted himself off.

"We'll wait," she crooned, guiding him back to the wall. "We'll sit right here and wait. They'll come back. They'll *all* come back. We just have to trust them. Trust them, and be patient."

Jordan had less trust and patience than Annon's purse had gold. He resisted Althea's efforts to cheer him and in the end infected her with his sour mood. Then Drum returned, muttering that his guild would not allow him to work in Britain City.

" 'A villa tinkerer,' that's what they called me," the farrier sputtered, "—as if I were some gypsy! May the sun march backward across the sky . . . I'm ready to go home. Past ready—Where's your damn brother and Squirt?''

Althea explained and gave Drum the same advice she'd given to Jordan with no better result. The farrier paced the courtyard, pausing occasionally to fling stones at the walls. Jordan flinched each time one struck. The blinded man said nothing, but Althea caught the drift of his thoughts: frustration, jealousy, and self-pity. She gave his fist a reassuring squeeze. Jordan became unnaturally still, but not at all calm.

A solitary tear trickled down Althea's cheek. She did not blot it. Another woman might notice, but neither of her companions was remotely aware of *her* misery. The tear had dried before Balthan returned.

With a smile on his face and the feathers in his rakish hat curled over his shoulder, Balthan strode through the broken gate. He'd found an apothecary who was desperate to off-load her stock before the Inquisition paid her another mind-numbing visit.

''Her blood moss was blue with mold; and I wouldn't want to meet the dog who dug her mandrake root, but she'd have paid me to take it, if I'd bargained harder. Spider silk's her specialty—or it was—''

''We don't care what kind of bargain you got,'' Jordan groused. ''Unless you learned how to spin spider silk into gold.''

Balthan studied the scene and the players. He shed his good humor. ''Where's the boy? The thieving squirrel ran off with Annon's purse?''

Althea explained that things weren't quite that bad: they still had her share and Jordan's—but the boy could be anywhere and huge clouds were mounding above the southern horizon.

''It might be rain,'' she concluded, ''but it might be miasma. After breathing it once, we don't ever want to breathe it again. We've got to leave before curfew's rung.

We've got to find a foodseller, but we can't—not until he comes back. If he comes back. If nothing has happened to him."

Balthan unslung his sack. "The Squirt will be back," he sighed confidently. Kneeling in a spot of shade, he extracted two pots from its uncanny depths and set about making In Lor glyphs that were mostly smoke and sparks.

The clouds flattened, turned dark. Balthan raised a shimmering glyph. Drum took a nap. And finally Darrel eased up to the battered gate. Unlike Drum or Balthan, the boy studied the courtyard before announcing himself. He expected a scolding and was absently grateful that Jordan—who, beside Lord Ironhawk, was the only person fast enough to catch him and determined enough to keep him—wouldn't be able to thrash him in the bargain. The happenstance thought lingered and Darrel flushed with shame. He'd let himself be thrashed bloody if it brought back Jordan's sight.

"Your brother's back," Balthan announced for Jordan's benefit.

Anticipation shot through the courtyard. Jordan felt it; his other senses were sharpening. He stood and confidently faced Darrel.

"Get over here! What, under stars, possessed you to run off like that? Get over *here*!"

Darrel twisted his shirt until the cloth was stretched tight. They were all looking at him. Even Jordan. Especially Jordan, despite the blindfold. He gulped and trekked across the courtyard.

"I'm talking to you, Squirt! Get over here!"

By then the boy was in reach.

"I'm here," he whispered as Jordan followed the sound and caught him.

The story tumbled out. Did they remember how he had disappeared from the Hunter's Horn the day the miasma made everyone sick? Did they recall how, eluding the Inquisition, he stumbled into Annon's hiding place? Even Balthan knew that story by heart. Darrel told them what happened between the Hunter's Horn and the bolthole: how he got lost on the rooftops and found himself nose-to-glass with a toymaker's attic. He'd resisted the temptation to steal a painted warrior, and this morning, the Eye of Destiny rewarded him for his virtue.

"We walked by it. I wanted to show—*tell* you, but I knew we didn't have any money. I didn't mean to remember where it was, but when Annon gave us the money . . ."

Jordan raised the blindfold. His eyes watered, adjusting to light his mind could not perceive. "Give it over." He held out his hand.

Darrel unwound the hem of his stained and very wrinkled shirt. He removed an object that he pressed against his chest before placing it gently in Jordan's palm. Shame roughened his voice. "It's a—" he croaked.

"I know what it is!"

Jordan didn't have to wait for an explosion. He could imagine what Darrel saw in that attic, what he'd risked a thrashing to buy. After all, they were brothers. They shared a father who decreed that his sons would never be allowed to *play* with anything. The toy had been carved from lightweight wood and painted with smooth enamels. It stretched from Jordan's wrist to his fingertips, much of that a long sliver: a sword, a bastard sword like the one Jordan still slung from his hip. He closed his fist. There'd been no explosion, still he knew the toy had the yellow hair he—but not Darrel—inherited from their mother. Jordan could crush the toy; he was strongly tempted to do so.

"I wanted a harpy; but there were only dragons. I didn't have enough for a dragon." Darrel shook his shirt. Copper coins showered the ground.

Jordan couldn't breathe. He closed his eyes and willed his fingers open. "Take it." He thrust the miniature sword in Darrel's direction. "Take care of it. Don't let Lord Ironhawk find it. You're important to him now, and he'll show you no mercy.''

Carefully, Darrel returned the warrior to its safe place in the hem of his shirt. ''You'll get better, Jordie, you'll see—You'll *see*—''

Jordan wrapped the blindfold over his eyes again, ignoring his brother. He waited for another voice, but no one spoke. ''Can we get out of the city before the miasma comes?'' he asked with an irritated sigh. ''Althea says we need food. How much can we afford?''

Althea answered. ''A week's worth, and we'll need another basket—unless, Balthan, we can use your sack?'' The magician's scowl answered that question. ''And if we're going to walk, Darrel needs sandals.''

''I do not. I *like* my boots just the way they are.'' Some days back he'd slashed them to uncramp his toes, which he wiggled at her.

''You've got to wear proper shoes!'' Althea's voice rose, she was thinking of the detested buskins Drum and Jordan agreed she must wear. Despite the intervening weeks and miles, they were still stiff and unforgiving. ''You can't walk on a metaled road like that!''

''Enough!'' Jordan silenced the courtyard. He could still lead them—when he chose to. ''We'll see what's left after we buy food.''

Balthan brushed ash from his sleeves. ''I saw wagons and market stalls in the square beyond the apothecary.'' The reagents vanished into his sack without a sound.

Althea's education, under the watchful eye of Lady Ironhawk, had been as exacting as Jordan's. When she led them into the market square she knew what she wanted and didn't see anything to match it.

''They've been selling since dawn,'' she muttered. It was midafternoon. ''There's hardly anything left. We feed our pigs better—''

"We're not at Hawksnest, Thea," Jordan reminded her. "Do the best you can, we'll survive."

She picked through loaves of coarse brown bread, mold-flecked cheese, and bundled strips of smoked meat that could pass for leather. She got good bargains partly because the farmers were eager to sell before the miasma arrived and partly because Drum, looming behind her, counted every copper coin she exchanged. After they bought a basket, there were five copper pence left.

"If we could find a cobbler," Althea mused. "Maybe he could patch the ones he's got."

Darrel gestured at the threatening clouds that now covered half the sky. "There's no time!"

Althea appealed to Jordan, but the bustle of the market square left Jordan as sullen as the sky. He didn't care about Squirt's protruding toes, the number of coins left in their purse, or the brewing weather. He wanted to be left alone by friends and strangers alike. They forgot the cobbler and followed the farmers through the city gates.

In the weeks since he'd been blinded, Jordan had been advised to accustom himself to a staff. Individually and as an uncommonly united group, they'd tried to persuade him with compassion and sarcasm; neither worked. The trek from Yew hadn't been so bad: They met a farmer with an empty wagon who'd been grateful for company, but they had no similar luck at the Britain gates.

They began with Jordan hanging on to Althea's elbow. When she was wearied by his jostling, he clamped his hand on Darrel's neck. They'd gone a mile, then the sky turned black and the rain came in howling sheets. Within moments they were drenched, after that there was no reason to seek shelter. They kept going at the same tedious pace.

Summer squalls were common along Britanny Bay. The late-afternoon storms were intense, but short-lived. The travelers trudged in grim silence, expecting the weather to lift, slowly realizing that this was no ordinary squall. The ditches alongside the embankment filled quickly; the roadway became a maze of puddles through which Squirt struggled to guide Jordan.

The sun, hidden by the storm, sank below the horizon. A miserable afternoon became a treacherous evening, with them all nearly as blind as Jordan. Not that Jordan cared or noticed. The brothers were each determined to march until the other called a halt. Althea waited in vain for Drum or Balthan to intercede.

"It's getting too dark. We've got to stop before someone gets hurt." They ignored her and so, with desperate drama, Althea refused to take another step.

Balthan tugged her hand. "It can't be far to the charterhouse, a couple furlongs. You can make it."

He hadn't used that tone of voice with her since she was six and their reprobate father died. She freed herself, planting her fists on her hips. "I've walked this road before; you haven't. It's twelve miles from the gates to the first charterhouse, and that's a damn bit farther than a couple furlongs."

Balthan was owl-faced. "Thea, I've never heard you use such language."

Althea would have enjoyed his consternation more if rain weren't pelting her eyes. "And I've never drowned before. I'm wet; I'm cold; my feet hurt; and I don't care."

"A mile. Two miles—at the most." He reached for her; she eluded him. He was successful the second time. "Let's go."

Drum finally spoke: "We can camp under those trees yonder. You can make us a fire—"

"A fire? Farrier—you've lost your wits. We're going to the charterhouse." Towing Althea, Balthan surged forward. "The sooner we start—the sooner we'll get there."

Drum placed his hand on the magician's chest. "Forget

the charterhouse. We could walk all night. A three-legged ox is faster—''

"It's not Jordan's fault we're in the middle of nowhere!" Squirt broke in. "We've let *you* set the pace. You're the slow ox."

The air became dangerously thick.

"Jordie?" Althea studied him through the gloom; he was pointed at the trees. "Jordan—what should we do? Should we keep going, or camp under the trees?"

"Doesn't matter to me."

His monotone was more than she would endure. "Nothing matters to you anymore. You wouldn't care if we were all struck dead here and now!"

Her reprimand pierced Jordan's defenses. "All right, how far are the trees? What's between us and them—plowed land or fallow? Flooded?" He listened to Drum's answers: a furlong, fallow, and probably flooded. "Is there nothing else—a hedge, a wall—?"

"There's a charterhouse—with walls, a roof, and a fire to dry our clothes. All we've got to do is keep walking—''

"Forget the charterhouse, Balthan. We're camping under Drum's trees."

Cursing, clinging to each other, they made their muddy way to a grove of trees.

"At least it's warm," Althea said, scuttling to the highest ground. "Not cold and raw like it was when we left Hawksnest. And the sun will be shining tomorrow."

Althea was right about the temperature. They were wet, but not cold, beneath their woolen cloaks. She was wrong about the sun. Dawn came in shades of grey. The wind was gone; the rain continued. During the night, the field between them and the road had become a full-fledged bog.

Squirt didn't care about the weather and Jordan didn't care about anything, but the other three hesitated on the verge of the mud.

"Just my luck to return to Hawksnest in the skirt of a hurricane." A moment passed before Balthan realized Althea and Drum were staring at him.

"A hurricane?" the farrier asked anxiously. The huge, infrequent storms were rumored to be the aftermath of weather-magic gone awry.

"Maybe—the rain's steady and warm. We're well north of the worst—" He realized he wasn't reassuring the farrier at all, and got to the heart of the problem: "Magic doesn't make weather."

"You can change the way the wind blows," Althea reminded him. "You said that Felespar made more Wind Change scrolls than any other kind, and that you could cast the spell yourself . . ."

"Rel Hur works over water." Balthan gave his attention to the bedraggled feathers in his hat.

"This isn't water?" Drum gestured at the bog.

The magician adjusted his hat over his forehead. "An *ocean*, Drum. Rel Hur doesn't change the way the wind blows, it creates a very big illusion over a very big body of water."

"That's all magic is: illusions, tricks, cheats." Drum shrugged the basket straps over his shoulders. "And dishonesty." He strode into the mud before Balthan defended himself.

After the field, the road was easy. The wind gusted, bringing drenching rain, but they were never dry anyway and maintained their established pace. In the midst of a downpour they came to the charterhouse and took shelter under its eaves. Their hopes of remaining until the weather broke were dashed when Squirt peered through a window and spotted the black-robed silhouette of an Inquisitor.

"There's never just one of them," the boy said sagely. "They've all got their tail of informers."

They returned to the road.

"We'll never walk twenty miles before dark," Balthan muttered. Twenty miles was the mandated distance between charterhouses on this road. "We're going to sleep in the mud again tonight."

Althea shushed him, but he was right. Downpours dogged them all day. By late afternoon the Old Paladin's Road had been transformed into a dike meandering through flooded countryside. The ditches beside that dike were swift-running streams that threatened to breach their banks. Four of the five bedraggled travelers studied the avenue of trees reaching toward them across a newborn lake. The trees marked an estate road. The wooden bridge from their road to it had been undermined by the ditch stream. It lay in pieces a furlong downstream.

As much as they wanted the hospitality the estate would certainly give them, if they reached it, none of them dared to leave the Old Paladin's Road.

"I wish we'd stayed in Britain City," Squirt lamented. "There was nothing there worse than this."

No one gainsaid him, or acknowledged that he'd said anything at all. Drum started walking, the others followed slowly and silently. Althea walked with Jordan, leaning against him as much as he leaned against her.

The road was empty; they hadn't seen a soul since leaving the charterhouse. Balthan suggested they might camp on the road itself; that roused Jordan.

"Too exposed, too dangerous," he decreed.

"Exposed to what?" the magician retorted. "Everybody's holed up under their own roof or in a charterhouse waiting for this to break."

Jordan nudged Althea, urging her forward. "Not everyone. Teamsters live in their wagons and they drive at night if they need to make up time. We might get run over."

"Or the gypsies," Althea added thoughtfully, remembering the old crone with her painted cards and mysterious table, and wondering if the images she revealed to Althea, Drum, and Jordan were true destiny or mere conjury. "We might meet the gypsies again—"

"Or *brigands*!" Squirt slashed with an imaginary sword. "But we could be ready for them. We could kill them all and take their horses—"

"Brigands are smart enough to realize that no one with anything worth plundering would be on this road right now," Balthan snarled.

No one mentioned trolls.

Perhaps Balthan was right. They saw no other travelers the rest of the day. And when, as the gloom of evening descended, they came to a turnaround that the teamster's guild had thoughtfully protected with a dike, no one mentioned that it might be unwise to spend the night in a place where teamsters, gypsies, and worse avoided the costs and scrutiny of a charterhouse.

There were several muddy hearths in the turnaround, a small woodpile, and a stone anvil for repairing travel-worn wheelrims. Scraggly trees buttressed one end of the dike. An unspeakable cess pit flooded the other.

Jordan sniffed the fouled air and grimaced. "Set out anything hollow to collect the rain. No one drinks ground-water unless it's been boiled."

Althea queried Balthan with a glance: her hearth-fire magic was not equal to the task of making fire with sopping wood, was his? The Second Circle initiate shrugged. After securing his sack on a tree limb, he went to the woodpile. He gingerly lifted an arm-sized branch; water streamed between it and the ground.

"You're asking for miracles, not magic," Balthan complained, but he carried that branch and another to the hearth farthest from the cess pit.

Three
ΥΥΥΥΥ

The feeble fire was worth the effort, both practical and magical, it took to keep it burning. Nothing appeared as grim in the ruddy glow of firelight. Althea threaded morsels of bread, cheese, and sausage onto greenwood skewers. Savory aromas began to permeate the smoke, providing something pleasant to anticipate.

When the edge was off their hunger and the hearth was hot and dry enough to sustain the fire, Althea filled their cone-bottom pot with rainwater, soaked peas, and groats. She relished pease porridge no more than her companions, but the peasant food was all they could afford. She crumbled sausage bits into the pot to forestall—if that were possible—complaints about the bland taste.

The pot yielded a steaming, mealy porridge a few hours later. Balthan's expression, when he tasted the first spoonful, was especially eloquent, but he gagged it down. Drum and the boy were too hungry to complain. Jordan had accepted the skewered bits eagerly, but he did not react to the sound of Althea ladling out the porridge.

"Jordan? I've got your supper—" Althea was certain he heard her; she saw him flinch when she called his name, then he became still as death. She squatted beside him and used her gentlest voice. "You must be hungry."

She put the spoon in his hand and set the bowl on his thigh. Once her hands were empty, she massaged the rigid muscles in his neck. She thought that he was relaxing when, without warning, he sprang to his feet. The bowl flew into darkness; Althea landed in the mud.

"Just leave me alone!"

"I—I'm sorry. I was only helping—"

"I don't want your help . . . or anybody's!"

Across the fire, Squirt linked his fingers, appealing to the all-seeing, all-knowing Eye of Destiny. He didn't approve of the way Althea coddled his brother; it was unmanly. But what else could anyone do when Jordan refused to care for himself? Jordan *could* get better—they'd all heard the magicians say so—if he would *try*. Squirt held his breath: perhaps Jordan was ready.

"Let him starve, if that's what he wants," Drum chided. "He's not fit for honest company as he is."

Squirt breathed again. Jordan had his back to the world; Althea was crushed and pathetic. The boy watched her lips shape an orison: *Please . . . please let me help you . . .* It was not any wish he wished to see granted. He made another: *Tell her to go away!* Nothing happened. Blindness notwithstanding, Jordan had grown up and he was amenable to Althea the way cheese was amenable to mold. The boy changed his orison: *Please*, don't *let it happen to me. Don't let me surrender to some weepy woman.*

Setting his bowl aside, Balthan stretched and got to his feet. "Thea," he said wearily, "when Jordan wants your help, he'll ask for it."

Althea gasped and jumped a foot away from Jordan. She forgot she had an audience. She walked away with exaggerated grace—as if she were balancing a crystal vase atop her head.

"I'm sure you're right."

Any other time the magician would have found all this quaintly amusing. Although Drum was the oldest among them by birth, Balthan was the only one who'd lived alone in the world. He was proud of his sister's beauty, even her artless wiles. Jordan Hawson didn't have a chance. Sooner or later he'd be eating from Althea's hand—literally. There was one large, ominous problem: his sister preferred a helpless Jordan Hawson while he needed a restored and vigorous one if he were going to redeem himself with Annon.

"I'm disappointed in you, Jordan," Balthan whispered when only Jordan could hear him.

"You shouldn't be."

They weren't friends. From the moment Erwald Lord Ironhawk brought the orphans home after a Peerage Conclave, Balthan and Jordan brought out the worst in each other. Erwald responded to their natural antipathy by forcing the foster-brothers together; he believed it would strengthen their character.

"You've never given up before. This blindness—it's no worse than when Lord Ironhawk swore you'd fight left-handed until you could disarm him—"

History lay between them: experiences shared, however unwillingly, binding them more tightly than mere friendship.

"It's beyond me," Jordan confessed. "If I don't move—If I don't talk or even think, then for a moment I forget. Everything's dark and peaceful; I'm floating somewhere far away. But once I move, everything closes in on me. I imagine tomorrow—what I'll be doing . . . not doing. I panic and I want to be dead."

Balthan hunkered down. "I've been making glyphs. I've mastered it, Jordan. I can help you. Take off that damned blindfold, open your eyes, look at my glyphs, and go to war with your eyes."

Jordan reached for, and found, Balthan's arm. "Give it up, Balthan. It's not your fault. I wasn't rescuing you, I

was proving something to Lord Ironhawk. He'd cheated me
and I meant to make him pay. But it was lies, all lies. I'm
not meant for a Virtue Quest, for Hawksnest, or glory . . .
especially glory. Don't feel guilty. By the Eight, the Three,
and the One-All-Around—I'm grateful to you: I've learned
the truth.''

Balthan pondered. He could say Jordan's logic was ab-
surd—but that was too refined. He could say it was stupid—but that was insufficient. Harebrained, asinine,
wooden-headed, and puerile, each failed to capture the essence of his opinion. He wracked his memory for the perfect
word on which to impale his foster-brother. Suddenly, it
was there.

"Of all the *pissant*—''

But before Balthan could reach his conclusion, the heavy
mood of the camp was shattered by clattering harness bells
and the bawdy refrain of a tavern ballad. The singer had a
throaty voice that might belong to a man or a woman.
Balthan's perfect reply vanished from his tongue and even
Jordan turned to the raucous sound.

Jordan used Balthan's arm for support. "What the. . . ?"
His other hand touched the blindfold but stopped short of
removing it.

"A teamster," Balthan and Drum said together.

Squirt asked and was told that Lord British issued licenses
to itinerant clans, vouching for their honesty and granting
them privileges in exchange for hauling consigned cargo
across Britannia in their great wagons. They and their car-
goes had Lord British's, now Regent Blackthorn's, personal
protection and they announced themselves to any brigand
who might have the foolish notion of waylaying them with
a multitude of brass bells.

The jangling and singing came to a halt on the road above
the turnaround. Steam rose from the flanks of two huge
horses, visible in the light of mirrored lanterns bracketing
the driver's bench.

"Ware the fire! Have you room for one more?"

The voice conjured the image of a hard-living teamster, but it was a woman's voice all the same. The attention of the Hawksnest travelers met above their fire. Althea shook her head. She knew all she wanted to know about women who held their own in the world of men; she didn't want one joining them.

"Give me your word!" The driver stood on the bench of her wagon. "I'm Seanna Jormsheir of clan Coulterquit. Willie, Tom, and I would like to bed down by your fire." When she landed on the ground, she was not dwarfed by the horses.

"Are you all deaf? You heard the bells—I mind my business; you mind yours. I don't care that you've got a magician"—Balthan's head shot up—"just tell me if there's room for the team and the wagon."

Balthan and Drum looked at each other, and at Althea who scowled back at them.

Balthan shrugged. "There are three of them, and they've got the teamster's right."

"Tell her, then," Drum replied.

The magician scrambled up the embankment. "There's room, but precious little else—" A wedge of mud and gravel gave way and he reached the metaled road on his hands and knees. "You'll need scrollcraft to get your team and wagon down there without breaking something."

"So, then, do I pay you now or after?"

Balthan made his owl face.

"You are a magician, aren't you?"

As proud as he was of his talent, Balthan did not like to be recognized as a magician. Magicians were absentminded, untidy folk with stains on their threadbare robes and spider silk in their hair. Balthan cultivated the same elegance in his appearance that he sought in his craft. He might be damp and road-worn, but he did not look like a magician.

"Don't take offense. I've got no quarrel with magic or

magicians—though how you got that fire going on a night like this without a magician beggars *my* imagination. Magicians come in all shapes and sizes—just like horses.'' Seanna slapped the nearest rump for emphasis. ''Maybe there are a few traitors, maybe not. So long as they don't bother us or what we're hauling, *I* don't care which side they're on.''

The way Seanna spoke about magicians and traitors disturbed Balthan—or perhaps it was simply that when she looked him in the eye, she did it levelly. He cleared his throat. ''Well, we're nothing more than travelers a bit down on our luck and headed home. Tell Willie and Tom they're welcome to join us, but it's up to them to get this rig down safely.''

''Tell them yourself!'' Seanna leapt up to the bench, swept up the reins one-handed, and snapped them together. ''That's Erwillian. Grab his bridle; he'll follow you and Bobbintom will follow him!'' Seanna released the brake.

Horses were not Balthan's favorite animals. He knew nothing more about them than he absolutely had to—and these were the largest horses he'd ever stood beside, with hooves like platters and teeth as long as his thumb. Pride compelled him to grab the rein.

''Come easy, now,'' Balthan said weakly and pulled Willie's head around. He expected disaster at the very least, possibly death itself, but Erwillian and Bobbintom were surefooted. Balthan was drenched in his own sweat by the time the wagon was level again, but the descent had been entirely uneventful.

Squirt was awestruck. ''Did you ever see such *big* horses?'' He gaped at Balthan who did not bother answering. Willie shook free. With friendly curiosity the great horse thrust his nose at the boy and sent him sprawling.

''Jordie—you *gotta* see this,'' Squirt rhapsodized from the mud.

Blindfold in place, Jordan was already moving. Having

no desire to come between a peer and prime horseflesh, Balthan got out of his way. Vision would have been nice, but it was scarcely necessary once Jordan got within arm's reach. His hands flowed knowingly, approvingly, over the animal's flanks. When Willie swiveled his head around, Jordan knew exactly where to scratch.

The brake was set and the reins were tied, Seanna could have climbed down, but she lingered on the bench, taking the measure of her new companions. The slender dark-haired one with the ludicrous feather hat—he had to be the magician, despite his denials. The light-haired one with the rag over his eyes—there was something sad about the way he got nose-to-nose with Willie. He hadn't been blind for long—his build and movements were wrong for an invalid. The boy was lively and, by the looks of him, the brother of the blind one.

"Jordan! Be careful!"

Seanna looked to her right. Another woman was coming. A scowling, hulking man—the last of her new companions—trailed behind. She focused her attention on the woman. Delicacy of bone and manner was not an asset in a teamster. Seanna needed a man's strength to handle the rig and a man's outlook to survive. She liked her life and her freedom, but she felt an unexpected pang of envy when Althea wrapped her tiny hands around the blind man's arm and led him away.

"Willie wouldn't hurt him."

Althea glanced over her shoulder, meeting Seanna's stare and rising above it.

Lord British decreed that Britannians should pursue their aspirations. A peasant could become a Peer; the path might be steep and treacherous, but it was never barred. A woman could become a swordmaster in Serpent's Hold or place her fate in the hands of a husband. Lord British's decree made no judgments.

Althea made judgments. Who was that woman dressed in

leather? Her hair was loose, wild, and shorter than Balthan's. Her skirt barely covered her boots. She probably ate with a knife, but never a fork. She was coarse and dirty. She never had to look to someone else for sustenance and protection. Althea shuddered. It wasn't fair. She was merely doing what she did best—what she *wanted* to do—yet her cheeks were burning.

Seanna wasn't angry and certainly not ashamed—simply uneasy, the way she felt any time she encountered a woman whose skirt swirled gracefully even when it was mud-caked and who, after wind and rain did their worst, looked winsome, not wracked. Life wasn't fair; that was the long and short of it. Never had been; never would be; and there wasn't any sense brooding on it.

"Give me a hand with the horses," Seanna hailed Drum, whom she'd mistaken for a servant, and got Squirt in the bargain.

Balthan interceded before the boy had undone two of the harness buckles.

"I want to help!" Squirt got free, as he almost always did, but Balthan caught him again and spun him toward Jordan.

"Go bother your brother. He needs it."

By the time Darrel caught his balance he was at the campfire. Everyone was acting strangely—even Drum who was talking to that teamster woman like they were long-lost friends. The boy consoled himself: they'd go to sleep. The wagon would go away. Life would settle down. But it didn't.

First Drum—of all people—proposed to sleep in the wagon, out of the rain. Seanna was hauling pigiron for a Peer who, despite his estate's location on the Cape of Heroes, south of Trinsic, distrusted ships, sailors, and salt water. The load was heavy, but small, and there was ample room in the dry wagon for them all. Squirt couldn't argue with that. Then, when morning promised another day of

steady rain, Seanna said that since the road might be undermined, she'd have to travel slowly. Drum, Balthan, and
Squirt could walk in front or behind, but Jordan and Althea
could sit on the bench beside her, or stay out of the rain
entirely beneath the canvas shrouds.

Althea wasn't happy—even the boy could read that much
from her expression—but she was tired of walking. She
clambered into the covered wagon. Jordan sat beside
Seanna. They hadn't gone a furlong before Althea left her
shelter and wedged herself between the other two.

Squirt caught up with Balthan, who was walking ahead
of the wagon. "What's going on with them?"

"There's a fox in the henhouse."

The boy spun on his heels and walked backward. It would
be hard to imagine a more uncomfortable-looking threesome. "Which one's the fox?"

"Can't tell yet."

Hours and miles rolled by. They reached the next charterhouse. Seanna expected a bonus if she delivered the iron
ahead of time. She'd wait in the yard, she said, if they
wanted to purchase provisions, but not for long. Althea
confessed sourly that they had no money. The wagon kept
rolling.

With rain still falling, and the land already flooded, it
was not surprising that they heard the stream before they
saw it. Even so, they were shocked to see a pair of stonework
walls poking out of the raging water instead of the bridge
itself.

"We've got to go back to the charterhouse," Althea said
simply.

Seanna waded into the stream. "Road's solid." She
stamped her foot through the water for emphasis. "Bridge
still spans the deepest part."

"That stream's three feet over its banks if it's an inch,"
Balthan countered, feeling his sister's eyes on the back of
his neck.

"And it's still raining"—Seanna slogged back to the wagon—"in case you haven't noticed. This water will rise another two feet—and that *will* take the bridge out. So unless you folks want to spend a week *outside* that charterhouse—I suggest we cross now."

Her plan was simple: one able-bodied person at each wheel, to warn of washouts and help to keep the wagon on whatever remained of the road. A fifth would rein Willie and Tom.

"I don't think I can," Althea demurred.

"I already figured that."

Althea's voice and eyebrows rose. "You can't expect me to brace a wheel hub—"

"Drum, Jordan"—Seanna pointed at the rear wheels—"your brother and me—" She pointed at the front ones. "The boy can take the reins. All you have to do is not fall off."

Squirt whooped, almost drowning out Althea's final objection: "Jordan's *blind*."

But Jordan heard her and went rigid.

"Look, 'Thea," Seanna said with false friendship. "He's going to eat so much muck, he won't know if he's still got that blindfold on. What do you say, Jordan? You're the one who'll be on his knees in muck." She thumped Jordan's thigh.

He stood up. "I can do it."

Althea grabbed his shirt; he nearly lost his balance. "Jordan—you can't. It's dangerous. You could get hurt."

Jordan brushed her arm away. "I'm already *hurt*."

He jumped down. Squirt wanted to run to him, but Balthan pinched his neck again. The magician wasn't as strong as Jordan or Lord Ironhawk, but he knew exactly where to put his fingers.

Althea's concerns were, however, valid. The stream was dangerous. Seanna retrieved sturdy ropes from a chest beneath the bench. They all tied themselves to the wagon.

Then she gave Squirt a nod. He climbed to the bench, slapped the reins, and the horses entered the water.

Seanna had been born in this wagon; the road was the only home she knew. For three years, since she'd turned sixteen, she'd handled the rig by herself. She knew every trick of the teamster's trade. On the other hand, it was a flooded stream just like this that made her an orphan and she wasn't as confident as she pretended to be.

The horses reached the submerged bridge, then Drum's front wheel wedged where the road joined the bridgework. The wagon lurched and slid against the downstream wall which immediately began to give way. Seanna had been right about the muck—Jordan didn't notice that he lost the blindfold as he struggled to help the farrier. He got his shoulder where it needed to be. The road was washing out beneath their feet. They'd get one chance, and one chance only.

"Now!"

Squirt slapped the reins; nothing happened.

"Use the whip," Seanna gasped; she was caught between the wagon and the crumbling wall.

He struck Willie, then Tom. They lunged against their collars and after a heart-stopping moment, the wagon rose onto the bridge.

After that, it was easy. The ground on the far side seemed firmer, the sky seemed brighter, and the rain, slackening.

Jordan was coughing the stream out of his lungs when a vision of Seanna—squeezed between her wagon and the wall—exploded into his mind. He realized the blindfold was gone. He looked up, Althea was beside him long before his magic-addled eyes yielded another image.

"You've lost your bandage. I'll make you another."

Listening to her fight with her wet skirt, it occurred to Jordan that he should help her tear the wet cloth. Then—remembering Seanna again—he decided neither he nor Althea was the one who needed help.

"Don't bother. I don't need it."

Althea won her battle. "You do," she assured him as she
held the dripping cloth against his face. "Your eyes . . .
change. I didn't notice until we were with Annon. Better
people think you're blind in the usual way."

Jordan didn't have any idea what she meant—except that
she was probably right. The spheres exploded again. He
saw Althea marching toward him with a fierce scowl and,
beyond her, Seanna leaning against Willie coughing water
out of her lungs.

"Hold still—or I'll catch your hair in the knot."

He pulled the cloth from her hands and threw it into the
stream. "I said I don't need it!" He stormed past Althea to
Seanna who was, by then, examining the team for their
injuries.

"Bruised ribs, nothing worse," she assured him.

It was only natural to hold the bridles while Seanna finished her examination. Excluding his sword—currently
lashed to the iron inside the wagon—horses were the best
part of Jordan's life. One horse in particular, a Valorian colt
named Fugatore, whom he'd raised and trained himself.

We needed money and a mule while we were after Balthan, so I loaned him to an estate outside Paws—sold him,
really. The loan's overdue and even if I had the money,
what do I need with a Valorian?

"You shouldn't pretend, Jordan Hawson," Seanna replied.

"Pretend?"

"You're not crippled and you're not blind. I don't know
what's wrong with you—everybody's got a different
story—but it's no reason to turn your back on the things
you love."

Jordan wandered away in silence.

Four
ΥΥΥΥΥ

T he storm lifted at sunset. Moonlight shone on silvery marshes that stretched to the horizon. Stars sprinkled the sky between the shrinking clouds. Jordan stared at them until his neck hurt, until every constellation exploded into his memory. He hadn't realized how much of his world he took for granted, how little he could recall.

"Ready to try my glyphs?" Balthan asked. He'd assembled the necessary reagents.

Relying on memory, Jordan joined him. "Lay on."

Jordan's swordmasters and tutors never complained about his dedication. He did what he was told, and he did it relentlessly. He stared at one glyph until it vanished, then another, and another until everyone else was asleep and Balthan couldn't keep his own eyes open. The magician's hands shook as he mixed reagents. The glyph sparked and scattered.

"Enough," he groaned. "I'm spent."

Jordan grumbled: "We've done twenty-seven. Can you tell how much we've accomplished?" implying that he could not.

Balthan was too tired to lie. "Spit in the ocean. We should try something else."

"Whatever you say." Jordan shrugged. "You're the master. I'll stare at as many as you can raise. Whatever it takes. We could sit inside the wagon tomorrow. It's dark back there—"

The magician wondered how many glyphs it would take: a hundred. . . ? a thousand. . . ? *ten thousand*? How long would it take to raise ten thousand glyphs? Jordan's mind-numbing tenacity had always confounded him. Erwald Iron-hawk's eldest son wasn't simple, but there were times when Balthan was convinced his foster-brother had no imagination whatsoever.

Balthan never lacked imagination. Pure luck had kept him from making rash promises; in his heart he'd been convinced that two or three glyphs, a dozen at the very most, would burn through Jordan's blindness. He was willing to try anything while the notion of ten thousand In Lor glyphs haunted his thoughts. He lay awake refining his glyph-raising strategies. He had to have Jordan restored before they got home.

Hawksnest was Balthan's home, insofar as he needed one. Erwald Ironhawk had been a better father to him and Althea than Simon the Wanderer. Lord Ironhawk treated his wards exactly as he treated his sons. He was virtuous and unstinting, and he believed that children were never too old to obey and revere their father. When Balthan would neither obey nor revere, Ironhawk vowed to break him.

Balthan's years at Hawksnest were not unpleasant, especially after Simon's drunken brutality, more like a protracted siege in which the occasional outbursts of rage and hostility embarrassed both sides. Still, the thought of picking up where he and Ironhawk had left off—Balthan could not believe there was an alternative—was less appetizing than Althea's pease porridge.

After a breakfast of that cold, crusted porridge, Balthan and Jordan retreated to the interior of the canvas-shrouded wagon. The magician delved into his sack, seeking the gnarled, grotesque limbs of mandrake to mix with, and hopefully strengthen, the glyphs he raised from lumps of sulphurous ash.

"I think it's better this morning," Jordan said while Balthan laid out the reagents.

"How so?"

"The images are so sharp they hurt. I can move them in my mind and bring them closer." He described the ceramic pot in Balthan's lap. "I can see the cracks in the glaze . . . The chipped rim . . . The potter's mark on the base . . ."

Balthan examined the pot. It was exactly as his foster-brother described it. If better meant compleat, then Jordan was completely better. But Jordan *saw* nothing. The explosions of vision remained unpredictable, the visions themselves remained frozen. As far as Balthan was concerned, they'd gotten nowhere. He wasn't raising glyphs to clarify Jordan's memory, he meant to restore his mundane eyesight.

"We'll try something different."

He took a pinch of the reagent mixture and held it in the palm of his left hand. He summoned an engendering spark from within himself. Nothing happened. The wellspring from which Balthan drew his magic was empty. Balthan knew that every magician's resource was limited, but he'd never tried to kindle a spell and failed. The wellspring would be restored but for the moment he was without magic as he had never been before. He hid his face behind his hands.

"This is 'something different'?" Jordan growled when he finally saw the hunched-over magician. "Is this your idea of helping me?"

The blinded fighter seized Balthan's hair before the magician could explain. Using wrestler's tricks, Jordan twisted Balthan's spine and bent him backward, then he wrapped his left hand over Balthan's jaw and pulled sideways until he met resistance.

"Is it?"

Balthan couldn't answer. His neck was so tightly wrenched that any move, his own or Jordan's, might break it. He and Jordan had brawled countless times, with Jordan winning more often than not, but not like this. Looking up into his foster-brother's eyes, Balthan saw nothing intelligent or familiar, not even the remnants of his own misguided magic. He was exquisitely aware that Jordan didn't realize he was about to commit murder.

"Road's out up ahead!" Seanna struck the bench with the whip butt to get her passengers' attention. "Put away your magic, it's time to do some honest work!"

Jordan blinked. He didn't see the magician's desperate, pleading face, but he felt what his hands had been about to do and withdrew his strength from them. Balthan hit the floor hard, grateful to be alive.

"What happened?" Jordan asked himself. The usual spheres had become a bloodred curtain; it lifted and the greenish blobs reappeared. "Whatever you tried, Balthan—I don't think it was a good idea."

The magician sat up slowly. His neck would ache until his magic was restored enough to heal it. The wagon halted; Seanna joined them, getting out ropes again. Balthan made himself small against the siderail trying to remember where he'd seen such dead-eyed rage. Terror had shattered his thoughts; he could hardly remember the thought-path to his magic.

Jordan remembered little of his sudden murderous rage. When they'd crossed the flooded stream and were drying out, he listened to Balthan's narration with unfeigned horror.

"Is it the glyphs?"

"It shouldn't be." Balthan chose his words carefully. He'd healed his sore neck and finally remembered where he'd seen that rage before. "Rage runs in your family, Jordan. Talk to Ironhawk."

"Are you saying I'm like my lord father?"

"I'm saying Ironhawk can control his rages. He never came *that* close to murdering me."

The red curtain hovered at the very edge of Jordan's consciousness, bleeding rage over his thoughts and the exploding green spheres. He scratched sweat from the stubble on his chin. He compelled the red to retreat. "Will you still help me? Can you raise more glyphs?"

Balthan was very willing. His desire to fulfill his promises before the wagon reached Hawksnest grew stronger with each passing furlong. "Anytime I've got the strength for it and Seanna doesn't have us tied to the wheel hubs."

The magician was true to his word, although as they continued south the road grew steadily worse. Those landlords whose estates straddled or bordered the road were responsible for its maintenance, but their attention and labor was focused on the flooded fields. When their crops were secure, they'd repair the banks and bridges—until then Seanna's wagon and its passengers spent most of the time in the mud.

Six days out of Britain City, the wagon reached the boundary stones of Malamunsted estate where Jordan left Fugatore as surety on the now-defaulted loan. Althea, Drum, and Squirt had no great affection for the animal, but they wouldn't object to the benefits of hospitality: hot meals, hot water, a modicum of privacy. For his part, Balthan welcomed anything that would postpone Hawksnest. Jordan yearned to see Fugatore, even if true *seeing* was still impossible. There was no way he could redeem the animal. Seanna's opinion, though, was the only one that counted. She looked at the quagmire masquerading as a cartway and said:

"You can walk, if you want, and all the way from here to Hawksnest, but my wagon's not going in there."

No one took her challenge; the wagon continued south. The streams had crested; the floods were receding. Each day the summer sun baked more mud into brick-hard dirt. Four days later they came to the northern boundary stone of Hawksnest and its cartway junction. Comparing his memories of Malamunsted and home, Jordan advised Seanna against using it and for once he got the brusque treatment the others knew so well.

"I've lost my bonus—Destiny knows that hurricane scoured the Cape of Heroes." Seanna guided the wagon onto the cartway. "I need to arrange some business here to cover my costs."

The cartway was a mud-rutted ruin. The verdant fields were cross-hatched with flood trenches. Staring out the back of the wagon, contemplating each new frozen image, Jordan was satisfied that the herds hadn't suffered and most of the crops had been salvaged. Still, it might be years before the storm was forgotten.

Willie, Tom, and Seanna had navigated a little over a mile of cartway less dedicated creatures would have considered impassable when they came to Rosignel, the original villa (and the name of the estate until Erwald changed it). Though fallen into disrepair, Rosignel remained the home of Lady Barbara's elderly grandmother, her tiny household, and the half-score men who supervised Ironhawk's stud.

"Let's stop here for the night," Althea suggested. "We can send someone up to Hawksnest. They'll know we're back. We can make ourselves presentable."

Althea understood that appearances *were* important and they'd need every small advantage when they faced Lord Erwald after their misadventures. She expected Balthan to understand, too; he fussed more about his appearance than any woman she knew. But Balthan had more worrisome thoughts between his ears and everyone else said there was no point to stopping when they were five miles from the Hawksnest villa itself.

Those five miles were among the worst they'd encountered. Nightfall found them two miles from the villa, at the bottom of the switchback road up the escarpment, and completely exhausted. Destiny decreed that they would spend one more night in the wagon.

Conversation was in short supply throughout the evening and the spirit of celebration was conspicuous by its absence.

"He'll be glad to see us, won't he?" Darrel whispered to his brother.

"Mother will be," Jordan answered an easier question.

Lord Erwald would be relieved to have his sons back, but, as Balthan said, rage ran in Ironhawk's blood. Jordan flexed his shoulders. After five hundred thirty-two glyphs his memory was thick with detail and texture, but his sight remained frozen and chancy. Jordan could withstand his father's rage; what he feared was rejection. He desperately needed reassurance, but Lord Erwald proclaimed both loud and often that affection weakened a son's character.

"But what about our lord father?" the boy persisted.

"We'll see—*You'll* see," he corrected in a ragged whisper that frightened Squirt away.

Jordan didn't try to sleep. He sat all night on the driver's bench. Erwald Ironhawk conceded that fear was inescapable, but a warrior conquered fear with Courage. A warrior embraced the Virtues of Honor, Sacrifice, and Valor that were derived from Courage. In the dark hours between moonset and dawn, Jordan Hawson armored himself in courage and waged war on his fears.

When the first rays of sunlight touched his face, he shivered and sighed: "I won't care. I don't care."

Like a rigid corpse, Jordan sat on the bench while his companions performed their morning rituals. He heard their queries and glimpsed their faces. They were worried; he wasn't. His fears were gone, along with hope and caring—regrettable, but unavoidable sacrifices of the night's battle.

Seanna chose to walk beside Tom, but Balthan braved the bench.

"Whatever you're thinking, Jordan, it won't work."

Silence.

"You can't pretend you're not here . . . Ironhawk will think you've lost your wits as well as your eyesight." Still unable to evoke a response, Balthan grabbed Jordan's shirt. "You weren't the only one who didn't sleep last night. I *heard* you talking to yourself. Personally, I don't care either. Throw everything away. I'll go back to Britain City and tell Annon that I did my best. But the rest—they do *care*, Jordan, and they *need*—"

Jordan's hand closed over Balthan's wrist. The magician had gone too far. "Jordan—?" he whispered as Jordan hauled him to his feet.

Jordan's eyes were horrifying to behold—the irises seethed like molten sulphur, each pupil throbbed independently. The pain in Balthan's wrist intensified; Jordan's calloused grip felt strong enough to reduce bones to bloody pulp.

"Don't *tell* me anything."

For a heartbeat, Balthan's shoulder was on fire, then he was flying through the air. He landed badly on his ankle. Animal reflex spun his legs out of the path of the iron-rimmed wheels. The wagon rolled harmlessly over him and stopped. Drum, Seanna, Althea, and the boy crowded around Balthan.

"What happened?" Althea asked.

They'd heard nothing of the conversation. One moment both men had been talking; the next, one was seething and the other sprawling. Balthan grabbed Drum's arm and hauled himself upright. He nearly fainted when his foot touched the ground.

"Anabarces!" he swore, once he'd caught his breath. "He's gone berserk."

They looked at the bench. Jordan sat rigidly, as if nothing had happened. Through the silence of the moment, they heard the villa tocsin: Lord Ironhawk knew visitors were approaching.

"What next?" Seanna demanded.

"We keep going," Althea answered uncertainly.

Seanna was no longer interested in meeting, much less doing business, with Lord Ironhawk. "Some homecoming," she muttered before turning to Balthan who stood like a stork with his knee bent and his boot poised above the mud. "What about you?"

He willed his toe to the ground; the ankle wouldn't bear his weight. "It's just a sprain," he insisted and tried again. Seanna caught him before he fell and put him with the pigiron in the back of the wagon.

"I'd keep my head down, were I you," she advised quietly, tying the canvas shrouds over the opening. "If it is berserkerang, somebody's going to blame you."

Balthan wrapped himself around his ankle. Erwald Ironhawk should know that Jordan's berserkerang had nothing to do with magic. *Maybe I* did *blind him*, the magician thought sourly, *but the berserkerang was always there in his blood*. He tucked his hat's sweeping feather under his chin and scuttled into a corner where Jordan was unlikely to see him from the bench.

Jordan didn't and couldn't know what was happening to him. Ironhawk kept his curse under rigid control and allowed no one to speak of it. Balthan hadn't puzzled out the truth until he was at the Lyceum where the subject was debated. Magic, the high-circle magicians insisted, could not cause the berserkerang, but, they conceded, it could awaken it. With his mind's eye, Balthan saw the scapegoat's horns waiting for him in the Hawksnest yard.

"Sweet mother of midnight, moonlight, and magic . . ." He found his reagent sack and plunged his arm into its deceptive depths, seeking the pouch in which he kept a mixture of ginseng and spider silk. "He's going to throw

me to the wolf.'' After extracting a thumbnail-sized lump
of felt, he cupped it against his nose and mouth. *"Mani!"*
he whispered, evoking the spell.

Mani was the simplest healing spell in the arcanum, and
the only one Balthan knew. Applied directly to the skin, it
made minor cuts and bruises vanish. Inhaled, its power
touched the mind, lifting the recipient above pain and panic,
strengthening the will to survive. Balthan's thoughts steadied: Seanna wouldn't linger, he assured himself. She'd be
glad of anybody's help getting the wagon back to the road.
All he had to do was stay put.

Althea would be distraught when she learned he was
gone, but not as distraught as she'd be watching Ironhawk
and Jordan wring his naked neck. Annon would understand—he'd have to understand. Balthan pulled a piece of
canvas around himself. With a little luck, he might even get
a nap.

Jordan's jaw was numb from grinding his teeth. He'd
gotten sight of Balthan's leg stretched across the wheel's
path. He knew disaster had been averted, but that didn't
diminish the image in his memory. He was appalled. He'd
conquered his fears and put himself beyond hope—and this
was his reward. He wanted to call a halt while he thought
things through, but the tocsin clanged. No time. No time.
No time.

The wagon climbed the escarpment to the Foregate. Jordan strained his neck, hoping to glimpse a familiar face, but
nothing replaced the wheel and Balthan's leg. Willie's and
Tom's iron shoes echoed off a wooden bridge, then clattered
over cobblestones: they were in the Foregate where Drum's
kindred and other artisan families lived and worked. A few
unrecognizable voices hailed them as they passed. Jordan
ignored them. A whispering undercurrent rose in their wake.
The wagon lurched to the right and stopped.

"My lord! Your sons return—alive and whole!" This

time the voice came from the guard porch overlooking the main gate.

Jordan made a frantic orison to his brother's Eye of Destiny, or any higher power that might listen. His eyesight did not clear. Seanna drove the wagon through the gate, into the gravel yard. Chaos erupted as the household surged forward, but Jordan could not tell if his parents were among them.

"Jordie! Come down!"

Squirt or Althea—in the commotion Jordan couldn't distinguish their voices—tugged his arm. He grasped the offered hand, then, in the quirky way of his affliction, the frozen, recent past exploded into his memory.

Erwald Lord Ironhawk looked older than his son expected. His hair was silver-streaked, his eyes were shadowed, and his cheeks were hollow, not ruddy. He stood alone on the steps above the yard, as if he knew the guard's proclamation was a half truth.

Trembling, Jordan misjudged the last step, but caught his balance. The air turned silent, as if the household had vanished. The lump in Jordan's throat sank like hot lead through his gut. He tried to feel the sun on his face—he knew the orientation of the villa steps, if he could feel the sun he'd know where to walk—but the sun was hiding.

After two strides he collided with someone and knocked them down.

"You can't see! You can't see me!"

Lady Barbara's voice. Her hands clung to him as she stood. Jordan couldn't feel the sun, but he felt his mother staring at him. She took his hand and pressed it against her tear-streaked face. A terrible weakness welled up inside Jordan. For the first time since his nightmare began, he found himself weeping.

"Who is responsible!? I'll see him hang!"

Within the wagon, Balthan threw aside his covering. It had been years since he'd heard that voice—he thought he'd forgotten it. Compelled by curiosity, he peeked between the shrouds. He felt a twinge of empathy for Jordan, hemmed in by hysterical parents and losing his composure, but his empathy faded as Ironhawk's tirade continued.

"This is Balthan Wanderson's handiwork! Whoreson traitor! Damned magician! Bloodsucking viper!"

Balthan sat back. Why did Ironhawk blame him instantly? He wracked his memory: Althea, Drum, and Jordan left Hawksnest without warning or explanation. Squirt? The boy said he escaped unnoticed. Of course, the boy also claimed Lord Shamino helped him, and that Lord Dupre, last of the Trinsic paladins, explicitly forbade Ironhawk to pursue his children. One clung to a shaky branch when one believed the Squirt.

The magician parted the shrouds again in time to see Althea plead with Jordan: "Tell him my brother had nothing to do with it!"

Jordan's reply—if he gave one—didn't reach the wagon. Althea's pathetic wail—coupled with Ironhawk's apoplectic silence—did not bode well. The magician expected the household to swirl around the wagon like the floodwater they'd seen so much of lately. He clutched his sack—not that it contained anything useful. A magician had to reach the Seventh Circle before learning the secret of Sanct Lor—Invisibility. Balthan, trapped in the Second Circle, only had his wits and Seanna's wagon for protection. He crouched in the darkest corner, waiting for the canvas shroud over the back opening to move.

But the shroud didn't move. The yard was very quiet. Curiosity reset its hooks in Balthan's vigorous imagination. He crept to his peephole and wished immediately that he had not.

A black-robed figure stood beside Lord Ironhawk. His sour face cowed the entire assembly, including Erwald. The

ominous stranger stroked his thin, lead-colored beard; he
stared over the crowd at Seanna's wagon.

The novices at the Lyceum on Verity Isle learned tricks
that were not quite magic. Tricks were things anyone could
do, and the novelty of knowing them faded quickly. Balthan
could not remember the last time he'd glanced out the tail
of his eye searching for the faint aura of consciousness that
surrounded all humans and many animals. But he narrowed
his eyes and turned his head.

He bit his knuckle to keep from crying out. The stranger
had a shadow, not an aura. The shadow wasn't as deep as
the one surrounding Blackthorn, but it was unmistakable.
The magician had his answers. Lord Blackthorn handpicked
the Inquisitors, but Balthan knew what had picked Blackthorn. Those evil wraiths who first appeared in Balthan's
dreams and later, when he rejected their temptations, hunted
him across Britannia had set an ambush at his home.

Panic enveloped Balthan; he beat it back. Yes, the wraiths
were evil and powerful; they were also limited and fallible.
They'd driven him to the cave from which Jordan had rescued him; but they'd lost him—since his rescue, Balthan's
dreams had been mundane. There was an Inquisitor waiting
for him here at Hawksnest, but no one *knew* he was coming.

A hand reached into the wagon, raising the rear canvas.
Panic returned.

"You were wise to make yourself scarce," Drum said
matter-of-factly. He climbed into the wagon. "There's an
Inquisitor here, and he's been telling tales about you. Lord
Ironhawk's ready to have your guts for garters—"

Inspiration struck. "Chase me," Balthan requested.
"Lead the household across the stream, into the woods."

"With that ankle, you wouldn't get far steps before I
caught you."

The magician hurriedly explained that he wanted Drum
to chase an imaginary Balthan hither and yon while the real
one got away.

"I don't know, wouldn't you be better off staying right here? Seanna's leaving. That's why I'm gathering our stuff."

What little remained of Balthan's rational mind agreed, but it was not strong enough to keep him from bolting. He grabbed the front of the farrier's vest and restated his wishes. Drum nodded; he leaned out of the wagon.

"There he goes," the farrier announced. "There goes Balthan Wanderson through the Foregate, across the stream, down the cliff, into the woods."

The recital should have failed, but the Inquisitor had performed his own role well. The tocsin clanged and the household took up the chase.

Drum withdrew into the wagon. "What now?"

"Join them, you idiot. Chase me!"

"But you're here—"

A feral growl rattled in Balthan's throat. He seized the farrier's cloak and basket. "*Pretend* to chase me while I *pretend* to be someone else."

The magician's voice was soft but his teeth were showing. Drum decided discretion was the better part of valor.

"Wait for me!" he yelled as he left the wagon.

Several moments later, his silhouette disguised by the basket and cloak, Balthan limped from the wagon and out through the gate.

Five

J ordan cursed silently. He sat
on the floor of his room,
rocking from hip to hip. Each time his shoulder struck the
chair that had tripped him. His left palm burned fiercely.
He had tried to break his fall as wrestlers did, striking the
floor with his hand, before he hit. Maybe it had helped;
nothing was broken. He spat on the splinter, then tried to
remove it with his teeth; that drove the barbed wood deeper
into his flesh.

"Hythloth take it!"

"Hawson?"

Hearing Hugh's sincerely worried voice in the room with
him, Jordan stopped rocking.

"Hawson, can you hear me?"

Did his armiger think he was deaf as well as blind? Jordan
assumed he'd be alone once he got to his room—but like
everything else, the assumption was wrong. Ironhawk's rage
and rejection were worse than Jordan dared fear. Althea had
run in the opposite direction when the household chased
Balthan. And Lady Barbara—whose face was never far
away each time his affliction allowed him a glimpse of the
world—was unrecognizable in her hysteria.

Jordan had escaped from the yard as quickly as he could, caroming against everything in his path, stumbling and weeping until he reached the sanctuary of his own door.

"Hawson?"

Where had Hugh come from? Had he been in the room before Jordan shot the bolt? Had he followed him from the yard and witnessed every lurching humiliation? Jordan couldn't know. He hadn't visualized anything since he left the yard.

"Hawson? Where are you?"

The scrape of Hugh's lame leg against the floor was uncomfortably loud.

Hugh made no unnecessary concessions to the knob of fused bone the healers left where his knee had been. When it was clear that Hugh would never ride or hunt again, Erwald suggested that his lifelong friend become his three-year-old son's armiger instead. For the last fifteen years Hugh watched over Jordan's property—his clothes, his arms, and his armor—and everything else as well. All that time Jordan had taken him very much for granted.

"I'm here, Hugh. Where under the bloodred sun do you think I am?"

"It's dark as midnight here, Hawson. We hung shutters during the hurricane and haven't had a chance yet to take them down. May I strike a light?"

Hugh took Jordan's silence as permission. He worked with flint and steel.

"You changed the room," Jordan grumbled.

"No, Hawson, your mother would not allow anyone in after you left—until the storm, of course . . ." More limping and the acrid smell of a freshly lit oil lamp. Then the thump of the chair being righted. "That's a nasty bit of work you've done to your hand. I'll get an awl to dig it out."

Jordan didn't protest. Magic and healers notwithstanding,

Britannians knew better than to leave puncture wounds un-
treated. He eased himself into the chair and braced his
upturned hand along the carved arm. He listened as Hugh
opened the wardrobe. A single drawer rasped open. Hugh
knew where everything was.

The armiger had made one unsuccessful assault on the
splinter when the mayordomo announced himself at the
locked door. Leaving the awl in Jordan's lap, Hugh limped
across the room. He didn't need to ask for instructions;
Jordan didn't need to eavesdrop. Instead, Jordan tried to
remember how many drawers were in his wardrobe and
what each contained. His vision cleared; he saw that there
were six, one of which was open and trailing bits of thread
and leather laces. For his life's sake, Jordan could not remember what was in the other five.

The doorway conference became louder.

"There will be no need for *that*. Hawson will be ready
for supper!"

Hugh was the only person who called Jordan "Hawson"—unless he was displeased and Hawson became a
grudging "my lord Hawson." Everyone else in the villa
tended to use his nursery-name, Jordie, which he detested.

"No, Hawson does not wish to join anyone in the hypocaust. We'll have a bath brought up here."

The mayordomo was not pleased, but Hugh won the
battle. He usually did. Jordan imagined the lame warrior
smiling as he turned from the door.

"Thank you, Hugh. I can't face Lord Ironhawk right
now—especially in the—"

"Your lord father is not in the hypocaust." The sound of
a smile was absent from Hugh's voice. He gripped Jordan's
hand firmly enough to make the young man wince. "Hold
tight."

Jordan took the advice. He looked the other way, too.

"Old habits die hard, don't they, lad? I never go upstairs
but I don't try to bend my knee."

"I see a little," he said stiffly. To Jordan's credit he didn't jump when the awl jangled a nerve.

Hugh tsk-tsked and probed deeper. "Shadows and light like an old man. More's the pity for you, Hawson. Nothing goes according to plan. May they do the same and worse with that whoreson when they catch him."

Jordan flinched, but not from pain. He'd been shaken by his father's rage and mortified by his own tears, but his courage had not failed him, nor his wits. He'd known exactly how he was going to account for his misfortune, but when he opened his mouth, his tongue belonged to someone else:

With his own blind allegiance to the darkest power of magic Balthan Wanderson did assault me as he assaulted our dear regent, the virtuous Lord Blackthorn . . .

Beads of cold sweat bloomed on Jordan's face. He would not live long enough to forget, or understand, what had happened in the yard. He'd betrayed Balthan and let the household course after him like hunting hounds. The voice had been his own, but those words? Jordan knew the florid speech of courtiers and used-goods merchants—he was related to members of both professions—but he didn't speak it and in his whole life he'd never called anyone "dear," not his mother, and especially not Lord Blackthorn.

Jordan leaned against the chairback, close to fainting.

Hugh set down the awl and slapped Jordan's cheeks. "Hawson, lad, come around now—the worst's over."

"It was Balthan's magic maybe, but not Balthan, and he never assaulted Blackthorn. I said it backwa—"

Hugh sealed Jordan's lips with a frown and a finger, cocking his head at the door as he did. Jordan missed the subtleties and brushed Hugh's hand aside.

"I lied." Confession restored Jordan's strength. "Something came over me—like that damned miasma in Britain City. I *lied*. By the Eight, the Three, and the One, I'll go to Lord Ironhawk now and tell the truth!"

"You're blind, Hawson—that's truth enough!"

They wrestled. The lame man was no match for Jordan, with or without his eyesight. Jordan was fumbling with the bolt moments later when a green explosion revealed Hugh's worried face. Jordan left the bolt in place.

"What's going on, Hugh? What's wrong? What's wrong beside me?"

"It's difficult to begin."

"Begin when you realized I was gone," Jordan suggested. He found the chair again and, once settled in it, stared at Hugh with the same intensity he brought to Balthan's glyphs. Hugh wrung his hands and swallowed; Jordan heard both sounds. "My brother said our lord father put on quite a performance, smashing statues and turning so red our lady mother feared for him. Does it begin there?"

"No, later—"

After a month of blindness, Jordan heard things he would not have seen in the past: the quaver in Hugh's voice telling how truly wrong things were. "How much later, Hugh?" he asked more gently. "When Squirt came after me?"

"No, Lord Erwald roared like a dragon, but Lord Dupre calmed him. We worried, of course, with both of you missing, but no one argues with Dupre, not even your father. No, it was after—when our *guests* arrived . . ."

Jordan leaned forward to catch every word and glimpse.

Three men came to Hawksnest. They said they were refugees from the black fog of the cities and begged hospitality. The tradition of hospitality was older than the philosophy of Virtue. Lord Ironhawk, who started life as a merchant's son, scrupulously adhered to old noble traditions. No one was ever turned away from Hawksnest, not even when the defects of his character were etched as clearly on his face as the Inquisitor's were on his.

"Lohgrin!" Hugh interrupted himself. "Other peers and landlords began complaining about their unexpected guests, but the worst of them was not half of Lohgrin."

The Inquisitor refused the luxurious accommodations
Lord Ironhawk provided. He said his calling demanded austere surroundings and insisted on a shabby suite of store-
rooms that, coincidentally, overlooked all three interior
courtyards. No one from Lord Erwald down to the scullery
drudges could go from one part of the villa to another without risking a glower from the Inquisitor's windows.

Once he'd selected his rooms, Lohgrin was in no hurry
to leave them. His churls, Ivo and Dench, unloaded their
wagon, dismantled it, and stowed the planks as well. It
went without saying that no one had been inside Lohgrin's
quarters since he occupied them.

A large villa could accommodate a snoopy, sour-faced
eccentric, but Lohgrin's intrusions went beyond eccentric-
ity. Each night at supper, the Inquisitor recited the eight
new laws that reduced the Avatar's elegant virtues to easily
subverted formulas. Then, while the household tried to eat,
he upbraided the guilty with the infractions he'd observed
from his windows and administered the punishments personally with the dessert.

"Lord Ironhawk permits this?" Jordan interrupted. "In
his own cup hall?" He couldn't see the hurt and outrage on
Hugh's face, but he heard the armiger's silence and that was
answer enough. "I should have sent Squirt home—Should
have brought him back myself. With both of us gone, Ironhawk lost heart. I saw it in the yard. I should have understood. No wonder he blames Balthan."

Hugh attempted to explain the changes that had come
over his old friend without casting doubt on Erwald's virtue.
Hugh hadn't found an explanation that satisfied himself, and
he didn't find one while talking to Jordan.

"Erwald has always kept his own counsel. He's a wise
man; he must have reasons for saying nothing . . . *doing*
nothing."

Jordan heard the dismay in Hugh's voice, but before he
could pursue it, the outer corridor rang with the clatter of

buckets and the solid thump of the wooden bathtub hitting the floor.

"You must bathe, Hawson, and shave. I'll take your mail to the armory—they'll clean and repair it—and we'll burn the rest. Men come home from hunting trolls not smelling this bad."

The moment for confidences had passed. Servants rapped on the door, announcing that the water was losing its steam. Hugh reverted to his usual form: interested in Jordan's presentability above all else, and hiding his own thoughts behind an impenetrable veil. Moreover, once the notion of sinking into a steaming bathtub entered Jordan's mind, all other concerns vanished. Jordan shrugged out of his mail, which he'd worn constantly for fear it would rust solid if he removed it. He'd grown so accustomed to its weight he felt giddy without it. His arms rose like bird's wings—then he got a whiff of his shirt. Ignoring the laces, he tore the dank cloth from his body.

"It's yours. Get rid of it."

Hugh plucked the shirt from Jordan's hand. "The pants, too, my lord Hawson."

A knee-deep bathtub did not compare to the villa hypocaust, which was a luxurious heated pool, but it was a thousand times better than ditch water. Though Jordan gasped when his toes breached the water, he recovered quickly, and immersed as much of himself as he could. He closed his eyes and listened to his body unwind. He felt too good to argue when Hugh offered to wield the razor over his chin. Once the novelty wore off, a man was willing to be shaved by another. The armiger also took the shears to Jordan's tangled hair.

When Hugh was finished, the water was tepid and the scents of cleanliness were replaced by the harbingers of supper: meat roasting on the spit and torrid Trinsic chowder simmering on the hearth. Jordan hadn't complained about the pease porridge, but like his father he believed vegetables were primarily ornamental and not to be eaten. He suffered buckets of cool rinse water in blissful anticipation of the coming feast.

Hawksnest maintained an army of servants. Jordan had grown up surrounded by people whose lives depended on his well-being. When he was Squirt's age—old enough to contemplate abstract ideas like justice and equality—he insisted on doing everything himself until Hugh set him straight: you are the fruit of their labor, Hawson. They tend to you because when you thrive, they thrive. They love you as they would a prized ox. You must treat them with Virtue, but never demean them by refusing their labor.

Very much like a prized ox, Jordan endured his grooming. He raised his arms; a clean shirt drifted around his shoulders. He sat; his toenails were trimmed before sandals were laced around his ankles. His thoughts wandered to the cup hall and platters of succulent meat. The image was so potent Jordan forgot his affliction until Hugh reminded him.

"The mayordomo wished to know if you will bring a knife to table, or wish him to cut your meat."

Jordan's appetite died. He couldn't take his place if he couldn't carve his own portion from the roast. He'd wind up sitting on Hugh's left side, eating with his fingers like an infant. Everyone would laugh at him or, worse, avert their eyes and pretend he wasn't there.

"Neither. I'm not going to the cup hall. I'm not hungry. Maybe later I'll get something cold from the kitchen." He did not add: *something I can eat without help*, but the words were on his tongue.

"My lord Hawson—" Hugh was displeased. "We all understand you've had a terrible loss, but that's no reason to behave poorly. You're expected in the cup hall."

"I'm not going!"

Berserk rage contorted Jordan's face. It took Hugh by surprise: though he knew about Erwald's berserkerang, he'd convinced himself over the years that Jordan had been spared. Then Hugh saw Jordan's eyes. Erwald's eyes were black and cold when the rage was on him, not like Jordan's; the seething sulphur irises lent credence to Lohgrin's accusations.

"What did that whoreson do to you. . . ?"

The other servants saw what Hugh saw. They jostled each other in their hurry to be gone.

"Balthan has nothing to do with it!" Jordan shouted. He groped about until he found something—one of the rinse buckets—to heave at the wall. "Forget about Balthan!" The bucket chipped the plaster.

Hugh attempted to break the berserkerang. He held Jordan's wrists and looked closely into those uncanny eyes. "Hawson! You're berserk. Jordan Hawson—*control yourself*!" The tactic worked with Erwald, and Jordan claimed he was not completely blind.

Jordan blinked. Hugh thought he'd reached the young man. Then Jordan blinked again and Hugh felt himself lifted up and flung aside. By the time Hugh had his good leg under him, Jordan had found the razor. The armiger had no choice but to leave and seek help wherever he could find it.

"Hugh? Hugh?"

The rage ebbed as quickly as it arose, leaving Jordan weak-kneed and gasping. He remembered the look of horror, despair, and recognition on Hugh's face, then everything faded to red. He didn't remember picking up the razor he still held loosely between his fingers. Jordan felt his way back to the hollow safety of his room. He should have guessed when he turned on Balthan. He should have guessed the cause of his father's legendary rages years ago, but he'd never let his thoughts wander to their logical conclusion.

"Blind and berserk," he whispered, letting the razor glide over his fingertips. There was a melancholy temptation to think he'd been cursed. Balthan's glyphs might cure his vision, but nothing cured the berserkerang. Except death—which Jordan held in his hand. The Avatar's philosophy was silent about suicide; Regent Blackthorn's laws were quite specific: a man who lost his honor was bound to take his life. Sitting on his bed with green spheres floating before his eyes and the incoherent memories of his rage fresh in his thoughts, Jordan was as far from honor as a man could be. He stroked the sharp edge one more time, then folded the blade into its staghorn case.

"Not for *dear* Blackthorn. And not for any Inquisitor, either."

What had Balthan said about the wraiths haunting his dreams? He said they tempted him to betray everything he believed in. Jordan smiled ironically: Balthan, who was no more virtuous than a weathervane, resisted the temptations, while he succumbed to them. Of course, courtesy of Balthan's magic and Erwald's legacy, Jordan judged he faced his temptations at greater disadvantage; still, now he was forewarned. He'd turn away from the razor until he could undo what he'd done.

Grand resolutions were easy. Action was more difficult. Jordan flopped across the bed, arms open wide and facing the window from which the shutters had been removed. Almost blind and apt to go berserk, Jordan couldn't count on seeing the Inquisitor much less overwhelming him. He had betrayed his most logical ally, Balthan, and, he suspected, mortally offended his friends. His brother might rally to his side, but any enterprise that relied on the Squirt was ill-omened from its conception.

Jordan was suspended between despair and the aromas wafting ever more strongly through the window. Several moments passed before he realized his eyes burned and green spheres had merged into a white-hot blob.

He'd been staring at the sun.

Sitting bolt upright, Jordan rubbed his eyes until the burning stopped. Everything was a uniform, velvety black, then, as if through rippling glass or a film of oil, Jordan saw his hands. His fingers moved—the first movement he'd seen since Balthan's cave—and he saw the movement as it oc-curred. Then, before he could appreciate the miracle, the greenish spheres filled his vision again.

Annon of Britain said to use magic against magic, so Balthan raised glyphs. Jordan turned toward the warmth. The power of the sun was greater than magic. His eyes burned and watered. Self-protective instincts pulled his eye-lids together; martial discipline kept them apart. His freshly rasped cheeks stung, but he stared at the sun until he heard footfalls in the corridor. Then, shuddering with relief, he turned toward the sounds. As before, his vision cleared.

Jordan saw his father lead the charge ahead of Hugh and a host of servants.

"Father!" Jordan forgot the stiff formalities of filial re-spect. Grinning through his sunstruck tears, he launched himself across the room. "Father! I can see!" But as quickly as Jordan shouted his triumph, the affliction returned. His arms encountered nothing until they touched the rough plas-ter walls: his father had sidestepped his son's embrace.

"He's mad! By all that's virtuous: he's *mad*!" Erwald's voice was harsh with revulsion; it paralyzed Jordan's heart and will. "You've ruined everything!" He clouted his son from behind, crashing him into the open door. "As Destiny is my witness, you're no son of mine!"

Shock had dulled Jordan's wits. "I can see . . ." he repeated, though the statement was patently false.

Conversation—if it could be dignified with that word—disintegrated further.

"Is this how you thank me, how you honor me for all that I've given you?" Ironhawk took another swipe at Jor-dan's head.

It was a measure of what Erwald Lord Ironhawk had, in fact, given his son that blind and numb as he was, Jordan knew a blow was coming and got his arm up to deflect it.

"What possessed you to run away and ruin yourself?" Erwald answered his own question before Jordan had a chance: "Balthan Wanderson! I should have seen him for what he was when the peerage brought him to me. I thought being with you would give him Virtue, but it's been the other way 'round all along." He paused, and Jordan flinched from a blow that never came. "I'll be damned before you and he ruin me, boy . . ."

The tirade continued, punctuated by slaps and punches. Jordan caught a glimpse of Ironhawk's twisted face and the fear that held all the servants, even Hugh, helpless. If anyone in the room was mad, it was his father, not him.

After that realization, the blows and the acid words lost their power. Jordan detached himself from his physical pain and floated above it, as he'd been taught. He looked for explanations: Lord Erwald had kept an iron grip on his berserkerang madness all Jordan's life. Now, something made his father lose it. Was that something his own blindness? Had Balthan's errant magic reached out of his eyes to drive his father mad?

Jordan hit the door again, the greenish spheres became sharp-edged, then red. He wanted to strike back, berserk against berserk; he was confident he was stronger. But Jordan swallowed the red and smothered it in his gut. It was better to be blind than berserk. He dropped to the floor, protecting his head. Something worse than blindness had happened to his father; something worse than anything Balthan with his borrowed scrolls could concoct.

As Ironhawk rained blows on his back a prolonged, shrill scream came through the window.

Six

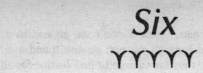

Althea ran in the opposite direction when the household took off after her brother. Like Jordan, she ran to the security of her room, the little room beyond the herb garden where she threw herself on the narrow bed and sought the oblivion of heartrending tears. She lay there for hours, wishing the heavens would swallow her and end her misery. She didn't expect visitors. Drum wouldn't come into the villa and didn't know where her room was within it. Balthan—if, Destiny willing, he'd been lucky—was miles away; she didn't want to lure him back to this cursed place with her wishes. And as for Jordan, *her* Jordie had betrayed them all.

She was startled when a gentle hand began to rub her back. She blinked back her tears and saw Lady Barbara, who smiled sadly and opened her arms.

"Tell me what happened, 'Thea. Tell me the truth."

While Hugh nursed Jordan's injuries, Althea clung to Lady Barbara, unburdening her spirit. While Jordan sat in the wooden tub, Althea dried her eyes on a corner of the quilt.

"It's a nasty business," Lady Barbara confirmed,

smoothing Althea's hair. "And I don't see an end to it. Your brother slipped through the net; no one found him. We can hope that he runs far enough to find Justice for all of us. In the meantime we must be very quiet. Destiny be praised, this Lohgrin has no eye for women—except to scold us for our weaknesses—we can be grateful for that."

In a wavering voice Althea reiterated what had happened during their first visit to Britain City, and what her brother said about the malign wraiths surrounding Blackthorn. Lady Barbara's lips tightened.

"I grew up at Rosignel, and Rosignel was here long before Lord British. My family endured evils the Avatar never faced or vanquished, Althea, and we'll endure this. Now, come along to the hypocaust. I've had the louvers dropped; no one will bother us. When you take care of the little, ordinary things, the great, extraordinary ones take care of themselves."

Lady Barbara's maternal reassurance was easy to believe and Althea wanted desperately to feel clean again. After gathering her soaps and linen, she followed Lady Barbara through the gardens, past the kitchen where the cooks were noisily preparing supper, along the open colonnade beneath Jordan's rooms, to the hypocaust in the most private of the three interior courtyards. As Lady Barbara promised, the water was steaming and the louvers made one quarter of the pool their private refuge.

Althea was grateful for the privacy. The hypocaust was seldom empty when the furnace was roaring and all the voices she could hear were masculine. She especially did not want to encounter Jordan, and simply assumed he and Darrel were among those on the other side of the gaily painted louvers.

Lady Barbara excused herself to oversee the final preparations for supper—one of those ordinary things she considered important. The menials who'd stoked the furnace washed the sweat from their bodies and went to their other duties. The water began to cool. The hypocaust was quiet except for water dripping from the walls and louvers.

Althea undid the knot between her breasts; the sheer linen bath sheet drifted away. Her thoughts had no more substance than the last steamy wisps rising from the water. The long journey to rescue Balthan and the long day of their return to Hawksnest remained in another world. She floated in aimless spirals, and would have stayed there, except that the menials returned with their skimming poles to clean the water. She swam over to her bath sheet and wrapped it around her as she climbed out of the water. A drying sheet of thicker, rougher linen hung from a peg; her filthy clothes had vanished moments after she shed them. Shivering, Althea slicked her hair from her face. She clutched the drying sheet around her shoulders and nudged the door open with her foot.

The courtyard was empty, unless she counted the old man weeding Lady Barbara's rose garden or the aromas wafting out of the hive-shaped kitchen. The gardener could be trusted not to notice her. The hypocaust was a favored trysting place among those who could not scavenge privacy elsewhere.

After her long bath, Althea was more interested in sleep than food. She walked slowly down the colonnade.

"Thou art a nymph born under the sea wave . . ."

Althea leapt into the air. When she landed, the drying sheet had slipped and she was facing the Inquisitor.

"Forgive me, I was overcome by your beauty. I did not mean to frighten you."

Althea was speechless and apprehensive. Even if Lohgrin told the truth, the churlish pair looming behind him had obviously carnal thoughts. She tugged the rough linen over her shoulder.

"I thought I was alone." She retreated a half step without turning away from them. "I've got to get back to my . . . work."

"Wait." Lohgrin caught Althea's wrist. His fingers were cold and dry like parchment. "Surely your *work* will wait another moment." His eyes were hard and bright as black jet beads. "Do you know who I am?"

She twisted her wrist to free it, as Jordan had taught her, but the Inquisitor knew the countermove.

"I've been told there's an Inquisitor here at Hawksnest," she said. "By your clothes and manner, you must be him." Ignoring the pain, Althea jerked free; the drying sheet slipped through her numbed fingers. It touched the ground and though she was still clothed by the bathing sheet, Althea felt naked and shamed.

"I am Lohgrin, of Verity Isle." He retrieved the drying sheet, then draped it around her neck. He caressed her arm before withdrawing. "And you are Althea, Erwald Ironhawk's fosterling, Balthan Wanderson's sister, are you not?"

Althea knew her face blazed scarlet, but her blood was ice. She wanted to run, but her feet were nailed. The gardener whistled calmly, ripping the weeds from the rose garden.

"Do you dream about the future, Althea? Do you wonder what it holds for you? Your only blood kin is outlawed. Ironhawk's eldest son is berserk and blind. Perhaps you hoped to marry him?"

Wet strands of her hair tangled in Althea's eyelashes. Lohgrin smoothed them against her temple, stroking her cheek as he did.

"I do not think about the future." She tried to sound brave, but her voice quavered.

"You should, my dear. A beautiful girl should always think about the future. Like the rose, her bloom will fade and she'll be left with thorns. Are you afraid of your future, Althea?"

She nodded slowly, unable to turn away.

"You need not be. When our regent sent me here, I thought Destiny conspired against me. How could I guess that Balthan would return? Or that he had a sister of such pristine beauty? With one hand"—he crumpled his fist—"I'm a hero quashing a traitor. With the other, I reach for my bride."

"You haven't got Balthan! You'll never catch my brother!"

Lohgrin's smile revealed dead-white teeth. "You sound so certain, my dear. Do you share in his secrets? In his treason?"

Althea's eyes widened—the only part that moved as the Inquisitor's words savaged her imagination. She had neither protectors nor protection. If this ghastly man wanted her, she would find herself in his hands. And he did want her. He had the look of a cat, ready to pounce.

"I'd die first. I'd kill myself before I'd let you touch me."

His smile broadened. "Such a waste, Althea." He touched her arm lightly with his smooth, dry fingers, then seized it. "A virtuous magician can restore life, at a price. Death need not be permanent."

"You wouldn't," Althea whispered. "You wouldn't *dare*." The Avatar had discovered the secret of Resurrection but the spell confounded destiny in ways neither virtue nor magic could repair. Since the Avatar's withdrawal from Britannia the spell had not been cast.

"Think of it, Althea!" Lohgrin's hand shook as he drew her closer. His stale breath was hot with excitement. "Consider the power your beauty has over me. See how it distracts me from my duties, my responsibilities—" He paused, and when he spoke again his voice was utterly calm. "If you satisfied me, I might forget your precious brother."

Althea loved Balthan, but there were limits to the sacrifices she would make on his behalf. "My brother"—she raked Lohgrin's face with hooked fingers—"can take care of himself!" Red beads appeared on the Inquisitor's cheek; his grip loosened. "And so will I!"

She spun away but had not gotten two steps before Lohgrin's churls surrounded her. Dench, the blue-eyed one with blond, wispy hair and a jagged, purple scar across his face, threw her over his shoulder.

"Take her upstairs."

Althea screamed with all the strength she could muster. She lashed out with her fists and heels, writhing like a cat in the washtub. But it was a lost cause from the start. Dench feared his master more than any pain Althea could inflict, and Ivo quickly locked his hands around her throat.

"Don't kill her—you maggot-brained cretin. She's no use to me dead."

Ivo let go. Althea's breath came in ugly, unconscious gasps.

"You said—?"

"Never mind what I said. Just get her upstairs and keep her—"

"Keep her for what?" It was Erwald Ironhawk, surrounded by retainers, with enough of the berserkerang left in his voice to stop Lohgrin in his tracks.

"Keep her quiet of course, my lord—until she's recovered. I'm no healer by trade, but before I left Britain City I visited Milan's infirmary and filled my apothecary box with restoratives. I'm afraid that the circumstances of her brother's treachery, revealed as they have been at the end of an arduous journey, have proved too much for her. She swooned coming out of the hypocaust, and became hysterical—"

"That is unlikely, my lord Inquisitor," Lady Ironhawk interrupted. She led a contingent of the menial servants: the gardener with his trowel, a stout milkmaid with the stomp from the butter churn, and a butcher with his stained apron and shining cleaver. Her lord brought more men in his tail, but hers were armed. "Althea is not hysterical. Nonetheless, at Hawksnest we care for our own." With a nod of her head, Lady Barbara sent a man to relieve Dench of his burden.

Dench awaited a similar gesture from his master. The courtyard filled quickly as men and women answered the third tocsin alarm of the day. Jordan stumbled to the stairway landing above the courtyard. There, invisible to the household and with the late-afternoon sunlight falling on his face, he tried to sort out the scene with his ears. When his eyes were watering he leaned around the newel post and watched Lohgrin give the signal to release Althea. Frustration and disappointment were evident in the Inquisitor's face; defeat was singularly absent.

"As you wish, Lady Ironhawk," Lohgrin said as the exploding spheres reappeared. "But I remind you, the Law of Compassion commands that we help those in need, lest we suffer that need ourselves. I abide by the laws I enforce, my lady, and I would advise you to do the same. Neither Compassion nor Humility guide you, my lady. I see distrust in your eyes. I hear dishonesty in your voice. Be warned, Lady Ironhawk: you are not immune."

Jordan waited for his father's response, but it never came. His mother muttered an awkward apology and dismissed the household. Sandals and bare feet scuffed across the paving. The stairs creaked and shifted as an unknown number of unknown men climbed. For all Jordan knew it was the Inquisitor and his churls. He could not run, so he crouched down, ready for the worst. But it was only Hugh and a few others.

"Come away, Hawson," the armiger whispered, tugging Jordan's sleeve in the correct direction.

"What's happened? Where's Althea? What about my lady mother? Lord Ironhawk—he let that slime—"

Jordan began at a whisper, but rose swiftly to a normal pitch and beyond. Hugh gave the sleeve an imperative tug.

"Mind your voice! Althea's safely away with Lady Barbara. Lord Ironhawk stands directly below with *him*." He kept a firm grip when the younger man lunged. "You'll accomplish nothing!"

Other hands grabbed Jordan's shoulders and arms. If he had not been so certain of Hugh's voice, he would have suspected the Inquisitor. He was wrestled to the wall.

"At least someone stood up for what's right," a familiar, but unrecognized, voice rasped.

"By the ninth virtue of tempered steel, Jordan—you picked a bad time to disappear and a worse one to come back with your head in a sling."

"Donsal—Donsal Doublehand? Is that you?" Recognition and surprise ended Jordan's struggles. "I thought you took a three-year contract with Thrud at Windemere?"

"I did and I left. That place is crawling with black-robes. I came back here, thinking it would be better—" There were a thousand words of regret in Donsal's momentary pause. "I'd put my knife between his shoulder blades if I didn't *know* what comes next is worse."

"How worse?" Jordan demanded. He placed both hands on Donsal's face, trying to discern the other man's expression. "What's worse than that—that toad pawing Althea? What's worse than him insulting my lady mother's virtue and Ironhawk letting . . . letting . . . let—" His palms were slick. His lips were flecked with rage. Donsal retreated.

"Fight it!" Hugh commanded. "Rein it in! Now! Before you get used to its power."

Jordan doubled over. He pounded his head against the wall, forcing the berserkerang inward until it broke. Sliding to the floor, with his cooling face hidden behind his hand, Jordan waited for his heart to recover its rhythm.

"Rotten luck," Donsal commiserated. "Just what you didn't need, just when you didn't need it."

"Aye," Jordan sighed, stretching his legs in front of him.

He felt like he'd been through a four-on-one skirmish. He'd sweated enough to need another bath.

"Things always seem worst ere they get better," the third man, still unglimpsed and unrecognized, said. He grabbed Jordan's wrists and hauled him upright.

There was no condescension. In the arena they spent as much time helping each other up as they spent knocking each other down—and Jordan Hawson had spent more time in the Hawksnest arena than anywhere else. He hugged the man gratefully, and realized that he could hear his father's voice. He backed up until he felt the wall behind him.

"I've got to catch my breath." Jordan flashed the wry smile any arena veteran would recognize and honor: I've injured my pride; no witnesses, please. If Hugh had been the only other man on the landing, it wouldn't have worked, but—thank the stars for little favors—the armiger wasn't alone.

"Come on with us, old man," Donsal said. "Jordan needs twice as long to figure anything out." Backs were slapped and leather echoed on the stairs.

Jordan shrugged off the familiar insult. He stared at the planks between his feet. If he was going to glimpse something, he didn't want it to be Hugh. It was true that he was better at fighting than thinking, at least he was good at something. Or he had been.

The stairwell was quiet, and so were the colonnade and courtyard. Jordan worried that Ironhawk had gone with Hugh and the men-at-arms. That meant the Inquisitor and his churls were on the prowl and that was an encounter he wasn't ready to have. Idle worries vanished when Jordan heard Lohgrin's resonant voice and were replaced by deeper ones.

"You do not seem to understand: I cannot easily overlook what has been done," the Inquisitor explained smoothly. "You brought treachery to your estate, adopted it, nurtured it, and endowed it."

"He was twelve when I adopted him," Lord Erwald sputtered. "I sent him to the magicians years ago. He's nothing to me. Look how he's repaid me. My son is ruined, worthless because of that whoreson. No one's suffered more than I have already."

What have you suffered? Jordan countered silently. Were you there? Do you see the world in frozen slices? Did Grandfather Chandeller ever call you "ruined" or "worthless"?

"You have not suffered, Lord Ironhawk." The Inquisitor said what Jordan could not say, and paused for dramatic effect. "You have been repaid. Had you not intervened, Simon's children would surely have followed him to an early grave—"

"It was an act of Virtue, sanctioned—requested!—by the Peers! No one could know what he'd become."

In his mind's eye, Jordan could see the flush rising on his father's cheeks.

"My lord Blackthorn, our regent, is not easily swayed by the excuse of ignorance."

Jordan could not guess where the Inquisitor was leading, but Erwald Ironhawk did: "I suppose that you could plead my case better than I?"

"My position is much stronger than yours, Erwald Chandeller, known as Lord Ironhawk. If I pled your defense, I would expect to succeed."

"If you pled my defense . . . And how much would that cost me? Five hundred gold crowns? A thousand?"

"I would not think of taking gold for the defense of Virtue."

"What would you think of taking?"

"My path has not been so easy as yours, Erwald. I was not born in a fine house overlooking Trinsic Bay. I never knew my father; my mother died when I was five. No one took me off the streets. No one endowed my education. While you put your own name on your wife's estate and built your proud villa, I was assaying gold in Lord British's treasury. I'd be there still—and to the day I died—but for the chaos Lord British wrought when he vanished. Regent Blackthorn called for help; I answered the call. I find myself at the high water mark, and I must take advantage of it.

"I have no family, Erwald—no sons to carry my name nor daughters to indulge. I have no comfortable home for my declining years. I would have these things: a healthy, young wife to give me children and a home where she can care for me."

"You can't mean Hawksnest. Never! I've lost the best of my sons, but I've got another. I'll make a man of him—"

"Hawksnest!" Lohgrin laughed with hollow merriment. "You do me a disservice, my lord. I would not dream of breaking your inheritance. All I want is Althea's hand, and the dowry you surely meant to settle on her."

Lord Ironhawk hesitated; on the landing, Jordan dared to hope his father would redeem himself by refusing the offer. He cleared his throat. "I'd thought to marry her to someone her own age . . ." he said weakly.

"With you, and your sons, the question is simply one of virtue, but with your foster-children, the question is in their blood. The bend toward magic runs in families. The bend toward treason as well: you heard her defend him. Lesser men than you and me might take the easy path and lock her away before her contagion spreads. But we are men of virtue—of compassion above all. And I am blinded by her beauty. No one would question the virtue of an Inquisitor's wife.

"We would all have what we want."

There was a long silence. Jordan tightened his fists until his palm bled. Sacrifice was one of the eight virtues, but this wasn't sacrifice. This was tragedy; this was wrong. He waited for his father to speak.

"We are in agreement then?" The voice was Lohgrin's. "If the girl consents—"

"We do not have the luxury of persuasion, my lord Iron-hawk. Need I remind you, Balthan Wanderson has already been condemned to corporal and spiritual death for his part in the Great Council's treason? My lord Ironhawk—we cannot *prove* it, yet, but we of the Inquisition believe in our hearts, souls, and minds that Balthan Wanderson is hand-in-glove with whoever—whatever—waylaid Lord British. We *will* catch him, and he *will* sing his song before he dies. We will seek all who abetted him, and after that there will be no time for consent."

Ironhawk cleared his throat. "We'll speak with her in the cup hall. I'm certain once she understands the risks."

"She is an orphan, dear Erwald; you are her guardian. She does not need to understand anything, so long as you do."

Seven
ΥΥΥΥΥ

Jordan gasped as his father
and the Inquisitor sealed Al-
thea's fate with a hearty handshake. He heard their footsteps
depart separately from the courtyard colonnade; he was too
stunned to move. Althea was beautiful, and she made his
blood do strange things. Four months beyond his eighteenth
birthday, Jordan hadn't spared any thoughts for marriage,
but he'd marry her in a moment if it would keep her out of
Lohgrin's hands.

He was still in the throes of outrage when Hugh's step-
drag echoed off the steps.

"Lohgrin means to *marry* Althea—and Lord Ironhawk
will allow it!" Jordan sputtered as he got to his feet.

Hugh did not answer until he was within arm's reach.
"There's shame, but no surprise in that," he said with no
indication of either in his voice. "She's a beautiful young
woman. The only wonder is that Lohgrin wants her. Except
to chide their virtue at supper, he's shown no interest in
women. Rumors have been thick—"

"He wants a wife to give him sons and Althea's dowry
in exchange for squaring Hawksnest's role in Balthan's supposed treason with Blackthorn."

Hugh nudged the young man toward his room. "Life can be hard for a beautiful girl living on charity. Virtue can be a very brittle thing." He meant to sound wise, and sounded desperate for wisdom instead. "Ironhawk means well—for you, for Hawksnest, and even for Althea—but it's a difficult passage. Innocent people often suffer, Hawson; nothing goes according to plan."

Jordan shrugged Hugh's hand aside. "It can't be allowed! Althea may not be blood kin, but she's not chattel. She'll never consent."

Hugh was ready when Jordan tried to plunge down the stairs. "She'll give her consent, Hawson. Ironhawk's already gone to remind her of her debts, and the danger Balthan's brought to us all. How often have *you* held your ground against Ironhawk—especially when he's right." Hugh's words were hard as flint, just as sharp, and spoken directly into Jordan's ear.

"Damn them both." Jordan meant his father and Lohgrin. He grabbed the newel post, then propelled himself to the door. "It can't be right when Althea's forced to marry. I'll stop them, Hugh, I swear it." He caromed against the doorjamb hard enough to shake the wall. "Find me my best jacket—the one I wore last Midsummernight—and my belt with the gold buckles. They'll look at me and they'll listen." He commenced a flailing search for his comb.

Hugh worked at the wardrobe in silence, but when Jordan knocked a second bottle onto the unforgiving floor, he shoved the neatly folded garments on the shelf. "Is this what you're searching for?" he said with sarcastic politeness, rapping Jordan's knuckles with the bone teeth.

In a heartbeat Jordan closed one hand over the comb and the other over Hugh's wrist. "Damn you, Hugh—"

"Damn me because I can see and you can't?" Hugh said softly. "You won't make a bad thing better with childishness. Sacrifice is a virtue, too. An adult—man or woman—understands that hard choices must be made. He does not run from them. He faces their consequences with honor, valor, and all the other virtues as his safekeeping."

Swallowing hard, Jordan released his armiger and attacked his hair instead. Hugh had never been rich or powerful, but he was a Peer by his own right. The medallion beneath his shirt carried two stones: a smooth crimson carnelian for the virtue of Honor and the faceted ruby of Sacrifice. Hugh knew about hard choices and their consequences. He left Jordan fighting his doubts and the snarls in his hair.

"But it's still not right," Jordan muttered, throwing the comb onto his bed.

"If the choice is between right and wrong, there's no sacrifice." Hugh handed Jordan a linen jacket.

The previous summer, when Jordan wore it for the first time, the jacket had been comfortably loose. Now the sleeves were tight and the loops strained to meet their corresponding buttons. Hugh interceded immediately.

"I'll say this much for your journeying"—the armiger yanked sharply on both sides of the jacket, forcing a loop over the appropriate button—"it's put meat on your bones. You're past coltish and starting to grow into your arms and legs—" Hugh prepared for another yank and another comment, but left it unsaid.

"Go ahead—finish it."

"You'd better not sneeze or these buttons will fly into the soup."

"That's not what you meant to say."

Hugh reached for and dropped Jordan's belt. "Balthan's got a lot to answer for. You, his sister, that magician Felespar, and—for all anyone knows—the disappearance of Lord British himself, just as the Inquisitor says—"

Buttons did go flying as Jordan lifted his armiger off his feet. "I'm not saying this again: Balthan's not responsible for any of this. He was scared silly when Blackthorn came for Felespar; he ran halfway across Britannia thinking he was followed; and when he cast magic in that cave, all he did was protect himself from his enemies. Real enemies, Hugh. There were three harpies guarding that cave: *harpies*! The Squirt gave him one of the feathers for his hat—you should have seen the look on Councillor Annon's face when he saw it. Balthan's not the enemy, Hugh; Balthan's enemies are the enemy.''

Jordan's thoughts raced ahead of his tongue. He remembered the moments in the Hawksnest yard when he condemned Balthan with words that did not feel like his own. He also remembered Balthan saying that his enemies came to him as dream temptations, and that although he'd resisted them, he hadn't realized their nature until he saw Blackthorn possessed by malignant shadows. If Blackthorn, a Companion of Lord British, could fall into temptation—what about Lohgrin? What about his father? What about himself? Did the berserkerang make one especially vulnerable to enemies?

''Balthan put up a fight. The wraiths couldn't corrupt him, so they hounded him with nightmares and harpies. When that didn't work, they turned to those who were closest to him . . . and weakest.''

Jordan shoved Hugh aside; to maintain his balance, Hugh held on to Jordan's arm. They were equally oblivious to the figure in the doorway until it was too late.

''Don't hurt him, Jordie!''

Squirt launched himself across the room. In his mind, men were giants and he was no bigger or stronger than he'd been the first time they put a sword in his hand, and laughed because he couldn't hold the point steady. Now he was nearly thirteen, and for all his effort and practice, both his arms weren't equal to one of Jordan's. On those occasions when Darrel wrestled with his big brother, he left nothing in reserve. He was astonished when all three of them collapsed on the floor. He was also the first to recover.

''Don't hurt him!'' Squirt pummeled Jordan's ribs.

Despite dire predictions from the swordmasters and wishful thinking from many menials, the Squirt was growing up. He might never be a match for Jordan, but his punches were well aimed, well thrown, and they hurt when they struck the bruises Ironhawk had left a scant hour earlier. Doubly handicapped by blindness and the red rage, Jordan would dismember his brother if he allowed himself the least retaliation.

"Get him off me!" he bellowed.

Hugh considered Ironhawk's second son an expendable nuisance, but he heard the urgency in Jordan's voice, and ignoring the ache in his ruined knee, he clamped one hand on Squirt's neck and the other on his breeches. Darrel lashed out with fists and feet.

"Have you lost the wits you were born with?" Hugh knew he wouldn't be able to hold the eely boy. He didn't wait for the inevitable escape, but threw him immediately at the wall.

Darrel gathered himself into a wary crouch. Being on the receiving end of a grown man's anger was nothing uncommon. He took pride in shaking the clouts off as if nothing had happened—he didn't cry, or apologize, or let on when he hurt. But something distinctly out of the ordinary was happening—again: Jordan remained on the floor, all tight and twisted as if he were in horrible agony.

Darrel made a fist, stared at it, then at his brother. "I didn't hit him hard enough to hurt him."

"It's the berserkerang—the third bout today." Hugh took a thick candlestick from the night table; he held it like a club. "It's consuming him. He's fighting himself . . . and losing."

The boy wanted to close his eyes or cover them, but couldn't. So much was suddenly clear—like a puzzle he could have solved a thousand times over, but never did because he didn't want to see the final shape. Unlike Jordan, Darrel knew his father bore the berserkerang—people ignored him, they talked in front of him as if he were a piece of furniture. The boy was certain he'd inherited it—how else to explain the pesky demon that gave him ideas and got him in endless trouble? And he accepted his fate because everyone thought Jordan had been spared.

Watching Jordan pound his forehead against the floor, Squirt was forced to recognize that, private demon or not, he was the one who'd been spared and that his brother—his exemplary brother—had inherited the curse. He crawled across the room and rested his hand carefully on Jordan's arm.

"I'm sorry, Jordie. The Eye of Destiny knows I'm telling the truth: I didn't mean to—I never put things together right. Come on, Jordie . . . *stop*."

"Leave him alone—you'll make matters worse." The armiger raised the candlestick. When Ironhawk first asked him to look after Jordan, they'd understood it might come to this. Hugh never kidded himself that it would be easy, but caught in Darrel's reproachful stare, Hugh found that murder was impossible; he heaved the candlestick into the corner.

"It's why the swordmasters always came here, to Hawksnest. It's why Jordan never went south to Serpent's Hold, or anywhere else for fostering. It's even why our lord father wouldn't nominate him for his Virtue Quest." Squirt wasn't asking questions. His gaze never left the spot where he touched Jordan's arm, where the bunched muscles were finally beginning to relax. "Ironhawk was afraid of this. He didn't trust Jordie, either."

Jordan shuddered. He rolled over; his back arched hideously, then with a prolonged groan he collapsed. Darrel's spirits soared; Jordan had won his fight. But Jordan wasn't moving.

"Come on, Jordie—you've got to be better. Don't be dead!"

Hugh caught the boy before he sprinted through the door, and for once Squirt did not struggle.

"Give him a moment to come around," the armiger advised.

After a few moments during which Darrel himself forgot to breathe, Jordan stretched his arms like a man rising from a peaceful sleep.

"Don't do that again, Squirt," Jordan said wearily. "Don't rush me or take me from behind—" His vision cleared momentarily, then clouded just as quickly. Fighting the berserkerang eroded the affliction in his eyes, but it was even more risky than staring at the sun. Nonetheless, Jordan had seen his brother in Hugh's arms. "—Unless you're spoiling for a rough fight. You're too big now." He reached out, man to man, for a boost.

Nothing could have made Darrel prouder. He clasped Jordan's wrists and pulled. At first it seemed more likely that Darrel would crash into Jordan's stomach, then the boy threw his head back and Jordan rose from the floor. Hugh was right there to steady them both.

"So, tell me whatever it was that brought you charging in here."

Fraternal affection had definite limits; Darrel retreated a respectable distance. "Balthan got away. Everyone came back empty-handed—even the ones who rode after Seanna and searched her wagon—"

"They stopped and *searched* Seanna's wagon?" Jordan tried, and failed, to imagine the teamster tolerating such a gross violation of her rights.

Darrel snickered. "They said so. Our lord father believed them, and so did that creepy Inquisitor. All that matters is that they didn't find Balthan. And that's good—isn't it?" When Jordan did not immediately respond, Darrel's voice shrank. "You didn't mean what you said in the yard, did you? That was something you and Balthan arranged beforehand, wasn't it—all that time you were together with the glyphs, you were really planning what to do when we got to Hawksnest, weren't you? And Seanna was in on it, too. . . ?"

"I wish it were true, Squir—Darrel." Jordan made an ineffective grab in his brother's direction.

"But it's good that Balthan got away . . . isn't it?"

"I suppose so. There's no guessing what he'd do if he knew what's happened—" Then briefly, but too melodramatically for Hugh's taste, Jordan related the encounters between Althea and Lohgrin, their lord father and Lohgrin, and his suspicions about the Inquisitor's influence over their father.

"But you won't let it happen, will you? You won't let that happen to Althea? . . . Jordie?"

Jordan wished for a moment of clear vision or, better yet, a plan. He got another cascade of sickly green spheres. He rubbed his eyes, as if that would help, and found his way to the chair.

"There's nothing I can do, Squirt. I can't see worth a tinker's damn and I'm . . . I go—" He could not say the word. "There's just nothing I can do."

"Then I'll do something. I'm big now, you said so yourself. I hid the sword you got me. I'll get it, and I'll sneak up on loathy Lohgrin and thrust it between his ribs, clean through his heart—if he's got one. I'll go like this—" Squirt mimed a deadly twist of the hilt. "And then I'll pull down and out." The boy had mastered some of his lessons. "He won't bother anybody ever again."

"Don't even think about it."

"He's a scribbler, Jordie. There's ink under his nails. How will he stop me? You heard what he said about magicians—he's not going to crack the seal on a kill scroll."

Jordan buried his face in his hands. He couldn't see; he couldn't fight—his thoughts kept turning into hopeless wishes. His gut was rumbling—it could be hunger, or it could be berserkerang. He almost hoped it *was* the berserkerang: a man wasn't responsible for what he did while berserk. It was tempting, and then the gong summoned the household to the cup hall for supper. The sound echoed inside Jordan, assuring him that he was in no danger of going berserk, nor did he care if all Britannia watched him eat with his fingers instead of a knife and fork.

Hunger was the one problem he could solve.

By the time the gong clanged the hurry-up, Jordan was sewn into his too-small jacket and Darrel had been made presentable in clothing scrounged from the bottom of the wardrobe. Hugh accompanied them as far as the high doors of the cup hall at which point, seeing the grim faces at the head table, he chose to exercise a retainer's privilege of eating in the kitchen.

"Is it that bad?" Jordan asked Darrel. His vision had not cleared since leaving his room.

Lady Barbara sat in her customary place. Though she wore her finest jewels, her hair was untidy and her expression was cast in stone. Ironhawk spoke loudly and expansively with Dench, as if the sullen, scarred churl were an old friend, as if this were an ordinary supper at the end of an ordinary day. Dench's master was absent, but Althea waited stiffly beside an empty chair. Her coppery hair was dressed with pearls, and like Darrel, she wore borrowed clothes: a pale green gown with flowing, fingertip sleeves. She appeared smaller and younger than she was. Her cheeks were red, also the rims of her eyes. Darrel felt her look at him. He smiled and she looked away.

"It's that bad," he confirmed to Jordan. "If we both sit at the high table there won't be room for the Inquisitor."

Lohgrin entered the cup hall before Darrel guided Jordan the length of it. Instead of his usual austere black, the Inquisitor had decked himself out in a variety of clashing crimsons. Ivo, whose features were handsome when he wasn't sneering and whose manners were casually refined, walked slightly behind his master, carrying a tasseled presentation pillow on which sat an ornate enamel box.

"You should see him. He looks like he's come to a masquerade," Darrel whispered scornfully. "He's a scribbler for certain! Lord Ironhawk can't keep from smirking."

Jordan did get a glimpse of Lohgrin parading through the hall. He was growing accustomed to these untimely visions and could study them without interrupting himself—but the frozen image of Lohgrin in matchless, moth-eaten velvets and satins nearly undid him.

Before he'd been struck by magic, Jordan took an opponent's measure quickly and often missed the subtleties. Now, he scrutinized the smallest details in his memory. Lohgrin couldn't know how foolish he looked. He was Blackthorn's man, but as Jordan had overheard, he wasn't wealthy. At Hawksnest, Jordan and his family took certain things for granted. Jordan detested the formal garments he had to wear once or twice a season, but they were always made to fit him alone, as were the comfortable clothes he wore every day. Only a fool would march into the cup hall dressed like a jester. Lohgrin was neither a fool nor a jester; it followed, then, that he did not know how he looked.

Jordan pinched his brother. "Mind your virtues, and *stop* laughing."

"Jordie—you haven't seen him—"

"I *have* seen him. He's proud as a peacock—"

"He's a scribbler, a scarecrow!" Darrel tried to wriggle free.

Jordan tightened his grip until pain forced the boy to be still and silent. "Either he mocks us in moth-eaten velvet—which I doubt—or he prays we will accept him as a peer."

Darrel wouldn't believe a word Jordan said, except his parents were both glowering at him and everyone else was giving the Inquisitor more respect than they'd give Lord British. The hall was so quiet when Lohgrin placed the pillow on the table in front of Althea that Darrel could hear pigeons cooing on the roof.

Lohgrin's presentation box, like his clothing, had seen better days. The clasp broke in Althea's trembling hands; the enamel flaked as she wrestled with what remained.

"I can't," she complained in a whisper that reached the darkest corners. "I can't open it."

The Inquisitor snatched the box from her hands. He wrenched the top off and threw it into the straw, then held up his betrothal gift. A gasp rippled through the hall, and Jordan's vision cleared long enough for him to see a huge freshwater pearl surrounded by garnets and hung from a short gold chain. Like all freshwater pearls, it was irregular in color and shape. It was impressive, but grotesque, not beautiful. The green spheres returned; the frozen pearl hovered in his mind's eye. Jordan cursed beneath his breath and almost missed what Althea said:

"It's too much. I cannot take it. I have been told that if I consent to be your wife, you will not persecute my brother and will protect my lord's family from retribution—this promise is all that I will accept in exchange for my consent. With it I will obey you as my lord and become your wife, asking nothing nor taking anything from you again."

Jordan wished to see her face, but the spheres did not yield. "What's happening? Is he giving her his word? I can't hear . . ."

Darrel waited a moment before answering. "You can't hear him, 'cause he's not talking. He looks *very* angry, but he's put the necklace back in the box. He's giving the box to the other guy. He's leaving—Jordie—he's giving up and walking out! She didn't take it; they're not betrothed!"

"She gave her consent, Squirt—that's all it takes: a woman's consent, freely given before witnesses. She refused his gift, but she's still his to marry."

Eight

ΥΥΥΥΥ

Althea lingered in the cool courtyard. Unexpectedly—miraculously—she was alone. Midway through her grim betrothal feast she'd stood up, walked out, and become alone. Althea had wished that no one would notice her departure, but while she had mastery over linear, or domestic, magic, neither she nor any living soul could grant wishes. Wishes were magic's magic and forever inexplicable.

The fountains splashed musically. A nightingale resumed its interrupted song. The cloying sweet scent of orange blossoms was balanced by the crisper essence of sandalwood: Lady Barbara perfumed the lamp oil for that very purpose. Althea sat beneath the nightingale's tree and shut her mind to everything but its song.

When all was said and done, courage was a very simple thing; simpler than love or truth—the other two principles that underlay the Avatar's philosophy of Virtue. Her life had been in tumult since Regent Blackthorn disbanded the Great Council of Magicians and set his Inquisitors in their place. But tonight when Lohgrin held up that ugly pearl, everything was clear and easy. If an orphan's fate was to be bartered like swine or cattle, she, as that orphan, would at least name her own price.

Lord Ironhawk had visited her room and explained why he was giving her to the Inquisitor, but he lacked the courage to demand acknowledgment of those hopes from Lohgrin.

Althea had always accepted that she was weak, naive, and ignorant of the ways of the world. From the beginning, when Balthan protected her from their father, she expected someone else to fight her battles for her. But when her darkest hour finally arrived, and she was utterly alone, Althea found that she had courage to spare. All the words, and the strength to say them, came from the darkness itself. She'd known from the moment she pulled her fingers away from the pearl how the Inquisitor would answer.

He hadn't accepted her bargain, but she'd forced him to make the refusal public.

The cup hall was amazed and silent when Lohgrin walked out. No one believed the Inquisitor could be denied—not when Lord Ironhawk spun so easily in the wind—especially by a woman-child who never spoke above a whisper. No one praised or congratulated her; no one spoke to her at all after the Inquisitor stormed out. She'd been surprised by the shunning, and hurt. Her worst fears about Ironhawk's family seemed amply confirmed. Jordan had stared at her—insofar as he could be said to stare at anything—but *he* never found the courage to speak. She drank two goblets of wine in quick succession; they gave her the courage to escape.

The nightingale sang with the fountains. The courtyard had worked its particular magic. Floating on the wine, Althea cast her doubts and fears into the night breeze. Surely when she reached her little room with its narrow bed and horsehair mattress, she'd sleep the deep, dreamless sleep all warriors earned when their battles were over.

Althea counted the doorways along the dark corridor with her fingertips until she touched her own. Iron locks were too expensive to hang on a room that contained nothing more valuable than herbs and fragrant oils. A knotted string descended from a hole in the planks. She pulled it; the inside latch rose, and the door swung open. Once inside Althea yanked the string through the hole, looped it over a peg, and pushed the door shut. The pivoted latch clicked into a grooved plate protruding from the door frame: not as good as a sliding bolt or a key mechanism, but locks only kept honest people out.

There was a dish of charcoal near the door. Althea dipped her fingers in the powder, then snapped them. Cold light coated her hand and winked harmlessly as she shuffled out of her borrowed gown. Althea was fastidious with her possessions, checking her clothes carefully for stains or tears before returning them to the cedar chest, but the gown wasn't hers. When it circled her ankles, she simply stepped out of it and left it where it was.

Handfire didn't last very long. The nimbus was already fading when she heard boot heels in the corridor. That was a little odd—except for the four-year-old son of the pastry cook all the residents of this corridor were women. Married men dwelt with their families in cottages; single men slept in a dormitory near the arena unless their duties assigned them elsewhere. Still, it was hardly scandalous for a woman to invite a man to share the greater privacy of her quarters—especially when the family's attention was elsewhere.

The handfire expired and Althea plumped her pillow into a soft ball. Her eyes were closed when she heard the latch rattle against the plate. She sat up; the rattle was not repeated. All the doors looked alike; he probably miscounted, then corrected himself when the door did not swing open.

Althea's thoughts were far away when wire scraped through the string hole. She didn't recognize the sound for what it was.

The latch string was on the inside of a closed door as often as not. Most people had a wire hook dangling from their belt along with a knife and a bit of flint. Fishing the string through the hole was a tedious but not particularly difficult task. Still, one usually knocked first, unless one knew for certain that the room was empty—or one knew that it wasn't empty but didn't dare make any noise.

Wide awake, Althea swung her legs over the edge of the mattress. "Balthan?" she whispered, and wished her charcoal wasn't on the other side of the room.

The string unwound from the peg above the hole, the hook was swiftly withdrawn, and the latch bar rose out of the groove.

"Balthan?"

A mote of sizzling light sped to the ceiling where it adhered and grew. Althea was momentarily blinded, then reassured. Her brother was a Lyceum magician with Circle magic at his command. No feeble handfire for him, but an In Lor spell to place a steady light exactly where he wanted it.

Althea sought her sandals as the door swung open and bumped against the wall.

"Balthan—thank heavens you're safe."

Balthan stared at the flickering light above him. The difference between where he was and where he might be if the Inquisitor had caught him was growing less distinct with each passing moment. Intellect told him that no more than six hours had passed since Drum had shown him the bolthole in the forge-yard. He knew he wasn't going to find a better place so he jumped down and Drum replaced the grate.

The bolthole had been cut when the forge-yard was built. It had a stone bench where a man could sit until his butt grew numb and nothing more. Balthan could lie down, if he kept his knees bent; even so his feet were in the ashpit directly under the grate. He could, of course, stand in the ashes. He could even leap up and hang from the grate, but so far he hadn't found a way to move it while he was dangling there. Before it got dark, he'd torn a page from his spellbook and, using the bench as a desk, covered the parchment with a self-serving message to his sister.

Ironhawk's men had come through the forge twice. The second time they announced that the traitor—which was to say, Balthan—had made good his escape. The Foregate alarm and curfew were repealed. That was a good many hours ago, and intellect notwithstanding, Balthan had begun to wonder why the smiths needed a bolthole in the forge-yard and if the farrier meant to starve him to death. He'd already eaten his supply of garlic; the ginseng was next, and then the blood moss. If he got out of here alive, he was going to start carrying food in his sack.

If Drum had heard Balthan's thoughts, he would have agreed that supper was taking too long. He expected his return to be noticed, but he hadn't expected it to become a clan celebration. There was nothing he could do for the magician until everyone went to bed. The kitchen opened into the forge-yard that was, itself, surrounded by the walls and windows of the residence. Drum had seen Balthan's knuckles hooked over the grate several times. His neck was stiff from cringing, waiting for the sound of iron scraping over stone—a sound he hadn't heard.

Drum had told his parents who he'd hidden in the bolt-hole. They'd been scandalized, but agreed to keep his secret until dawn, and not a moment longer. The lives and liveli-hood of the clan could not be jeopardized for Balthan Wan-derson.

Although years had passed since Balthan's last visit to Hawksnest, the precocious magician was not at all forgotten. In addition to the usual failings of peerage sons—marked tendencies toward drunkenness, disorderliness, and de-bauchery—Balthan Wanderson wreaked havoc with undis-ciplined magic. A glance from him and cream refused to separate from milk, bread dough rose like foam on a fresh poured mug of beer or else lay completely flat, roosters crowed themselves to exhaustion, and tarts simply vanished from the sills on which they cooled.

When pressed, it was conceded that the mercurial youth could be inventive and helpful—when it pleased him. He could magic the churn-stomp to make butter in half the usual time. He could level a shelf on the first try or squint and see exactly where a wheel needed rounding. The problem was that no one ever knew which Balthan was crossing the threshold until it was too late. It was his changeableness they neither forgave nor forgot.

Even now, when the beer pitcher sat on the table and everyone was mellow, Drum knew most of his family would gladly deliver Balthan to the Inquisitor if they had an inkling that he was in their forge-yard. If Drum had not felt the black fog in Britain City or seen Lohgrin with his own eyes, he could not have revealed the bolthole to the frantic magician when he came stumbling into the forge. There was something unpleasant about the Inquisitor, something that made Balthan Wanderson seem bright and trustworthy. After listening to the Foregate version of the misery that had overtaken Hawksnest since he left, Drum was certain he'd made the right decision—but that didn't keep him from glancing anxiously at the grate.

Ned Nearhand, his father's brother and the patriarch of the family, clapped Drum on the shoulder. "Itching for tomorrow, aren't you, lad? Itching for the weight of a hammer in your hand and the fire wind on your face? You've got the roaming out of your spirit; time to settle down to a life's good work. You've had your taste of chasing after Virtue and come home again safe. I feared for you, running off like that. No denying that I thought you were daft and I said so, too. You'll hear it about and around. But I'm glad you've come back with your head squared. We kept your place. You're not Krist. Not like Krist at all."

Drum winced. "I'm grateful, Uncle Ned, and itching—just like you said." Drum was a hair taller than his uncle, not enough to make any difference, especially when the subject was Krist, the black sheep of his grandfather's generation and the last member of the family to abandon the life of fire and iron.

"Then—to bed with you!"

The others took the patriarch's words as a command and started for the door. Drum suppressed the urge to glance into the forge. He'd done the right thing today when he rescued Balthan from his pursuers, but tomorrow morning he'd be a member of his family again, forever. Tomorrow morning, hiding Balthan in the bolthole would be wrong. Two months ago Drum didn't believe right could become wrong overnight—as if right and wrong were as changeable as Balthan Wanderson. Much had happened in the last two months.

"A moment, Uncle Ned—a moment to be alone in the dark, with the fires banked and my family sleeping above me. To know that I'm home again, and where I belong." In the last two months he'd learned to tell an honest lie.

Ned Nearhand scrutinized his nephew. "Have you gone philosophic on us, Drumon?"

Drum met his uncle's eyes without hesitation. "No, I just need to be alone."

The older man was unreassured. "By all the iron that's been dug from the ground or fallen from the stars—I never needed to be alone. That's what comes of leaving your family, Drumon—you begin to get a taste for it. Next thing you know, you *are* alone—plumb alone for the rest of your natural days."

By tradition, Drum should have knuckled under, but he neither bent nor broke; it was Ned who backed down. "Have it your own way. Sit up all night, alone. You'll hammer your thumb bloody come morning. It's all the same to me."

The patriarch left. Drum was alone—except for Balthan, of course, and a cousin who emerged from the shadows behind the oven as soon as everything was quiet.

"He's here, isn't he? You locked him in, didn't you?"

The cousin was Minette. She was Ned Nearhand's youngest daughter, a few years younger than Drum, and like others her age who weren't taken into the family trade, she worked for wages in the villa. Drum had not shared his secret with her.

"Your mother told me," Minette explained. "After I told her what happened."

"After *what* happened?" Drum placed himself between his cousin and the forge-yard.

Minette hefted the beer pitcher, realized it was empty, then sighed as she sat. "It's a long story—too long to tell. There was another alarm—two actually. Loathy Lohgrin was spying out his windows, as usual, after he left the feast. He said he saw someone scale the walls. He sent his churls to sound an alarm—the first—he went to Althea's room. He said she was unconscious when he found her, poisoned. No one else saw anything, but the Inquisitor hauls a big hammer in there—"

"Althea? Will she live—?"

"Too soon to tell." Minette shrugged. "Lohgrin brought her to his rooms. They've dosed her with everything in the apothecary cabinet. I guess—but she's still unconscious. They don't know what kind of poison it was. Loathy says it was magic—"

"Get me out of here, Drum!" Balthan's knuckles looped over the grate.

Minette ducked under Drum's arm and raced across the forge-yard. She got to the grate first and stomped on Balthan's fingers. The magician dropped to the ashes with a groan.

"Not so fast," Minette addressed her cousin. "If it's magic, he's the likely suspect."

"Drum! Move her and the grate—" Balthan whispered urgently.

"Or what?" Minette wrapped her skirt tightly around her

legs. She didn't move off the grate. "Will you blast me
with fire? Poison me as I stand? What will you and your
magic do?"

"Drum! You know I've been down here for hours. I
couldn't be two places at once, could I? Come on—the
Inquisitor's lying."

"No, Minette's right: you've done strange things with
your magic—things no one else would think to do. I
wouldn't put anything past you."

"I didn't poison my sister. I couldn't and I wouldn't.
Anabarces' ghost, Drum—she could have done it herself.
Remember the harpies!"

Minette queried Drum with a glance, and after a reluctant
moment the farrier conceded that Althea had indeed mistak-
enly poisoned herself during their travels.

"I saved her then, Drum—I'll save her now."

"You'd give yourself to the Inquisitor to save your sister?" Minette's tone was both uncharitable and incredulous.

When Balthan answered correctly and without hesitation,
Minette relented and stepped aside. Drum lifted the grate
and pulled Balthan up.

"Maybe I could get in and get out without the Inquisitor
catching me . . . I could do just what he said I did: scale
the walls! I'll need rope—And garlic. You must have some
garlic."

He headed for the herb racks. Drum was right behind
him. Minette cleared her throat nervously.

"Whether you poisoned her, or she did it herself, it's
better to leave her as she is."

Both men gave Minette their full attention. She'd stayed
in the villa to help with the sudden feast, but hadn't been in
the cup hall. What she knew about Lohgrin's dower-gift and
Althea's refusal was secondhand, but believable. "I could
understand if she tried to kill herself, or if you'd murdered
her for mercy. She's better off in the ground than in *his*
bed."

Drum sagged against the wall. His breath was shallow, as if he'd been struck in the gut. Balthan cursed and smacked a fist into his palm. He paced the kitchen, favoring his stiff ankle.

"I've got to get in there—There's got to be a way."

"There're guards—the Inquisitor's churls and Hawksnest retainers. I saw them when I left. No one trusts you, Balthan, you won't get near her," Minette said simply, factually.

The magician went weak with regret. He eased into a chair. "Drum, help me—Please? I've got to save her—"

"Save her for what?" Drum seized the magician's shirt, hauled him upright, and one-handed him against the brick wall. "Hammers and bells—you're not going anywhere near her."

Balthan's legs gave out, he collapsed on the stone-hard dirt. "Is this what you want? I'm on my knees pleading with you—I can save her life, Drum. I can save Thea's life—"

"For what?" the farrier's voice was anguished. "So that the Inquisitor can make her his *wife*?"

"We'll get her out—"

Balthan rolled out of the way of a thrown bucket. Upstairs, someone called for quiet; someone else demanded to know what was going on.

"It's all because of you!" Drum declared, standing over Balthan. "None of this would be happening but for you." He pulled the magician to his feet. "I should take you to the Inquisitor's myself—just to make it stop."

"You'll have to kill me first."

Drum was considering the idea when Minette interceded. "You're fools—both of you!" She was used to burly men and not at all intimidated by them. "You"—she brandished her fist in front of Drum's nose—"how are you going to hand him to the Inquisitor without letting on that he's been hiding *here*?" She turned and brought her anger to bear against the magician. "And you—so smart, so sure. You can save your sister; you can get her out of Hawksnest. You want this; you want that. What about her? From what you say, she's taken care of herself, by herself—"

"Killing herself is not taking care of herself!" Balthan shoved Minette away.

People were moving inside the rooms that surrounded the forge and kitchen courtyard. Lamps were lit; stairs were creaking. Minette grabbed Balthan's wrist with a new urgency.

"Get out of here!"

Balthan found the audacity to laugh at her but Drum, who'd been sobered by thoughts of the Inquisitor interrogating his family, had an answer. "The stream," he said, taking Balthan's arm from his cousin. "Follow the stream." He pushed the other man toward the back of the forge-yard.

Balthan fought until he was close enough to the bolthole to grab his sack, then he allowed himself to be propelled out of the light. Drum gave him a final shove and he slid down an embankment. The water was knee-deep and ice-cold.

"I'll get her out," Balthan whispered at Drum's silhouette. It was a promise and a warning.

"Don't come back here."

"There's a piece of parchment in the hole. Give it to"—inspiration flashed in Balthan's mind, and left a name behind—"Jordan."

"Hammers and bells—he's blind, what good will it do him?"

Balthan felt the current swirl around his boots. "Burn it, Drum. Do what you want." He followed the water until he hit a wall and felt the lip of the tunnel that dove under it.

"Where will you be—if they ask?"

Balthan laughed once, then surrendered himself to the tunnel.

Nine
ΥΥΥΥΥ

*B*althan Wanderson sought
shelter beneath a spreading
oak. He was soaked to the skin and suspected there was
mold growing in his boots, maybe between his toes as well.
Since being rescued from his cave, his life had cycled from
sticky damp to wringing wet. He had been dry—he'd even
been dry since emerging from the Foregate sewer—but
those moments were merely aberrations in an otherwise
soggy existence.

This particular watery episode began with a sunrise thun-
derstorm, then the clouds transformed a mist blanket and
drizzle that might well last forever. It was not the torrential,
wind-driven hurricane that had plagued them on the road
from Britain City, but that hardly mattered: the fields remained waterlogged from the earlier flooding. Mud wallows
were revitalized with the first raindrops and the trenched
hillsides where the broodmares grazed were as slick as any
ice-covered slope. Balthan's once-fashionable garments had
the stains to prove it.

He plunged his arm shoulder-deep into his magic sack,
feeling his way past the reagents until he found a warm,
parchment-wrapped meat pastry that he withdrew and began

to eat slowly. The delicacy had shouted his name as he crept around the outside of the Rosignel kitchen; he'd felt guilty taking it. Minette's accusations hurt because they were true: the people of Hawksnest didn't trust him. His fellow magicians didn't trust him. His family—and he included his adoptive family as well as Althea—didn't trust him. Balthan didn't have to worry about his friends; he'd never bothered acquiring any. Indeed, as far back as he could remember, he'd put his efforts into confounding all those who crossed his path.

With a dramatic sigh, Balthan rewrapped the pastry and tucked it away in the depths of his sack. The magically woven interior was jammed with rolls, fruits, sweetmeats, sausage, and an entire wheel of his favorite blue-veined cheese. He'd never have to eat his reagents again. He should have felt better than he did. Perhaps it was some lingering effect of the magic he'd wrought in the cave. Maybe his desperate passage through the Flame of the Avatar *had* changed him. Or possibly mold was growing in his brain.

He'd never meant to need anyone—including Althea. He'd actually tried to leave Hawksnest two nights ago. He'd gotten as far as one of the sentinel stones, but he hadn't been able to climb the embankment to the Old Paladin's Road.

It wasn't magic keeping Balthan on Ironhawk's land. He would have recognized magic, and overcome it. No, this was more insidious than magic; it was Truth, Courage, and even Love: the underlying Principles in a philosophy of Virtue he'd never completely embraced. It wouldn't be enough to get Althea out of the villa. He was going to have to free Hawksnest from the corruption Lohgrin—and all that stood with Lohgrin or behind him—brought to it.

And he'd have to do it by himself—because no one trusted him.

Balthan didn't have the slightest notion of how he was going to accomplish his self-imposed quest. He could fill every blank page of his spellbook with questions he couldn't answer—but he did know that Althea was still alive. The estate cemetery lay outside the walls of Rosignel and from the oak it was clear that there were no new graves. He'd tried to learn more by creeping up to the open windows under cover of night, but the handful of people living at Rosignel did so because they weren't interested in what happened in Erwald Lord Ironhawk's household. They spent their evenings reminiscing about the old days when Hawksnest was Rosignel and Lady Barbara's father was the tenth of his lineage to be the landlord. Listening to them one would not know that Lord British had been missing for six months. One would not know that the Avatar had come to Britannia a century ago, raised the Codex, and formulated the philosophy of Virtue before returning to his native world. One would not even know that this was Britannia, not Sosaria where sorcerers of every moral stripe confronted each other.

Balthan kept watch on the graveyard while he waited for inspiration. Intuition said the key lay in what Minette said. A magician always started with intuition and then attacked with the hammer and chisel of logic until the truth emerged like a statue from stone. Balthan tried, then he'd hear Minette say: *No one trusts you* and lose himself in some better-forgotten memory.

It happened again.

He was back in the early summer of a drier year. He was in this very field, rubbing all the foals with mint oil and garlic. The broodmares couldn't tell which belonged to whom. Ironhawk knew who was responsible, even though he never quite figured out what had been done. And Jordan got stuck bathing the foals and reintroducing them to their dams—

Balthan remembered everything except why he'd played the prank. He didn't like horses, and surely the foals hadn't cooperated—

The magician heard a foal squealing and the distraught whinny of its dam. He heard the sounds several times before he realized he wasn't remembering them. The mare was not far from his tree. At first he couldn't see the foal, then he saw it struggling in one of the trenches. Without another thought, Balthan went to get a better look. The mare charged, then stopped short without completely blocking the magician's path. She stretched out her neck and lowered her head. Balthan licked his lips nervously and stayed where he was. Ironhawk kept these mares for breeding, not riding; they were halter-broken but it took a firm voice and a steady eye to control them—neither of which Balthan possessed.

The foal squealed and struggled. Balthan saw the problem and turned quickly away. It had lost its footing and slipped into one of the muddy trenches. He'd done that himself, but the foal had broken its leg. Balthan knew what had to be done: slit its throat; end its misery, but his hands weren't getting the knife out of his right boot. He was still gathering courage when the mare butted him down. Sprawled in the wet grass, Balthan watched her advance. Her nostrils flared. Her eyes were wild and her teeth were as long and yellow as a boar's tusks.

"Go away," Balthan pleaded. She butted him again; he scrabbled backward across the grass. The foal's head thrashed against his hand.

Balthan didn't faint at the sight of blood—his own or anything else's—but he'd never personally killed anything, and mercy or not, he wasn't going to start by slitting the throat of an unweaned foal. He'd have used magic; there were spells that could drop a dragon in flight, but hornets were more potent than anything in his Second Circle arsenal.

"There's nothing I can do," he explained to the mare.

The mare whickered and butted him gently.

"Nobody trusts me. No mortal soul will give me the benefit of the doubt—but some half-feral *horse* thinks I can work miracles!"

He couldn't work miracles, but there was nothing in the extensively annotated catechisms on the Lyceum shelves that prohibited a magician from healing animals. The formularies were written for humanity and Balthan's limited experience was with humanity, but bones were bones and, in point of fact, he'd never set the bones of man or beast.

The foal thrashed when he touched its leg. Balthan sat back on his heels, pondered awhile, and tried a different tack. The animal had to be calm; it had to trust him before he could even try to examine its leg. He felt foolish crooning nonsense and petting the creature as if it were a dog, but petting worked.

The rain stopped; Balthan never noticed. The sun burned through the mist and went to work on the mud. Balthan stripped off his shirt and bound it tightly around the foal's straightened leg. Then he picked the exhausted creature up and set out for Rosignel: a hard, half-mile hike through rutted, muddy fields, with the broodmare ambling behind.

Insofar as he had thought things through, Balthan meant to carry the foal to the stables and jury-rig a sling for it in one of the stalls. Then he'd go back to the oak—detouring past the kitchen to lift himself a bit of dinner. Spell-casting, especially healing, left a magician ravenous. All that got pushed aside when a grim-faced sword-bearing man rode out to meet him.

The corridor where Darrel crouched with his back against the wall and his knees touching his chin was, like most of those in the villa, open on one side. During the morning, water puddled on the floorboards. Now that the rain had stopped, a sliver of sunlight was drying the wood as it progressed toward him. Darrel had never watched sunlight move before. He guessed he was learning something—or seeing the proof of some lesson he hadn't learned. Either was preferable to being where he was supposed to be: with Aldonar, his tutor; or doing what he was supposed to be doing: copying three whole pages, letter by excruciating letter, from Aldonar's *Treatise on the Applications of the Virtue of Humility*. Watching water evaporate wasn't as boring as copying philosophy, but it was still boring. Darrel could follow any whim as far as it went and the splinter of sunlight wouldn't have moved more than a nail's breadth.

Mostly Darrel's whims led him to hope his parents—specifically his lord father—would forget he'd been born. Yesterday morning Lord Ironhawk came to his youngest son's bedroom and announced that the tutors who hitherto had kept themselves busy bettering Jordan's mind and body would henceforth devote themselves to Darrel, instead. If that had simply meant more hours in the arena practicing swordwork and horsemanship, Darrel would have rejoiced, but so far all he'd gotten were extra hours of reading, writing, and *philosophy*.

This morning, when Darrel explained that the last virtue he'd need if he was supposed to replace Jordan was Humility, Aldonar reached for his switch and the boy raced for the door. He'd expected to lead the scholar on a merry chase through the villa until noon, when he'd let himself be caught in time for lunch, but Aldonar hadn't chased him. The tutor went directly to Lord Ironhawk, and now there were surly retainers everywhere with orders to bring him to his father on a spear butt, if necessary. It had already been a very long morning. The afternoon promised to be even longer.

As sunlight touched his big toe, Darrel wrenched his wayward thoughts from his misfortunes to the more challenging task of overcoming them. He'd already tried his most reliable gambit: he snuck into the weaving room and asked his mother to intercede for him. But Lady Barbara said he had to "take hold." She wouldn't get up from the loom to give him a hug, and was stiff when he tried to give her one.

There was no point in appealing to Jordan. Two men were shooting dice in the corridor outside Jordan's room.

Moreover Jordan hadn't come out of his room since Althea got sick—

Althea.

He hadn't thought about Althea. She couldn't help him reconcile with his father or Aldonar, but he could visit her and maybe make her feel better. He got the croup every winter and knew what it was like to be trussed up in a dark room, surrounded by medicines that smelled bad and tasted worse. He would even offer to read to her—provided the book had pictures and no more than three or four words on a page. That way he could say he was practicing Humility and Compassion and Sacrifice *and* reading—which was surely better than copying what Aldonar had to say about Humility alone. Besides, the challenge of getting past the Inquisitor's churls to Althea's room appealed to him.

Stairways were out of the question, also any path that crossed a courtyard. That left the roofs, which were steep and tiled with interlocking sections of clay pipe. They were treacherous in the best weather; the servants drew lots after every serious storm; the loser climbed the ladder and made the inspection. But Darrel was light-footed, agile, and dangerously bored. The spiral masonry columns on the open side of the corridor beckoned, and leaving his sandals behind, the boy answered their call.

Shinnying along the crown tiles of Hawksnest was much easier than wandering the rooftops of Britain City. Here, Darrel knew where everything was and never found himself facing a blank wall or a sheer drop. The worst moment came when a tile cracked beneath his weight and a piece disappeared over the eaves. He heard it smash on the ground, but no one else had.

It was more exciting than frightening to slither headlong down the tiles to the eaves once he'd reached the right spot. Then he thrust his head and shoulders over the edge, looking for Ivo and Dench. He could see their feet sticking out on the paving, some thirty feet straight down, and took that to

mean it was safe to lock his arms around another column
and swing his legs from the roof to the corridor.

There were two doors on the corridor, one with the latch
string dangling outside and the other with it drawn in. Never
wanting to work harder than necessary, Darrel put his eye
to the latch hole with the dangling string. He didn't see or
hear anything worrisome, so he pulled it. The door opened
away from him.

"Althea?" he whispered, not wanting to alarm her, and
not wanting to alert the churls, either. "Althea—it's me,
Squir—Darrel, I've come to see how you were feeling."

No answer. He pushed the door shut behind him and
waited for his eyes to adjust to the darkness. Maybe she was
asleep. Maybe he shouldn't disturb her.

"Althea?"

The solitary window was not only closed but covered with
dyed parchment that turned the light an eerie, uncomfortable
shade of red. Heartbeats came and went before the boy could
make out shapes in the gloom, then he realized that the bed
had been dismantled. A mound of ropes, blankets, mattress,
and planks filled one of the corners. Obviously Althea
wasn't here, and if his purpose was to visit her there was
no need to creep farther into the room. But Darrel had heard
the tales of Lohgrin's arrival and how Ivo and Dench had
carried everything, including the cart, upstairs. No one from
Hawksnest had gotten a chance to examine any of the chests
and baskets before they vanished and no one, to the boy's
knowledge, had ventured behind the closed door.

This new opportunity was too great to resist and after
peeling the parchment from the window, Darrel opened the
nearest basket. It was filled with hard, shiny objects he
mistook for beads until he held one up to the light and
realized it was a beetle husk. He'd seen similar things in
Annon of Britain's bolthole when he stumbled in there and,
mistaking it for a demon's lair, nearly wrecked it. Annon
had about a dozen of what he said were scarabs, and they

were gem-colored, not oily and black like the hundreds and hundreds Lohgrin had in one basket.

Darrel wondered what an Inquisitor—a man sworn to hunt down traitors, most of whom were magicians—was doing with dead bugs. Then he wondered if they were truly dead—or if they might come to life. He imagined them surging out of the basket with sharp prickly feet and clacking pincers. The image nearly sent him screaming into the corridor.

His demon did things like that. Nothing like berserkerang that afflicted Lord Ironhawk and Jordan—but a mischievous gremlin-demon that got him in trouble no matter how hard he tried to behave. When he read, it made the letters wander and the words meaningless. When he tried to write—well, he preferred not to try *that* very often.

When he ransacked Annon's bolthole, Annon stopped him with a spell that calmed the demon. The effect of the spell hadn't lasted long, but Darrel could recall that precious sense of being himself, just himself: alone and calm. A Council mage couldn't very well follow a boy around, casting the appropriate spell whenever that boy's private demon reared its head—but Annon had done something better: every man, the Councillor said, was a powerful magician in the realm of his own mind. Darrel didn't need a runic alphabet or reagents to charm his demon.

"Calm. Be *calm* . . ." The boy emptied his lungs. "Those bugs have been dead for years. Lohgrin's a horrible man, but he's an Inquisitor, not a magician. Not like Annon. There's nothing to be afraid of—"

The magic worked, at least where the demon was concerned. Darrel felt the urge to panic escape between his lips. What remained was reasonable doubt and equally reasonable fear. Balthan talked as if his kind of magic—Annon's kind of magic—with its eight reagents and Eight Circles, corresponding to the Avatar's eight virtues, were the only kind of magic, but Darrel knew otherwise. He never missed an

opportunity to visit Rosignel and listen to his great-grandmother tell the legends of mighty Sosaria with its wild
magic, its heroes, and its evil sorcerers.

Darrel inserted his stiff fingers into the scarab-filled basket. He removed a handful and funneled them into the hem
of his tunic, which he sealed with a knot. He'd show them
to the cook and the gardener and the other folks who lived
at Rosignel. They'd remember—

The unmistakable sound of a man climbing the stairs
shattered Darrel's reverie. The Inquisitor's storeroom would
be a bad place to be found. He could see a half-dozen places
large enough to hide a scrawny boy; he could see them
because the red-stained parchment was still peeled back
from the window frame. He should hide; he should fix the
parchment, or hiding wouldn't do any good.

Footfalls reached the top of the stairs. They came down
the corridor, heels striking hard on the planks. Squirt could
see Lohgrin's black robe snapping around his ankles; heat
didn't bother the Inquisitor, he never showed a sweat. Darrel
could see Ivo and Dench behind Lohgrin . . . His dilemma
resolved itself. He dropped to his knees behind the scarab-
filled basket and the chest on which it sat. He banged his
forehead on the floor and sent a desperate orison to the Eye
of Destiny.

The footfalls stopped . . . right outside the door! The
latch rattled and the door swung open. He came into the
room, across the room, and stopped on the other side of
the chest. Squirt didn't dare move, not even to lace his
fingers in a luck-sign. He heard the basket move and expected to feel Lohgrin grab the back of his neck. The iron-
strapped lid of the chest slammed against his head. Somehow he managed not to groan or cry out.

The Inquisitor searched without finding. He cursed, invoking a name, Nosfentor, that the boy had not heard before
and hoped never to hear again. Lohgrin mauled his posses-

sions: objects struck the floor with thumps and shatters. He didn't notice that the room was brighter than it should be.

Squirt drew a much-needed breath. Something bounced against his face. He opened his eyes to look at it and stared into the palm of a large, leathery, but unmistakably five-fingered hand. He wanted to panic. He wanted to scream and bolt for freedom, but his private demon, contrary as always, held him frozen until the Inquisitor found the objects of his quest.

" 'A dragon's gall, a gazer's caul, steeped in the blood of an unborn soul and dried in the dark of the moon—' That should keep her under control."

Then the Inquisitor laughed—a sound that got into the spaces between Squirt's bones and made him shiver. This was like a nightmare. He wished it were a nightmare, so he could wake himself up. Lohgrin left, leaving his unspeakable possessions wherever they had fallen. The door slammed shut, but nothing had been a dream. Everything was as real as the ghastly hand. Squirt trembled when he reached for it. He could taste his own tears as he pushed it away and crawled out of his hiding place. He didn't want to look at the gaping chest or the objects beside it, but he did. If he'd eaten since breakfast, he would have gotten sick, but the best his empty gut could manage was a feeble churn.

Among the least offensive objects was a book propped against the chest: a leather-bound book with a broken clasp. The demon stirred; Darrel *had* to lift the cover. The script was the color of dried blood and probably was. The vellum was finer than any in Lord Ironhawk's library; Squirt didn't want to guess what animal it had come from, but he did. He tried to read the words, but no amount of blinking unscrambled the odd-shaped letters or translated their words. He let the cover fall back against the vellum.

"Be calm," he whispered, as he had earlier. "Think.

Think what you've seen. Think who you can tell—'' Annon's face loomed in the boy's memory. The boy shook his head sadly and made the image disappear. Lord Ironhawk's face rose. Surely *what* he had seen was more important than *why* or *how* he had come to see it? And any punishment his father might concoct would not contain dragon's gall or gazer's caul—whatever they were. Then his father's image laughed—not as eerie as Lohgrin's laugh but just as devastating. Lord Ironhawk would never believe him—at best he'd insist on a public inquiry and in his heart of hearts, where the demon made its home, Squirt knew Lohgrin would hide the evidence. Lord Ironhawk's face followed Annon's into oblivion.

"Think, *think*. Somebody's got to believe me. Somebody—"

Another face formed in his mind, and this time Squirt and his private demon were in complete agreement.

Ten

ΥΥΥΥΥ

      *E*ntrusting himself to the protection of the All-Seeing Eye of Destiny, and the chancy wisdom of his demon, Squirt slipped into the corridor, which was empty, although not silent. The other door—the latchstring-locked door—was wide open; he had a good view of Dench's blond head. He had a momentary urge to eavesdrop, but stifled it, and shinnied directly up the column. The rooftops were clear, and his destination window was wide open. He swung through and caught his balance lightly, making no more noise than a pouncing cat.

He opened his mouth to announce himself, but the words didn't come. His mind chewed an extra moment on the scene before him: his brother, half-naked and sweaty, sitting cross-legged on the floor, staring grimly at a candle flame. Jordan's breathing was ragged, as if he were in the last furlong of a footrace, but except for that, he was utterly still. After the ordeal in the Inquisitor's storeroom, Squirt leapt to catastrophic conclusions:

Sweet Eye of Destiny—Jordie's lost his wits altogether! He'll be no help. I'm on my own— Darrel returned to the window.

111

"You don't have to go. I should have known nothing would keep you out."

Relief left Squirt grinning and weak in the knees. There was no mistaking that weary tone: Jordan knew exactly who he was.

"You can see me! You can see. You're well again!"

"Better, anyway." Jordan mopped his face with his shirt before pulling it over his head. He ground his knuckles into his eyes, then squinted at the window. "It's midafternoon, isn't it?"

"More or less. The Eye does see everything, Jordie, truly it does. We've got trouble, Jordie. You've got to come and see, now that you *can* see—"

"What kind of trouble have *we* got, Squirt? What did you break this time?"

"I didn't break nothing," the boy snapped before blurting out: "I sneaked into the room where I thought Lohgrin had Althea—except he didn't have her there. An' then he came in, so I hid, and I listened because he was talking to himself while he was looking for things—awful, creepy things: worse things than Balthan collects. He swore something terrible, and said he was going to make Althea obey him—"

Jordan's interest sharpened. "He said *that*—exactly that: he was going to *make* Althea obey him?"

"I don't remember *exactly*, but that's what he *meant*. Jordie, he had a basketful of black bugs, and he had the hand of a hanged man—all turned into *leather*!"

"A hanged man? Not just a dried-out hand, but a hanged man's dried-out hand?" Jordan wet his fingers and pinched the wick. "You almost had me. I'd believe anything about Lohgrin . . . But a *hanged* man? How do you know he was hanged? How do you know it even came from a *man*? Did it talk?"

The boy groaned. He didn't mean to lie and exaggerate; and he hadn't lied. The withered hand was so repellant he simply assumed it came from a criminal. "I *saw* it, Jordie.

It was a big, old hand, and maybe it didn't come from a hanged man—but it came from *something*." He shook his fists in frustration and the bugs knotted in his shirt bumped against his hip. He fumbled with the knot. "Here—look at these!" Squirt grabbed his brother's hand and filled it with the greasy husks.

Jordan frowned. He squinted, and then he recoiled, scattering the bugs into every corner of his room. After wiping his hand many more times than necessary, Jordan narrowed his eyes once again and sought his brother's face.

"You're still blind," Darrel exclaimed angrily. "You can't see." As far as he was concerned Jordan's deception was far greater than his own.

And Jordan accepted the judgment with a sigh. "I didn't say I could see. I said I was better, and I am. Flame works as well as the glyphs. The sun works best of all—but then I might truly be blinded. I've been going at it day and night. Mostly I can see things now, as they happen, sometimes fuzzy, but sometimes it's no good, and my eyes clench up, and sometimes I see nothing at all."

Darrel fidgeted one foot behind the other and tugged the seams of his clothes. "You can't help me. Nobody can. I saw *things* in that room, Jordie, awful things. He's an evil man. Evil."

Another scarab fell out of Darrel's shirt. Grimacing, the boy flung it away. Jordan snatched the husk out of the air and, holding it by one sawtooth leg, examined it closely before lobbing it out the window.

"I said better; I meant better. Another day, maybe two, and it *will* be gone."

"Can you fight?"

Jordan folded his right hand over the invisible hilt of an imaginary sword. His arm tensed, then relaxed. "No, I wouldn't dare." His voice was very soft and he wasn't thinking about his eyes. Darrel wouldn't look at him so he caught the boy in an arm-lock. "I'm not going to give up my sword—if that's why you're looking at your toes. I'll figure a way through our family curse, the same way I figured out how to use the candle to get the magic out of my eyes."

"But I *need* you, now," he whispered.

"Tell me what happened—exactly what you saw, what you heard. Don't make it into a story."

The boy complied, omitting the parts between himself and his demon. He would have confessed those, too, if Jordan had asked *what made you think that*? but Jordan didn't ask anything until the very end.

"Lohgrin said 'keep her under control'? Those were his very words—you're not making them up to bait me?"

"I swear it." Darrel crossed his forearms and thrust them forward. It was the traditional gesture of submission in combat and fealty. Jordan should have taken the boy's wrists and given them a symbolic shake to test their strength. When Jordan didn't, Darrel feared the worst. "Who else *but* Althea could he have meant?"

Sharp replies jostled on Jordan's tongue; teasing Squirt was nearly irresistible, but he did resist. This time the boy was telling the truth; and Althea was in greater danger than he had imagined. A comfortable pair of sandals was within arm's reach; Jordan left them alone.

"It's not going to be easy," he muttered, beginning a search for the sturdy buskins he'd worn on their journey. "There might not be anything we can do . . ."

The boy didn't believe that for a heartbeat. He was at the age where strength and prowess were the best solutions to any problem, which meant that there was nothing his brother could not quickly resolve—provided he didn't break his neck getting there. "You can't wear those on the roof tiles. You'll slip and fall off."

Jordan jabbed the leather thong at one of the buskin grommets. His jaw jutted forward and his eyes were half-closed. He missed and tried again before threading the thong through the hole. Someone else might think Jordan was careless or preoccupied; Squirt knew better.

"We have to use the roof, Jordie. The Inquisitor's set guards at the bottom of the stairway. They won't let us up."

"I'm the eldest son and heir of the lord of this villa." A frustration tear tracked across Jordan's cheek, but his voice was firm and his fingers began lacing the buskin competently. "You're the second son, second heir. There's no place in Hawksnest we may not enter unless our lord father himself forbids us."

"He won't go up there himself."

Jordan snugged the buskin against his leg and knotted the thong. "We go up the stairs like we have every right to, Darrel, or we don't go up at all, we don't look for Althea, and you don't get to show me your hand 'o'glory."

Since Darrel wanted to do those things very much, he followed Jordan through the door without arguing. He'd heard the expression hand 'o'glory whispered before, but he had no idea what it was. He'd never thought to ask Jordan, who was not considered much of a scholar either. Perhaps he had underestimated his brother.

"What's a 'caul'?" Darrel halted on the landing and clutched the newel post, as if the answer might physically unbalance him.

"Something else Lohgrin's got hidden away?" Jordan suggested and then, noticing the unusual apprehension on his brother's face, gave a more serious answer: "It comes with birthings. Babies have them when they're born but the midwives whisk them off and burn them, or bury them—"

"*All* babies?"

Jordan's eyes had clenched again, and he didn't enjoy displaying his ignorance. "Not all. Some. Maybe just a few. Hythloth, Squirt—if you're interested ask Lady Barbara—or ask Agatha, the old hag's sure to know."

"She once scolded me that I had a black caul and that I'd come to no good because of it." He thought the old woman had seen his demon. He ran to the hayloft, stripped, and examined himself thoroughly. He couldn't see the demon, but who knew what old Agatha could see?

"I don't know if it was black or not—" Jordan's eyesight didn't budge. He struggled to get an arm around the boy without punching him. "But Agatha made hue and cry the night you were born. Lord Ironhawk roared right back that it was nonsense and threw the thing into the hearth. I didn't get a close look, but it seemed no different from the slink that comes off a miscarried calf or foal."

Darrel shuddered. "It's nothing that makes me look—*different*—now? Nothing Agatha could see when she hollered at me?"

At that exact moment Jordan couldn't see anything, but he made a dramatic show of examining the boy's face. "Two buggy eyes. Two holes in your nose. A very big mouth. You know, you *do* look remarkably like a *toad*—" He blinked and his vision was perfect. "Better start looking for weepy warts—" He mussed Squirt's hair and tickled his ribs. The boy wriggled free and shot down the stairs.

"I don't have warts!"

"Not yet. One morning, you'll wake up black, and green, and covered with slime. You'll *hop* out of bed!"

Hawksnest had endured many identical afternoons: Darrel's screams echoing off the courtyard walls as Jordan tormented him. The elder brother could have caught the younger at any time, but running—the thrill of seeing clearly enough to run—was more enjoyable. He didn't lunge until a stab of pain lanced his eyes. The world became dark and burning.

"Enough!" Jordan steadied himself on Darrel. He shielded his eyes from the sunlight.

"Say I don't look like a toad."

Jordan didn't say anything. His eyes continued to burn, if anything the irritation was getting worse each time he blinked. Tears leaked down his cheeks; he felt like a fool.

Half the world—half the household, at least—must have heard them, seen them. And if their escapade wouldn't have drawn more than a weary yawn in other years, things were different now.

"Say it!" Squirt persisted. "Swear to the All-Seeing Eye of Destiny—"

"You and your Eye." Jordan balanced on his own feet, wiped his face, and blinked hard. The blurring was too bad to guess if he could see movement. "Where are we? Who's watching?"

The boy gasped when he saw his brother's eyes: where they should have been white, they were bright red. He marveled that Jordan's tears weren't the same awful color.

"Where are we?" Jordan repeated. "What's happening? Is anyone coming?"

"Your eyes, Jordie—" Darrel's voice cracked, he swallowed and tried again. "They're filled with *blood*." He caught Jordan's wrist. "You'd better get back to your room. I'll get Hugh." He tugged Jordan's arm without moving him.

Jordan blotted his face. His sleeve was wet through; his eyelids seemed lined with sand. "It's the light," he croaked, fighting the impulse to rub his eyes. "If no one's here, just lead me the rest of the way. I'll be all right once we're in shadow. The sun's too bright—that's all." He relaxed the hand in Darrel's grip and shielded his eyes with the other one. The burning agony became bearable.

"You're sure? If you're blind again, it's not going to do any good to go upstairs."

Darrel wasn't sure if Jordan were growling or moaning, but there was no one else in the courtyard, no one—not even the churls—between them and the stairway to Lohgrin's suite. Head down and shoulders up, he led his brother. He expected something terrible to happen but nothing did and they were standing outside the first of two closed doors on an empty, quiet corridor.

He released Jordan's wrist. "Which one first?" he whispered. "This one's got the bugs, the hand, the book, and the other stuff. The other one, I don't know. It's where Lohgrin went, so maybe it's where he's keeping her."

Jordan held his breath, lowered his hand, and gingerly opened his eyes. The burning pain came back with a rush, but dry; he'd used up all his tears in the sunlight. At first everything was colorless and blurred, then it resolved. Straight ahead: light above dark; the plaster walls above the darker floor and wainscoting. A little to the left: the open colonnade, dazzling bright and painful. He shut his eyes and turned to the right. Darrel: wide-open eyes, wide-open mouth, a light-colored shirt changed to tan as he stared. Jordan blinked—it hurt, but the result was a bit clearer, he let out his breath.

"I can see . . ."

"Your eyes look worse than they ever did before, when you couldn't—"

A shrill laugh interrupted them. Not nearby. Not Althea. Probably a kitchen girl surprised by her swain or a ribald joke. Not repeated and not significant in itself, except as a reminder that sound carried on a quiet summer afternoon.

"The room where you were," Jordan said quickly. "Let me see what's there, then we'll look for Althea. If we find her, there might not be time after."

The storeroom was exactly as Lohgrin and Darrel had left it, with the dismantled bed and unpleasant objects strewn across the floor. The boy pointed at the hand that he wouldn't touch on a dare, but Jordan hefted without hesitation, studying it by touch and his still-chancy sight. Its palm was broad. Its fingers were long and capped by thick nails that narrowed and curved like a dog's or bear's. Whatever twisted purpose it served, it hadn't been hacked off any hanged man's corpse.

"A troll—" Jordan's mind filled with the memories of the one time he'd encountered trolls and killed them. "Don't grieve too much." He tossed the hand to the floor. "They'd harvest worse trophies from you, if they caught you. What else? You said there was a book—"

Considering the sort of trophies men took from the creatures they hunted, Darrel decided not to ask what might be worse, but pointed at the chest and the thick, leather-bound object leaning against it. After Jordan's behavior with the hand, the boy was surprised when his brother got down on his knees and examined the book without touching it.

"Get me a stout piece of straw from the mattress."

"It's just an old book."

"An old book that looks like Balthan's spellbook—the pages of which he treats with arsenic paste, just in case the wrong person starts licking through them."

Darrel gulped; he'd never suspected. "How does he turn them, if they're poisoned?"

"I don't know, Squirt—maybe he's lying about the arsenic. Maybe magicians aren't harmed by their own poisons. Maybe I don't want to find out. Get me the straw."

The boy wiped his fingers vigorously and fetched the straw. Jordan raised the cover, revealing the same squirmy script that had defeated Darrel earlier. Jordan scowled and squinted and stopped himself just short of rubbing his eyes.

"Can you read it?"

"No." Jordan wedged the straw randomly between the vellum sheets and flipped the page open. The dull, brownish script was as elusive as ever, but there was a drawing that was easier to decipher: a butcher's chart of red meat, edible organs, and offal—except the butchered animal was a man.

"I don't like that," Darrel whispered. "I didn't see anything like that in Annon's study."

"Written in blood." Jordan sat back on his heels and raked his hair until it stood straight up. "His own?" he asked himself. "*Hah!* We should be so lucky. Runes, but written under some sort of spell. A spell. What kind of spell—? Who would have cast it for h—? Fool!" Jordan sprang to his feet and kicked the book shut. "Balthan—you bloody fool!" His voice rose, he turned toward the open window. That was a mistake: the light hurt his eyes. He covered them with his hands and continued in a whisper: "You had all the pieces but you didn't put them together right!"

"Jordie?" Squirt tugged on his brother's sleeve. "Jordan? Are you all right?"

Jordan lowered his hands. "It's clear as winter crystal—Everything comes together. The dreams Balthan had—something trying to get him to steal the Word of Power. Later Blackthorn came, trying to get the same thing. Then the Inquisitors—not just enforcing Blackthorn's stupid laws, but hunting down magicians. The dark smear across Althea's talisman . . . the harpies guarding Balthan's cave . . . the miasmas in the cities making everyone turn on each other. It's all one and the same—" He sucked in his breath as if he'd been struck hard in the stomach. "By the Eight, the Three, and the One-All-Around—" Jordan took hold of his brother's shoulders and turned him so their eyes met squarely. "It's all one and the same."

"What's all one and the same?" Jordan wasn't holding him firmly enough; the boy wriggled free with little effort. Whatever "it" was, he suspected Jordan had succumbed to it, too. "You're not making sense."

"It's magic—Blackthorn's a magician! Not Balthan's kind of magician, or Annon's, but some other kind. Maybe something ancient from old Sosaria. I don't know. But they're magicians, Squirt. Blackthorn, the Inquisitors—Lohgrin anyway—and they're eliminating everyone who could stand against them."

Darrel couldn't follow all the curves of Jordan's logic, but he caught enough to feel there was truth behind them. "We'd better find Althea quick, then—before it's too late. And then what should we do? Run away? Fight—*kill* Lohgrin and his churls?"

"Althea." Jordan turned away and covered his eyes again in a failing effort to catch up with his own thoughts. If Lohgrin was a magician—Jordan did not doubt his own conclusion—if he practiced a form of magic powerful enough to poison the air of Britannia's cities, what chance did he or any untalented man have against him? Was certain defeat a sufficient reason to surrender without a fight? "We have to try," Jordan answered his own question. "By the Eight, the Three, and the One-All-Around—for everything that we believe in—we have to try. Come on."

Darrel didn't like the grim look settling on his brother's face, not with those bloodred eyes and the fact that neither of them carried anything more substantial than a meat knife. "Maybe we should go to the armory? You could get your sword—"

Jordan ignored him—if he heard him at all. Darrel figured he hadn't, considering how things had been going. He'd be lucky if Jordan didn't go *berserk*. His big brother didn't look left or right when he stepped into the corridor that was, fortunately, empty, and when he got down to the other door—the latch-locked door—he was in no mood to fish the string out patiently.

"I'll do it," Darrel intervened quickly, getting between Jordan and the door before Jordan could start pounding on it. Darrel's hands trembled; he had to try several times before he caught the string with the hook and drew it through the door to release the latch. He gave the door a little shove—it swung open easily.

Much too easily.

They'd found the room where Althea was. They'd found the room where Lohgrin was, with Ivo right beside him brandishing a knife almost long enough to be called a sword. The Inquisitor raised his arms. Ivo lunged. Darrel didn't know whether to charge or run away. In the end, it didn't matter for he couldn't move a muscle; confusion or magic, he didn't know which. Jordan surged forward, so it wasn't magic. Darrel managed to find his legs and started for the bed.

"Thea—come on. Let's get out of here!"

Althea saw him. He'd swear she saw him and recognized him, then she made a horrible face and began to scream—a single unwavering note that had to hurt her throat as much as it hurt his ears. He reached for her anyway, but a pair of arms came out of nowhere and locked around him: Dench, who'd opened the door and waited behind it. Dench was brutally strong, but he didn't know the tricks to hold Erwald Ironhawk's eely son. A heartbeat later, Dench doubled over clutching his crotch. Althea hadn't paused for breath; Jordan was on the floor wrestling Ivo for the knife; and Lohgrin was three unfamiliar syllables in a magic spell.

The boy dove for the door as a singularly foul odor filled the room behind him. Too frightened for Virtue, he scrambled to his feet and up the column to the roof without once glancing back to see what had become of Jordan.

Althea kept on screaming. She still hadn't paused for breath.

Eleven
ΥΥΥΥ

                    J ordan didn't know what hit
                    him. One moment he'd been
wrestling with Ivo—and winning—the next, his nose was
squashed against the floor and Ivo's knee was spearing his
spine. He'd swear magic had been used against him, if he
could have been certain that the accursed berserkerang
hadn't won again. He was still piecing things together when
he heard the Inquisitor's voice.

"Bind him well."

Ivo and Dench obeyed their master swiftly and competently. Their prisoner's arms were wrenched behind him and
bound from wrist to elbow with a dampened leather thong.
Jordan could bear the pain more easily than he could bear
the insult and humiliation of being trussed up like an animal.
He struggled until the sinews in his left shoulder snapped
and the muscles in that arm did not respond to his will. It
was no accident that Dench chose that injured arm when he
hauled Jordan to his feet. The heir of Hawksnest bit into his
tongue and managed to stand unaided.

"You're a dangerous man, Jordan Ironhawk's son. Who
knows what you might have done if no one had been here
to stop you? You bear the berserkerang and you display

neither the strength nor the inclination to control it." Lohgrin's voice was silk with concern, and utterly at odds with his twisted smile.

Jordan swallowed his own blood. Seeing that sneer, he knew he hadn't succumbed to the berserkerang. He could stand proud. "Save your lies for those who might believe them." The room was dusky; his eyes weren't troubling him. He could meet Lohgrin's glower with one of his own.

"But they *will* believe me, when I tell them what you meant to do to my betrothed."

"Althea won't bear witness to lies, Inquisitor."

Lohgrin showed his teeth. He directed his gaze behind Jordan. The young man turned around. Althea sat impassively on the mattress. Her linen shift was torn from neck to waist. Tangled coils of hair fell across her face and breasts without concealing them. She stared straight at Jordan without recognizing him or making any effort to cover herself. Jordan had seen corpses carried to their graves with more color to their flesh.

"What have you done to her?" he demanded. "She's not herself." Jordan struggled against his bonds until Dench struck him between the ribs with a weighted, supple truncheon, then his struggle was simply to stay upright.

"She's twice betrayed: once by a brother who poisoned her, again by a foster-brother who wanted to ravish her. I've saved her life, but you're right: she's hardly herself."

"You lie. Balthan never harmed her. I came to rescue her. It's all lies. Thea—?" Jordan pleaded for recognition. "Thea—it's me: Jordan. You've got to tell the truth—"

They let Jordan move toward the bed. He was a half step away when Althea finally roused from her stupor. She crossed her arms over her heart. Her hands grasped the misshaped pearl at the hollow of her throat. She began to scream: the same high-pitched, unwavering scream as before. Jordan retreated and found himself in Dench's unfriendly embrace.

"Silence. Cover yourself," Lohgrin said; Althea obeyed. "Follow me," he said, and they all obeyed.

Althea, barefoot and apathetic, followed the Inquisitor. Ivo was nearby, ready to catch her if she stumbled or fainted—either of which seemed likely. Then Dench and Jordan, with Dench working Jordan's ribs with the truncheon.

"Ease up! I'm coming. I can walk on my own." Jordan squandered his strength trying to pull free.

"You'll crawl, if he says so. You'll hump the ground like a worm."

To emphasize his point and power, Dench gave Jordan's bad arm a vicious twist. Jordan moaned, as the churl expected, but moved into the pain rather than with it. Dench found himself rammed into the wall.

"You'll be feeding pigs the hard way—"

Jordan shoved again, forcing the air from the churl's lungs. He raised his knee, quick and hard. Dench went rigid with shock. Jordan would have struck again, but Ivo's hand had closed around his throat. Ivo stuffed a fist into Jordan's gut, forcing Jordan against the open railing. The bright light hurt more than the punch; neither diminished the satisfaction of seeing Dench on his knees. The red berserkerang crowded Jordan's awareness; if he accepted it, he'd have the strength to rip the thong from his arms and tear everyone limb from limb. He might be able to stop before he attacked Althea, then again, he might not. He had a scant heartbeat to make his decision. In that moment he saw a shadow move through the light.

In the last weeks he had learned to decipher the smallest mote of vision: the shadow was Squirt's scrawny leg swinging down from the roof. There was no deciphering what the boy might do out of loyalty or heroism. Jordan stifled the berserkerang.

"Run!" he shouted. "Hide!" Dropping to his knees, Jordan did what little he could to protect himself as Ivo kicked him again and again. Dench hobbled over; his blows were weak, but with the truncheon, they didn't have to be strong. Jordan felt himself losing consciousness, not even the berserkerang could save him from oblivion. "Enough!" Lohgrin called off his churls. "He's no use dead."

Helpless, barely conscious, Jordan sprawled on the planks.

Darrel clung to the hot clay roof tiles, wishing he could absorb the abuse he heard the churls doling out to his brother. He was absolutely certain they'd been thwarted by foul magic. The stench of it lingered in his nostrils and between his ears. He wanted desperately to swing down to the corridor and join the fray, but Jordan was right: one of them had to stay free.

Jordan groaned when they stood him up and, by the way the building shuddered, a moment later, fell down again. Darrel could spare one fist for his anger; he pounded a tile so hard it cracked. He felt a little better then. But the roof was no place to be after a long hot day. He was roasting on top, baking underneath. He asked his demon where he should go, but the only thought it released into his mind was: *Find Annon*, and that wasn't remotely possible until midnight when he might be able to sneak into the stable. His pony, Dragonfly, was old and more of a pet than a mount. If he wanted to go to Britain City, he'd have to take a horse—no, worse than that, he'd have to take one of the Valorians.

If anything important depended on him getting a Valorian out of his lord father's stable and all the way to Britain City—well, he might just as well give it up before he started.

Lohgrin snarled orders Darrel heard with half an ear, then he led his companions down the stairs to the courtyard. Darrel scrabbled over the crown tiles and eased himself to the other side, where it was even hotter. The Inquisitor hailed one of the menials.

"By Law and Virtue, where is your master?"

Darrel could not hear the reply, he did hear the menial yelp.

"He chooses a fine afternoon for hawking! His sons have disgraced him. You—hie yourself to the tocsin and summon everyone to the great hall for the meting out of justice! The laws of the regent apply to everyone. No exceptions will be made!"

Darrel pressed his forehead against the searing tiles. It *was* a fine afternoon for hawking—the sort of afternoon Lord Erwald would always spend with his beloved hawks—unless something very urgent kept him indoors. Althea languishing in a locked room; Jordan locked in another; even himself on the run from Aldonar—none of that would seem urgent to Lord Ironhawk.

Darrel sighed, and nearly lost his grip. Not long ago, Lord Ironhawk would have taken Jordan's word over anyone's, but that trust had vanished. Darrel had a good idea how Ironhawk would react when he came rushing in from the fields to hear Lohgrin's charges. It didn't bode well for Jordan. He didn't want to watch; he didn't want to listen; he didn't want to be anywhere near the great domed hall and for a moment the boy considered sneaking away altogether and forever—but only for a moment.

Retreat could be virtuous, if it prevented capture, injury, or death *and* was used to regroup for a counterattack—anything less was cowardice and cowardice was the most unvirtuous principle Darrel could imagine. He refused to believe he had imagined it, and blamed it on his demon instead.

"I'll find Lord Ironhawk, you hear," he told it. "I'll tell him not to listen to that Loathy Lohgrin. I'll tell him what happened and he'll believe me because I'll tell the truth—" Laughter reverberated in his skull. Darrel blamed that on the demon, too, though it sounded exactly like his father's scorn. "He *will* believe me, because it *is* the truth!" Darrel cast the calming magic Annon had taught him. The laughter shrank, but doubt lingered.

The tocsin clanged. Squirt snapped out of his brooding thoughts. Lord Erwald would ride into the villa yard, dismount, and then walk to the domed hall. The boy bargained with the Eye of Destiny:

"Let me get to the yard first; I'll take care of the rest by myself."

He stood up and ran across the roof tiles as if he'd been raised in a steeply sloped world. The Eye of Destiny fulfilled its half of the bargain: Erwald Ironhawk hadn't reined his horse to a stop when Darrel first saw him. Fulfilling his own half was going to be a bit more difficult: the roof edge where he stood was thirty feet above the ground. Decorative masonry on the walls provided a variety of secure handholds—but if he used them, he'd never get down in time. He looked for another way, and found it: a mound of compost the gardeners left by the courtyard archway.

The boy was almost positive it would break his fall.

"Ironhawk!"

Lord Erwald looked up to see his youngest son leap off the roof.

"Virtue protect—" The reflexive invocation died on Erwald's lips. He loved Darrel, but it wasn't easy. There was something seriously wrong with that boy. If it had been Jordan—if Jordan had ever been the sort who would put himself on a roof's edge—then Erwald would have known heart-wrenching horror. Jordan didn't have his younger brother's luck—or his perversity. As soon as Erwald saw the compost mound, he knew what Squirt was doing and knew he would land safely.

"Ironhaw-w-w—!"

There wasn't quite enough time for Darrel to tuck his limbs beneath him. He hit the pile spread-eagled and facedown. Fortunately, he got his mouth shut. He sprang to his feet none the worse for the experience. The same could not be said for his clothes. Lord Ironhawk retreated as his son approached.

"Stop—stop right there!" he commanded. "What is the meaning of this? Are you trying to scare the life from me?"

The tocsin clanged again, giving Darrel an extra heartbeat to phrase his reply.

"My lord father—The Inquisitor. Everything is *lies*. You can't believe him. He's put magic on Althea to make her tell lies. He's got thousands of slimy, dead bugs in a basket and a hand from a hung man or troll. His magic's *foul-smelling*—"

"Love of Virtue, boy—how would you know?" Erwald gave his son a stiff-armed shake to rattle the boy's teeth. The lord's first thought was to call the horse-grooms and have them lock Squirt in a stall until after he'd dealt with the alarm, but his wife was forever telling him to go easier with the boy, especially now that Jordan was maimed. Pain accompanied that thought and made Erwald pause. His son Jordan, on whose well-raised shoulders he'd placed all his hopes. His son Jordan blinded by that ingrate Balthan, and possessed by his inheritance: the damned berserkerang.

"My lord, Father—you've *got* to believe me. I'm not lying." Darrel couldn't get loose and he hadn't found the words he needed. Then inspiration struck. "Jordan can *see*. He's almost all better. He believed me—once he saw what I'd seen."

Erwald released his son lest he do the boy harm. He gathered his will and his strength and banished his old enemy: the red berserkerang. "You go too far," he warned softly. "What possesses you to say these things—? To do these things to me day after day?"

"I don't know," Darrel lied. He was suddenly and supremely aware of the malodorous clods clinging to him. "But nothing possessed me today. I wanted to see Althea, that's all. I went to the room where I thought she was, but she wasn't there. This bad stuff was there instead, and Lohgrin came in. He said terrible things, so I went and got Jordan, so we could get Althea—"

"Enough!"

The tocsin still clanged. Greater and lesser household members streamed through the yard; the foregate leaseholders were coming through the gate. All of them noticed Darrel and his father, but pretended not to. Erwald was not pleased that the Inquisitor would presume to summon everyone; though, thanks to Squirt, he had a forewarning of what was going to happen. Erwald Ironhawk could feel his life slipping through his fingers; he couldn't make a fist to stop it. The Inquisitor and Darrel were, oddly enough, similar: they could be predicted, like the weather, but never controlled, never understood. Erwald would rather be rid of them both—but Darrel was, inescapably, his son; and Lohgrin—

Lord Ironhawk clutched his side; he rode out the spasm and let his arm fall. In his prime he'd slain a dragon single-handed, without the fearsome aid of his berserkerang. Lohgrin didn't wear a sword, he'd never gone on a Virtue Quest, and he wasn't a Peer of the realm. Neither he nor Blackthorn had the right to impose their will on Hawksnest. But whenever Erwald considered challenging the black-robed Inquisitor, his insides turned against him.

Darrel hadn't moved. "Father, my lord—I beg you: please don't listen to him."

"Don't beg. It's not Humility, and it won't get you anything. I've listened to you; I'll listen to him. Then I'll listen for the truth between my ears." Erwald turned his back.

"You'll never hear it," the boy said loudly enough for everyone to hear. "You'll only hear what the Inquisitor wants you to hear, not the truth at all. Don't go in there if you ever want to hear the truth between your ears."

Erwald winced. Darrel had ambushed him, probing his doubt and shame without mercy. He regarded his son not as an incorrigible boy, but as a young man. "Cowardice is no less vile than falsehood, Darrel. If you would accuse someone of either, and cannot do it face-to-face, you are the one who stands without Virtue. I will not consider anything you've said, unless you have the courage to say it to the Inquisitor's face, in the hall.''

Darrel clenched his teeth and started walking. The Inquisitor was a man with a silken tongue; he was only a boy who reeked of last year's manure. He wouldn't win. Anything he said would get broken, put back together, and used against him. But this time he wouldn't retreat. His lord father was right: if he couldn't make his accusations to Lohgrin's face, then he was the one without Virtue.

Everything was as bad inside the hall as Darrel imagined it would be, maybe worse. Lohgrin stood on a platform beneath the dome. (Darrel assumed Ivo and Dench had dragged it there.) The Inquisitor stood grimly with his arms folded, greeting everyone with a stare worthy of the Avenging Avatar. Althea stood beside him, looking frail in her torn shift. They'd put Jordan in one of the spots where sunlight streamed directly through the open second-story gallery. Tears streamed down his cheeks and his eyes were so hideously red that they seemed to glow with their own fire when he opened them.

A few steps into the hall, Lord Ironhawk looked away from the Inquisitor and confronted his youngest son.

"Strength of the Avatar—what have you done?"

Darrel studied his filthy feet. There didn't seem any point in answering or marching closer to the dais. The Inquisitor knew he was here—their eyes had already met and the black-robed man had actually grinned. Darrel looked around for Lady Barbara: he'd be safest in her shadow. But he couldn't find her in the crowd.

No one in Britannia—including Lord British or his bardic Companion, Iolo—had a better flair for drama than Lohgrin as he waited for Erwald Chandeller, Lord Ironhawk, to make his way through his assembled household to the platform. It became clear that there were no steps attached to the dais. Erwald was a good decade past the days when he could

leap that distance with grace or confidence. The lord of
Hawksnest seemed to grovel at Lohgrin's feet as he mounted
the platform. He was upright quickly enough; he towered
over the Inquisitor, but the image of him on his knees
lingered in everyone's mind, along with Jordan's crimson
eyes.

Lohgrin began by saying that he'd let Althea tell everyone
what had happened in her own words; he hoped they'd be
very quiet so they could hear her.

Darrel invoked the Eye of Destiny, as he did in any crisis.
He found, however, that his faith was much reduced. "Just
make it be over quick," he mumbled and tried to lose
himself in the crowd.

Althea told the story she was meant to tell: how Jordan,
knowing she was ailing and defenseless, forced his way into
her room. How he proclaimed that he would prevent her
from marrying her betrothed: he'd take her himself in the
old, disreputable Sosarian tradition of summary consumma-
tion. Althea's voice was remarkably steady as she described
what had been prevented, which didn't surprise Darrel at
all, as the words were not hers—especially at the very end
when she said she did not ask for Jordan's death, merely
his eyes and his manhood.

The Inquisitor intervened. "It is not for you to decree
punishment, my dear. Our regent, Lord Blackthorn, has laid
down laws to protect innocent victims from the so-called
Justice of unaccountable lords and peers who do not embrace
Virtue but return to the brutal customs of Sosaria—"

Darrel followed the angle of Lohgrin's stare and finally
found his mother. Lady Barbara's family traced its lineage
to Sosaria; there was no doubt who the Inquisitor was blam-
ing for Jordan's traditional corruption.

Lohgrin began to sermonize on the Virtue of Compassion.
Darrel felt his anger rising. He knew he'd do something
stupid if he didn't get out of the hall. He wove through the

crowd, but the Inquisitor nailed him before he reached the threshold.

"—Jordan Hawson was not alone in his crime. He brought his brother to witness his so-called marriage. My beloved Althea has shown her Compassion by withholding his name. Darrel Hawson is, of course, a child and not responsible for his actions—especially when he's spent his life subject to the same influences which have shaped his older brother, and—lest we forget—the traitor Balthan Wanderson—"

Darrel knew he didn't want to be in the hall to hear the next words. He put his head down and charged the door.

"—Stop him. Catch him! Bring that scoundrel up here immediately!"

Hands reached out from everywhere, clutching the boy and his clothes, but not tightly enough. He squirmed, kicked, bit, scratched until he was free, and then he was gone.

Twelve

ᚱᚱᚱᚱᚱ

S eanna wrapped the reins around her hand. She slapped the loose ends against the footboard, making an impressive noise to get Willie and Tom moving at a faster pace. The wagon was light; she had delivered her pigiron and gotten her bonus as well, even though she was late with it: the man was astounded she'd gotten through at all and was desperate for raw metal. He had not, however, given her a return cargo, nor would anyone else on the Cape. They said it was because of the hurricane. Seanna suspected otherwise. After Hawksnest, she was on the watch for Inquisitors and seeing them everywhere.

Rarely was Seanna without a cargo, a destination, and a deadline. She was anxious, but the team responded as any horses would: they were loafing. They ambled through the hot, hazy afternoon with notions of sweet grass filling the cavity beneath their flaxen forelocks. Like guilty children caught in the act, their heads rose and the wagon lurched forward as the reins snapped.

"There's a teamsters' call tonight," Seanna said quite loudly. Four pointed ears swiveled to catch her voice and a taste of her worries. "I'd like to get there in time to find myself someone who knows more about what's been going on lately. So, if you don't mind—'' She snapped the reins again and the team began a heavy-footed trot.

The geldings maintained their pace after the reins went slack again. They were typical of their breed: stolid, stalwart, hard-working, and loyal. They'd keep the wagon rolling smartly until Seanna's voice faded over the horizon of their minds and meadows without horizon replaced it.

Seanna was as distracted as her team. Teamsters' call was usually in autumn, on Dedication Day, when all Britannia commemorated the Avatar's quest for Virtue. A midsummer call was extraordinary, and could only mean bad news; good news could always wait an extra month or two. Coulterquit clan answered the call at a charterhouse on the Western Road north of Spiritwood, but for this extraordinary call she'd go to an establishment north of Trinsic, some twenty miles ahead.

Teamsters' call was a time for gossip, betrothals, and—most importantly—guild business. Seanna had balanced her accounts the previous night. She kept her tallies and receipts in a locked box beneath the driver's bench. The notched boards and jagged-edge scraps of parchment were a regular part of her haul, registering them with the guild and paying her road tax was the official purpose of any call. Because she had no cargo, she was carrying consignment collateral, a nest-egg of gold coins that was normally scattered and safe in the treasure rooms of the estates and hamlets for whom she regularly worked. A teamster's wagon was under royal protection whether it hauled cargo or collateral, but carrying her own gold made Seanna nervous.

"Damn all Inquisitors to the endless night of Hythloth," she muttered, unaware that she spoke aloud. Willie and Tom picked up her voice through the jangle of their harness bells; they leaned into their collars and the wagon rolled faster.

"Sticking their noses in every chest and sack. There's not a roof along the Old Paladin's Road that doesn't have a prowling black-robe under it. It's not enough that they've cordoned off every moon gate looking for magicians and Resistance fighters—now they've clamped down on *us*! We're as honest as the day is long—" she shouted, not at all forgetting that the length of a day varied considerably over the course of a year. "We pay tolls, taxes, tariffs, customs, *and* duties—but now they want a silver shower of their own. And they *still* want to poke into everything and if they find one thing they don't like it's off to the Inquiry chambers."

She shivered despite the heat. People were missing bits and pieces when they came out of the Inquiry chambers—if they came out at all.

"Who wants to take a chance? Not me. I had the one from Hawksnest already, one was enough."

Willie tossed his head. A fly swarm transferred itself to Tom's dark, shiny flanks. Seanna didn't need Willie or anyone else to tell her to keep her mouth shut about Hawksnest. Confiscation and bribes were a sideline for the Inquisitors; their true trade was intimidation, and though it galled Seanna to acknowledge it, they were doing very well. Years would pass before she'd forget the black-robed man with the flinty eyes ordering his men to search her wagon for Balthan.

As a rule, Seanna had little sympathy for magicians. Their wind-commanding Rel Hur scrolls gave ships and sailors an unfair advantage in the competition for cargo. She made an exception for Balthan Wanderson without quite knowing why. He dressed like a city fop on a prolonged losing streak. He was long-winded and arrogant, and he made her team as skittish as they made him. He tickled Seanna's mischievousness. She encouraged Willie to pluck that ridiculous hat from his head whenever it was the magician's turn to help her tend the team. Balthan could have begged off the chore; Squirt would have gladly taken up the slack, but Balthan didn't. The magician whined and complained, but he never shirked the way Drum did. The farrier kept to himself, as if a man that size could be overlooked!

If Balthan ran from the Inquisitors, then his reasons were probably good. And the Inquisitors' reasons for chasing him were undoubtedly bad.

"We'll hie ourselves to Minoc, my friends, and lose a few seasons hauling trees out of the forests. We won't get rich or fat, but we won't get questioned, either—and until Lord British comes back, that's all I care about. Let the magicians and the Resistance brawl it out with Blackthorn and his Inquisitors while we're far away."

Tom whickered. The ever-present flies returned to Willie.

The pitched roof and palisade of a charterhouse shimmered in the distance. Seanna stretched until her joints popped, and checked the locked box. A line of bright, big wagons was laid up along the palisade. A crew of stableboys and apprentices had cordoned off a substantial part of the charterhouse yard as a paddock for the team horses that were too big for an ordinary straight-stall.

"Clans are gathering behind the stable, but the roadmaster's on the porch with two witnesses," the tallest of the apprentices shouted as Seanna halted her team. "They'll register your tallies right away . . . if you've got 'em ready. You don't have to stay the night."

Seanna couldn't hide her surprise. The roadmaster was registering tallies *before* sunset? Teamsters not staying? She'd been so busy thinking about her problems, she hadn't considered that every teamster was getting the same hassle. Some of them might have enlisted in the Resistance. And some of them might be working for the Inquisitors. She wanted to stay, but finding the right person to talk to would be an unexpected challenge.

"I'm staying the night."

The apprentice was her own age, maybe a bit older. She was young for a journeyman teamster, exceptions had been made because she was an orphan. He felt free to ask her a question he would not dare ask another driver. "How many do you think are running for one side or the other?"

Seanna didn't want to guess or answer. She took the harness from his arms and stowed it in the wagon herself and kept the shrouds drawn tight with her signature knot—lest anyone look inside. She let the apprentice lead Willie and Tom to the paddock. Team horses were more important than politics. Besides, she could watch the cooling, grooming, and feeding from the charterhouse porch where the roadmaster had her counting table.

"Seanna Jormsheir! How goes the road?"

She completed the traditional greeting: "Smooth beneath my wheels," then clasped the older woman's hand firmly for a boost to the porch. Not that Seanna, or any teamster, needed assistance, but it was unforgivably rude to disdain a roadmaster's help when it was offered, and the weathered woman with the harness rings dangling from her ear had been a roadmaster as long as Seanna could remember. Her name was Greete. One of the witnesses was Coxford, a master Seanna recognized but who was not part of her clan. The other she did not even recognize.

Greete settled behind her table, adjusting her ear-links so her shoulder supported their weight. "I can register you now, Seanna Jormsheir, if you like." She opened a heavy book to a clean page.

Seanna unlocked her box and opened it carefully. She made heaps of wood and parchment on the counting table. Greete used her left hand to accumulate them on the abacus and her ink-stained right hand to record the totals in the book. When the roadmaster was done Seanna's heaps were tidy piles and nine months of her life had been reduced to a column of script notations and a companion column of numbers. After a flurry of beadwork on the abacus, Greete read off Seanna's road tax, which was a few pence less than Seanna had calculated herself. She opened her box again to pay it.

"Plus two gold crowns for your bells."

The heavy lid slipped through one hand and struck the fingers of the other. "What?"

"Regent Blackthorn has declared that teamsters must re-purchase their bells at each call, or forfeit them."

Seanna looked to the witnesses. "That's not fair. It's not right. We buy our bells just once, when we take our first wagon. What if I lost a cargo during the year? Or when I have to replace Willie and Tom?" Then she considered that this was an extraordinary call. "What about Dedication? Will I have to buy them *again* in three months?"

Coxford's jaw was clenched, the stranger stared at the horizon. Greete spoke for the guild. "You could skip the call of course, but if the Inquisitors caught you with the wrong seals on your wagon, or forged seals . . . Of course, you could surrender your bells . . ."

"I might as well become a gypsy or a brigand!"

Greete nodded grimly. "You could join the Resistance."

"Or hire yourself to the Inquisitors directly." Coxford took the heat out of the summer afternoon with his scowl. He hawked into the sand beyond the porch. "They've always got cargo to move secretlike, and no one will bother you while you're hauling it—but don't sleep in your own wagon."

Seanna couldn't feel her throbbing fingers. She couldn't feel anything below her knees. It took forever to fill her lungs with useless air. The charterhouse porch wobbled like a warped wheel.

"No," she whispered with her eyes squeezed shut. "This can't be happening. It's a dream—" But dreams reminded her of Hawksnest, of magic-blind Jordan, and the tales Balthan told around the campfire.

The stranger's voice interrupted Seanna's plummeting reverie. "Or pay the two crowns now and hope that Lord British comes back before the next call."

His wasn't a voice of landlord peers or virtue, but a

workingman's voice of compromise and survival. Drumon the farrier couldn't have said it better. Seanna caught her breath with a shudder and dug into her box for the coins. No wonder teamsters were getting back in their wagons and rolling on.

Greete rested a hand gently on top of Seanna's cold, clammy one. "Take yourself to the stable. There's a fresh-tapped keg of ale and mutton roasting over the fire. Take what your guild can offer and gather your wits. Sigwein's here with his wife and sons."

Seanna stared past the grey-haired roadmaster, remembering Sigwein's red, green, and yellow wagon. The apprentice she'd spoken to in the yard was Sigwein's eldest son and heir.

"It's no time to be driving alone," Greete warned, guessing Seanna's thoughts or in cahoots with Sigwein. "Laws make outlaws, and folks get desperate. Come winter the wolves will walk on two legs."

"I'm going north, to Minoc and the timber camps."

"You and everybody else!" Coxford snorted. "That forest will be as crowded as Britain City on his lordship's birthday."

He didn't think about his words until after he'd said them. The mention of Lord British left a bitter taste in his mouth; he hawked again. Seanna locked her box and headed for the stable. She had no appetite, nor interest in conversation, but neither did anyone else. Even the children sensed something lurking just beneath the surface. They foreswore their usual screeching mayhem and contented themselves with quieter games. Sigwein sat on his box with his arms folded across his chest and a scarf wound low over his eyes. Seanna nodded at his wife who stood by the hearth cranking the mutton spit with the questionable help of her two youngest children. She couldn't remember the other woman's name.

"Tell me when it's my turn," Seanna offered, taking a wooden mug and filling it with sun-warmed ale.

"Later. I just started," the wife replied without looking up.

Seanna found a shady spot and claimed it with her up-ended box. She drank half the ale without pausing for breath. The tart, potent brew quenched her thirst and made her eyelids unbearably heavy. As a herald might use his saddle for a pillow, she settled against the box. She pulled her hair forward so it covered her face like Sigwein's scarf. The ale closed her eyes and left her arms limp, but Seanna couldn't sleep. Her thoughts churned, fueled by the sun and the ale. They always came back to the Inquisitors, Hawksnest, Greete's warning, and Jordan Hawson—though not necessarily in that order.

Other voices—other teamsters and their kin—joined the gathering. Most fell silent quickly, but a few talked and Seanna listened. She learned Coxford was right: she wasn't the only one headed north to the timber camps. But most of the talk was about the will-o'-the-wisp Resistance. Everybody, it seemed, had been questioned about it and believed it existed, but no one belonged, or admitted belonging. The heat of the day began to wane. A breeze freshened and, bearing the aroma of succulent sheep, drove the muzziness from Seanna's head.

She was refreshed, and more cheerful than she had any right or reason to be. Refilling her mug, she joined the knot of people waiting for the meat to be carved.

"It's the magicians' fault. If they'd just give our regent what he wants, there'd be none of this," someone snarled. "It's not as if he wants power or riches or anything else out of the dungeons. All Lord Blackthorn wants is to find Lord British. I heard him say so himself. It's the magicians who block him. They're the ones who've stirred up the landlords and peers. They're the ones who've stirred this Resistance to what's lawful and right. Regent Blackthorn wouldn't need Inquisitors to help him keep the peace, if the magicians obeyed him."

Seanna's spirits fell, but before she could locate the speaker or put a name to the voice she heard, Coxford launched a rebuttal.

"Forget the Council! Forget dungeons! Forget Words of Power. Wherever Lord British is, no magician put him there." Coxford shook his head vigorously. "Lord British taught the magicians everything they know. *He* gave them the Words of Power to seal the dungeons after the Avatar went home. There's no way *his* magicians could have surprised him or harmed him. If he was surprised or harmed, it has to be by someone from somewhere else."

An involuntary gasp rippled through the crowd. Lord British came from "somewhere else," as did the Avatar and the Companions. It was unthinkable that the Avatar could turn against Lord British, and the Companions were Lord British's trusted friends. But because they all aged with glacial slowness they were all magical even if some of them claimed not to be magicians. Regent Blackthorn was a Companion who claimed no magic.

"That's treason," someone whispered, then added: "To Lord British."

There was a murmur of agreement. Coxford was repudiated and chastened. He had retreated from the crowd when another voice piped up.

"Well, I think Lord British is in the underworld—in a horrible dark and cold cave, and held there by evil."

Seanna had no trouble locating the speaker this time: his neighbors edged away from him. They nailed him with stares meant to establish that *they* were no part of his madness. If it were madness. Seanna thought again of Jordan Hawson who'd been blinded while rescuing a magician from a cave.

Greete asked the first question: "What makes you think that, Thykel?"

Thykel was not the boldest of teamsters. Like Seanna he was a journeyman and drove his wagon alone. The similarities ended there. Thykel had been a journeyman for thirty years. He lacked professional ambition; his lack of a wife and family was also a lack of ambition. Seanna could not remember him speaking up before, and judging by the raised eyebrows all around, no one else did either—which made his answer all the more interesting.

"I was on the road above Spiritwood, bound for Britain City with a wagonful of mead and honey from the abbey. I'm careful of Spiritwood. There's places I lay up, places I don't. A place that I do is a hermitage just off the road. They say a holy man, a druid, dwelt there planting the trees and hallowing the ground. I figure it's a little safer."

Seanna scratched her neck impatiently. At the rate Thykel was going, the mutton would be charcoal and cinders before he was finished. She longed to tell him to get to the point of it, but the roadmaster was weighing Thykel's every word. As long as Greete was content to hear the yarn exactly as the journeyman played it out, no one else would interrupt.

Thykel had apparently visited the hermitage within the last month—despite a wealth of unnecessary details, the man was stingy with the particulars Seanna wanted most to hear. There were two people dwelling there: an elderly man with an aura of holy magic and a woman of some beauty and considerable strength, who was moon-mad. The old man said he'd found his companion wandering the snow-covered forest. She was battered, fevered, and starving. He'd nursed away her bodily hurts before realizing that her wits were addled.

"She was docile enough while the sun was shining. She had a way with the horses, too, and a fascination for the short sword I keep beneath my bench. But, came the night, she raved—"

Shanna—by day she answered to the name, but that night Thykel said she cried it like a lost child—put the fear of the ever-after into Thykel with her dream-fueled ravings. She mistook simple things like the table and stools, the ropes of dried onions hung on the rafters for boats and rocks and serpents. She had a variety of names for the old man: Arionis, Geraci, Meridin, Noin, and Roin. When she saw Thykel, she called him Remoh, then she turned around and called the old man "Lord British."

"That old man, he was sharp; 'Shanna,' he says, 'where are we?' and she begins to tell us about a cave so big it was a hollow mountain. 'Shanna,' he says again, 'what has happened to us?' and she tells about magical creatures and monsters and *wraiths*. She no sooner said the word than she screamed that there were three of them right behind us. And I tell you, I was glad I wore my brown trousers."

Seanna rolled her eyes. After all these years of mousy silence, Thykel finally opened his mouth to tell a joke that was older than Lord British and not particularly amusing. Other teamsters agreed, and turned their attention to the mutton. Seanna thrust her platter forward for her share. Thykel was still talking.

"—They rode with me and the hives and the honey all the way to Britain City. The old man thought Milan the healer might restore her wits. The black fog was down when we got there and the gates were shut. I went to the end of the line to wait for morning with everyone else. It was foggy and the air was foul, the way it is when the miasma settles. The old man and I tried to rest, but Shanna started raving something fierce. It was the three wraiths again, and Lord British, and the next thing I knew there was an Inquisitor on either side of us. *They* didn't think she was moon-mad."

Against her better judgment, Seanna rejoined the throng around Thykel. The journeyman showed the marks on his arms where the Inquisitors had prodded him with hot iron. He repeated their questions: What had the woman said; the old man? Why had he been in Spiritwood? Had he been in a cave recently himself; did he know anyone who had been? Thykel said he told the truth each and every time. They released him at dawn.

"I've had dreams ever since—*her* dreams. Cold misty caves with shadows so dark I can feel them. And wraiths: shadows with burning eyes. I haven't seen Lord British, but he's there someplace—I know he is. The wraiths guard him, and they're real. I try not to sleep now, especially at night—''

Seanna nearly dropped her platter. Balthan slept easily while he was in her wagon, but he kept a pouch of ginseng and garlic close by because he'd had nightmares. He spoke of cold shadows and called them wraiths. But he'd been in a cave north of Yew, while Spiritwood—This time she did drop the platter. The southern verge of Spiritwood was, in all likelihood, the northwest boundary of Hawksnest.

She salvaged her meal and ate in thoughtful silence. Did she—Seanna Jormsheir, journeyman teamster—believe in Destiny? In coincidence? In *luck*? Did she continue to Minoc, to the glutted timber camps? Or did she return to Hawksnest?

If she did return to Hawksnest, she could hardly roll up to the gate and say: *Greetings, my lord, the secret of Lord British's disappearance lies northwest of here—that's why you've got the slimiest of slimy Inquisitors fouling your table*. She had nothing but the shivers racing along her spine to back up her suspicions, and the memory of that Hawksnest Inquisitor rummaging through her wagon. The memories were compelling, but the shivers were just shivers, nothing more. Maybe she was catching a fever. She hoped it was a fever.

Seanna decided to go directly to her wagon and go to bed. She figured to be better in the morning, or worse. But she wasn't. She dreamt restlessly the whole night. Not about caves or wraiths—thank Destiny—but about Jordan's brother, Squirt, who'd climbed up a tree and couldn't get down. All night Seanna tried to get him out of the tree, finally she stood on the back of a mettlesome stallion: a mettlesome, grey Valorian stallion. Jordan's grey Valorian stallion: Fugatore.

Shades of pink and lavender painted the sky when Seanna descended from her wagon and rinsed her mouth at the well. She got rid of the night-mouth and the cobwebs between her ears, but not the questions:

Did one, or did one not, believe in destiny? wishes? or luck?

There was some activity around the charterhouse, but none in the teamster camp. No one paid attention when she brought her team out of the paddock. She harnessed Willie first, then Tom. She pulled Willie's head down so they could look into each other's eyes.

"I hope you were born lucky, Erwillian, because I'm about to take us on a fool's errand, and if I'm right, we're going to need all the luck we can muster."

The sun had barely risen when the stableboy opened the palisade gate. She was headed to the estate where Jordan claimed he'd left the horse.

Thirteen

ΥΥΥΥΥ

D arrel's favorite daydream
was running free through
Hawksnest. He fancied himself hiding, foraging, and generally leading grown-ups on a merry chase. For three days
he'd lived his daydream and found it somewhat less than
blissful. He couldn't get near Jordan's prison. Many of his
favorite hiding places were hot, stenched, and swarming
with wasps. And everyone was looking for him.

No sooner had Darrel escaped from the great hall than
the Inquisitor held up a purse of coins and promised it to
whomever captured him. The menials and wage-servants
set aside their prejudice against Lohgrin. They chased the
boy and the reward with equal vigor, and they knew the
backways of the villa as well as the Squirt himself. He left
his mark on the shins of his pursuers, and reearned his name
more than once, but it wasn't easy. He'd grown in the last
months. He was longer and stronger and escape routes he'd
used all his life were painfully tight.

Yesterday evening he'd been caught foraging in the
cheese larder. He bolted into the winecellar where a ground
window allowed air in and him out. It had been a squeeze
the last time he used it, around midwinter, but yesterday,

when he'd needed it most, it was impossible. He got hung-up: shoulders wedged against the masonry, legs flailing. Someone grabbed his ankles—he believed his desperate game was over—then, instead of being pulled, he was pushed into the herb garden.

His benefactors were gone when Darrel looked back into the winecellar. He made his way to the crawlspace beneath the copper dome of the great hall for the night. He'd shivered until dawn, but now the sun was beating on the metal. It wasn't noon yet, but the heat had already sucked him dry. He was going to have to find another bolthole and something to drink.

Darrel ventured down into the great hall. He found a mug abandoned since who knew when. Once it had been filled with ale, now it was half-full and swarming with gnats. He thought anything wet was better than nothing and raised the mug to his lips, which would not part. He'd have to find fresh water.

The tocsin clanged midday; Darrel cracked the door. He'd have to run across the yard in full sight of the tower guards to reach the villa proper. By habit, the boy invoked the Eye of Destiny. He caught the orison before it escaped and banished it. If he was too big for the winecellar window, then he was too big to beg favors from the Eye of Destiny. He sprinted for the nearest shrubbery and dove beneath its tangled branches. The yard filled with agitated birds, but no one noticed, and after a few moments he started for the kitchen.

Darrel and the cooks were weather-wise. They knew no one would want a hot meal while the sun was up. The big stone-walled room with its hearths and ovens was deserted. The fires were banked. Later, after sunset, the cooks would do the baking. The boy got himself water from the drinking barrel. Then he saw the large bowl of fruit sitting in splendid isolation on the sideboard. His stomach knotted and the water no longer satisfied him. His demon teased him with the sweet taste of juicy grapes and berries. His mouth watered. Darrel twitched, then froze again. He resisted temptation until he knew where he would take the prize: the furnace room beside the hypocaust. Like the kitchen, it would be deserted until sundown. Moreover, it was near the storeroom where Jordan was imprisoned. He snatched the bowl and ran.

The only reason Darrel had not followed Balthan's example and fled Hawksnest was a stubborn hope that he'd find a way to set his brother free. It was a faint hope. The Inquisitor didn't trust Lord Ironhawk's security. He confined Jordan in the windowless hole beneath his storeroom, and the churls were doing a competent job of guarding their prisoner. The furnace room on the opposite side of the courtyard was as close as Darrel could get.

The furnace-room door was open; Darrel left it that way. He secreted himself against the back wall, atop a woodpile. No one would see him unless they came inside and let their eyes adjust to the dim light, but he could see most of the nearest courtyard, and a good deal of the one beyond it. They were both empty; he dove into the fruit. The fruit was nearly gone when he found a folded parchment packet.

As soon as he lifted it, Darrel noticed that it was ink-marked. He almost cast it aside without further investigation. Writing—especially the scribbly sort of writing on the parchment—could be of no use to him. His fingers, however, told him that there was something flaky *inside* the packet; that kept his attention. There was a second packet inside the first; it had been soaked in oil to make it waterproof, and sealed with dark wax. The flakes were inside the second packet. Darrel curbed his curiosity long enough to unfold the outer scrap entirely. Maybe, now that he was big, writing would yield its secrets.

And, perhaps it would—but not that afternoon. Darrel smoothed the sheet against his thigh. The marks weren't writing, but four pictures: a square with a dot in its center;

a lopsided pitcher; a stick-figure with its tongue stuck out
and its hands over its gut; and, last, another stick-figure
lying down with a droopy flower rising out of its gut. He
deciphered them: if the flakes were added to water, whoever
drank the water would get sick and die.

Someone was plotting murder. If whoever left the fruit
on the sideboard was the plotter, who was the intended
victim? The person who ate the fruit? No, that didn't seem
likely. It did seem likely that the person who ate the fruit
was supposed to use the flakes to murder someone else.
Was he, Darrel, supposed to murder someone, maybe the
Inquisitor—? It seemed unbelievable—except that someone
had helped him escape from the cellar yesterday and there
was no good reason for the bowl to be sitting lonesome on
the sideboard.

Darrel was willing—even eager—to take the risks, if he
could figure out *how* to take them.

There was movement in the courtyard. Darrel stiffened,
then relaxed; it was only the gardener with his dog cart. The
old man began watering Lady Barbara's roses, examining
every branch and bloom as he did. Darrel—who was having
no luck figuring out how to get into Lohgrin's bedcham-
ber—found himself watching every move. When all the
roses had been attended, the gardener began digging along
the back wall of the storeroom. More roses, Darrel thought.
Jordan was trapped on the other side of that wall, and his
lady mother was thinking about roses.

The cart was nearly full before Darrel noticed that the
excavation was directly below a roof downspout. The gardener was going to get a thorough scolding. Roses, Lady
Barbara always said, did not like to have their feet wet.
She would never allow her precious roses to live under a
downspout.

A downspout . . .

Darrel set the bowl aside. He crammed the sealed packet
into the hem of his shirt and crept to the door. Hawksnest

was almost new, as villas went. It had been built after
Lord Ironhawk's marriage to Lady Barbara and hadn't yet
experienced the countless alterations of whim and fashion
that had turned the old villa, Rosignel, into a maze. At
Hawksnest, wherever there were downspouts, there were
catch-basins and ground windows like the one in the winecellar. Lady Barbara must have had the basin filled in and
covered when she had the courtyard converted into her rose
garden.

Darrel thrust his head into the sunlight for a better look.
Red-orange brickwork winked between the gardener's legs
as he worked. Suspicions and hopes confirmed, Darrel withdrew into the shadows and hugged himself. Now everything
made sense: his lady mother was telling him what to
do—she was his new Eye of Destiny. She couldn't look for
him, but she knew he'd get hungry and she knew his favorite
foods. She knew he couldn't read, so she'd drawn stick
figures to explain the poison. She knew where the Inquisitor
held Jordan, and sent her trusted gardener to reveal the other
way in: the way only she remembered!

The youth's mood of celebration lasted until Ivo strode
into the courtyard to confront the elderly gardener.

"What's the meaning of this?" the churl demanded,
cocking his arm, then hesitating when the old man did not
cower. Darrel strained his ears but could not catch the gardener's reply. Ivo retreated, scratching his chin and staring
at the exposed brickwork. The old man's explanation did
not satisfy him, but it must have been plausible—at least to
a man who knew little about architecture and less about
roses—because he went back to his post on the other side
of the storeroom where the stairway rose to Lohgrin's suite.

The churl's visit reminded Darrel that poison packets
and excavations notwithstanding, getting Jordan out wasn't
going to be easy. It became less so moments later when the
drowsy peace of the afternoon was disturbed by the thuds
and shouts of conflict. The gardener scurried behind the

dog cart; from the way he watched his excavation, Darrel understood that Ivo was venting his frustration on Jordan. There was a thud powerful enough to shake the storeroom walls, then, not a heartbeat later, a wail of pain. Birds rose from the courtyard and elsewhere; Darrel slumped against the wall.

"I'm not big enough. I'm never going to be that big."

Jordan howled once more, then silence reigned. The gardener hurried off, leaving his work, his tools, and the dog cart behind. Darrel fingered the oiled parchment and waited for inspiration.

The afternoon continued its hot, oppressive progress toward evening. Clouds piled up above the estate. They billowed toward the sun, turned grey, then black. Gusty winds swirled from every quarter. The gardener's shovel, which he'd left propped against the cart, crashed to the ground, waking the dog who began to bark. Dench came running. The churl picked up the shovel. He swung it at the dog, which had the size and shaggy appearance of a sheep—but not their timid temperament. It lunged for Dench's throat but, hampered by the heavy cart, fell short. Dench swung again, striking the dog in the ribs and breaking one of the shafts attached to the harness. He raised the shovel a third time, this time turning it so the edge of the blade would strike the dog.

The dog bared its fangs, Dench hesitated. A spear of lightning struck the great hall dome. Thunder pounded the villa with sounds that were more felt than heard. Sheets of wind-driven rain swept over the roof. Dench threw the shovel away—he was not the smartest creature under the sun, but he knew not to brandish a sword, or a swordlike object, to a thunderhead's face. The dog recognized its reprieve; it bolted for shelter, dragging the damaged cart as lightning struck the dome a second time. Dench called Ivo and together they chased the dog through the next courtyard and beyond.

Another thunder fist hammered the villa. The ground quivered, or perhaps it was merely Darrel's knees quaking. Erwald Ironhawk's domed hall—the pride of Hawksnest—attracted lightning like stables attracted flies. Darrel couldn't banish his storm fears completely, although he knew—as Ivo, Dench, and the dog did not—that Lord British visited Hawksnest when the dome was raised. Britannia's greatest magician set protective runes in the copper and left precise instructions for the forging of long chains that hung from the dome's edge and were anchored deep in the ground.

While the storm gathered strength for another futile assault on the dome, Darrel splashed across the rose garden. He called Jordan's name from the excavation. There was no response. He got down on his knees and pressed his dripping face against the window grate, realizing as he did that it, unlike the one in the winecellar, was set solidly in the bricks. He begged Jordan to come to the window, but barely recognized the bruised and bloodied man who appeared.

The sound of Darrel's voice and the fuzzy sight of his face renewed Jordan's spirit. His injuries were not as serious as they appeared. He threw his considerable strength into wrestling with the grate. With the help of Darrel's knife and the pouring rain, they got it loose, but no amount of struggle was going to get Jordan through the opening. The storm was beginning to die down when they conceded defeat.

"Go upstairs and raise the trapdoor," Jordan advised from the floor where he sat rubbing his abraded shoulders. "Hurry. Those two'll be back. Lohgrin's put the fear of fire into them."

Darrel hurried. He took the stairs two at a time and skidded to a halt on the slick planks. Lohgrin was taking no chances, there was a great heap of sandbags piled over the trapdoor, then Darrel saw the rope rising from the center of the heap and the tackle block hanging below the roof beam. The boy launched himself at the pulley rope, hitting it with some speed and all his strength. The sandbags didn't rise an inch. Darrel hooked his feet in the railing and pulled the rope. The bags budged, but there was no way to move them off the trapdoor. This was as hopeless as getting Jordan through the window. He'd have to hack the sandbags from the rope one at a time until he could shove the reduced heap aside. The Avatar might return before his mortar-dulled knife accomplished *that*—of course, the Avatar would be big enough to work the pulley one-handed.

"Squirt!" Jordan's shout rose through the floor. "Squirt!" It was louder the second time, louder than the dying storm.

Darrel stamped on the planks. "Shut up!" he shouted—every bit as loud as Jordan—and attacked the pile. He kept his ears pitched for the returning churls, figuring he'd escape to the roof if they returned before he had the pile lightened. He didn't hear them, or anything else untoward, until a hand fell on his shoulder, at which moment he shrieked, jumped, and landed on the far side of the sandbags.

"Fool! *Changeling*! Rotten . . . idiot . . . gremlin!"

Darrel didn't know Drum's cousin, Minette, but once his heart was beating again he formed an opinion of her that Balthan would have appreciated. Minette hurriedly concealed what little damage Darrel and his knife had inflicted on the sandbags.

"There's no time for this nonsense. *They're* coming back. *Now*!" Minette paused in her rearranging to look squarely at Darrel. "I thought I made it perfectly clear: put the powder in their wine, wait for them to fall asleep, and *then* get your brother out. Are you *that* stupid?"

He was Erwald Lord Ironhawk's son, and no wage-laboring laundress was going to call him stupid and survive—Then Darrel heard Ivo scolding Dench as they came through the courtyards.

"Not as stupid as *you*," he sneered as he wrapped his arms around a column. "They're going to find *you* here."

Minette's expression paled. "Wait." She caught Darrel's ankle just before he swung up to the roof. "The powder I left for you—do you still have it?"

"Let go!"

She held on. "Give it to me!"

Darrel threw the packet to the floor, and hauled himself to the roof. The churls could see him, if they looked up—but the last rain of the storm kept them watching their feet until he was panting safe on the other side of the crown tiles. Their feet were thudding on the stairs before Darrel got himself secured against a chimney.

"A melon—ripe for the squeezing!" Dench exalted.

Darrel panted hard and felt sorry for the haughty laundress: no one, especially a young woman, deserved Ivo or Dench. He braced himself for her screams and suffering, but they did not come. Instead she laughed at their coarse comments; taunting and teasing and telling them that they should fortify themselves with a glass of wine if they wished to have their way with *her*. She played a dangerous game. Could Minette's poison work faster than Ivo and Dench? From the safety of the roof, Darrel linked his fingers and made a wish.

He heard a crash, a frightened, feminine yelp, then he rammed his fingers into his ears, willing himself to hear nothing more. Heartbeat by counted heartbeat, he tried not to think about what was happening. He lowered his fingers cautiously, expecting to replace them, but there were no sounds at all coming from the corridor below.

Eye of Destiny—had they killed *her and run away?*

Visions of hounds tearing out the throat of their prey and the slaughter yard when the herds were culled in autumn battled for Darrel's imagination. He did not want to creep over to the colonnade side and peek under the eaves—but he could not resist. Part was duty—if a Hawksnest servant had been butchered, then he, as Ironhawk's son, should sound the alarm—but the larger part was morbid, shameful curiosity. It took him a moment to sort out what he was seeing.

"Well—*help* me, damn you!" the girl whispered hoarsely.

Minette was pinned beneath the two churls. She sounded angry, not injured.

"Are you hurt?"

"No—but you will be if you don't get over here. Help me up—these two aren't going to sleep forever."

Darrel swung to the floor and grabbed Ivo's inert foot. She had whispered, so he did too: "They aren't? Haven't you killed them?"

The girl made a superstitious gesture at the clearing sky. "On my Virtue—I hope not." She got her arm under Ivo's shoulder, shoved, and sighed as he rolled onto his back. "It's not my place to kill. That's for landlords and peers—for Lord Ironhawk, when he comes to his senses."

Dench groaned as they moved him; his head made a hollow sound when it struck the floor and for a moment he was not breathing. Minette made her skyward gesture; Darrel scowled and kicked the fallen man in the floating ribs. Dench breathed again and they pushed him off Minette's legs. She quickly pulled down her skirt. Her lips quivered and Darrel understood that she was not quite as unflappable as she pretended to be.

"You and Jordie—you've got to get away from here—Get away and get help. Someone with the power to send the Inquisitor away. He's an evil man, with evil habits."

Darrel wasn't listening. Not a respectful Lord Hawson, not even a polite Jordan, but *Jordie*—as if her interest in his imprisoned brother were personal and private. Darrel sneaked a reappraising glance as he deposited two sandbags on Ivo's chest. It wasn't hard to picture Jordan getting moon-eyed with the laundress the way he got with Althea. He'd have to ask Jordan later, if there was a later. In the meantime he took two more of the ham-sized bags and dumped them on Dench.

When half the sandbags sat on the churls instead of the trapdoor, Minette whispered that they could raise the rest with the rope. When the weights were flush against the roof beam and they'd each secured the rope on the rail, Darrel grabbed the metal ring in the trapdoor and lifted. He'd raised it a few handspans before something locked around his ankle and pulled him off his feet. The heavy door slammed down on his shin. He gasped with surprise, then with pain. Minette lifted the door and retrieved his battered leg but by then Darrel's tears were flowing and he lacked the will to make them stop. Strong, sweat-smelling arms carried him down the stairs. Jordan's arms—but that only made Darrel feel worse.

"I'm sorry, Squirt. I heard a scuffle, then nothing. When the door lifted, I seized my—"

They'd reached the courtyard. Jordan got one stride into the sunlight before his eyes burned and drove him back into the shadows.

Fourteen
ΥΥΥΥΥ

Minette trilled. "A lot of help you two'll be to anyone! Lame and blind together!"

Darrel sniffled thick, salty tears and wriggled out of Jordan's arms. "I'm not lame." He balanced all his weight on his sore leg, not knowing that he told the truth until it held him. Then he hopped for good measure. "See—it doesn't hurt at all." That part wasn't true, but moving it, even abusing it, didn't make the pain worse. Still, he obeyed when Jordan ordered him to stop.

"And I suppose you're not blind, either."

"You try walking into sunlight after three days in a pit!" That, too, bent the truth without completely breaking it. Jordan's eyes were among the very few parts of him that the churls hadn't battered. Like Darrel, Jordan had to prove himself in front of a woman: he marched boldly into the sunlight again.

"Can you see?" Darrel asked.

"Aye," he replied, though his eyes were streaming and he couldn't pretend he saw clearly. He remembered his manners. "I owe you thanks, girl, for the help you've given us. I don't suppose I could persuade you to help us further by, say, hiding us in your room until sundown, or venturing into the armory—?''

"And you say you can see! Hammers and bells, Jordie—you don't even recognize me!'' Minette swung at Jordan's arm; Darrel held his breath. ''What's the use of getting you out if you're still cursed and blind?''

Jordan didn't recognize her, but she cursed by metal, like Drumon, and that narrowed the possibilities. Jordan wiped his eyes and shaded them.

''Minette.'' His voice softened. He took her hand lightly and kissed it.

''Eye of Destiny!'' Darrel turned away in disgust. ''Now, they're moon-eyed!'' He spoke loudly enough for them both to hear, but they were ignoring him.

''I owe you my thanks, and more,'' Jordan said.

He had his arms around her and his mouth against hers. The tongue-tied awkwardness that plagued Jordan when he was in Althea's company did not hamper him with other young women. Darrel looked around for a bucket of water. Finding none, he hissed through his teeth like a snake. Jordan opened one eye, then made a crude, but easily understood gesture with the fingers of his unoccupied hand.

''We have to get away. They aren't dead, *Jordie*. We don't want to be here when they wake up—do *we*?''

Jordan took his time releasing Minette. ''We need food for several days traveling and weapons—I'd prefer my bastard blade, but any will do—and my mail shirt. And horses—'' Jordan's thoughts shot to the grey Valorian, Fugatore; they returned empty and aching. ''No, we'll get horses later.''

Darrel whooped for joy. Minette tottered backward, wiping her lips on her arm.

''I can't,'' she whispered, suddenly conscious that they were in the archway beneath the corridor and readily visible from several directions. ''I've done all that I can. More. I risked everything getting the sleep-herbs. You can't ask—My family. If I got caught helping you escape, they could lose everything.''

Jordan seized her arm and pulled her against him. Doubt flashed in Minette's eyes: Jordan was a peer's son. One could assume that he'd been educated in the principles of Virtue, just as one might assume the Inquisitor and his churls had not. Lord British made Britannia a realm of opportunity, yet it remained true that physical strength expanded opportunity—if Minette had more strength herself she'd be swinging a hammer at one of the family's fires instead of beating laundry for wages inside the villa. Jordan was a young man with tremendous opportunity.

"What about your cousin, Drum. Would he help us?"

Jordan's tone was more desperate than threatening—though Minette took little comfort there. She shook her whole body saying no, trying to get free.

"Minette, I assume you want us to help you—and your family—by getting rid of the Inquisitor and his churls. You won't kill them yourself—guild principles, I understand: smiths don't compete with assassins—but I'd wager my inheritance that you don't care if *I* kill them—"

She belted the mottled purple swelling on the side of Jordan's face. He staggered and Minette took her own opportunity to raise her knee. Jordan was fast, inured to pain, and aware of his vulnerabilities. He spun Minette off balance by pressing his thumbnail into the nerves of her wrist. Her knee missed; its momentum pushed her further into Jordan's power. The pain shooting from her wrist to her elbow left her speechless and afraid to move.

Jordan seemed equally paralyzed. The muscles along his jaw began to pulse. Darrel recalled the berserkerang.

"Please, Jordan—no! Don't hurt her." He clung to his brother's wrist, trying to pull it and Minette toward him. "Let her go! We don't need her, or Drum, or anybody—we've just got to get out of here . . . NOW!"

Jordan purged the red veil with a sigh. He released Minette but did not apologize. "We need your help Minette—yours and your family's . . . *I* need your help. I don't know how I'm going to do what has to be done. I need food because my meals haven't been exactly generous lately. I need a weapon because . . . Because I do.

"You've come this far—you can't throw up your hands and pretend you haven't."

Minette studied the crescent mark Jordan's nail left on her wrist. The storm left the air cooler, if no less humid. Servants would hurry to complete those tasks the storm had interrupted. She and the Hawsons had been standing, talking—arguing—in one place far too long. They'd been seen—the fact that they had seen no one convinced Minette of this. The household was, in effect, protecting itself from the perils of witnessing her with Ironhawk's fugitive sons. Minette knew the sympathies of the foregate and household as well as anyone because she shared them. The Inquisitor held Lord Ironhawk in his sleeve. Together, they held power over the entire villa—except for Ironhawk's sons.

"I need an answer," Jordan interrupted. "If you and yours won't help me, I might just as well throw myself back into the pit—"

That was more than Darrel could endure: "*I'm* helping you. *I* would have gotten you out without *her* help. We're enough, just the two of us."

Jordan covered his face, gently. He was unaccustomed to pleading his cause to a woman and incapable of controlling his overeager brother at any time. *If it were up to him . . .* but it wasn't. Squirt was with him and so was Minette. He lowered his hand.

"We can't cross open ground until nightfall. We'll have to stay inside the walls until then. Go to your cousin—tell him what's happened. Tell him: if there're swords or armor in his forge for repairs—No, *ask* him to bring what he can to the postern gate an hour after sundown. He knows where it is. Tell him—" A variety of explanations stirred in Jordan's mind, but not one of them were guaranteed to persuade the farrier. "Tell him: Destiny willing, my brother and I will be there, but he must do what he wills to do."

Minette looked down at her apron. It was streaked with laundry bluing. "We're not like you," she said softly. "We're common folk who want nothing more out of life than a roof over our heads and food on our table. We rely on a landlord to protect us. We're not peers. We don't think about Virtue Quests. We're not ready to become heroes." She raised her eyes to meet Jordan's.

He chuckled. "You work hard; I get the hard work."

Minette's cheeks flushed. She wanted to lash out, but Jordan was armored with the truth. "I'll tell Drumon," she murmured. An unpleasant thought entered her mind, she launched it at Ironhawk's heir, to make him feel guilty. "Ivo and Dench will remember me when they wake up. They'll come looking for me. They'll follow me, maybe Drum, too—if he decides to help you."

Darrel nodded vigorously. "Let's kill 'em while we've got the chance." He brandished his nicked and dulled knife. "This'll rip 'em up good."

The youth was right. Valor and Honor notwithstanding, the Inquisitor's churls were too dangerous to leave alive. Jordan should have attended to the matter the moment he was through the trapdoor—when his desire for vengeance was the greatest. But he'd thought they were dead, and with his brother hurting, he hadn't given them a second thought. Now, when he gave them that second thought, he couldn't do it.

"I can't kill a man while he's defenseless," Jordan explained, looking at Minette, not his brother. "Unless your herbs were stronger than you meant, they've been reprieved. You best stay out of sight, yourself . . . after you've talked to your cousin."

Subtle shifts in posture and gesture passed between Minette and Jordan like shuttlecocks in a game Darrel watched without knowing the rules or scoring. He thought they were both being ridiculous. "I'll do it myself," he announced. The air moved at his back, but Jordan missed. Darrel started up the stairs two at a time.

"Stop."

Darrel caught his balance and froze. They dubbed it "Mother's Voice," because its effect was demonstrably magical. Yet it contravened all known laws of magic: it was not invoked with runes. It required no reagents whatsoever, nor ritual gestures beyond those needed to form the necessary words. Women seemed to learn it at childbirth, and used it liberally in the education of their children, hence its common name. The Inquisitor had it as one of the many components of his dark charisma. Lord Erwald, in contrast, could rant and rave and chew the plaster off the walls without uttering a single word that *must* be obeyed. Jordan had never shown an aptitude for magic before, yet Darrel knew he did not dare move again until his brother gave him leave.

"I won't have you doing for me what I won't do myself," Jordan continued. "That would make you the same as them, and me the same as the Inquisitor. I won't have it. If they come upon us, you can carve to your heart's content—but not while they sleep."

Lips pursed and eyebrows furrowed, Darrel descended the stairs. "Then, let's just *go*. I've about run out of places to hide in—" He looked at the puddles on the paving stones. "We're going to leave tracks . . ."

Jordan flashed a confident, lopsided grin and ruffled his brother's hair. "Trust me, Squirt—there are places you haven't found yet."

Darrel, who had at that moment decided he liked being called Squirt no more than Jordan liked being called Jordie, answered Jordie's smile with a sneer.

Minette had had enough and ran off for the villa kitchens. Then, as promised, Jordan led Darrel into the unknown—a series of man-high tunnels, knee deep with fast-flowing water the current of which they followed. The tunnels were pitch-dark, slick underfoot, and filled with odors.

Darrel balked when their tunnel began a steep descent. "You can't be serious. This place reeks."

"Listen to who's talking."

Something soft and wormlike brushed against Darrel's bare leg. He leapt with surprise, lost his footing, and slammed into Jordan, whereupon they were both swept down into a wider, deeper tunnel. It was not the first such ride for Jordan. He remembered exactly where an iron ring was mounted in the side wall. He snared it with one hand, Darrel with the other, and swung them both to a shallow shelf.

"Do you have any idea what this is?" Darrel swore as he shook every part of himself. "Do you know what's *in* this water? Do you? It's full of shit!"

Jordan laughed. He hurt when he laughed, but he couldn't stop. He leaned against the wall, clutching his ribs, moaning and giggling until amusement and agony were both sated. "Where did you think it went? Does someone march into your room every morning and carry the chamberpot to the stables or do they wash it down a sump hole?"

The darkness shielded Darrel from the most visible effects of his embarrassment. He was thirteen years old—there were some questions he hadn't gotten around to asking. Which led to one that seemed worth asking: "How did you find out?" He, himself, would naturally have explored the sewer, if he'd suspected its existence, but Jordan? Perfect Jordan? It was hard to picture.

"You know where the postern gate is?"

"Aye." The little-used rear entrance through villa walls opened to a sheer drop that, depending on the season, was twelve to eighteen feet above the same stream that flowed through from the foregate.

"Well, one summer it hardly rained; the stream almost dried up. I saw this huge cave below the banks. I guessed what it was. I'd say we're under the great hall right now. The sewer goes everywhere.''

"You explored the whole thing?'' The fact they were up to their ankles in questionable water implied the answer, but Darrel still couldn't imagine Jordan groping through the dark passages.

Jordan stifled another round of laughter, remembering. "Not that year,'' he chuckled. "You think it reeks now? The stream's nice and high; it just rained. Imagine if it hadn't rained for a good three weeks and the stream was too low for the shunt.''

The youth did, and groaned. "But I don't believe you. You wouldn't go into a cave on a dare, no matter how sweet it smelled.''

"Depends on the dare. Balthan dared that I couldn't find my way to where the water's drawn down from the stream. Couldn't let him win.''

That made sense. When Balthan got prankish, anything was possible. Darrel knew very few of the magician's legendary pranks and escapades through personal experience. Of course, he still strained everything he drank through his teeth—one mouthful of tadpoles had been enough for several lifetimes. If Balthan Wanderson dared, then no true son of Ironhawk would refuse the challenge.

They were both silent a moment, remembering their foster-brother.

Darrel broke the melancholy first. "How did you know I didn't know?''

"The smell clings,'' Jordan conceded. "Our lady mother—she doesn't really approve. If you'd ever found these tunnels, Agatha and her perfume bottles would have found you, and you—would have raised the dead in protest.''

Sometimes Jordan sounded as stuffy and pompous as any weak-wristed tutor. "How did you know? You don't know everything. Maybe I wouldn't have,'' Darrel protested. He couldn't see his own hand at the end of his arm, but he knew the expression that was forming on Jordan's face.

"Squirt—when have you *ever* gone quietly into a bath barrel? I'm not talking of an ordinary bath in the hypocaust—I'm talking about Agatha putting sweet-soap on your hair and holding your head under the water until you're near drowned."

It sounded as if Jordan might have firsthand knowledge. Darrel stayed as far from his mother's personal maid as possible. The woman was a witch; a denizen of the underworld disguised as an ill-tempered woman. Her hobby was his misery. It would be just like her to rise, eellike out of the water while they were talking—

"What if they follow us? Could anyone follow us? Could they take us by surprise?"

"We'd hear them. Unless they've got magic, handfire at least. Can't get this far carrying a lantern—" Again Jordan used the voice of experience. "But it's even safer closer to the stream. Come on."

They waded on, always with the current, always descending, until they came to a dimly illuminated, smooth-walled chamber. Its floor was completely covered by a pool of water. Light rose from the bottom of the pool.

"Magic!" Darrel exalted.

"The outflow to the stream," Jordan corrected. "They can't surprise us. When it's dark, we'll go out—you can see it isn't far—but watch out, we're right below the mill and the current's brutal."

When the water was lower and the pool confined to the depression in the center of the chamber it would be possible to sit on the floor. As it was, with the stream flood-swollen and the sewer itself carrying runoff from the earlier storm, the pool rose to Darrel's calves and there was nothing to do but stand in cold water until he was numbed through.

Jordan was too tall for the chamber. He squatted down before his neck got stiffer. He suffered the aches and indignity with the same practiced detachment he used in the arena. Darrel imitated him, and imitated him well. They didn't talk, merely waited until the light from the pool was gone.

Jordan stood and groaned. "Once you surface, come back to this side of the stream. We go up the bank to the wall, then along the wall to the postern. It's steep and crumbly. Try not to slip, but if you do—don't cry out. Grunt. Swine come here often enough; a little grunting won't alert anyone—" Before all this started, in another lifetime, Jordan, at Lord Ironhawk's command, stood duty in the guard-porches; he knew their routines and habits.

"Swine? You mean *boars*?"

Whenever peers gathered to discuss the most ferocious foe they'd faced on their Virtue Quest or since, someone always mentioned the full-grown male pig. Though the tusks of the domesticated variety were carefully extracted, a breeding boar weighed as much as a horse, ran as fast, and feared nothing under the stars.

"Don't worry about it," Jordan advised before he jumped into the water.

It was good advice. The night air was clean and fresh after so many hours in the sewer chamber. The moons had risen, stars were beginning to appear; there was ample light and no boars whatsoever. Darrel was born to stealth; he picked his way through the scree without dislodging an audible pebble. Jordan was not quite so light-footed; he sounded a bit like something foraging for dinner, but the guards coming on duty in the nearest tower, at least a hundred yards away, took no notice.

Drum waited inside the postern gate.

"I've brought you swords—we had them in the forge for repair—and food and all the silver I could gather."

Which was more than Jordan had allowed himself to hope. He gave the farrier the sincerest embrace of their short, prickly friendship. "Your Virtue climbs high—"

One of the peerage's traditional compliments, uttered by habit, almost without thought.

"Or my mind's completely addled. Jordan, I've taken the measure of this Inquisitor. There's nothing to be done against him—no more than can be done in the cities when the miasma falls."

"No one will ever accuse you of false hope," Jordan said, getting the feel of the larger weapon before belting it over his hips. "By the Eight, the Three, and the One—did you weight this club with lead?"

"I doubt we'd have it in the forge-yard if someone hadn't complained about it. But the edge is good—I sharpened it, and the other, myself."

Jordan pressed his thumb on the edge, and whistled appreciatively. There was little danger he'd cut himself; sword steel didn't take, or need, the keen edge of a good knife. With his strength behind it, though, it would sever an arm or slice through ribs. "It does you credit, Drum." He eased it into the scabbard and made certain Darrel had done the same. "Thank Minette, too, and tell her she must have a bard's silver tongue to persuade you." He tore into a loaf of bread.

Drum hooked his now-empty hands in his belt. "I'll tell her, but I stood ready to help you, lord's son."

That pricked Jordan's ears. He stopped chewing and gave Drum the courtesy of his attention.

"I was wrong. Balthan had no wrong part in this. I did not believe him and didn't help him when I had the chance. Now I make amends." He reached into his belt-pouch for the vellum sheet Balthan left behind. "Tell him so, if you ever find him."

It was too dark for reading. Jordan tucked the vellum in the sack with the rest of the food. "I'm coming back, Drum. This *will* be set to rights." He shrugged the sack into the least uncomfortable position on his shoulders.

"Don't be a fool. When Lohgrin heard you'd gone, they

say flames shot out of his mouth. But he *never* asked if anyone had seen you go, nor sent anyone after you.''

Jordan paused with his hand on the open gate. ''Meaning?''

''He's got ways—dark ways, just like Balthan's enemies. Swords won't help if he doesn't need men to find you.''

''You always know how to cheer me up, Drum. How do you drag yourself out of bed each morning?''

The farrier ignored the question by asking one of his own; the same question he'd asked Balthan. ''Where will you go?''

''First—to Rosignel: roust ourselves a couple of barren mares. After that, who knows? When I'm ready, I'll be back, and you'll know it.'' He herded Darrel through the gate, down the scree to the stream.

''You're not serious about *mares* are you?''

These were the first words out of Darrel's mouth once they were across the stream and headed through the fields. In the youth's rigidly ordered world boys rode geldings, codgers and magicians rode mules, women rode mares, and men rode stallions. Anything else was unnatural.

Jordan swatted his brother on the neck. ''You can walk . . .''

His voice trailed. A cold breeze had touched his cheek—not cool, but cold. He walked backward, studying the villa that displayed only the ordinary lights and sounds of a hot summer night. He was anxious, jumping at shadows, or breezes, then—as his mind fitted the lit windows with their rooms—he realized the Inquisitor was watching them.

''Run!'' he shouted to his brother.

''Where?''

It took a moment to decide, then the icy breeze touched Jordan's cheek a second time. ''For the stones atop the moon-gate hill!''

''What?''

"Don't argue—RUN!" He caught Darrel's sleeve as he passed and dragged the youth until he got his legs working.

Althea stood by the window of her new room—Lohgrin's room when he was here. And he was here, behind her, muttering into an ink-filled bowl. The air in the room was deathly still, she'd come to the window hoping to find a breeze. She felt better now than she had a few days ago; better but not good. She was tired and weak, as if her mind had shrunk while she was ill and no longer filled her entire body.

"Do you see them?"

She shuddered, as she did whenever he spoke to her. She still hated him, and feared him, but in her reduced state her greatest rebellion was silence.

"Tell me when you see them."

Them? It was not her will to remain there, watching the darkness, but she did, and wondered, without emotion, what horror he meant to show her. The Inquisitor had that power. He'd moved into her dreams right away; now he had her waking thoughts as well. She saw something move—saw it with unnatural clarity. For a moment she hoped, then the horror came. Jordan and his brother were running away from the villa. Her left arm rose; she seized it back. Her jaw dropped; she clutched her throat, imprisoning her voice.

"Ah—you've spotted them. I trusted you would."

Althea left the window. She was drawn to the center of the room where her betrothed wove complex symbols in the air above his scrying-bowl. His right hand was grotesque, then Althea realized he wore another hand over it like a glove.

"Go to them. Bring them back to me."

Althea moved toward the open window but this time the command had not been meant for her. Smoke and tendrils of viscous slime spun out of the Inquisitor's clawed fingers. Althea found herself able to retreat and cower in the corner by her cot. The manifestation danced and grew midway between the bowl and the window. When it was as thick as a man's heart, Lohgrin spread his mismatched hands. Althea whimpered as a bloodshot eye opened in the hairy palm. Lohgrin moaned, himself, as the eye floated away from him and was absorbed into the manifestation. Glancing at him, Althea saw that his eyes were white. The Inquisitor was blinded—or, rather, his vision dwelt in the gazer swimming out the window.

Her will told her that this was her chance: while he was blind and enthralled she could bludgeon him out of her life. But her legs did not answer to her will and her hands tightened around her throat until the room went black.

The beatings, the heat, the meager meals, took their toll on Jordan's stamina. He was lagging many yards behind Darrel. The night was silent except for their desperate ascent to stones reared in a circle at the top of moon-gate hill. The silence frightened Jordan more than hoofbeats or shouts could have done: whatever tugged the hairs on the back of his neck was not part of the ordinary world.

"Get inside the stones!" he gasped to his brother who was nearing the circle.

He prayed in an incoherent way to an unnamable power that they would not have to enter the gate that would translate them instantly to somewhere else—perhaps to safety in Trinsic, perhaps not. Magicians knew the mechanics of gate travel, but even they admitted that mistakes happened and could not be corrected. Only Lord British knew all the secrets of the shimmering blue light. *He* said the gates were not magical at all, yet he'd hallowed the ground where they appeared, forbidding those with evil or malicious intent passage through the stone sentries. This was the source and substance of his faith: Darrel and he would be able to pass between the stones; whatever pursued them would not.

He'd know in another few steps if his faith was true.

Darrel stumbled as he breached the imaginary wall, but he passed through. Still on hands and knees, he looked back the way he'd come. What the sweating youth saw filled him with terror: a malignantly luminous visage—dead silent and swift—loomed just above Jordan. Its eyes were blood and fire, its teeth like patterned steel, its mouth as black and vast as heaven beyond the stars.

"Faster! *Faster*! Don't look back! Just *run*!"

Jordan needed no encouragement. A fetid wind poured down on him. With his last strength, Jordan passed between the stones. The visage deafened them both with its shrieks. It swirled outside the stones at blinding speed, seeking—not yet finding—a way between them.

Fifteen
ΥΥΥΥΥ

The apparition did not persist once it, and the intelligence behind it, determined that Ironhawk's sons were beyond its power. It shrieked a last time and was swallowed by the night. The fear of it lingered in the brothers. They stayed within the sentinel stones after the gate flared at midnight and they were crowded against the stones by a column of incandescent blue. As wide as Jordan was tall and twice as high, the gate gave off a bitter, metallic tang, and made their hair stand on end.

Balthan had led them through a similar gate near his refuge cave to the prime gate of the city of Yew. The Hawksnest moon gate, like Balthan's, was a secondary gate, bound to Trinsic's prime moon gate as Erwald Ironhawk maintained his citizenship in that city. If one entered the vibrating blue light of the Hawksnest gate, one should emerge a few miles south of Trinsic—unless something went wrong. If the apparition had pierced the stone sentinels, the young men might risk the trip. But it didn't; so they didn't.

"Get some sleep," Jordan suggested, carefully arranging himself in the grass between the stones and the gate.

"Shouldn't I stand guard?"

Jordan shielded his eyes from the gate's light. "Suit yourself, but either we're safe or there's not a damn thing we can do to protect ourselves."

Darrel resolved to sit at Jordan's feet until the gate closed and dawnlight brightened the horizon. He lasted half that time. He fell asleep with his back against a sentinel stone. He woke up with the sun shining on his face an arm's length beyond it. His horrified yelp awakened Jordan.

"I guess we made it," he said, scurrying back inside the circle.

Jordan's sole comment was a groan. His bruises had stiffened in the dew and he needed help getting to his feet. He limped badly when he tried to walk.

"You're hurting."

"Just stiff. Come on. Lohgrin probably thinks we used the gate. Don't want him seeing otherwise from his window."

"You think *that* came from the Inquisitor?"

Jordan belted his sword and shrugged the food sack onto his tender shoulders. His silence answered the question.

"So he's a magician—like Balthan and Councillor Annon?"

"Not like them—but a magician. You're the one who showed me his stuff—what did you think he was? A peddler?" Jordan shook his head with disgust. "Wouldn't mind seeing Balthan right now. I'd admit he'd been right, and ask him to work on my back." He groaned and clutched his floating ribs.

Darrel dropped his sword belt. The metal rings clashed against the scabbard. He flushed with shame: surely Jordan heard the racket. But Jordan was still trying to walk. They started slowly. Ground mist hovered in the valley between Hawksnest and Rosignel. The sun would burn through long before they arrived. The day promised to be as sultry as the previous one.

"Are we going to look for Balthan?" Darrel asked when Jordan's walk was steadier and his lips weren't a pair of thin, pale lines.

Jordan remembered the vellum Drum had given him. Darrel sat cross-legged on the moist grass while Jordan dug it out of the sack. Jordan stood while he unfolded the much-abused sheepskin.

"Damn."

"What's it say?"

"Nothing." He slapped it into Darrel's hand. The words—there had been a great many of them—were smeared together. Drum had given the vellum the best care he could, keeping it, probably, in the waistband of his trousers. He was illiterate; he hadn't considered what a hot day in the forge-yard would do to writing.

"Where will we go?" Darrel discarded the useless vellum.

"We'll hike along the road looking for gypsies—for a certain old gypsy woman with a magic table—"

"And Lord Shamino! They'll know we're looking for them!" The boy leapt up. His conclusion was not farfetched: the forest-wise Companion and the itinerant gypsies were known to travel together, pooling their mysterious knowledge. If any people could tell them how to save Hawksnest from the Inquisition, Lord Shamino and the gypsies could. "Let's go!" He ran into the thinning mist.

Jordan felt more like eighty than eighteen. He couldn't run this morning if his life depended on it. Squirt waited for him at the fenced-in field where Lord Ironhawk ran the least valuable of his broodmares with a promising young stallion. He spied a dark brown mare, hardly a beauty, with lopsided ribs and swollen knees. Once she'd been very special to him. Unlike his brother, Jordan didn't let himself be hampered by tradition. If the best horse Lord Ironhawk volunteered was a mare, he took her and rode her with love and pride.

He called her name. She raised her head and looked

straight at him. For a moment she seemed to remember,
then she went back to grazing. One afternoon several years
ago, a herald had thundered into the yard. He demanded, in
Lord British's name, the best horse in Lord Ironhawk's
stable for the next leg of his very important journey. The
brown mare served the herald well—far better than he
served her; he broke her knees, her ribs, and her wind getting
to Trinsic before sunset. She could never be ridden again,
and ten-year-old Jordan learned always to hold something
back when he gave out his love.

There were other mares in the field who could be ridden,
once the brothers got bridles and saddles from Rosignel.
Darrel spied the guard on the ramshackle porch above the
gate moments after he spied them. Jordan strode ahead of
his brother and remained ahead as they approached the
closed gate.

"They won't let us in."

"They will," Jordan corrected grimly. He was prepared
to demand obedience with his sword if he had to. But it
didn't come to that. The guard recognized them and opened
the gate once they were closer. More importantly, the net-
work of observation and rumor stretched between the old
and the new villas. The guard knew what was happening at
Hawksnest.

"Lord Ironhawk said if the moon gate hadn't killed you,
he would. You're disinherited. He's settling everything on
Althea. It's a crime against Virtue." The man gave a respectful nod toward Jordan's livid bruises. "There's not a
man or woman on the estate who won't join you when you
rise up against your father. I'll tell them that you've come
through safe."

Jordan shook him off. Tempting as it was, he wasn't
ready to challenge Lord Ironhawk, and he wasn't interested
in the help of those who so easily set aside their oaths to his
father. "We'll take what we need and be gone for now."

Rosignel's harness room was furnished, as were all parts

of the now-neglected villa, with old-fashioned goods and Hawksnest castoffs. While Darrel investigated the wonders of the former, Jordan picked and chose among the latter.

"You're a welcome, unexpected sight."

Jordan shouldn't have been surprised, but he was. The saddle fell through his hands. One hand gripped his scabbard as he spun to face the door, the other seized the hilt. A foot-long section of sharpened steel glistened in the light. The intruder wisely retreated. His voice was vaguely familiar, but the silhouette in the doorway was not. But, then, Jordan never expected to see Balthan Wanderson in torn clothes, with naked knees, and a frayed kerchief bound over his hair.

"Anabarces' ghost—don't tell me you're still blind!"

Balthan approached warily; when he was at sword's length, Jordan proved he could see quite well by snagging a tatter of the magician's sleeve on the tip of the blade. "You look like a peasant. You've been *working*." He lowered his weapon and took Balthan's arm.

The magician did not struggle against Jordan's grip. He knew he would not break free and he hated to fail at anything. He didn't respond to the accusations because they were true.

"You've been swimming in the sewers . . ." He sniffed loudly, melodramatically. "And coming up second in a two-man fight."

"Third among three."

The appropriate greeting rituals thus observed, Jordan released Balthan's arm and allowed the magician to examine his bruises with a feather-light touch. He winced when the inspection neared his swollen cheek.

"Table leg," he explained.

"They broke a bone. Fortunately, I've had experience recently with broken bones. First, though, we get rid of the swelling. It won't take long—They tell me you're not staying. I'll tell you what little I've learned."

"I'll tell you what chased us up moon-gate hill last night. Maybe you'll know what it was."

Balthan led them to a room in a decrepit part of the villa where only the most diligent searchers would discover it. He alternately grunted and nodded as Jordan, then Darrel, described the apparition, Althea's strange behavior, and the objects in the Inquisitor's locked storeroom.

"There were *thousands* of them," Darrel concluded his description of the bug-filled basket.

"A reagent," Balthan said. He plunged into his sack for a flat ceramic pot and a tangled wad of spider silk. "Not one of ours," he added unnecessarily. Absently, expertly, he divided the silk, felted each piece into a shallow cup shape, then filled the depression with ruddy powder from the pot. "Lohgrin's a magician." He sealed the felt cups by folding them. He raised one to Jordan's cheek. *"Mani!"*

"We guessed as much."

Jordan dodged involuntarily. The little bundle fell to the floor. Balthan hissed and threw the spent reagents into the chamberpot. He picked up another felt lump.

"Hold still. I imagine all the Inquisitors are."

"He's controlling your sister the same way he controlled that apparition." Jordan flinched when the silk touched the bruise, and another useless lump flew into the chamberpot.

Balthan laid the third in the palm of Jordan's hand. *"You* hold it wherever it hurts the most; *I'll* do the rest."

"You can do magic that way?" Jordan fitted the lump against his cheek.

"The proper way isn't working. *Mani!"*

There was a flash of light, a tiny *pop*, and the sound of Jordan staggering backward into the wall. A wisp of smoke curled around his fingertips. His mind said: light, smoke, fire, pain. His skin said: ice, and after a moment *a-a-ahh*. The throbbing stopped.

"I guess it does work." Balthan shrugged away his misgivings and handed Jordan another lump. "Let's do it again.

I doubt it,'' he returned to Jordan's earlier assertion. ''A gazer—the grimoires call what you saw a gazer—belongs entirely to the magician who made it. Althea has her own soul. *Mani!*''

The soothing ice spread across Jordan's ribs. He could and did breathe deeply without gasping. ''You just said he's not one of you. Maybe his magic's different.'' He took the next-to-last bundle and pressed it against his shoulder.

''Different reagents, different invocations— *Mani!*—But magic doesn't change. A gazer's a gazer—it is what it is no matter who or what created it. It has no soul, no will. Althea does, he can enthrall her, but he can't control her soul.''

''You're splitting hairs.'' Jordan stretched both arms high; his palms pressed against the roof beam. He bent over, pulling on his ankles until his forehead touched his knees.

Balthan watched the martial exercises with a bemused frown. ''All magic is splitting hairs. May I assume that you're sufficiently healed?'' He scooped up the last bundle and was ready to dispose of it when Darrel caught his eye.

Please?—the boy mouthed, raising his trousers to expose his contusion. Balthan held out the bundle.

''You can touch it; I won't jump.''

''Well, sit down first—'' Balthan motioned Darrel to the primitive pallet with its straw mattress. ''But if you kick me, Squirt, so help me, I'll wring your neck.''

Darrel believed him. He got a death-grip on the boards and twisted his neck so he couldn't see what was happening. He was scarcely aware of Balthan probing the injury or arranging the felt over it. There was a naked sword in the corner of this room. Its pommel and guard were like no others the youth had seen, the blade was nicked on both edges. Obviously it was a relic from his great-grandfather's days—and yet the rust had been whetted off. The hilt leather wasn't even dirty; it was, however, poorly wrapped.

''Mani!''

The icy sensation took Darrel's breath away. For a moment he thought Balthan had maliciously wrought harm rather than healing. Then the soothing surrounded the ache. The reagents collapsed into a fine powder. The angry contusion shrank and faded before Jordan's astounded eyes.

"You're good at this," he muttered, as if he'd never quite believed it before. "You're truly good."

"Are you surprised? Was that a compliment?"

"No . . ."

The air was suddenly as cold as Mani magic, and not at all soothing.

Jordan strove to extricate himself: "I mean, yes . . . No and yes. No, I wasn't; yes, it was—I guess."

Darrel sat up between them. "Is that your sword in the corner?"

The magician became as flustered as Jordan. "There's nothing against a mage having a sword."

He tried to hide the relic blade behind him. Tradition inhibited magicians from carrying steel. It was an understandable tradition: like magic itself, swordwork was a skill best learned in childhood and a solid education in one didn't leave enough time for practice in the other. Yet Balthan, like Jordan and Darrel, was a Peer's son. He had not been ordained for magic, to the exclusion of all other learning, until he was in his teens. In fact, both his father and Lord Ironhawk tried mightily to beat the talent out of him.

When Erwald finally admitted defeat and endowed a scholarship at the magician's Lyceum on far-off Verity Isle for his foster-son, Balthan resolutely and without regret turned his back to steel—until he found himself running from Lohgrin. He knew the sword was an embarrassing relic. He practiced—played with it, if the truth were told—by himself. He was too ashamed of his barely remembered swordwork to ask the guards to practice with him.

Once Jordan saw the weapon and guessed what Balthan was doing with it, the magician buried his shame. He

squared his shoulders and met Jordan's questioning
stare—they were much the same in height, and though Jordan was much brawnier, book learning hadn't completely
softened the magician—with a hard, undecipherable glower
of his own.

Jordan blinked. "I'm not the one you have to prove it
to," he whispered as he sidestepped his foster-brother and
hefted the relic. The balance wasn't bad; the blade itself
was another matter. "Were you planning to *saw* through
the Inquisitor?"

Balthan growled and reached for his sword. Jordan
warded him away with his free hand.

"Just put it back. The Lady of Rosignel gave it to me
because your father's abandoned the promises he made when
he married Lady Barbara."

"But can you use it, Balthan? How much do you remember?"

Peerage children were acquainted with the sword as part
of their customary education. Balthan was ashamed of his
skill, but he knew more about swordwork than most men.
He couldn't hold a candle to Jordan. Jordan's skills went
far beyond custom; he was better than most swordmasters.
If Balthan attempted, for pride, to cross swords with the
hard-muscled man holding his sword, he'd lose. Of course,
if he admitted that he couldn't use the relic, he also lost. It
was a matter of which confession hurt more. He leaned
forward until he could feel Jordan's hot breath on his chin.

"I can use it."

A confrontation was ordained. They faced each other in
the yard between the kitchen and the stable. Darrel took a
seat on a pile of firewood. He was the only apparent specta-
tor, but certainly there were others. Balthan, who might
have thought he stood some faint chance of a draw, watched
Jordan settle behind his sword. No amount of luck was
going to save the pale magician.

Darrel shouted "Lay on—" from the woodpile.

The youngster knew how the bout would go, and how quickly: Balthan held his sword much too tightly, his stance was unbalanced, and mostly, Jordan was very good. Jordan feinted; Balthan swung. Darrel blinked. When he opened his eyes the magician was kneeling in the mud, without a weapon, clutching his wrist.

"Had enough?"

To Darrel's surprise, Balthan hadn't. He shook feeling into his hand and retrieved his sword. This time he centered his weight over his feet, but he still held the hilt too tight, and he still believed Jordan's feint. This time Balthan was still standing when Darrel reopened his eyes.

Jordan retrieved the relic sword and offered it, hilt forward. "Try again. Hold it gently—like a woman. You haven't forgotten *that*, too?"

The magician snatched the sword. He squeezed the hilt with every shred of strength remaining in his arm.

"I warned you—"

Jordan didn't feint. Steel rang on steel. Balthan's sword soared, end over end, high into the air. Darrel dove for cover; Jordan seized the stunned magician and hauled him out of danger. The sword came to rest hilt up in the rancid sweepings from the chicken coop. Balthan didn't rush to retrieve it. His arm was ringing from the elbow down. Darrel expressed his sympathy by braying like a mule. The youth laughed himself to his knees. Balthan started toward him and met the opposing force of Jordan's arms.

"You've had enough," Jordan said softly, giving Balthan a subtle shove away from the sword, away from his brother. Then he turned to Darrel. "All right, let's see what you've got."

The youth's laughter died. He gathered himself and drew his sword cleanly. He practiced his lessons in the same arena where Jordan did, though he seldom had the chance to measure himself against him. Darrel closed quickly. He did not believe the feints. He didn't retreat, or let his brother retreat: Jordan had longer arms; Darrel would never get inside his guard again if he let himself get pushed out. They circled warily and on the far side of the yard, Balthan sat in the mud and watched.

"All right—I'll attack you . . . now!"

Darrel knew where he was weakest. He defended himself successfully; he hadn't, however, actually seen Jordan's attack. He guessed where the next attack might fall, and got his sword up just in time; the shock went through his arms, his back, then down his legs. It was like being struck with a hammer.

"Your turn. Attack me."

"I'd rather defend."

"Lay on, Squirt," Jordan taunted, extending his arms sideward. "I've been in a hole for three days. Balthan's left me plenty of bruises. I still don't see well in the sunlight. Come on, Squirt—attack me."

Darrel was not fooled for a moment. The tip of Jordan's sword—a good two yards away from Jordan's supposedly weak shoulder—didn't wobble, didn't twitch. The tip of Darrel's sword was, maybe, a foot and a half from Jordan's throat. If, by some unforeseen accident, his attack succeeded; Jordan would be dead.

"Lay on, Squirt. *Try*."

Jordan's smile was all innocence and completely intolerable. Darrel lunged. Jordan parried the flat of the sword with his off-weapon arm. Darrel stayed behind his weapon, as he'd been taught. He was halfway through a complete orbit of the yard when the flat of Jordan's sword landed against his back, lifting him off his feet. If it had been the edge, he'd be dead. Darrel barely held on to his sword. He completed his spin and managed—by some miracle—to come to a stop in a credible stance and facing Jordan.

"I'm impressed. Can you do it again?"

Darrel swallowed, nodded his head, and braced for an onslaught.

Feeling crept back to Balthan's fingers. He made a fist. The throbbing ebbed, then got worse. The magician part of him said to go to his room and cast Mani spells until he felt better, but the part of him that wanted desperately to be a better man than his father had been kept watching and learning. Jordan wore Darrel down without even having the decency to break into a sweat. Finally Darrel and his sword parted company, each landing in the mud well away from the other.

Balthan could take some satisfaction: it had taken longer, but Jordan had made Darrel look and feel just as foolish. It was a feeble satisfaction, though, tempered as it was by the recognition that he, himself, could not have stood against Darrel.

Sixteen

ΥΥΥΥΥ

Jordan's muscles were coiled before he awoke.

There was someone else in the room. The room itself was unfamiliar. His ears told him that the softly humming stranger was a man pouring water some six or seven feet away. Slitting his eyes, Jordan confirmed each suspicion. Cautiously, feigning sleep, he hooked a leg over the side of the bed, then he sprang across the room.

The stranger yelped; his hands shot up. Jordan caught a pitcher just before it smashed against the floor. He missed the glass; it shattered. Belatedly, with water dripping from his face and hands, Jordan recognized the Rosignel architecture, the hearty breakfast on the sideboard, and Ventar, the man who'd been standing guard when he and Darrel arrived.

Ventar dropped to his knees, heedless of the glass shards. "My lord, I did not realize you were awake."

"I wasn't," Jordan admitted. He examined the empty pitcher before handing it over. He'd snatched it out of the air—clean and simple. His eyes and his body were back in thoughtless harmony. "I feel good." His slightly embarrassed grin strengthened into a smile. "By the Eight, the

Three, and the One-All-Around, Ventar, I feel like myself again.''

"I'm glad, my lord.'' The burly, plain-faced guard did not rise. "When you did not stir for so long, we began to worry.''

Jordan raked his hair. He rubbed his chin; the stubble was almost thick enough to be called a beard. Perhaps he'd look in a mirror before he shaved it off, although it still felt sparse and uneven. A nerve twinged when he touched the ridge below his right eye. He remembered Balthan saying he'd broken a bone there. He remembered Dench and Ivo beating him.

Everything came back to Jordan, as it might to any man who'd slept uncommonly long. He remembered sitting in the Rosignel kitchen. There was a platter of eggs and sausage in front of him; he said he was too tired to eat. He remembered looking up at Balthan—he must have fainted by then. Balthan was looking grim.

Jordan turned on Ventar. "Did that trickster lay magic on me?''

Ventar understood. "No, my lord. The young mage said you were bone-tired and we should let you sleep until you woke naturally. He came up once—to work on your face—but we watched him the whole time.''

"But no other time?''

"No, my lord.''

"How long have I been sleeping?''

"This is the third morning, my lord.''

Jordan stared out the window that faced east, away from Hawksnest villa. Three days—he'd hoped to have found the gypsies and Lord Shamino in three days. He couldn't begrudge the rest, not when he felt so much better for it. The beatings, his battle against the magic-induced blindness, the emergence of his berserkerang inheritance, each was sufficient cause for exhaustion. He found it harder to believe that Balthan hadn't meddled.

"You're sure there was no extra magic?"

Ventar raised himself to one knee. "Our Lady of Rosignel would not permit it, my lord. She was not easily persuaded to allow the healing. Magic has no place in a virtuous home."

Another of his great-grandmother's infamous quirks. The Lady of Rosignel—everyone called her that, including Lord Ironhawk—lived by her own rules and in her own world. The folks who chose to dwell at Rosignel rather than Hawksnest indulged, if they did not actually share, their Lady's delusions. Looking at Ventar Jordan could not tell if he was an indulger, or a sharer.

Jordan's sewer-stained shirt had been washed and patched. He pulled it over his head and looked for his buskins. "Three days . . ." he muttered. Anxiety gained the upper hand in his thoughts: anything could have happened in three days. He remembered Lord Ironhawk's favorite complaint about his grandmother-by-marriage: the Lady of Rosignel doesn't notice anything until everyone else has forgotten it.

His buskins had been scraped clean; they had new waxed-leather thongs.

"Who knows what the Lady would make of Lohgrin—"

Jordan unhooked his sword belt from the bedpost. It, like his buskins, had been cleaned and mended. The brass wires binding the scabbard had been washed in acid; they shone like gold. Every nailhead glinted in the light. Hugh had outdone himself.

Motion near the door caught Jordan's attention. As he looked up, a voice inside his head reminded him that Hugh wasn't here; Ventar was. The stocky man blocked the doorway.

"Our Lady was not fooled. She saw his shadow before she saw him and bid us hang herbs in all the windows. A noose of her own hair hangs from the gate to snare him or his kith should they come to Rosignel. Our Lady sees things differently, but she sees them true all the same. The Inquisitor has turned against Virtue. Evil attaches to him."

Sighing heavily, Jordan sat down on the bed. He studied the nailhead pattern. Seanna's wagon could have stopped at Rosignel before Hawksnest. He couldn't remember why they hadn't. So much could have been changed, possibly avoided entirely—"If only she and Balthan had spoken to each other."

His own voice startled him. He became aware of Ventar staring at him.

"Nothing goes according to plan, my armiger always says that."

"I admire Hugh, my lord. What will you do now, my lord?"

Jordan asked his memory about Ventar whose services he seemed to have acquired. The past yielded one image: a cottage boy in his best clothes waiting at the arena one summer morning. He asked to join the estate guard. Lord Ironhawk said he was more valuable as a swineherd. Jordan recalled that he'd been about Darrel's age at the time. He'd made a fool of himself asking his father how a swineherd could possibly be more valuable than a guard. Lord Ironhawk knocked him ass-over-elbows into the mud. His question had made a different impression on Ventar, though: the man was in awe of him.

"Is there something you want? May I serve you, my lord?"

Flustered, Jordan hustled to the sideboard where he ripped apart a loaf of bread. Although he'd always been called "my lord," it was a courtesy title only. Everyone knew that the true lord of Hawksnest was Erwald Ironhawk. Everyone except Ventar who lived, after all, at Rosignel.

"Tell me what my lord father's been doing while I slept—if you know." There was a bitterness to his voice that the bread could not hide.

"My lord, he and Lady Barbara have been in seclusion.

You and your brother are dead. The Inquisitor says he saw you run between the stones, into the moon gate. He says it turned bloodred and consumed you for your treachery against family, Britannia, and Virtue itself.''

Jordan forgot the bread. "That's a terrible lie, Ventar! No one would believe that."

"It is a lie, my lord, but there is nothing else to believe. No trace of you was found in Trinsic. Empty coffins stand beneath Ironhawk's great dome; graves have been dug to receive them. You're dead, my lord. Hawksnest is in deep mourning, my lord. Ironhawk has lost both his sons. He's made Althea his heir. The Inquisitor's word cannot be refuted without compromising Rosignel."

Jordan thought of his mother. There was no way he could spare her the needless grief. While they were believed dead, he and Darrel could look for help without watching their backs. At this moment in time, an honest message from her living sons would serve no purpose. Jordan's anguish was genuine and he could not get his mother's tear-stained face out of his thoughts until another thought erupted and covered everything else.

"Althea," he whispered. "He's made Althea the heir, and he's going to marry Althea!" Jordan seized Ventar's shoulders. "Did that bastard look anywhere for us? Did he actually *try* to find us?"

Ventar tried to free himself. "No, my lord . . . But you were on the moon-gate hill all night. Your brother—'' It was clear from his expression that Darrel told everyone about the gazer and that Ventar was unnerved. "The Inquisitor *did* see you there. And you meant him to believe you'd used the gate—''

Jordan shoved the other man aside. He aimed a fist at the wall, thought better of it, and pounded his palm instead. "We did *exactly* what he wanted. We couldn't have given him more of what he wanted if we'd tried!"

"My lord?"

"Lohgrin doesn't care about my brother or me. He doesn't really care about Balthan Wanderson. He cares about Hawksnest. He wants Hawksnest for his own, and we've given it to him on a pretty velvet pillow. Marry Althea. Wait a decent interval—a day or two—and slip poison into the lord and lady's wine . . ." Jordan released Ventar. He clapped his hands together. "Just like that: Hawksnest belongs to him. He owes nothing, not even to the regent!"

"Yes, my lord." Ventar kept a good arm's length between himself and Jordan. "Just like that."

"Two coffins under the dome, you say? He can't get married while they're there. He'll give my absent corpse full honor—just in case there's ever a challenge. Let's see—" Jordan ran through the funeral ceremonies in his mind. "Tomorrow, Ventar—he could bury us anytime after sunrise tomorrow and marry Althea anytime after sunset."

"Yes, my lord—" Ventar eased out of the room. His lord, after all, was known to go berserk.

"There's precious little time. Where are my brother and Balthan? They're around someplace, aren't they—?"

Ventar nodded. "I saw them on my way up here, my lord. I'm certain they were headed to the yard where the mage feinted with his shadow before you came."

Jordan was already seething with plans. He'd accorded Ventar's answer no more attention than a hive gave to any one bee. Still, he hadn't liked what he heard. He asked a second time and listened more closely as Ventar clarified his answer:

"They've gone behind the stable so the sound of steel wouldn't disturb your sleep." The former swineherd mimed a man thrusting with a sword.

"They wouldn't." All other thoughts drained out of Jordan's mind. "They're not *that* foolish."

But he was already past Ventar and charging down the stairs. He stopped short in the tiny courtyard. Rosignel was a maze. Whatever plan the villa had it had been lost as each succeeding generation imposed its needs and whims. Jordan was about to return to his upstairs window when he heard the unmistakable clash of steel. With the sound as a touchstone, he made his way to the back wall.

They were doing exactly what Ventar promised, and they were more foolish than he'd believed possible. Granted the Rosignel armory was not well stocked, but a moth-eaten jerkin would have been more protection than nothing—which was all Balthan and Darrel wore above the waist. Darrel had shed his sandals as well.

It was just possible that Balthan had honestly forgotten how dangerous an arena could be. He'd never paid any attention to the swordmasters and lately he'd been surrounded by scholars and magicians. There was no excuse for Darrel. The youth was the better swordsman, but he was far from a swordmaster. Jordan hesitated before wading between the foolish fighters. Unless his timing was perfect, he could cause murder, not prevent it. He drew his own sword quietly, and waited where they were not likely to see him.

He didn't expect to wait long. By appearances they'd been playing their dangerous game awhile and were wilting. Although neither of them declared an attack before beginning it, nor completed the disengage at its end, the weight of their swords and the extravagance of their movements were forcing them to pause between exchanges. All the same, the clean rhythm of cuts and parries blurred into random flailing. Jordan could not decipher one move from the next.

Each time steel met, Jordan expected disaster, each time it was narrowly averted by a tactic he considered inappropriate. Maybe he'd misjudged them. Maybe, but not likely—

Darrel's sword slammed into Balthan's. Jordan saw that the mage had learned how to hold his weapon. Nicks and burrs bound the steel blades momentarily together. Jordan would have pulled out of the attack. There was no way to anticipate the movement of the steel when it unlocked. He'd rather avoid a surprise than take advantage of one; not so Darrel and Balthan. They grunted and heaved until Balthan's relic blade broke from the strain. Darrel lacked the strength, or presence of mind, to alter the downward arc of his sword.

"Guard up!"

Jordan didn't hear his own shout. He committed himself to crossing the yard before Darrel's sword sliced across Balthan's unprotected throat. Jordan knew Balthan's broken sword was a serviceable weapon. It was shorter and unbalanced, but quite capable of parrying any attack or thrusting through unarmored flesh. Jordan also knew that Balthan would equate broken with useless and lower his arm.

The warning penetrated Balthan's thoughts. He traced the sound to its source and lost a moment to astonishment. Then he glanced up and lost another precious moment to terror.

Jordan was halfway across the yard. There wouldn't be time to beat Darrel's sword with his own, so he threw it aside and launched himself like a javelin at his brother's chest.

Impact knocked the wind from both of them. They sprawled on the ground a body's length from Darrel's last footprints. Darrel held on to his sword. The first thing Jordan observed as he propped himself up on his elbows was the runnel of blood in the groove.

"Damn—"

Jordan got to his knees, wrested the weapon out of Darrel's hand, and sent it skidding toward the wall. The youth's eyes were open. He was fully conscious, although not in command of his arms, legs, or lungs. He cringed when Jordan looked at him.

"Damn you—" He clutched his side where he must have taken Darrel's knee in the ribs. It hurt, but not enough to worry about. "—To Hythloth."

The youth started to blubber. Jordan pushed to his feet

and turned away. He expected to see a corpse, or a gaping chest wound, so the sight of Balthan curled up tight and moaning was, despite the blood, a relief.

"Easy now—" Jordan pressed his fingers against the magician's neck. With his other hand he rolled Balthan onto his back and looked for the wound. It was a deep gash from wrist to elbow along the outside of his forearm. Balthan's pulse was racing shallow; his skin was clammy, and as Jordan watched, his eyes rolled into his skull.

"None of that!"

Wrestling Balthan as if he were a scarecrow, Jordan got the magician sitting, then shoved his head forward between his knees. Blood pumped along the gash and gave no sign of stopping. Jordan looked for something to stanch it and spotted Balthan's shirt folded neatly nearby. After thumping Balthan soundly with what was meant to be reassurance, he went after the shirt and the tip of broken sword. When he returned Darrel stood over the magician, his own shirt trailing from his hand. The youth looked wobbly and green from fright. Jordan shoved him rudely aside.

"It was an accident. The sword broke."

Red fingers of the berserkerang caressed Jordan's mind. He could feel the pliable flesh of his brother's throat. Balthan's blood became Darrel's blood. It would be so easy—so *deserved*. And so very wrong. With the sleeve of Balthan's shirt draped over his thigh, Jordan made himself relax. The red retreated, but he did not risk looking at Darrel. Jordan probed Balthan's upper arm until he found the pressure point that slowed the blood, then he knotted the cloth over the broken steel and bound them together over the pressure point. Within heartbeats the flow was reduced to a trickle.

"There—the worst is over. You're going to—" He grabbed a hank of Balthan's hair and brought his face into the light. He almost didn't recognize the slack-jawed features. Balthan was always so cocky and intense. Jordan had

never seen him scared witless before. ''—Live. Believe it.''
He let go and turned his attention toward Darrel.

"It was an accident," the youth insisted, retreating as he
spoke. He saw the way Jordan was looking at his throat.
Closing the collar placket with both hands, he made a dash
for the gate.

Jordan caught him on the second stride, lifted him off his
feet, and pinned him against the nearest wall.

"I'll be damned if it was an *accident*!" Jordan's voice
was harsh, demonic. "I call it murder!"

Tears streamed down Darrel's face. He thought he was
going to die; he hoped he was going to die. Death couldn't
possibly be worse than the way Jordan looked at him. He
lost count of the number of times he said he was sorry, that
he'd never do it again.

"I was only trying to *help*," he wailed. "Like a swordmaster—Like you."

For one indrawn breath, the berserkerang held Jordan in
its claws. His heart pounded and he could not breathe. Then
he exhaled, and once again the red receded. He let Darrel
go; his hand was shaking.

"I'm not a swordmaster, Darrel."

"But you're good. You're the best."

Jordan shook his head. "I'm no swordmaster; I still want
to win. Swordmastery is beyond winning. Come winter,
when the dust has settled and the swordmasters are back at
Hawksnest, you can try to learn the difference if you want."

Darrel's spirit was reborn: he'd gone from abject disgrace
to a chance to learn the secrets of swordmastery, with Jordan. He wrapped himself around his brother.

"It's not about fighting, Darrel. It's about teaching and
learning and self-discipline; you might not like it."

Darrel squeezed harder—hard enough to hurt, so Jordan
used his longer arms to tickle Darrel's ribs until he shrieked.
He caught the youth's arms before he leapt away.

"Listen to me—if I *ever* catch you free-bouting without

armor, I'll break every bone in your hand and you'll never pick up a sword again. You understand?'' Darrel hung his head. ''Answer me!''

''I promise.'' He chafed the feeling back into his white-ringed arms. ''What if someone were in trouble, and there wasn't time—''

''Squirt!''

''I want to know. Stranger things have happened. Did you know we're both dead—that's pretty strange. That's why we were practicing—free-bouting. Balthan said we couldn't wait for you; we had to carry off Althea ourselves.''

''Aye,'' Jordan sobered completely. Events of the moment receded to their proper subordination. ''Tonight. The two of us, maybe more—maybe Drum, maybe Ventar.'' He retreated and looked at the sun: late morning. ''Get your sword.'' He started to retrieve his own. ''We need a diversion. Maybe Bal—''

A few stains in the dirt marked the place where Balthan collapsed. The broken sword was still there; the magician was not. Inspection revealed widely spaced stains trailing through the gate.

''Eight, Three, and One—where's he gotten to?''

''Probably his room.''

Scooping up the broken sword as they passed it, Jordan let his brother lead the way. They found Balthan wedged in a corner, apparently unconscious. There was blood smeared on his face and chest and completely covering his arm. He'd discarded the tourniquet; the wound must have reopened. Darrel back-stepped rather than cross the threshold; he collided with Jordan.

''Is he—?''

Jordan cursed and shoved the broken sword into Darrel's hand. Something black and shapeless darkened the floor near Balthan's limp, outstretched hand. Remembering how shadows figured in the magician's dreams, Jordan feared the worst. His sword was half-drawn when he realized that the "shadow" was the interior of the magician's reagent sack. He swore and slammed his sword back into the scabbard.

"Wha—?" Balthan's eyes opened partway.

"You healed it, didn't you?" There was a hint of disappointment in Jordan's voice.

"I tried." Balthan folded the "shadow"; it became a coarse cloth sack again. The movement left him panting. "It's stopped bleeding. I'll finish it . . . later."

"Don't. Leave it alone. Let it scar. It's tradition: a swordsman keeps his scars. The first one, anyway."

Balthan frowned eloquently. He understood Jordan's fascination with scars, he simply didn't share it. "I guess I'm not a swordsman, am I?"

"I wouldn't put money on you in a fair fight."

"That about covers it. I'm a magician. I should count myself lucky if I can cut my meat without slicing off my valuable parts."

Jordan extended his hand; Balthan ignored it.

"No peer's ever accused us of being *fair*."

"Cheer up. No swordsman fights fair unless he has to. You're not great, Balthan—you're not even good, but you've progressed from unbelievably awful to plain bad."

"I'm beside myself with joy." Balthan tried to stand but didn't have the strength.

Grabbing his good arm, Jordan yanked the magician to his feet. "Right now you're a better swordsman than most men of Britannia. You could take Drum, who swings everything as if it were a hammer. You could face down any drunken bravo—four or five of them, if you kept your wits—"

"But you'd kill me—"

"If I were foolish enough to draw steel against you. I'd look at that infernal sack of yours and I'd look at your sword. I'd see that you don't trip over it, so I'd have to figure you could draw it without gutting yourself. I'd have to think: a magician who wears a sword . . . What else does he know? Is it worth the risk to find out? I'd leave you alone.''

"I hate to admit this, but you're smarter than the average steel-skulled fighter. Lohgrin's churls would just run me through.''

"I'll take care of them. You're going after Lohgrin. A mage with a sword against a mage without one. I know where I'd wager, no matter what kind of magic he's got.''

They stared at each other until Balthan erupted with laughter. Weak from healing and woozy from loss of blood, he shook and listed dangerously to one side. Jordan caught him before he collapsed and propelled him toward the door.

"Food first, then plans—"

They faced Darrel who looked left out and jealous and held Balthan's blunted sword like a candle before him.

"I've got to get another sword. That one's beyond repair.''

Jordan plucked the broken blade from Darrel's hand and herded the youth ahead of them. "This is now a main gauche. I observe that you've got the instinct to defend with your off-weapon hand. I think you'll find this more durable than your arm.''

"A main gauche?'' Balthan took it into his left hand as they headed toward the kitchen behind Darrel. "Do I get another sword? Or is this it?''

Seventeen
ΥΥΥΥ

*N*othing goes according to
plan.

Or so Hugh, the armiger, said in every possible circum-
stance. It would become his epitaph someday, along with
the corollary:

*Plan for the worst; whatever happens will be an improve-
ment.*

Like so many of Hugh's homilies, they were partly true
and useful for curtailing optimism. Jordan resorted to them
constantly throughout the long afternoon, casting the pall of
probability over boundless enthusiasm.

"I don't think Althea will be with Lady Barbara putting
the last stitches in her dower linen." Jordan balanced his
stool on two legs and waited.

"It's what brides do, whether they're facing a love-mar-
riage or an arranged-marriage. It's tradition. My sister is
very traditional and strong-willed."

Jordan let the stool thump to the floor. He wagged his
finger at Balthan's nose. "Lady Barbara is burying both her
children at sunrise tomorrow; she's not going to be stitching
tonight." He added a second finger. "Althea's enthralled,
you said so yourself; she's not strong-willed." He added a

third, final finger. "Lohgrin can't be sure we're dead. He should expect something. He should have her near him."

The magician raked his damp hair with his left hand. He'd bathed and healed. He'd already eaten two roasted chickens, a loaf of buttered bread, and three portions of his favorite blue-veined goat cheese. He was waiting for a cherry pie to cool before eating it. Magicians were always hungry, never heavy.

"I'll grant the first two, not the third. He's a magician; he thinks you got sucked into the gate and never came out. Magicians," the magician confessed, "have their own prejudices."

"Ventar says there's poison in the postern gate. You saw what it did to his hand—"

Prompted by the memory, Balthan collected cheese crumbs on his fingertip and licked them off. "Corrosive acid, not poison. Might last a week, less if it rains."

"I don't care what it is, or how long it will last. It's there. Lohgrin suspects; Lohgrin expects. If he isn't expecting Darrel or me, maybe he's expecting *you*—"

Crumbs fell from Balthan's finger.

"Does this mean we're using the sewer tunnels?" Darrel asked in the silence.

Jordan considered: what could go wrong using the tunnels? "We could use them coming out, but going in—against the current—we wouldn't know where to climb out."

"We'll have Althea after." Balthan could play Hugh's game when he wanted to. "What about the forge-yard? It abuts the villa wall. Drum could pull her up on a rope."

"You never know about Drum. He sees Virtue differently."

Balthan sighed; he knew the farrier better than Jordan suspected. "He'll do it for Althea."

"Aye, he wants her, but she wants Jordie," Darrel agreed.

Jordan winced; Balthan noticed and vowed to remember.

"It's the sewers, isn't it," Darrel challenged. "Wading through garbage and turds."

"You haven't bathed since the last time—"

"Enough!" Jordan shouted. While he slept, his brother and the magician had developed a juvenile, name-calling camaraderie. "Forget the sewers. We'll work on Drum. I like the wall. There's a dead spot where the fruit trees have grown and blocked the view from the guard porch. Ironhawk's talked about cutting down the trees for two years now, but I don't—" The fruit trees as they appeared from his window flashed in Jordan's mind with a faintly green aura. Then everything became dark; panic raced down his spine. He blinked, and the Rosignel kitchen reappeared.

Balthan stared at him with professional curiosity. "See something?"

"No, nothing. I remembered that the trees haven't been cut, that's all. We'll use the wall. Let me think about it from there." He got up from the table. His balance was off; he thought he concealed it by reaching for the bread. "I'll leave you two here—you can eat and throw things at each other."

Balthan blocked Jordan's route to the door. "You're sure you don't want to talk?" he said softly. "You saw *something*."

"It was nothing. I'm fine." He sidled through the door.

Rosignel was quiet. The day's work was finished although the day was not. Jordan shielded his eyes and judged the hour by the angle of his arm: ample time to plan an assault on Hawksnest, ample time to consider that although he'd fought through his blindness, it, like the berserkerang, remained within him. There was an unnatural hole in his mind. It sucked in images he had not consciously seen, and spat them out again in exquisite detail. The fruit trees weren't the first. He could remember Darrel's sword slicing Balthan's arm. The memory was so complete it hovered in front of him like a ghost.

Jordan hoped this wouldn't happen too often. He supposed that if he could control the ravening berserkerang, he could adjust to seeing two different things—one real, the other remembered—on top of each other. He'd learned to fight left-handed; nothing could be more unnatural than that. Hatching stratagems was not particularly natural for him either—Jordan preferred to take life as it came—but in the absence of anyone willing or able, Jordan was learning to plot as well.

He found himself in the stable muttering: "It's not fair."

The stalls were mostly empty; the few that weren't held feisty stallions or mares with sickly foals. None were ridable. Jordan gathered lengths of rope and set out for the fields.

"Only fools and kings think life's fair." Another of Hugh's proverbs.

The sky was a cloudless amber by the time Jordan returned to the kitchen. Balthan—this strange, friendly Balthan—was debating obscure points of Sosarian legend with the cook. The whole household was there, including the Lady, though she was sound asleep. No one noticed Jordan until he filled his bowl from the stewpot. Balthan stopped talking; they waited for him to speak. Jordan considered letting them wait, but they were more patient than he.

"I've got horses ready. Four. One for Althea."

The cook made a luck-sign as did several others.

Darrel fidgeted. "Mares?"

Jordan nodded; Darrel wrinkled his nose. "Men don't suffer riding mares. You're not old enough to worry, anyhow."

The youth stuck out his tongue. He didn't want to take chances.

Nonetheless, when the sun had set and the brightest stars

sparkled in the dusk, the youth mounted a chestnut mare
and rode through the gate. Naturally Jordan took the best
horse; but he had the second-best and held the reins of the
spare animal. Balthan needed both hands to control his
docile mare; the way he sat in the saddle, he'd be lucky if
he could walk when they reached Hawksnest. He fussed
with his scabbard, thumping the mare's ribs with it, until
Jordan took it away from him.

"How did you get from one place to another while you
were with Felespar?"

"Moon gates, mostly. Boats. He had a carpet—"

Jordan spurred his horse forward. He thought he'd
planned for the worst, but Balthan rode like a bucket of
water. They'd walk the horses and stay on the cartway for
the mare's sake. At this pace, they'd come up to Hawksnest
after the moons rose, when any fool could see their silhou-
ettes on the wall. On the other hand, Jordan would have
more time to refine the persuasion he meant to use on Drum.

The wind freshened. Darkness flowed down from the
north, covering the stars, one by one. The moons would not
be visible. Jordan was starting to feel encouraged when,
heels and elbows flapping, Balthan came abreast.

"I don't like that." He raised his hand, still holding the
reins.

The mares bumped together. Jordan cursed and, not quite
accidentally, kicked Balthan in the shin.

"Storm coming, I guess. It'll be slippery on the roofs,
but the tunnels would be impossible."

Balthan stared at the sky. "It makes me nervous."

"What do you want me to do?" In winter storms came
down from the north; in summer they usually came from
the south or east. The wind was wrong, too: rising steadily,
without gusts or breaks. "We've got to go on. It's tonight
or never."

"Let's make it quick." Balthan shivered though the wind
was not cold.

The sky was midnight dark when they came to the fore-gate house where Drum dwelt with his kindred. Wind whistled along the narrow street, rattling shutters, obscuring all other sounds. This was the chanciest part of Jordan's plan: if Drum did not let them in, if he sounded an alarm instead, they could forget about Althea. They'd be lucky to escape themselves—which was why Darrel and Balthan stayed mounted while he hammered on the door. The odds were against Drum answering the door; Jordan was not surprised when Ned Nearhand, Drum's uncle and the clan patriarch, appeared before him.

Jordan took a deep breath. "Good man, I come to ask for a favor—"

"Lord Hawson? Is that you? I can hardly tell for the darkness. Who's with you? Come in. Come in quickly, all of you."

Dumbfounded, Jordan led his horse into the passageway. Hugh's voice in the back of his head recited another pithy adage: If something seems too good to be true, then it is not true. The forge-yard, at the far end of the passageway, was lantern-lit and quiet; anyone could be waiting there—if anyone had known they were coming.

The others crowded behind him. Jordan shook his wind-blown hair out of his eyes and, leading his horse, kept pace with his host. "Good man, they're burying me tomorrow—how did you know to look for me tonight?"

Ned did not answer. Jordan's vague apprehension flared into panic; the red fingers of the berserkerang caressed the back of his neck. He came into the courtyard ready to fight for his life. Something came at him from the shadows. His hands were on his sword before he recognized Drum.

"I knew you couldn't be dead. It had to be a trick. His or yours. I knew you'd get here in—"

Balthan clambered out of the saddle, into the light.

"Balthan! They found you. I gave Jordan your message; did he tell you?"

The magician flexed his knees; forgotten muscles were making their presence known. He grunted in Drum's direction, then hobbled to a bench. He plumbed his sack for spider silk while Jordan persuaded Drum to help them.

"We could use extra hands on the rope at the end to bring Althea over the wall."

The big man's shoulders sagged.

"There's no risk. Almost none. Just stay hidden until we need you to pull the rope—"

"I could do more. I could come with you. I could carry her—that way you'd have both hands free for your sword, if you needed it."

This was not what Hugh meant when he said nothing went according to plan. "What do you think?" Jordan turned to Balthan. Drum and his uncle were watching him expectantly.

Balthan was no help. "It's all the same to me. You're the battle-lord."

"*I* think you should let him come." Darrel wedged in front of Jordan. "You and he can get Althea. I want to show Balthan the storeroom, especially the book and that big, hairy hand."

The wind stopped as abruptly as it had begun. The air was still and heavy, ready to give birth to a cataclysm. They looked to the magician for explanations; he squinted at the clouds.

"The cities have another name for miasma, don't they? Black fog?"

Jordan nodded.

"Well, we've got it here at Hawksnest."

"Miasma? Black fog?" the patriarch demanded. "What are these things? What new insult visits us?"

Drum described the danger: "Your head hurts bad enough to kill. Lock away the knives—" He glanced around. Knives were among the lesser dangers in the forge-yard.

"Keep everyone inside and quiet. I'm going with my friends."

"Put herbs in the windows," Jordan suggested. "It's what they've done at Rosignel." He omitted the noose made from his great-grandmother's hair. "It might help."

Balthan rummaged through his sack. At times his arm seemed to disappear into the paving stones of the courtyard, but with the fog wisping down, the lanterns were flickering and nothing looked quite right. Before Ned could demand an explanation, the magician produced a rope of braided garlic and a much-smaller pouch. He tore off a bulb before passing the rope to Drum's uncle. "Put those *everywhere*."

The patriarch held the rope at arm's length. "They're contaminated by magic."

"*Use them!*"

Raising his head like a check-reined horse, Ned looked for the source of the command still echoing between his ears. Then the part of him that would always be childlike and subject to maternal authority took him out of the forge-yard. Drum's mouth hung open; Jordan looked away and covered his face; Darrel chortled openly. Balthan went on with his craftwork, drawing gem-colored threads out of the pouch, weaving them into a supple hollow cord into which he stuffed cloves of garlic and tiny black seeds. He broke the cord and offered a length to each of them.

"Shouldn't you say something?" Darrel asked as he knotted it around his neck.

Balthan obliged: "In Vas Sanct."

Nothing happened. Magic, Balthan explained with evident irritation, was more than mixing reagents, reciting runes, or even innate talent—or else he'd be able to cast any spell. Real magic was passed from one adept to another in circumscribed rituals. Because Balthan had an excess of innate talent, his superiors spent more time thwarting his curiosity than teaching him. Life at the Lyceum had been no different than life at Hawksnest, until Felespar took pity on him and made Balthan his amanuensis, although Balthan did not mention this last to the others in the forge-yard.

"If there's no magic, what good will this do?" Drum countered.

"It is the form and substance of great protection. *Believe*, and you'll be protected."

Balthan felt Drum's and Darrel's belief. He couldn't give them the protection Felespar could have given them, but they were no longer naked. A magician couldn't lie to himself, although he donned a fragrant necklace to strengthen their belief. Jordan hadn't been caught either; he smiled wanly as he slipped the cord inside his shirt.

They scaled the wall at the back of the forge, crawled to the blind spot, and dropped their rope over the inside edge. The fog had grown thicker. The guards could not have seen the ground, much less the rope dangling on the wall. Jordan realized that his head wasn't pounding as it had in Britain City, although the miasma was denser, and getting worse the closer they got to the Inquisitor's rooms. He kept his realization to himself. They linked hands at the bottom of the stairs and climbed together.

"Here's the storeroom door." Darrel's voice was muffled. He might have been thirty feet away rather than at the end of Balthan's arm.

They separated. Jordan put one hand on Drum and the other on the wall. The air was odorless, tasteless, and utterly dark; it resisted them as they walked forward. The latch string was inside the door, but the latch hadn't been set. The door swung open to Jordan's touch, and although it seemed impossible, the darkness was more profound inside the room. Again Jordan laid his hand on the wall and led the way. He hoped Althea was asleep. He'd have to clamp his hand over her mouth to awaken her. Maybe he should let Drum do it instead—

Jordan's knee struck the bed; he knew immediately that it was empty. "She's not here," he whispered. He ran his hands over the linen and found it undisturbed. "She hasn't been here."

Drum jostled the bed, confirming Jordan's assertions for himself. "Just as well, I don't like to think of her breathing this—What now?"

"Look around, see what you can find. I'll get Balthan and my brother."

"How?"

"Use your head, Drum."

Not caring whether the farrier took him literally, Jordan found his way to the storeroom where Darrel and the magician were groping unproductively through the black air. Neither the spellbook nor the hand 'o'glory came easily to hand. Balthan wouldn't open the chests or baskets.

"Forget about it," Jordan advised. "Thea's not next door. We've got to split up and look for her."

"Lady Barbara's sewing room?" Balthan returned to his earliest suggestion.

Jordan's grimace went unappreciated. "Why not? Darrel, go with him. Drum and I will go to her room, maybe she's there. We'll meet at the forge." He felt them file past him into the corridor, heard their footsteps on the stairs, then nothing: no sound at all from anywhere, no light or odor, nothing but the pressure of his feet on the floor to say that he was where he believed himself to be. Terror seized Jordan's spirit. The need to curl into a tiny, cowering ball was overwhelming—until it encountered the simmering ber-serkerang. The compulsions were well matched; Jordan balanced between them. He chose to stand erect, to walk away, to leave both behind—if Destiny willed. The doorway was where he expected to find it.

"Drum—come on, we'll check her old room."

"I've found something. Come. Listen."

Jordan entered the room. The farrier was crouched in a corner. He had Jordan press his ear against the wall. Muffled voices could be heard.

"I can't find a door. Where does it come from?"

There wasn't time for Jordan to explain that a villa, where unrelated folks of unequal status lived cheek-by-jowl, was much more complicated than the forge-yard. He wouldn't have known the right words, anyway. In silence he felt along the wall until he found a hollow panel. The panel slid to one side and the muffled voices were louder, though still indistinct.

"Does that sound like Althea to you?" Jordan asked, but as usual, Drum had no opinion.

Jordan went through the low, narrow opening first. A ripe draft rose from a lower chamber. It kept the black air at their backs, but otherwise, it was hardly an improvement. Sallow light glimmered at the bottom of a short stairway. The voice was clear, now. Not Althea, but Lohgrin himself. Drum was ready to leave as soon as he recognized it, but Jordan restrained him.

"I'm going down for a look," he said in his softest voice.

"Not me," Drum averred, somewhat more loudly.

"Stay quiet, then."

Jordan hadn't known that these rooms were connected to the tunnels, which surprised him somewhat—he and Balthan had been very thorough the summer they spent exploring them—then he noticed the fresh pile of dirt near the foot of the stairs. He realized that Lohgrin—or more likely Ivo and Dench—had excavated their own passage. Retrospective fear made him shiver: he and Darrel had been luckier than they imagined when they escaped to Rosignel.

If Jordan could trust his ears, the Inquisitor was not near the bottom of the stairway. There was no way to guess where the churls were, which way Lohgrin faced, or to whom he was speaking. Jordan descended carefully, his hands on the hilt of his sword.

"Your will, my lord. As always and ever, your will alone."

Lohgrin couldn't mean Lord Ironhawk; Jordan begged Destiny that the Inquisitor didn't mean Lord Ironhawk. He eased down the last step and shot a quick, intense glance into the chamber before withdrawing. He closed his eyes, listened to the Inquisitor prostrate himself, and waited.

"As you, my lord, wait in the trackless depths of infinity, I wait here for you. Take these bodies to sustain you, my lord Nosfentor, so I may hear your voice with my mortal ears and, thus hearing, be commanded."

Jordan's knees buckled, bile scorched the back of his throat, an image exploded out of memory: Ivo and Dench suspended above a seething pit. The Inquisitor wearing the hand 'o'glory, the palm of which emitted a tendril of black, miasmic fog. There was a rumble of distant thunder. It pushed the image from Jordan's mind. A heavy hand landed on the back of his neck, but it was only Drum.

"Lohgrin. Lohgrin, my servant . . ."

The voice, Nosfentor's voice, was faint and distant. It was also powerful and unspeakably evil.

"A mistake was made and you must correct it. There were two witnesses when we took Lord British: a scribe and a female knight. We found and consumed the scribe. The female was not with him. We assumed she was dead, like the others, until a hermit brought her to the Britain City, by chance, on a day when we were there."

"An interrogation?" Lohgrin's voice was eager and obscene.

"Blackthorn unraveled her mind for our inspection. There is nothing left. You may see for yourself after you have retrieved the box."

Jordan's mouth hung open. Every suspicious thread knotted together: from Balthan's nightmares last year, through Lord British's disappearance, to Blackthorn's regency and the miasma. The enormity left him stunned as Nosfentor

explained that the scribe had made a record of the ill-fated
expedition and, sensing his own doom after Lord British
disappeared, enclosed the parchment in a sandalwood box.
How a scribe came to possess a sandalwood box was a moot
question, what mattered was that it was gone when the
wraiths found him.

*"We have chosen you as our tool. Commit this to your
memory—there are many entrances to the Maelstrom caverns. This is the path the female knight took, which you will
take—"*

Deep-pitched vibrations shook the villa foundations.
Mortar rained down from the ceiling. Jordan roused from
his stupor as lightning flashed inside the chamber. If there'd
been time he might have hatched a better stratagem—or he
might have decided to escape with what he already knew.
But there was no time. Jordan knew that if he tried, he
could remember whatever Nosfentor revealed better than the
Inquisitor himself. He peeked into the chamber.

Jordan did not want to see the wraith, but the genius of
his memory was also its weakness: it absorbed everything,
or nothing. He saw Nosfentor—a shadow swirling around
the churls, whose limp bodies could be glimpsed between
its coils. Its eyes blazed like miniature red stars in an endless
night. The blackness streaming from Lohgrin's hand
'o'glory shaped itself into forests and craggy hilltops.

An iridescent serpent emerged from Nosfentor. It slith-
ered through the forests, around the hills until its diamond-
shaped head rested between Lohgrin's feet. Light rippled
along its back; a pinprick in the forest blinked a counter-
point.

"I see the path, my lord. I will remember."

Jordan didn't know why those hellish eyes failed to notice
him, but they didn't.

"Within the cavern, these are the places we know—"

The hills hollowed, the forests became the crystal interior.
The snake became a swarm of luminous insects.

"Here is where we consumed the scribe." An insect light settled on the crystal. *"Here is where the female's memory ends. She does not remember him concealing the box. It must lie between these two points. You will find it and destroy it."*

The cave began to dissolve like wax in a flame. Jordan saw a man-made cairn by a river; he would remember it.

"I will, my lord. Absolutely. Immediately."

"Now! You rotting offal—I know your thoughts, your lusts. Your bride can wait! You will leave NOW!"

The twin suns merged. A ray of crimson light fell on Lohgrin's face.

"Jordan—" the farrier whispered from the safety of the stairwell.

Jordan hesitated. The crimson ray became orange, then yellow.

"Jordan—now would be a good time for us to leave, too."

A flash, a scream, the smell of singed hair and fouled clothing. The Inquisitor raised his hands beseechingly. "Sundown, my lord. Sundown tomorrow. She'll be mine—"

The crimson light pulsed again, faster and stronger. Jordan pushed Drum up the stairs. They took the last three in one bound, squeezing through the open panel as white-hot light seared the air behind them.

Eighteen
ᵞᵞᵞᵞᵞ

T he miasma emanating from Nosfentor absorbed its anger. The roar of the wraith's voice was reduced to menacing susurrus. Thick, black air was, however, no protection from the tremblors shaking the entire villa. The first jolt threw Drum against the corridor; Jordan collided with the open railing as the floor planks rippled like waves on a lake.

Cowardice, the specific infection of Nosfentor's miasma, had imprisoned the Hawksnest residents in their unnaturally dark quarters. But when the ground began to move, cowardice yielded to panic. The screams, like Nosfentor's roar, were absorbed by the fog. That they were heard at all was testament to their desperation.

After the ground betrayed them, it could not be trusted. Jordan clung to the railing and scuffed the planks like a skater, not daring to lift his feet as he walked. The farrier crawled. When a second tremblor turned the corridor to quivering jelly, he lay flat and would not move until Jordan pulled his earlobe rudely toward the stairs.

"We've got to get away before the roof falls on us."

Drum feared the ground more than the roof—until a third tremblor, more powerful than the other two, showered them with debris. He and Jordan supported each other until, by a miracle, they were at the bottom of the stairs. The smash of masonry striking the pavement blended with the screams, the low pitch of the wraith's voice, and the otherworldly keening of the trembling ground. Drum and Jordan pressed together like frightened children. Each felt the other's pounding heart.

When the ground was quiet, they shoved apart. Neither admitted fear nor thanks.

The screams were getting louder and clearer. Jordan recognized some of the voices. Then someone cried: *"Fire!"*

The tocsin's clang was dull, as if it and the mallet were wrapped in fleece. But it was struck repeatedly. Jordan turned toward the sound. He couldn't see the tower, but he could see Drum's silhouette: charcoal in black. The fog was lifting.

Alarms, warnings, and gut-wrenching cries came from every quarter. The air remained too thick to smell the fire or locate the injured. Jordan hopped from one foot to the other. Should he go to the forge-yard? Should he stay in the villa? Then he heard one absolutely identifiable voice:

"Injured and children: to the courtyards! Men and women: form bucket lines at the wellheads! Avatar come help us! Does my dome still sit above the hall? Somebody tell me—does it still sit intact?"

No coward malignance from beyond the stars was stronger than the possessive love Erwald Ironhawk had for Hawksnest. His voice was everywhere, though that, perhaps, was a trick of the fog. The panic faded; that was no trick, that was Ironhawk restoring order with brute force.

Jordan stumbled. He drew a deep breath, filling his lungs with air that was itself filled with Nosfentor's miasma. Jordan had no way of knowing the nature of Nosfentor's malignity—only that he was hollow inside and that the image of Lord Ironhawk hovering before him filled that emptiness with terror.

"Fire! Fire in the foregate!"

The unnatural black of the miasma became the greys, purples, and blues of midnight—except where it revealed the blood-rust colors of firelight. Drum took the lead and Jordan followed. They raced to the wall where, after a frantic search, they found the rope.

Later, in the morning and the years to come, Hawksnest would reflect and be grateful that misfortune struck at the height of summer when hearths were cold and no one kept a brazier by their bed for warmth. Widespread fires would have overwhelmed them, transforming misfortune into catastrophe. As it was, there was a fire in the villa kitchen and another at the foregate baker's. The forge-yard, toward which Drum ran recklessly, suffered shattered nerves and a few broken roof tiles.

Two fires were, however, more than enough to keep every hand busy passing buckets.

Jordan made his way to the stream where the foregate folk mobbed together. Many people were shouting orders, no one was obeying them. The result was chaos. Jordan was thinking about his father and waiting for his heart to thaw when he waded into the stream.

"I'll fill the buckets!" he bellowed. "The rest of you form two lines, back-to-back. Right side: pass the filled buckets to the fire. Left side: pass the empties back. *My* right side!" He paused to fill the first bucket and shove it at the nearest hand. "*My* count: One! Two!—"

He was their landlord's son; he had no right to interfere with the foregate. He was, or had recently been, dead as well. With miasma cowardice stagnant in their lungs, the foregate folk shrank away from him. The baker's house burned until Drum strode forward with his kin to take the sloshing bucket. The farrier passed the bucket to a cousin, who passed it to another cousin, who passed it to Ned Nearhand. If the patriarch of the forge-yard could stand in line taking a Hawson's orders, then anyone could.

Jordan sent another bucket up the line. A bucket brigade could eventually extinguish a fire, but the blaze was bound to get worse before it got better. Jordan called cadence until he was hoarse; by then the rhythm was well enough established that they didn't need him. Children too small to stand in the line scrounged for anything with a handle that could hold water.

An hour passed, and another. Jordan's feet were as cold and numb as his heart. He stopped thinking about his father or about what he'd seen and learned in the chamber below Lohgrin's room. Somewhere in the long hours between midnight and dawn he heard another alarm sound from the villa tocsin, but it did not effect the stream where he waged his personal fight against disaster, and so he ignored it.

Drum and his kin left the line. The kindred returned, Drum did not. Jordan saw neither the departure nor the return. He never looked up to see the stars emerge from the clouds and the smoke. He forgot the fire itself and did not hear the cheer when word came down the line that it was doused.

"No more."

No one took the brimming bucket. No one held out an empty container for him to fill. Jordan blinked stupidly and tried to stand up straight. His bones groaned. He accepted a woman's hand and clambered to the bank. He lay on his back, staring at the amber dawnlight. Hard labor was cathartic. He could think about what had happened without reliving it. He could rehearse what he'd say to his father, Lord Ironhawk.

"Jor-*die*!"

Darrel's voice spiraled through Jordan's ears to his turgid mind. His brother was running toward him; he had survived. Jordan propped himself up in time to see Drum catch Darrel and fling him to the ground. Jordan leapt to his feet and assumed a brawler's stance. The farrier came to a wary halt beyond arm's reach. Darrel got slowly to his feet, favoring his right leg. It did not matter that Jordan regularly inflicted greater pain and indignity: he was the elder brother; he could treat the younger however he wished. No farrier had such rights.

"Try that with *me*," Jordan invited, showing his teeth as he grinned.

Drum declined, but did not retreat. "I had to stop him. He's possessed. The Inquisitor possesses both of them—"

"It's not true!" Darrel protested from a safe distance. "You won't listen to us. Balthan didn't do anything he didn't have to do."

As his indignation faded, Jordan felt weariness return to his legs. His thoughts moved like syrup catching a word here and there as Darrel and Drum traded accusations: Althea was alive and with her brother. The Inquisitor was also alive. He and his churls had stolen five horses and ridden north at first light. Jordan recalled the second alarm.

"The churls survived?" Jordan could scarcely believe that Lohgrin escaped the quaking chamber behind them, but the last he'd seen of Ivo and Dench they were hanging inside the wraith. "They went north. North to Spirit—"

"Don't say it!" Drum grabbed Jordan and shook him. "Hammers and bells! It's the only thing they don't know—the only thing that's keeping Althea safe!"

Jordan extracted himself. The bearded man talked nonsense, and yet his passion and belief were undeniable. Jordan glanced at Darrel and the knot of onlookers they'd begun to attract.

"You'll have to tell me the whole tale—" Jordan began and got no further as Darrel and Drum instantly complied. He extended a hand toward each of them. "By the Eight, the Three, and the One-All-Around—not both at once and not *here*!" Habit suggested retreat into the villa, but there were guards in the tower and the sixth sense at the base of Jordan's neck was warning him away. "Rosignel." He strode away from the stream.

"Be damned first," Drum blocked Jordan's path.

Darrel had a rock in his fist. He was taking aim at the farrier's skull and although Jordan was inclined to trust his brother over Drum at that moment, he wanted to hear the farrier out before anyone brained him.

"The forge-yard—is that a place where you'll tell your side?"

Drum breathed heavily through his mouth. The veins at his temples throbbed visibly.

"Where, Drum? You tell me where."

The forge-yard was acceptable so long as Darrel stood apart—in sight but out of earshot. "They're in league with each other," the farrier insisted.

Jordan shrugged. The movement brought Balthan's silk cord into sight. Drum tore it off Jordan's neck and ground it into the mud and gravel on the bank. He started for the forge-yard, nailing Darrel as he passed. Jordan scooped an arm around the youth and dragged him along.

Darrel hung close to Jordan's waist. "What happened to you and him?" he whispered urgently. "He's gone mad. And you wouldn't come out of the stream when I called." He wiped his face on Jordan's damp shirt. "I thought he and Balthan were going to kill each other. I couldn't make them stop. I didn't know what to do—"

Jordan ruffled the youth's hair before shoving him away. "Don't worry about it. I'm all right." Darrel looked skeptical until Jordan cuffed him behind the ear. "I'll listen to what he has to say, then you and I—we'll do whatever has to be done."

"We've got to get to Rosignel and help Balthan with Thea—that's what we—"

Jordan hushed him again and pushed him through the gate first.

The smiths had unbanked their forge fires before the wild fires were contained. There were red-hot lumps of bloom-iron being worked on each of the anvils. Ned drew molten wires from the furnace; the 'prentices clustered around him, cutting nails with sharp chisels and quenching them in a barrel of brine. Drum pointed to the well where he wanted Darrel to stay while he talked to Jordan; he had to point, there was no way the youth could have heard him above the din of iron.

Jordan allowed himself to be led to the stream at the back wall where they'd begun their assault not twelve hours earlier; the ropes were still dangling.

"All right, Drum. Tell me what happened to get you unstrung."

The farrier's distress, suspicion, and conviction surrounded Althea whom Balthan and Darrel had manhandled out of the villa through the smoke and the unspeakable black air. She was unconscious when Drum first saw her with a dark bruise on one side of her face and her wrists bound at the small of her back.

"They"—Drum meant Balthan and Darrel—"were bent over and coughing up soot. I thought I'd help them—set her free, but they were the ones who'd battered and bound her. They came for me like dungeon demons—red-eyed and roaring—but they were no match. I struck them down and set her free." He broke off to glower at the back of Darrel's head.

By then Jordan had a fair sense of where the story would end—he'd never forget the sight and sound of Althea screaming at him—but he let Drum get there at his own pace.

"She tore at me with tooth and nail, shrieking the whole time. I couldn't make myself known to her; she thought I was one of them; they'd terrified her so."

"Did she go after Balthan and my brother with the same fury?"

"Oh—aye, when she saw them trying to stand."

"And did she ever raise her hands to her throat where she wore a great black pearl?"

Drum tensed. He retreated a half step, regarding Jordan out of the corner of his eye. "How do you know?" He raised his fists.

Jordan flashed his most innocent smile, while deciding which of Drum's legs would be easiest to break if he had to fight. "Lohgrin gave her the necklace." He shifted his balance to the balls of his feet. "While she wears it, she does the Inquisitor's bidding."

The farrier's lips quivered; his fists did not. "She knew her brother. She knew him by his own name and by the name of that wraith we saw. Nos-fen-tor, she called it, just like that. I know what I saw. I know what I heard. In that chamber and right here in the forge-yard. Balthan belongs to that wraith, just as the Inquisitor does, and—may I drink molten slag all eternity if I lie—as your brother does since you left them together. You and I are the only ones whose minds are uncorrupted."

Jordan silently agreed that he, himself, remained sane; he reserved judgment about Drum. As for the others—"Drum, Balthan's no Avatar, and neither's my brother, but they don't *belong* to anyone or anything that would abduct Lord British."

"Balthan admitted it, Jordan. He swore by Nosfentor's power that he'd poison our well and our food if we didn't let him have his sister. He cursed me and all my kin in that wraith's name until we relented—"

A pit opened inside Jordan. He imagined the forge-yard: Althea raving, Drum standing between her and Balthan, everyone else crowding close, choosing sides. When his back was pressed against a wall, Balthan used threats, not persuasion, to clear a path to the door. Jordan's heart tumbled into the pit. "He kept swearing and cursing, worse all the time, until you relented?"

Drum sensed that Jordan was leading somewhere; it made him defensive. "He swore Nosfentor would take the temper from our steel and make our iron brittle. He said he'd put a

pox on us that would turn our skin blue and make our hair
fall off—''

"You relented—you surrendered Althea—because of
Wanderson's infamous, imaginary, turn-you-blue pox?"
Jordan lost his composure and began to laugh.

"It wasn't the pox. It was the iron. He said the wraith
would make our iron brittle. I believed—because of what I
saw in that chamber."

Jordan pinched his cheeks to stop laughing; when he felt
grim again he faced the farrier. "I know Balthan, Drum. I
know what's important to him. He'll say *anything* to get
what he wants when he wants it. You're the one I don't
understand. You're ready to believe the absolute worst about
him, then you surrender the woman you love to him because
of *iron.*"

He stalked away, signaling Darrel as he approached and
cocking his head toward a small paddock where two mares
waited, still under saddle. The youth met him there and they
checked the girths and bridles without speaking to each
other, or acknowledging Drum who hovered nearby. They
were mounted when the farrier seized the reins from Jordan's hands.

"Balthan lied to me," he insisted, as if that balanced all
the accounts. "If he'd been honest; if he'd tried to tell me
the truth—"

"Balthan tells people what they want to hear. He's a
magician. He's got a knack for it."

"Althea. She was bound and bruised. The way she
screamed at him. The way she used Nosfentor's name. It
was an honest mistake . . ."

Jordan pressed his heels between the mare's ribs, making
her sidle and toss her head until Drum got out of the way.
"Your mistakes are all Virtuous, Drum." He stroked the
mare's neck. When he looked up, Drum was staring at him.
The farrier's expression was an unhealthy mixture of shame
and rage. "We all love Althea." Drum flinched and re-

treated; Jordan's voice was as hard as the finest steel in the forge-yard. "We do and say things we regret." His voice was milder.

"You'll be at Rosignel?"

Jordan nodded. "I'll send word if anything changes."

The mare wanted out, she wanted home. Jordan let her run once they were out of the foregate, but she was almost as tired as he was and slowed to a drowsy walk after about a furlong. She stopped completely a bit after that. Darrel came alongside and took the reins from his brother's limp hands without waking him. They were spotted long before they reached the gate. Ventar was waiting for the mares; Balthan was waiting for them. Jordan paused by the well to pour a bucket of water over his head.

"I can't unclasp it; I don't dare cut it," Balthan said of the chain around Althea's neck. He'd already admitted drugging the water to keep her asleep.

Jordan knelt by her cot. He stroked her hair, tucking locks of it behind her ear. Her skin was cool; the bruise was gone. If they'd been alone, he might have kissed her, but with her brother and his brother crowding the room, that was unthinkable.

"It's a whole different pattern of magic than what I'm used to," Balthan spoke quickly. "I can't get my mind around it yet. The mess I made of your eyes was simple compared to this. But I'll get it, whatever it takes."

Balthan's sack was draped over the door looking, for once, completely ordinary and empty. His magical paraphernalia was strewn about the room. He described everything he'd tried, what he'd hoped it would accomplish, why it might have failed. Jordan examined a mandrake effigy, being very careful not to touch it. He stood at the window staring at nothing in particular until the magician's nervous prattle slowed and finally stopped.

"What's Nosfentor, Balthan?" he asked with his back still turned.

The magician sighed. He tried to stare out the window, but Jordan was already there so he stared at his feet before answering: "I don't know."

"But you *do* know Nosfentor? There is a reason Althea put your name and its together?"

"Drum told you." Balthan covered his face with his hands. He muttered through his fingers: "It's all behind me, truly. It's nothing to be concerned about. I shouldn't have said what I did there in the forge-yard. I panicked—"

Jordan turned around. "You told Drum what—By the Eight, Three, and everlasting One: look at me, Balthan!"

Ironhawk's son sounded angry; he wasn't, merely exhausted. Balthan didn't know that; his hands trembled when he lowered them. He expected the worst, and got a recounting of what had happened to Jordan and Drum in the chamber below the Inquisitor's bedroom. The anxiety drained out of Balthan's face; he leaned forward to catch each word.

"Now, I ask you again: What, exactly, is Nosfentor?"

"Exactly, I already told you: I don't know. Generally, Nosfentor's one of the wraiths that tempted me last year."

"You might have told us."

"I told Felespar—he understood. I passed through the damned Flame of the damned Avatar and I survived. What did I have to tell *you* for? I don't owe you anything."

They snarled at each other, poised on the brink of another venomous argument.

Darrel held his breath and made the linked-finger gesture of hope and luck behind his back where they couldn't see it. "Please don't fight," he wished aloud. Both men fixed their glares on him.

"He's right," Jordan said. "It's going to take both of us to finish this."

Balthan shook his head. "They've got five hours on us, Jordan. They could be anywhere—"

"I know where they're going." Jordan tapped the side of

his head. "Thanks to you—I remember exactly where they're going."

"My poor scrambled magic—it's still in your eyes?"

Balthan was seldom overcome by sheer joy. Once it pierced his habitual cynicism, he had no defense against it. He smiled, he laughed, he tried to catch his breath and couldn't. He staggered to the window where Jordan tried to hold himself aloof. After a moment or two, he stopped trying. Determined that he wouldn't be left out, Darrel wormed between them.

Althea thrashed alone and unnoticed on the cot.

Nineteen
ΥΥΥΥΥ

*I*n the hot, sunny days after the cataclysm both the villa and the foregate swarmed with laborers. Great piles of debris were assembled. Anything that could not be salvaged or burned in the winter was taken down the hill and abandoned in the marsh. Every wall, floor, and ceiling was examined for damage. Repairs were planned and begun. By autumn Hawksnest would appear exactly as it had in the spring—before the ground moved, before the hurricane, before Jordan and Althea began their wild quest.

The people of Hawksnest worked diligently—even frantically—to restore their home. There were few laggards or shirkers; everyone seemed eager to do his or her share, and a few did more, as if physical exhaustion were as important as restoration, which, in a way, it was. The Inquisitor had been among them for two months; the damage he wrought upon their spirits was more subtle, more painful to locate and repair, than loosened masonry. Folks awoke in the clean air after the fires, glimpsed their kin and neighbors, and felt the hollow ache of shame. A spontaneous, naive wish sprang up: if Hawksnest was restored, they would also be restored, and the Inquisitor's critical face would recede into the haze of nightmares.

Some would be lucky: their wishes could become reality. Others seemed to realize that their wounds would not be healed with wishes. They had a haunted look, bustling from one self-appointed task to the next. And no one looked more haunted than the Lord of Hawksnest. Erwald Ironhawk patrolled his home incessantly—inspecting, supervising, offering advice. He had not slept since the fire alarm was sounded; he ate standing. Menials, retainers, even Lady Barbara, stayed out of his way when they could.

The empty coffins were removed from the dais beneath the copper dome. The coffins were made of wood; they could have been saved for winter, but were instead weighted down with stone and sunk in the marsh. Ironhawk's sons were known to be alive. Jordan's streamside leadership had been witnessed by the entire foregate. Darrel had been seen by fewer people, but their word was accepted without question.

Questions about the sons might lead to questions about the foster-children, Althea and her outlawed brother; and that brushed dangerously close to the private shame no one would discuss.

Likewise, it was generally suspected, and left unconfirmed, that all four young people had taken refuge at Rosignel. When every crack had been plugged with mortar, every charred beam replaced, and every surface restored to pristine, sparkling white with lime plaster—when all that was done, then Hawksnest would invite its missing children to return home, as if they had never been away.

There were rumors that Jordan and Balthan had ridden out of Rosignel, with swords flashing at their sides and chain mail glistening on their shoulders. Rumors. Jordan would never expose a mail shirt to the summer sun while he was inside it. When he and Balthan left Rosignel, their

mail—smeared with sooted grease to keep it rust-free and
wrapped in the ample canvas tunics they would wear over
it—was stowed on one of the packhorses they led.

Hugh knew the truth. He'd gathered the armor and the
weapons, including Jordan's favorite bastard sword, and
given them to Ventar. He told Lady Barbara, and after
keeping the knowledge to herself for two days, she told
Erwald, thinking it might calm him. She was rarely wrong
about her husband's moods; this was one of those rare times.
Lord Ironhawk went to his library where the Avatar's sigil
of Virtue was inscribed in bronze on the mosaic floor. He
barred the door with books and could be heard, from time
to time, pacing the sigil, reciting his flaws, both real and
imagined.

Drum stood beside his fire, waiting for the rod he held in
the shimmering coals to turn red. An awning protected him
from the bright, blazing sun; nothing could protect him from
the heat and noise of the forge-yard. His was one of five
open fires, but the worst shimmering heat came from the
bloom furnace where his father and uncle smelted local bog-
ore into serviceable metal for wall braces and nails.

His cousin, Minette, offered him a pitcher of water. He
drank some and poured the rest over his head. What they
really needed was high-quality iron: the kind Seanna had
had in her wagon. The kind they could buy from any Trinsic
ironmonger. But they weren't likely to get any. The moon
gate flared each night, but only Lord Ironhawk could guaran-
tee that a wagon would get through safely, and Lord Ironhawk had locked himself away.

The rod was the right color. Drum called one of the
apprentices to roll it on the anvil. He began hammering it
down. When he'd reduced the diameter, he severed a hand-
length piece with a cold chisel. He put a point on one end
and flattened the other, then flung the finished spike into a

bucket. He could make two more spikes before returning the rod to the coals. He meant to lose himself in his work, as he'd lost most of the last four days, but the work no longer bound him. His mind began to wander.

Drum was aware of the shame affecting everyone in the forge-yard in part because he didn't share it. He'd been gone most of the time Lohgrin cast his pall over Hawksnest; he'd been with Althea and the others. He'd been gone; *that* was the source of *his* discomfort. Drum wasn't ashamed or guilt-ridden. He'd reconsidered everything and reached the same conclusions. He was a farrier, a journeyman smith; his obligations were in the forge-yard, with his kin. The Inquisitor, his churls, and the wraith had come and gone. Now there was work to do.

The trials of the privileged folk inside the villa were nothing to him—except that there was no pigiron. Three spikes were in the bucket. The rod was in the fire. Drum wiped sweat from his brow and waited.

If everything was honest and just—why did he see the wraith's damned map glowing in the coals of his fire? Why did he keep looking over the wall at the tocsin? Why was he hoping that Jordan and Balthan would return quickly, and fearing that they never would?

Drum was startled out of his spiraling thoughts. The apprentice pointed at the fire. The rod was bright reddish-orange: too hot to work into spikes. Conversation was difficult in the forge-yard; the husky girl's hooded and averted eyes said everything eloquently. Drum himself was suspect. He'd been contaminated by his association with the land-lord's children; he was no longer the proper temperature. Drum wanted to tell her that mistakes sometimes happen: no blame or shame. She might listen; she wouldn't understand, so he left the rod against the anvil and headed for the street.

Minette was waiting for him.

"Where are you going?"

He told her the truth: "Rosignel," then added, "there must be salvage metal there."

"If the landlord won't go there, why should you?"

"The landlord should go to Trinsic and get us the iron to fix his house."

Drum strode toward the street. Minette ran after him.

"You should have gone before—before Balthan and Jordan left. You should have gone with them, but you didn't. Now you're going because of Althea—"

"I'm going for salvage."

He kept walking. Minette stopped.

"Why aren't you taking the mule if you mean to bring scrap back?" Minette shot her final volley: "You're lying, Drumon. You're lying to yourself!"

That stung a man who valued honesty above all other virtues, but he kept going. He waded the stream and was refreshed by its coolness. He loped down the hill, something he had not done in years, then settled into a comfortable walk. He was out of sight of the villa, but still within earshot: the tocsin began clanging. He began to run again—if Jordan and Balthan were returning, they'd return to Rosignel, not Hawksnest. Drum was strong, but he was no runner. After a furlong, he was panting harder than he ever panted in the forge. His vision was narrow and his thinking got no further than his next step. He didn't hear the harness bells until he'd nearly run into them.

Drum didn't recognize the horses or the wagon until Seanna was on the ground upbraiding him. Even then, he couldn't get a word out between gasps. The teamster handed him a waterskin.

"What's happened that you'd run all this way to meet me?" It was, from her perspective, a reasonable question. She'd heard the tocsin and knew the lookouts had spotted her. Teamster wagons were like no others but distinctive from each other. Drum, she concluded, must have come out to meet her.

He shook his head. "No thing. Why. Are you. Here? Still. Hauling. That iron?" He took another swig from the waterskin and got his first look at Seanna's cargo, which was tied to the back of the wagon. "That's Fugatore. What's—?" The puzzle wasn't large or complicated, the pieces came together quickly. "Jordan's better, but he's not here. Better turn around. We'll go to Rosignel. I'll tell you what's happened."

They hadn't gotten halfway to the sleepy villa when they heard, then saw, Darrel whooping his way across the fields. Word had been passed to him that a teamster's wagon was rolling toward Hawksnest with a grey Valorian in tow; he meant to catch it.

"You're late!" the youth exclaimed. "Fugatore was supposed to be here four days ago. I wished for him so Jordan wouldn't have to ride off after Lohgrin on a *mare!*"

Seanna cocked her head at Darrel. "I dreamt up the idea to fetch him a week ago, but until four days ago the old baron wouldn't part with this beast." Her tone implied that the situation changed abruptly about the time of Darrel's wish.

"What happened four days ago?" Drum asked.

"He went wild. He killed a groom and savaged another stallion so bad they had to put him down. After that Baron Hrothgar was glad to get what I was willing to give for him. It was that or let the knackers have him."

"Has he been any trouble since then?"

The teamster shook her head, glancing between Darrel and Fugatore. "He's ambled along behind the wagon like a big, dumb baby." She settled her stare on Darrel. "Are you magical, boy?"

Darrel shuffled with embarrassment. "I had a dream, too. Jordan was riding Fugatore and the Inquisitor was dead. So

I wished for Fugatore so the dream could come true. I wish
for lots of things and they never happen, not even four days
late.''

"But you wished for Fugatore, and here he is. What if
I'd decided to go someplace else? Would I be rotting in my
grave like that groom?''

"I can't read.''

"What's that got to do with it?''

"Magicians go to the Lyceum, like Balthan. They read
and write and study all the time. I can hardly read. How
could I be a magician?''

Seanna said nothing. If Darrel didn't know the difference
between being a magician and having the raw talent to make
wishes, she wasn't going to enlighten him. "Untie the beast
and hold him while I get the wagon turned around.''

Darrel needed Drum's help to keep the Valorian quiet
while Seanna stood on the pole shaft between the horses
and, guiding them with her voice, her hands, and the butt
of her whip, got the wagon pointed back to Rosignel. The
maneuver would have been impossible a few weeks earlier,
but the ground was dry now and stayed firm beneath the
wheels. Both Seanna and Drum assumed that Darrel would
ride Fugatore to Rosignel, or at the very least lead him, but
the youth retied the rope to the back of the wagon.

"He belongs to Jordan,'' Darrel explained, although that
was only part of the story. For all his prejudice about mares,
mules, stallions, and geldings, the youth wasn't quite ready
to match wills with a Valorian, especially Fugatore.

The farrier snorted. "Valorians have more inside their
skulls than they need. They get ornery. You just have to
show them you're bigger, smarter, and meaner than they
are.''

They walked ahead of the wagon, much as they had done
on the Old Paladin's Road. The jingle of the harness bells
gave Drum the sense of privacy he needed before asking
about Althea. Darrel shrugged and said nothing.

"Well, is she better? Is she herself again?"

"She's better, I guess," the youth said reluctantly. "But she's not herself."

The farrier pressed for more information and received the same answer in a variety of ways. By then they were passing through the gate and he could see for himself.

A great, spreading tree dominated the Rosignel yard. For generations it created the cool shade where the family gathered to escape the summer's heat. The ancient Lady of Rosignel slept in a padded chair. A girl-child sat on the ground nearby amusing herself by drawing pictures in the dust.

Althea sat on a stool on the far side of the tree trunk. Her sunset hair was woven into a single plait that touched the ground as she sat with her chin pointing north, away from the gate and the noise of the teamster wagon. She twisted a length of gauze through her hands continuously, unconsciously. The rest of her could have been a statue.

Drum called to her. The old woman stirred in her chair, the girl pressed one finger against her lips, but Althea did not respond at all.

"I told you she wasn't herself," Darrel said. "Look at her neck."

Despite the sultry heat, Althea's gown was laced high and tight. It covered the necklace, but not the raw red blotches ringing her neck. Before Drum said anything, Althea raised a hand and clawed at her skin. The girl cast a dark, nervous glance Darrel's way. It was clearly her task to intercede; it was equally clear that she was afraid.

"We cut her fingernails to the quick, but it hasn't done any good. She just rubs and rubs." He lowered Althea's hands gently to her lap and held them there until she began to fuss with the gauze again. "Thea, Drum's come to visit you, and Seanna, too. You remember them, don't you? Thea—look at Drum."

She looked at the farrier but did not seem to recognize him.

"Hammers and bells! What's the matter with her!"

"Don't shout," Darrel cautioned in a soothing whisper. "Sometimes she gets upset like she did in the forge-yard. Before he left, Balthan said it was the necklace. She wants to take it off, but she can't."

"Then cut it off," Seanna suggested as she joined them.

From the back Althea looked no different from the last time Seanna had seen her, but from the front Althea left the teamster slack-jawed. The raw blotches were worst around Althea's neck, but there were abraded patches on her face, arms, and hands. Her green eyes were bloodshot and sunken; her lips were chapped and weeping.

Darrel released Althea's hands, but remained poised to grab them again if she reached for her neck. "We can't do that. Lohgrin enthralled it, and she might die if we tried."

"What have you got to lose?" Seanna demanded with her usual bluntness. "She's dying right now."

The men glowered at her and spoke with one voice: "She is *not*."

But the teamster was right, and they knew it. Althea was withering. She would obey simple commands, for a few moments at least. She ignored her plate when they brought her to the table, but if they put a spoon in her hand she'd raise it to her mouth and swallow. Not that eating did her any good, her flesh melted away.

"She's curst," the girl said from her safe place beside the sleeping old woman. "The milk sours. The bread won't rise. The horses sweat."

"It's high summer, Jinney," Darrel snapped. "Those things happen."

They did, of course, but he looked where she looked—at Seanna's wagon. Willie and Tom were more lathered than they'd been on the road. Fugatore, who'd been cool, was thoroughly soaked.

"She's curst," the girl repeated. "We'll all be curst."

Seanna's curiosity turned into worry when her team was

affected. She hurried to them, examining their eyes and ears, their legs and hooves. There were maladies that could consume a healthy animal in the course of one afternoon. She knew the symptoms to look for and didn't find them. She wasn't relieved. Althea didn't have a fever, wasn't recognizably sick, and yet she was dying.

"I'm taking them outside the gate," the teamster decided. "Fugatore can stay inside. It's up to you. I'm giving him to you, since Jordan's not here. I'm not staying. Every city's got its black fogs these days, every estate has a weasely Inquisitor—but Hawksnest is the worst. You've been singled out. The child is right: you're cursed."

She untied the Valorian's lead rope and left it dangling at his feet. Then she wheeled the wagon around and, true to her word, led it through the gate. Fugatore needed a few moments to figure out that he was loose. He looked at the gate. He looked at the people. There was something in the yard that wasn't right. It tickled his nose; it made him frantic.

Drum and Darrel watched his nostrils flare. His ears flicked and swiveled. They knew the signs.

"He's going to bolt!" Drum warned, in case Darrel wasn't paying attention.

They thought they knew where the Valorian was headed and raced for the gate, but Fugatore followed another path: straight at the tree. They shouted and waved their arms, which should have sent the animal galloping in the opposite direction. He veered, but came back toward the tree. Seanna heard the commotion and came to help.

"This is how he got at Malamunsted," she shouted. "Right before he killed the groom." It was a bit of knowledge they could have guessed and would rather not have heard.

Drum and Darrel gave the horse more space, which was fine with Seanna as that gave her the chance to use the whip she uncoiled from her shoulder. She cracked it in front of Fugatore's nose. He stopped short. For a moment the threesome thought they were going to catch him, then, with an enraged squeal, he flanked them: Althea had left the shade. She was marching to him.

"Thea!" Darrel sprinted toward her. "Go back!" He was waving his arms at Althea instead of the horse, and with even less success.

The farrier was right behind him, but they would have been too late if Seanna hadn't whipped Fugatore's nose. While Drum swept Althea into his arms and carried her from the yard, the teamster faced the Valorian. Fugatore came to a flying stop, all four legs stiff and digging into the ground. There were rings of white around his dark eyes, but he let her take the rope and lead him out of the yard.

Seanna gave serious thought to climbing onto the bench and heading back to the Old Paladin's Road. Jordan, whom she found attractive, and Balthan, who amused her, weren't around. The other two were completely caught up in Althea, leaving her with three sweated horses to look after. By the time she had them mopped and watered and moved into the shade she was ready to use her whip on Jinney.

"Where are they?" she demanded, feeding the braided leather through her hands.

"Way in back." Jinney weighed her responsibilities: the Lady of Rosignel who had slept through everything against the leather-clad teamster with her whip. "I'll show you," she decided.

Seanna followed the girl to the tumbled-down part of the villa where Balthan made his quarters. It looked completely abandoned; she thought she'd been duped and was fingering the whip again when she heard familiar voices around the corner. She dismissed Jinney, who scampered gratefully away.

They didn't notice her coming toward them.

"Thanks for all your help."

Darrel and Drum looked up and so, surprisingly, did Althea.

"You're welcome," she said politely, clinging to her companions' arms as she rose to her feet. "What did we do?"

"Nothing," Seanna said with a weary sigh. She threaded the whip through her belt and helped herself to a pitcher of water. It was difficult to get angry at a frail young woman who couldn't stand without help. "I've taken care of Fugatore. He's in the shade, cropping grass like he's never had another thought between his ears."

"Fugatore?" Althea took a tottering step on her own. "Jordan's Fugatore?" For a heartbeat she was smiling and hopeful, then her lips twisted and her hands rose to her neck. She began to writhe from side to side; Drum caught her before she fell.

"Jordan's not here. Seanna brought Fugatore back," the farrier soothed. He sat Althea on his knee and tucked her head against his chest. "Jordan's far, far away from here."

Althea sobbed quietly; her hands stayed around her neck. Seanna waggled her fingers at Darrel who hurried over to her.

"Does she want to see Jordan, or want *not* to see him?"

The youth shrugged. "Both, I guess. She can't seem to decide. She's at war with that necklace. . . ." His thoughts leapt ahead of his tongue. "That's it!" A huge grin brightened Darrel's face. "Althea's at war with the necklace!" He raced back to her and Drum with Seanna following behind him. "It's just like Annon said about Jordan's blindness—she's fighting the necklace and the magic's starting to fade."

Althea looked at him with tear-filled, red-rimmed eyes. "What necklace?"

"The necklace you're holding on to!" Darrel exclaimed before Drum could stop him.

Althea held her hands in front of her. She stared as if they'd suddenly appeared there at the ends of her arms. She shook her head, denying them; her sobs thickened. The farrier tried to wrap her in his arms again, but she'd been filled with an uncanny strength. The pressure of her fingertips on his breastbone was enough to topple him.

Darrel was astounded. "Did you see that?"

Seanna had, and she moved swiftly to get herself and the youth out of Althea's way. "This is some serious magic you're meddling with," she muttered, warning herself more than Darrel.

Drum rose to his hands and knees but no farther. Althea's touch had left his arms and legs tingling; he wasn't sure he could stand. But he could talk. "Do something! Stop her!"

Seanna disagreed: "Let's see where she's going." She didn't think the three of them together could stop Althea if they wanted to.

"She's after Fugatore, what else?" the farrier grumbled as he took an unsteady step.

The muzziness and tingling passed quickly, he caught up with the others and was proved right. Althea made a beeline for the tethered Valorian. Fugatore raised his head the moment Althea came through the gate. He flattened his ears and his neck, two clear equine warnings. Trembling and sweating, he backed away until the rope was taut.

"You'd better get your whip out again," Drum advised.

But Althea seemed to know exactly where to stop. Her hands returned to her neck. "Where's Jordan?" she demanded. "I don't see him. I must find him. He needs me. Where is he? Where is Lohgrin? I must tell him. Where is he?" She began to repeat herself, then she fell forward and fainted.

As soon as she collapsed, Fugatore stopped trembling.

"Are you wishing again, Squirt?" Seanna demanded, spinning the youth around. "If you're wishing again, so help me—I'll make you sorry you were ever born."

Darrel danced away. "I'm not doing anything," he protested—and lied. He was wishing. He was wishing that Jordan and Balthan were here—or if that weren't possible, that he could be with them. It wouldn't be all that difficult: Drum had been in the chamber with Jordan; he'd seen the map. And Jordan had drawn a map in the dirt for Balthan; Darrel remembered it well enough. They'd just have to go north by northwest—they could even take Seanna's wagon. There were old, but serviceable, tracks leading to Spiritwood. And if they weren't sure which way to go, they could let Althea wander a bit. It was hard to say whether she would look for Lohgrin or Jordan—but since Jordan was looking for Lohgrin, it didn't matter.

"I said: *Stop wishing*! I can see you making wishes—putting notions into my head!"

Twenty

ΥΥΥΥΥ

It was cooler in Spiritwood than in the lowlands around Hawksnest. Balthan judged this a mixed blessing as it made wearing mail possible without making it comfortable. Jordan was accustomed to the weight of a metal shirt, but for the magician it was a torture above the waist to rival the agony his misbegotten horse caused elsewhere.

"Snap out of it!"

Jordan nudged Balthan, who jerked upright and hissed.

"Your turn." Jordan pointed at an uninviting array of rock and shadow.

Balthan shrugged his shoulders; they jingled. He kneaded his thighs, trying to ease the aches. "If I get down from this beast one more time today, I'm not going to be able to get back on."

Jordan swung his leg over the pommel, then jumped down lightly onto the balls of his feet. The maneuver kept the horse between his back and any possible enemy.

"You love this, don't you?" Balthan snarled. He could dull the aches with magic, but spell-casting left him hungry and tired. And when the aches returned, as they inevitably did, they were worse. Although this, the eighth day of their wandering, was not as bad as the first few had been.

"You're not human," he shouted as Jordan climbed over the rocks. Jordan had a loose-limbed walk that the magician both reviled and envied. "Your knees bend sideways."

"It's a cave, all right. There's just a hint of breeze. You'd better dismount."

Balthan interrupted his cursing long enough to groan as he lifted his leg and dragged it over the mare's back. He slid slowly to the ground, clinging to the saddle for a few extra moments, until he was certain his legs wouldn't buckle. "If the hole's not windy, there's no sense going in."

They'd become experts in not finding caves. The hills of Spiritwood were cluttered with rock heaps, both natural and compiled by the long-dead farmers who'd tried to turn this stone-ridden land into fields. If the air was moving or, better, if it was moving and rank, a hole was also a cave. Spiritwood was spongy with caves, but none of the ones they'd found so far let a man get more than his own length beneath the surface.

With the reins of four horses wrapped in his hand, Balthan approached the black maw into which Jordan had disappeared. "Tell me I don't have to crawl in there after you."

No answer. The magician tested a branch for sturdiness and secured the horses. He removed his sword from one of the packs and, with it dangling from a thong around his neck, got down on his hands and knees just in time to hear Jordan humphing toward him.

"I found a place where the wind was foul. I don't know how big this Shanna was, maybe she could've gotten out. No way I could wedge in."

Balthan studied the treetops, gauging the time of day from the angle of the light. "We could call it quits for the night."

"We could give up entirely."

The young men glared at each other. Balthan's aches were all in his body, Jordan's were elsewhere.

"They all look alike," Jordan explained. "Nothing's clear in my mind anymore, I've looked at so many piles of stone and tried to overlay them. I'll never recognize it. Lohgrin could have found that box and gotten back to Hawksnest by now."

Balthan untied his horse and shoved his toe into the stirrup. Both he and the mare grunted when he landed. "He hasn't. Let's go."

"By the Eight, the Three, and the One—you're keeping secrets again." Jordan grabbed the mare's reins; Balthan pressed his heels against her flanks. The beast obeyed Jordan. "Tell me, damn you."

"Lohgrin's called for help."

Jordan looked up at the bright blue, cloudless sky. "There's been no miasma, no black fog."

"He called, nothing came. His memory's not as good as yours. He's probably lost worse than us."

"Impossible," Jordan snorted, but he released Balthan's horse and mounted his own. "Why should I believe you, anyway?"

"Because I feel it," Balthan replied, and before Jordan could challenge him, he pushed his sleeve up past his elbow and thrust his naked forearm in front of Jordan. The fine hairs were raised.

"You pick our direction, then."

"We're looking for a cave, not Lohgrin."

"We'll look for Lohgrin looking for a cave. Which way?"

Balthan got nowhere complaining that he wasn't a lodestone. In the end, unwittingly duplicating Jordan's tactics, he picked a random direction and they rode in silence. Jordan, leading the packhorses, kept Balthan in front, and Balthan kept stubbornly on the same meaningless course until one of the many serpentine stone walls some ancient farmer erected on the verge of his plowed fields cut across it. The wall was only waist-high, but that was high enough to stop the horses.

The magician let his mare decide which way they'd turn. She took her time cropping the grass at the base of the wall. There was more grass to her left, none to her right; she stepped left and the decision was made.

As far as Balthan was concerned, everything in Spiritwood—the trees, the meadows, and the innumerable piles of stones—looked alike. He could get a notion of the time of the day by looking at the sun, but he'd never thought to use that knowledge to determine direction. The ground was a carpet of decaying vegetation telling him nothing whatsoever. He didn't know one set of animal tracks from any other and when he saw animal droppings in front of him, he simply saw something to avoid.

Not Jordan. If he'd thought to bring a bow with him from Rosignel, they'd be eating venison every night; as it was, he set snares and kept them in small game. Thanks to his blindness, he was a better hunter than he'd been a year ago. Even riding behind Balthan, he heard grouse and partridge. He saw the man-high trails the antlered deer made between the trees and the lower paths of lesser animals. At Hawksnest there were men who could tell the age, sex, and points of a deer from its droppings. Jordan might never be that good, but he certainly knew horse droppings when he saw them.

He spurred his mare forward, clapping Balthan sharply on the shoulder as he came alongside. "Look! Horse turds! You've found them! We're on their trail." Jordan dismounted and used a twig to probe one of the mounds. "A day old, maybe two—not more than that."

Balthan stayed put. "How can you be sure?"

Jordan cocked his head and raised a cynical eyebrow.

The magician sighed. "Not sure that it's horses; sure that it's Lohgrin. Sure that we aren't back where *we* were two days ago."

"We haven't been here before." Jordan remounted. "That makes me think we're following Lohgrin. Keep an eye out for anything unusual."

"You jest."

"I jest," Jordan agreed. He took back the lead.

Lohgrin wasn't covering his trail; he probably didn't realize he was leaving one. Ivo surely did. Dench was gutterbred, like his master, but Ivo came from an estate somewhere. He knew how to fight and hunt. If Ivo thought they were being followed, he would have scrambled the trail. Or, perhaps, if he remembered hanging with Nosfentor's miasma swirling around him, the churl figured there was no use trying to hide.

Jordan figured they'd camp where their quarry had camped the previous night. He wasn't upset when one of the packhorses neighed loud enough to flush birds from a nearby tree. He was upset, and a little frightened, when another animal, somewhere in the distance, answered.

"Anabarces' ghost," Balthan swore softly.

"Get your sword. Stay close, but be ready to run. Don't let go of the packhorses, unless it's to save your life."

"I've run out of hands. Can't I leave the packhorse tied to my sad—?"

"Forget your sword. Concentrate on keeping the packhorses. Stay back a little."

More than ever, Jordan regretted not bringing a bow and arrow. He considered climbing a tree, then the hidden horse trumpeted again, and an equine chorus erupted behind him.

"Can't you keep them quiet?"

"I'm trying. I could slit their throats—would that be a good idea, my lord? Or should I slit mine instead?"

In his mind's eye, Jordan saw arrows sprouting everywhere—especially from his own body. He considered running, but for all his imagination, he'd actually seen nothing to make him believe there were archers. No one was trying to keep the other horses quiet. He held the reins in his left hand, drew his sword, then, hunched behind the mare's neck, urged her forward.

He found the horses first, five of them tied to a tree-line. They'd been fed—grain and grass were strewn along the line—but it was almost gone. They were hungry again, and thirsty; that accounted for the noise, and implied that no one else was nearby. Jordan kept his sword ready, just in case, and continued on until he reached the camp.

Wood was stacked neatly beside a stone-ringed hearth that had already seen at least one fire. There was no sign of saddles, packs, or the other gear three men and five horses should be hauling. Nor was there any sign of the men themselves. The camp dropped off abruptly on one side. Dismounting and holding his sword with both hands, Jordan covered half the distance before a familiar, fetid scent reached his nose. Relaxing a bit, he confirmed his suspicions: beyond the camp was the largest cave mouth they'd seen. Except for the sound of the stiff wind blowing from its depths, the cave was quiet. Taking one cautious step into the shadows, Jordan saw the missing gear stacked on a natural stone shelf.

"I guess we've found it."

Before Jordan's mind recognized Balthan's voice, his body had pointed his sword at the magician's throat. Irritation replaced wariness. "I didn't tell you to leave the horses."

"I tied them with the others." Balthan parried the sword with his forearm and entered the cave. "Anabarces! The wind is whistling. The cavern here must be huge." He sounded, and indeed was awed by the prospect.

"The fire's dead cold; the horses are hungry. They've been there all day."

Without warning, Balthan shouted "Hel-lo!" He was pleased with the echo and himself until Jordan spun him out of the cave and laid the sword at his throat.

"Announce our names while you're at it! Tell them we're

out here waiting for them to come out!'' He lowered the
sword. "Sound carries, you dolt—especially in the dark.''

The magician's instinct was to argue and quibble, especially when he knew he was wrong. It took some doing to
swallow his venom and apologize. "I wasn't thinking.
Sorry. It won't happen again.''

Shadows lengthened as the sun neared the treetops. Night
came quickly in Spiritwood. Both men sized up the hours
of light left.

Balthan spoke first. "Day or night. What difference does
it make?'' He assumed they were going in. "It's going to
be pitch-dark in there. We may as well start now and get it
over with that much quicker.''

"I say we sit tight here and wait for them to come out.
Wherever they are, whatever they find, and even if they
come out someplace else, they're going to come here for
their horses.''

"You don't want to go in?'' The magician reeked relief.
"We don't have to make a race to the finish? We can wait
for them to bring the prize out and then take it from them?''

"I could put an arrow in Lohgrin's back, if the opportunity arose . . . and I had an arrow.''

Balthan's head bobbed. "Hmm—We're more alike than
I thought.'' He climbed the rocks to the camp. "Let's make
ourselves comfortable. I'll make the fire, if you'll take care
of the horses.''

"You've been healing again.''

The magician shrugged guiltily. "I thought: if there was
going to be trouble . . .''

"Go easy on the food. We didn't bring enough for an
army or a heal-happy magician.''

Stars were shining before Jordan finished with the horses.
He'd laid a ring of snares around the camp and a trip rope
across the mouth of the cave. The snares were for tomorrow's dinner, which he believed would be a celebration.
The trip rope would give him and Balthan all the warning

they'd need to take out a trio of exhausted cave trekkers. He returned to the camp filled with a contented confidence he hadn't felt in a very long time. Balthan removed a brace of rabbits from the spit and gave Jordan the larger one along with a loaf of bread.

"To success," the magician said, saluting his companion with a juicy haunch of roast rabbit.

"To success," Jordan agreed, returning the gesture.

They ate in silence, a mutually agreed upon truce since their conversations tended toward arguments wherein Balthan bitterly decried the injustices of the entire world. They hadn't come to blows yet—something of a miracle considering their past history.

Eventually one of them would offer to take the first watch and the other would go to sleep. Jordan was listening to an owl and thinking of nothing at all when Balthan stretched and stood. He figured the magician was ready to take the watch, but Balthan had something else on his mind.

"Are you going to marry her?"

"Say what?" Jordan forgot the owl.

"When we get back to Hawksnest, are you going to marry my sister, Althea?"

"I don't know. I thought about it a while ago, now . . . I don't know."

"But you love her?"

Sitting wasn't comfortable with Balthan staring down at him. Jordan got to his feet. "What's got you riled? Of course I love Althea; she's family. What's that got to do with marriage? I'll get married someday. Althea will get married. *You'll* even get married."

"If you married her, then she'd be at Hawksnest with you. I could accept that. I can't leave her there with Iron-hawk. I'm of age; I'm her blood kin. I'd stand on my rights and take her with me."

"Hythloth—you're serious—"

"I won't let her stay. I've got nothing against you. You'll

still be my brother whether you marry her or not. But I've seen how Ironhawk cares for his children, and I reject him as my father, as Althea's father. I won't let Althea stay under his hand. You don't have a choice, not if you want Hawksnest—and don't lie to me, you *do* want it—but I have, and I have to make it for Althea."

"Shouldn't you ask her first? Find out what *she* wants?"

Balthan considered the notion. "No," he said after a moment's thought. "I've always taken care of Althea. I can't stop now. If you don't want to marry her, I'll endow her to the Lyceum, if she wants magic. I'll get my money out of Yanno Goldsmith somehow. Otherwise, she stays with me until I find a husband for her."

"I think you're wrong on two counts: I don't think Althea wants a husband right now—not me or anyone else. And I don't think she's going to go with you. It's her life. You've got to let her live it. If she wants to stay at Hawksnest, she stays at Hawksnest."

"Until Ironhawk decides to marry her off again!" Balthan's voice rose. "You said it yourself. We're all going to marry. If she stays at Hawksnest who's she going to meet? It's got to be you or someone Ironhawk chooses for her. Who else is there? The Squirt?!"

"There's Drum," Jordan said softly.

"Drum!" Balthan lifted his arms to the rising moons. "Anabarces—do you hear this? My sister and a damned farrier!" He stalked away from the fire, toward the drop-off.

Jordan let him go. He'd discovered that the magician cooled off quickly if left alone. It was tempting to goad him—Balthan's tantrums were entertaining—but not when Althea would be the battleground. Moreover, the discussion had jangled his own nerves. He did love Althea, and he had been ready to marry her when he thought that would save her from Lohgrin—but his readiness grew mostly out of a sense of duty and virtue. If *love* were the only criteria—

Jordan raked his hair and rubbed his eyes. He prodded the fire. He stared at the sky; there were clouds moving in. He checked the horses. None of this altered the ugly truth: if love were the only criteria for marriage, he didn't love Althea nearly enough. She didn't intrigue him, or make him feel flushed and light-headed the way she used to. It had nothing to do with the Inquisitor. He guessed she'd lost her charm that day at the flooded stream when she wanted him to be nothing more than a cripple.

"Jordan—" Balthan's voice had lost its fire and was flat with concern. "You'd better come take a look at this."

He felt the change as soon as he passed the fire. The cave was inhaling, the wind whistled in the other direction, drawing smoke from the hearth, over the drop-off, into the mouth.

"Fire's got to be doused. Let's hope it hasn't drawn enough smoke to warn them." Jordan started to kick the fire apart.

Balthan tugged on Jordan's sleeve and pointed up. "That's the least of what it's drawing."

Bile soured Jordan's throat. Trammel and Felucca, the twin moons, shed their silver light on an all-too-familiar wall of swirling clouds. As the men watched, black tendrils swept across Felucca, consuming it.

"This time his call was answered," Jordan whispered.

"This time he didn't call."

Jordan kicked more dirt over the fire. "The one thing I didn't figure: Nosfentor would swoop them up and take them home like heroes." He kicked again, sending sparks across the camp.

"Don't think so. If Nosfentor could carry them home, it could've carried them here. If Nosfentor could carry *any-thing*; I don't think it would bother to send Lohgrin."

"Huh?"

"Whatever Nosfentor is, it can get inside a person's dreams and mind, but it's not real."

"I was in that chamber, Balthan. The wraith is real, I swear to you."

"Not tangibly real. Not arms and legs, eyes and ears, hands and fingers real. Nosfentor made that map, but it couldn't touch it. The wraith will see the box when, if, Lohgrin sees it, but even then, it won't be able to touch it."

"You think the Inquisitor's found the box?"

"Maybe. But I told you, I *feel* Lohgrin—like nails scratching a mirror—and I haven't felt anything. Maybe he was supposed to do something and didn't, and Nosfentor's following his trail—"

"That's even better. We're right where Lohgrin was last night. It'll find us instead."

"It didn't find you before when you were in that chamber. It didn't even find *me*, and the wraiths knew me well enough to chase me clear across Britannia!"

Trammel's last white sliver vanished behind the cloud wall. The forest erupted with warning cries as the night creatures sensed danger and sought shelter. The horses, whose instinct was to run from danger, called to each other and thrashed against the ropes that anchored them. A wind sprang up suddenly. It seemed to blow against the clouds, but that was illusion: Nosfentor's black storm was breathing in, just like the cave. The last embers of the campfire scattered and vanished.

"We're safe—right?" Jordan growled as leaves, twigs, and other debris swirled through the camp.

Balthan lost his cockiness. Like the horses, his instinct was to run. It was, however, too late for running. He could just perceive Jordan's silhouette beside him; the ground in front of his feet was a complete mystery. Nosfentor might destroy them if they stayed where they were, but the tangled roots and undergrowth of Spiritwood surely would if they tried to escape.

"Find something solid—a tree or rock—hold on to it," he suggested, then added: "Don't fall asleep."

Jordan's reply was lost in the roar of the wind. They crawled blindly to the trees. Jordan climbed to one of the main branches, Balthan remained crouched at the base of the trunk. Then, as suddenly as it had begun, the drawing wind ceased and the forest was dead quiet.

"You still there?" Jordan called from his perch.

"I am. I think the horses pulled loose and bolted."

Balthan heard the first syllables of Jordan's curse, but no more than that. The lull ended; the wind came out of the clouds. It was howling, fierce, and filthy. Hailstones slammed through the trees. The beleaguered men tucked their heads and succumbed to formless, instinctive orisons as the onslaught continued. They had an idea Nosfentor had arrived when the hailstones pelted them from all directions. Their canvas-covered mail was the best protection they could have had, until the pellets began to melt and fuse.

The difference between now and forever grew fuzzy in their minds just as it was in the mind of every creature subjected to the storm's fury. The difference between better and worse was not noted until Spiritwood was again quiet. Then consciousness climbed out of its deep bolthole and resumed control.

Ice clung to Balthan's hair and clothes. Some of it fell as he stood, but most would stay put until it melted. He stretched and flexed, amazed that he wasn't hurt. The moons were glowing in the sky again. Jordan relaxed his death-grip on the branch and dropped heavily to the ground. He was less ice-clotted, more stiff in the joints. They walked slowly across the camp, mindful of the slushy hail. From the drop-off, which gave the widest view of the sky, they watched the black clouds retreat.

"What happened?" Jordan asked.

His voice sounded weak, as if he'd howled back at the wind during the storm, or Balthan had been deafened. The magician shrugged. Clots of ice broke from his shoulders. The other sounds he could hear came from the forest itself, battered tree limbs crashing to the ground, the waterfall of melting ice. There was nothing that sounded animal, much less human.

Jordan lowered himself over the drop-off.

"They left their gear. If they left—The trip rope's intact."

Balthan checked their packs. They'd fallen out of the tree they'd been hung in, but except for a few soggy loaves of bread, all was intact. The magician's sack was almost completely buried in slush. He lifted it by the cord and gave it a vigorous shake. The slush and debris fell away cleanly; the cloth wasn't wet. Balthan slung it over his shoulder without examining its contents.

He heard Jordan approach, felt a silent inquiry. "Magic," he explained.

Jordan turned away. He studied the sky. The moons were higher, but not yet at midheaven. The endless storm hadn't lasted very long. The night was young yet. He checked the horse lines. Balthan had guessed correctly: the knots were broken, the animals were gone.

"Maybe they'll wander back during the night. No point going after them now."

The slush was almost gone, turned to mud. There was only one dry place where they might sleep: in the mouth of the cave.

"I think they're long gone, tucked in their beds someplace, or drinking wine," Jordan suggested lightly.

"Then you sleep with their gear. I'll keep watch."

"You think there's still trouble coming?" Jordan spoke more soberly, but he took Balthan's offer and began making himself a bed.

"I think Lohgrin and his churls are in this cave. Whether they're alive or not. . . ?" He shook his head. He didn't say anything about entering the cave himself or with Jordan; he didn't need to.

Jordan settled on the ground with a sigh and a slither of mail. "We'll see about that when the sun's up. Wake me up later."

Twenty-One
ΥΥΥΥΥ

Sunlight entered the cave mouth. Balthan roused when its lengthening fingers touched him. His dreams evaporated; he awoke with no notion of where he was, or why. The magician was a restless sleeper; a moment of confusion while he yawned wasn't unusual, but this went beyond all expectation. He staggered into the light, into Jordan's trip rope.

Astonishment kindled the magician's mind; he knew his name and almost knew where he was when he hit the ground. He had the wind knocked out of him and had to start over. He hadn't moved when Jordan stood in the dirt beside him. The yellow-haired fighter apologized for forgetting the rope.

"No harm done," Balthan countered. He rolled onto his back. The sun was high; the morning was nearly gone. "Anabarces! We should've been up and gone hours ago." He started to rise, felt dizzy, and paused with his weight on one knee, his arms on the other.

"Gone *where*?"

The slush was gone, even the mud had dried. The sky was fair-weather blue, unmarked by clouds. But the storm had been real. There were broken branches and wilting leaves strewn about.

Balthan got to his feet. "No sign of Lohgrin." It wasn't a question. "What about the horses? Any sign of them?"

"Tracks. They're around. We'll find them, if not today, then tomorrow. After we catch one, the rest will be easy. When we've got them all, we'll head home."

Jordan started up the rocks. The magician hesitated. He studied the gear Lohgrin and his churls had left in the cave mouth. The glamour of an unfamiliar spell lingered around them, it would be gone by evening. Lohgrin had his churls secure the gear, then he'd protected it. He'd probably put a similar spell on the horses, but being living creatures, theirs eroded quicker. The Inquisitor's failings were extensive, but stupidity and waste weren't among them. He expected to get out of Spiritwood the way he'd entered, and he'd expected to get out of the cave before his spells eroded.

Balthan was convinced that the Inquisitor remained in the cave. The wraith had come, with its usual havoc, but it hadn't done anything because there was nothing to do.

"We've got to enter the cave," he announced, once he'd climbed to the camp. "Something's gone wrong. They don't have the box yet. We've got to try."

Jordan spun a wooden bowl at his companion. A pot of unappetizing porridge simmered in the firestones. "Give it up, Balthan. We tried our luck, and lost. At least we tried."

"Then I'll go in alone—while you're looking for the horses." Balthan filled his bowl and sprinkled it generously with pepper from his sack.

"You honestly believe he's in there."

"Honestly, Justly, Valorously, Honorably, *Humbly*, and all the other virtues: Yes, I believe, and I'm going in. Alone—if I have to."

He wouldn't have to. "We've come this far together. No sense splitting up just when it's getting interesting."

They stowed their gear near the other piles. They each carried a length of rope and a sword, in case they encountered their quarry coming out. Jordan carried a small shovel as well, in case they didn't and wound up digging for the box themselves. Balthan thought he'd abandon his mail shirt, but Jordan wouldn't remove his, so the magician suffered.

The cave was exhaling. Guided by the wind and a light spell Balthan kindled on the shovel, they moved from the cave's mouth into its throat. At first they walked abreast, then singly. They stooped, then they crawled. A cold stream of muddy water flowed across the rock. Balthan became grateful for the mail protecting his arms; he wished he had gaiters, too. The frigid mud was laced with pebbles whose arrow-head points were invariably attracted to his kneecaps. The magician yelped and grumbled; Jordan, being Jordan, endured it all in silence.

The deeper they went, the stronger the wind got until it tore apart Balthan's light spell. They were nailed by the darkness, then Jordan headed forward again, yelping a bit when he bumped his head or rammed his fingers into unyielding stone. Finally he swore with particular disgust; a heartbeat later, Balthan's hand closed over his ankle.

"What's wrong up there?"

"The damn thing divides! There's a big tunnel, and a little one not fit for worms. Guess which is blowing?"

That wasn't difficult. "The wormhole. Can you fit?"

There were curses and groans as Jordan thrashed his way into the hole, kicking Balthan in the process.

"I wager I know why they didn't come out!"

Jordan's shouted words were the last intelligible ones they uttered for a good while. Squeezing through the hole took concentration and strength. Reaching Balthan's subterranean bolthole had been child's play in comparison, and only the conviction that the Inquisitor had passed through the wormhole kept them going forward. Then Jordan whooped exuberantly. Balthan, bent in three impossible directions, heard the echo. Hope loaned him the strength to keep going until his straining fingers touched nothing. Jordan caught his wrist and pulled him out.

"Make your light. I want to see how big it is."

The magician obliged, although the gleaming shovel did little good. It cast its light into their eyes, not into the cavern. They could see each other—fatigued, trembling, and filthy—the ground at their feet, and the wormhole from which they'd emerged; nothing more. The wind had abated, but remained palpable. Jordan heaved a stone out of the light. They heard it land some distance away. He threw other stones, most of which traveled at least as far. Reaching down for another, he saw footprints.

"There's enough mud to hold a trail. We can track them!"

But not easily. Balthan's magic light, whether he attached it to the shovel or held it on his hand, created a sphere of light twice his height in diameter. They could see no more than three or four steps ahead and when the trail crossed rock, which it did frequently, they had trouble finding it again. The water-slicked rock was ice-slippery and tilted. The mud itself was even more treacherous. They laughed the first time they saw skid-marks, then they fell a few times themselves and it was no longer funny.

The spell flickered and died. Balthan reached into his sack.

"Do you have to put it all over the blade? Could you just put it on the front?"

After several failures—the spell tended to make a sphere around the object on which it was cast—Balthan stuffed reagents into the joint between the metal and wood. The spell stayed put, the dark shovel blade absorbed much of it, and the men, who were no longer *in* the light but behind it, could see farther.

Their immediate reaction was awe. Sheets of pale stone

flowed across the uneven floor, frozen cascades rippled
down the walls. Huge icicles descended from the darkness,
smaller ones hung everywhere; beneath each was a mound.
Sometimes icicle and mound met, and became a pillar.
Everything glistened. It was like snow. It was like water. It
was like nothing they'd seen before.

"When I was blind, this is how it was," Jordan whispered. "Everything was frozen so I couldn't tell how fast,
or how big. Is that flowing water or solid rock? Are we
in a hollow mountain, or peeking into a hollow nut? Did
Nosfentor make this last night?"

Balthan picked up a fractured stone. He fitted it to an
icicle. The surfaces locked. The senses he used in his healing
spells told him the fracture was recent, perhaps as recent as
the previous night, but the rock itself was ancient.

"This is bigger than Nosfentor," he answered. "The
world's egg." He put the broken piece in his sack. When
this was over, he'd study the stone and lose himself in it.

Jordan pointed to the far side of one of the pale flowing
rocks. The tracks began again. They left that chamber for
another narrow passage, and another chamber, and another,
until their senses were numbed by grandeur and majesty.
The air was still, now, and saturated. They saw miniature
clouds over flawless, miniature lakes. The caverns were not
completely quiet, water hung everywhere and eventually
fell, creating plops and echoes. When a drop struck his ear
Jordan leapt into the air and landed badly. He and the shovel
went spinning, sliding down a rock flow until they struck
one of the lakes. Darkness enveloped the chamber.

"Jordan. . . ?" "Balthan. . . ?"

Balthan made light around his hand. He saw a stone in a
nearby pool, reached for it, and was shocked by the depth
of the crystal-clear water. He looked for an easier stone,
cast a spell over it, and skidded it toward Jordan's voice.

Jordan hung on the edge of a dark pool. The shovel was
gone. Jordan was grateful for the glowing stone. He started

up the rock flow. Crawling was difficult with the stone clutched in one hand; he tried to stand and skidded immediately. He wound up back in the pool, in the dark.

"Stay there." Balthan unwound his rope and fed it down the slope.

"I'm not hurt," Jordan protested, and started up again, this time without light of his own.

"Stay there!" Balthan put magic in his words. "Wait for the rope."

Jordan stayed where he was until the rope touched his hands and Balthan said he was ready, not because of the linear magic, which had no power over him, but because the magician had been concerned enough to use it. Jordan conceded that it was easier to scale the flowing rock with a rope—

"But it wasn't necessary. I'd have gotten up eventually."

"That pool was dark."

"So?"

"So—this is the clearest water I've ever seen. That pool there, looks like a puddle but it's deeper than my arm. How deep do you suppose that black pool was?"

Jordan swallowed hard. He could swim when he wasn't wearing a mail shirt, carrying a sword, not to mention his buskins, and rope. Probably he could have shucked the extra weight before he drowned. His pulse raced: *probably* cut too close to the bone.

"Maybe we should run rope between us," he suggested.

The magician averred. "So we could both drown? No, thank you, I'll walk alone."

"I don't understand you," Jordan murmured.

The magician was genuinely perplexed. "If it's so important to you—Give it here. I'll tie it around me."

Jordan shook his head. "No, you've made your point and I can't argue it. If there were more of us, I would, but with just two, one falling would pull the other in after him."

"My thoughts exactly."

"Aye, once you mention it, I think you're right; but I don't think that way. I wouldn't, even if I could." He handed Balthan the entire rope.

The magician coiled it over his arm. The light danced crazily over the chamber surfaces. "I don't like being joined up. I'm responsible for myself. When someone's tied to me—I don't know what they'll do; if they'll do the right thing. Even you."

"I'm sorry for you. You don't trust anybody."

"Nobody trusts me—or have you forgotten?"

Jordan flashed a rueful half smile. "I'd forgotten. I thought I was tying you to me, not me to you."

The magician cringed; the light around his hand flickered. "You're scum. You're slime. You have no mercy, no Compassion. You know exactly what to say, then you wait until my flank's exposed and skewer me . . . with *trust*. Damn you." He hung the rope across his chest. The light around his hand continued to flicker; the spell had been hastily cast and then compromised by emotions. He pondered where to cast the next one, now that they'd lost the shovel.

The end of Jordan's long scabbard proved a viable alternative, except in the tight passages, where the shovel had also been useless. They continued to follow the tracks, losing all sense of time and distance as they did. Balthan began tossing ash-coated pebbles into the air whenever they entered a new chamber. He'd kindle the light spell once they left his hand. The men learned not to look at the incandescent spark but at the illuminated features. Sometimes ghostly light clung to scattered icicles or flows after the spark faded. They entered a huge chamber; the cool, eerie glow was retained by the entire back wall. Balthan decided to wait until the chamber was dark before kindling the scabbard. But the glow didn't fade, it was sustained by another light in the distance.

"We've found them!" Jordan whispered exuberantly.

Balthan agreed, but with less enthusiasm. He couldn't

see the distant light without wondering how it was sustained—and he didn't like the conclusions he reached. Casting the light spell on his hand where it would be easier to quench, he took the lead for the first time. The tracks eventually brought them to the base of the monumental rock flow that had retained Balthan's magic. From there they saw a seething radiance in the ceiling of the next chamber. Balthan looked away quickly, but Jordan was transfixed.

The magician held his hand a few inches from Jordan's eyes, breaking the enthrallment.

"Now we know what it did," he explained as Jordan shuddered and returned to his senses. "*Don't* look at it."

"It's hard—the colors move . . . like flames dancing. It's beautiful."

"You'd probably say the same about the dragon that ate you. Don't look at it. Tell yourself it's deadly and forget it."

Jordan repeated Balthan's words, fixing them in his mind, then he was ready to ascend the rock flow.

They had found the end of the trail. Nosfentor's malignancy illuminated a chamber best described as a hollowed mountain with a river running through its heart: the wraith's second vision. Three men could be seen on the river strand. Two were laboring: Ivo and Dench. The third paced.

"This is the place," Jordan whispered. "I recognize it now. They've dug up the cairn." He removed the strap that held his sword in the scabbard. "Let's go."

"Let's not. This may be the place, but they haven't found that box, and they've been digging awhile. They're going to be tired and careless once they find it. If we take them out now, we'll have to do the digging."

As before, Jordan found himself unable to offer a more Virtuous, less risky tactic. He accepted the magician's unpalatable suggestion. They stayed where they were, well above the strand where the churls labored. The river, unlike the water elsewhere in the cave, wasn't clear, but its appetizing color came from the unnatural light that continued to enthrall Jordan. From time to time, Balthan would tap his arm or, if that failed to get his attention, place his hand in front of Jordan's eyes.

"I can't keep from looking," he complained, chagrined by his failure.

"You're doing well, for someone who's head-blind, not a scrap of magic to call his own."

Jordan was not consoled. "I can see myself: sword in hand, head pointed at the ceiling—until a churl slices it off!"

"Good point." Balthan dug into his sack. "Look at me—"

Jordan obeyed. It was the magician who hesitated.

"I can't do it."

"Why not?"

"I can't. It's not right to meddle with magic."

"Balthan, I let you meddle when I couldn't even see you—"

"That was a different kind of magic." He put the reagents back in the sack. "This would be Sixth Circle magic, if I'd been initiated into the Sixth Circle, which I haven't been. I shouldn't be able to cast it; I can't cast it. It shouldn't work at all; I don't know why it does, and that's why I don't want to do it. I don't trust me." He was knotting the thongs when Jordan grabbed his hand.

As he'd done with Minette, Jordan pressed his thumbnail into the sensitive flesh inside Balthan's wrist. He bore down until the magician's fingers were stiff and the thong slipped through them. "Be a good magician and make your magic. I don't care whether you trust you or what kind of magic your masters let you play with. Right now, I've got a choice between that magic up there, and your magic." He squeezed harder.

Any other man would have been rigid, but Balthan calmly used his free hand to retrieve the sack. Except for his glazed

eyes, Jordan might have believed his foster-brother had no
nerves.

"I should learn to keep my mouth shut around you."
Balthan's voice was soft, his lips scarcely moved.

When Jordan released his hand, the magician cradled it a
moment, then fished the reagents out of the sack one-
handed. He mixed them in the palm of Jordan's hand; his
own was still trembling when he pronounced the words: *An
Xen Ex*. It was the same spell Annon had used to calm
Darrel, and as Balthan warned, he could not cast it properly.
The reagents were not transformed to weightless powder.
But when the magician described the light in the ceiling as
maggot-ridden offal and the poisonous ichor of a thousand
worms, Jordan found himself nauseous. When Balthan described the light as the vomit of vultures, Jordan staggered
away, wretching and groaning. He was still green when he
returned.

"I guess I deserved that." He coughed and wiped his
mouth on the filthy canvas covering his mail shirt. Nothing
this side of death could induce him to look up.

Balthan held out a small, bright red lump that Jordan
declined. "It's cherry treacle. It's got to taste better than
your tongue."

"I don't trust you *that* much, my friend."

With some difficulty, Balthan broke the lump in two.
"Truce. Pick your piece; I'll eat the other one."

"I've seen the things you put in your mouth," Jordan
muttered, but he took the larger piece, popping it in his
mouth a moment after Balthan. It was cherry treacle, and it
was wonderful.

The churls gave up making holes in the mud. Stripped to
breechclouts, they dove along the strand, fighting the current. It seemed unlikely the box would remain nearby if it
had fallen into the river, but then Dench surged up with his
hands high.

"I've got it! I've got it!"

His joy echoed through the cavern. Lohgrin himself deigned to kneel in the mud to take the nondescript box into his own hands before the churls helped each other out of the river. The Inquisitor gleefully wiped away the silt and held the box up to the light.

"Remoh's sandalwood box!" he shouted, and in the rocks above the strand Balthan and Jordan felt their hearts skip a beat.

"Is he calling?" Jordan demanded. "You said you could tell."

Balthan shook his head many times. "I can't tell. He is, he isn't. I don't think he knows himself."

"We can't take a chance."

The magician had no clever alternatives. "What do I do—other than stay out of your way?"

"Take out Lohgrin before he casts anything. He did something at Hawksnest. It knocked me off my feet and smelled like swamp gas."

Balthan thought a moment and went back to shaking his head. "Magically, I'm no match for him, Jordan."

"He doesn't have a sword, you do; use it. Stay out of sight when I come forward. Maybe you can take him by surprise. Like you said—they're apt to be careless right now."

The magician flexed the hand Jordan had mauled and made certain his sword would slide out of the scabbard when he needed it. "I've never killed anyone . . . anything before. I don't know if I can."

"Think of maggots breeding in your rotting guts," Jordan said as he started for the strand. " 'Cause that's what you'll have if you *don't* kill him."

Balthan muttered until Jordan signaled him to be quiet. Lohgrin and his churls were still celebrating. Jordan picked his target: Ivo, the better fighter of the pair, and flashed Balthan a victory smile before he broke cover. Balthan tried to return the gesture, but his lips were as numb as the rest of him.

"Ironhawk!"

Jordan drew his bastard sword as he leapt over the rocks and, wrapping his left hand below his right at the top of his swing, delivered a mighty cut across Ivo's back while all three—Dench, Ivo, and Lohgrin—were nailed by his warcry. Dench raced for his sword. The Inquisitor shouted something that had no noticeable effect.

"Ironhawk!"

Desperation gave Dench an agility neither he nor Jordan expected. He made an acrobatic dive for his sword, caught the hilt firmly between his hands, and got the blade up in time to parry Jordan's murderous slice. Momentum carried Jordan a stride beyond the impact; by the time he got turned around, Dench was bearing down on him. There was a brief moment when he could see that Ivo was moving and Lohgrin had his hands above his head like the pincers of some gigantic insect. There was no time to look for Balthan before he parried Dench's sword.

The Inquisitor cried out the name of the wraith: "Nosfentor!" and other unrecognizable syllables, invoking a thunderclap that lifted everyone and hurled them through the air before pinning them to the ground. Jordan closed his eyes quickly, but not before he saw the nauseating light dislodge and begin a swift, gut-curdling descent. As soon as the pressure lifted from his chest he rolled to his feet.

Balthan was the last to stand up. The thunderclap had been aimed at his chest. He was sure it had stopped his heart, and wasn't sure why he wasn't dead. Neither was Lohgrin. The Inquisitor wasted precious moments repeating the invocation without re-creating it. Balthan saw his opportunity, leveled his sword like a lance, and charged across the mud. Lohgrin's eyes bulged; Balthan thought he had his quarry. Then the Inquisitor uttered an alien syllable.

The rune was wrong, and so was the manifestation, but Balthan recognized an An Tym spell as it folded around him—it was, after all, one of those he'd used to such ill-effect on Jordan. Balthan knew ways to combat magic that the head-blind could scarcely imagine; all of them, however, took too much time. Lohgrin was smiling as he advanced. Balthan saw death coming for him. He recklessly borrowed magic and movement from his future destiny: he raised the tip of his sword, aligning it with the Inquisitor's heart.

Dead cold sprouted in Balthan's mind. He'd borrowed too much. He might never cast another spell. He wouldn't know until Lohgrin's spell wore off—if he lived that long, which, as the numbness spread, he guessed he wouldn't. He was completely helpless, but Lohgrin didn't advance.

The Inquisitor had seen his thunderclap fail to slay his young nemesis; he saw the inconvenient upstart move steel through his negation of time. He couldn't waste time finding out what else Balthan could do—at least not until he got the box to the wraith.

"Some other time," he said, and laughed at his own wit, then, clutching the box, he began the long trek to the surface.

Balthan read the Inquisitor's lips. He would have laughed, too, if he'd been able. He would have liked to tell Jordan that he'd been right: a magician who knew how to hold and point a sword was a formidable opponent. Balthan wouldn't get the chance. He'd meet his death as the Inquisitor's spell waned.

He wondered if his eyes would close before he died, if there'd be a burst of agony, or if death would come with a whisper. He wondered about many things and the sword began to feel heavy.

This is it, he thought.

There was a burst of agony, but it heralded restored movement and feeling, not eternal oblivion. As Balthan's muscles were revitalized, he turned to his right, away from the path of Lohgrin's escape, to see how Jordan fared. A thin mist cloaked the strand. Nosfentor's seething light had completed its descent. As the fumes penetrated his nose and burned into his lungs, Balthan understood that the mist was corrosive rather than poisonous, but it was deadly just the same.

The other three, having been farther from the source of the negation spell, had not been so profoundly affected. Jordan slowly, but handily, parried Dench's swordwork; he'd overpower the churl once opportunity presented itself—unless Ivo interfered. The wound across Ivo's back was a hideous mass of fused tissue. The fact that he could retrieve his sword implied that the Inquisitor's first invocation had imparted powerful healing magic. Ivo wasn't as good as new, but he was good enough to change the balance in Dench's fight, especially since Jordan did not seem to be aware of Ivo's restored potential.

Balthan didn't know what to do. His voice hadn't recovered, besides, he didn't know if a shouted warning would help. He had no magic whatsoever, not even as a distraction. All he had was his sword, its tip now buried at his feet. One hand wasn't enough to lift it, not even two. He released the sword and concentrated on getting both hands on the hilt of the main gauche, the broken relic, in his left hand. Aiming for the vulnerable organs below Ivo's ribs, he thought *run*. His body responded with drunken lurches; each unbalanced step brought him closer to a facedown collision with the mud. He thought *stop*; that made things worse. Balthan had no control over himself or the weapon when the fractured steel entered Ivo's body.

Sound wouldn't disrupt Jordan's concentration but he was ever alert for movement. Something large hurtled his way. He retreated, allowing it to pass between him and Dench. Jordan fleetingly chastised himself for forgetting Ivo. But Ivo was surely dead now; the rest of that screaming amalgam of arms and legs was of no interest or importance. Jordan prepared for a killing thrust and did not hear the splash.

For his part, Dench saw the death-grin on Ivo's face and
it unnerved him. In his nasty, brutal life, Ivo served as both
friend and mentor. Dench felt his loss and forgot his danger.
He also got his very first look at Balthan: the magician
who had caused so much trouble and now tragedy. Blind,
irrational hatred pointed Dench's sword at the river. He
would have leapt after them—if Jordan had given him the
opportunity.

Dench's death was swift. He went down smiling: the pain
was gone and he wasn't alone.

Jordan wrenched his sword free and came on guard. He
looked for the Inquisitor and found no trace. Shouts and
splashes rose from the river. He remembered Ivo, and realized that the noise and the extra limbs had come from Balthan.

As soon as he relaxed, Jordan's gut caught fire; he fell,
coughing, to his knees. He crawled to the river's edge. The
air was cleaner right above the water. He convulsed and
stuck out his hand.

"Come on."

Balthan waved him off. "The bloody thing's stuck!" he
explained before plunging under the water again.

Jordan reached as far as he could and got a handful of
canvas. "Forget it." He jerked Balthan off his feet and
hauled him to the bank.

The magician made a final, feeble lunge before the wisdom of Jordan's words percolated through his mind. He
stopped fighting and accepted help getting out of the water.
He retrieved his sword and his sack from the rocks where
he'd left it, then he followed Jordan away from the strand.
They did not pause until they were out of the acrid air and
out of the light. Jordan wretched until his lips were foam-
flecked and he was certain that he'd purged himself. He
slumped against the rocks, wheezing loudly but feeling better. Balthan was choking. Jordan followed the sound. He
pounded between the magician's shoulder blades and when

that didn't seem to be helping he clenched his arms around the other man's chest and squeezed violently. Balthan wretched and sagged helpless in Jordan's arms, but he was breathing again.

"You had me scared," Jordan confessed. "For a moment I thought you might die on me." He propped Balthan against the rocks and dropped the sack in his lap. "Magic us a light, will you? It's going to be dark soon."

"I can't," the magician said weakly, and, between gasps, explained that he'd squandered his destiny and his magic after Lohgrin hit him with the time negation spell. "I'm surprised I've survived this long. I thought I took everything."

A cold sweat bloomed on Jordan's forehead. His heart pounded; his lungs wheezed and burned. "You're not dead. You couldn't have taken *everything*. By the Eight, the Three, and the One-All-Around: I don't want to die blind."

"I'm sorry—"

"Don't be sorry—Try."

Reluctantly, Balthan slipped his arm into the sack. It was as empty and ordinary as it had been the day he'd gotten it. His worst fears were confirmed; he withdrew his arm.

"Try harder!"

"It's empty. I'm empty."

Jordan ripped the sack from Balthan's hands. It was just an ordinary, empty, coarse-cloth sack with a faint, musty smell. He held it upside down and shook it violently. He started to turn the sack inside out.

"Don't—!"

Balthan doubled over screaming. A moment passed before Jordan understood what was happening. When he did he realized his hand was filled with something warm, squishy, and not at all the texture of coarse cloth. His fingers stiffened and the sack slipped off his arm. Balthan snatched it and held it tightly against his chest.

"Inside—it's you?"

The magician nodded. He'd never really known pain or
terror until Jordan seized the bottom of the sack. The pain
was gone, but the terror lingered. He curled around the
cloth, sobbing like a child and shivering. Jordan towered
over him feeling crueler and more foolish as time passed.
He knelt down and put his hand gently on the magician's
arm.

"Come on, Balthan," he pleaded.

Finally the magician shuddered and rolled away.

"Are you going to be all right?"

Balthan gradually got control of himself. "Aye."

"I guess it wasn't really empty, was it? You just didn't
reach down far enough."

"No, I guess not." Balthan tried to laugh and moaned
instead. "Don't ever do that again."

Nosfentor's luminous cloud winked out. The cavern was
darker than the darkest night.

"I won't have to now that we both know you're still a
magician. Can you make light yet?"

"Not yet, but not long either."

Twenty-Two
ΥΥΥΥΥ

The storm cloud passed beyond Seanna's wagon just after sunrise. It was towering and solitary, black as soot, and wreathed with lightning. The thunder crash never reached them and although the branches bent upward to reveal the frosted underside of their leaves, the rain they predicted did not come. The cloud hovered above the northern horizon awhile, then dispersed.

Darrel and Drum argued about the nature of the storm cloud: was it the wraith, Nosfentor, or was it simply its messenger? Drum had been beneath the villa; he believed it was the wraith summoned by Lohgrin. Darrel disagreed. The swift-moving storm reminded him of the gazer Lohgrin sent to chase him and Jordan up moon-gate hill. He thought the cloud was a spy, sent by the wraith, to observe the Inquisitor.

"What difference does it make whether the wraith was summoned or came spying of its own accord?" Seanna interrupted. "It was no natural storm and I'm damned glad we weren't in its path. We would have been, if we'd followed her."

One by one, they looked across the camp. Althea sat by

herself on stones harvested from some poor dead farmer's field. She ignored them, watching squirrels playing in the trees, one hand resting in her lap and the other, as always, tucked inside the neck placket of her gown.

She'd been their sole guide and compass since leaving Rosignel a week ago. Several times a day, whenever the rough road they followed branched, Drum would lift her out of the wagon, carry her to the open road in front of the horses, and set her gently on her feet. Then Darrel would ask: *Which way, Althea?* Sometimes she whimpered. Sometimes tears flowed from her eyes. But after a few moments she'd lower her hand from the pearl and moments later she'd choose their path.

Last night, as the others made camp, she'd wandered away. Drum was in a roaring panic before they found her standing atop a ridge, arms outstretched, eyes closed in rapture, and facing that point on the horizon where the towering black cloud had hovered before it dissipated.

Seanna had been getting the wagon ready before she joined Drum and Darrel's argument. She had Willie's harness draped over her shoulder. Pulling her attention away from Althea, she looked first at her horses, then at the leather trailing through her hand. "I don't think we should follow her any farther. I didn't see anything like a road going across that valley last night. I'm not willing to take my team cross-country and into storm-wrack."

She expected that Darrel would say something reassuring. He had every other time she hesitated. In her mind Seanna knew that they were on a fool's quest; but when the boy spoke of his dreams, of helping Jordan, Balthan, and even Lord British, she allowed her heart to be swept along in his enthusiasm. She waited anxiously as Darrel bit off his fingernail, saying nothing. Althea gave them their direction, but Darrel kept them moving. His confidence that they'd find Jordan in time to help vanquish the Inquisitor and recover the sandalwood box had seemed unshakable. Until now.

"Have you come to the end of your road, Darrel Hawson?" Seanna asked flatly. "Did that storm take away all your luck and wishes?" Her mind was relieved, but disappointment sat heavily in her heart. They'd come so far. She would have taken the wagon across the valley for him, but she wouldn't do it for herself. "I'm going to turn around."

Darrel wished he were somewhere else, but he remained where he was. His wishes never had become real—it had only seemed that way when Seanna showed up with Fugatore tied to the back of her wagon. He'd made wishes, and he'd had the dream where Jordan was riding Fugatore and smiling because the Inquisitor was dead. He'd believed in the dream the same way he'd believed in the Eye of Destiny. The Eye had sustained him since he was a baby. The dream sufficed for less than two weeks. This morning he woke up filled with dread. He wished it were tomorrow. But it was today, and he was frightened. He wished Jordan were with him. He wished with all his might. His fears multiplied.

Althea had heard their conversation. She listened as Seanna crooned to Willie and fitted the harness to him and the wagon. It was always Willie first, then Tom. She heard everything they said, watched everything they did. She was very much alive and aware within herself, although her friends thought she was lost in a world of her own because she didn't talk to them. Althea had been lost, but not in a world of her own.

Listening, more than seeing, and much more than speaking, required no conscious effort. It was almost invisible. Althea listened to everything: the birds and the squirrels, the many sounds the horses made, even the sound of the flies buzzing around them. She thought that if she listened to everything, then nothing would notice that she listened to her friends as well.

Seanna said she'd turn the wagon around. Althea hoped the teamster would; she truly hoped—Her breath caught in her throat. Hope was dangerous. It left a trail in her thoughts that *he* could follow when he came to see what she was doing. Althea stifled it, and then hoped she'd been successful. She began to tremble. That was the trouble with hope, once it got loose, it was demon's work to get it caged again. There was only one sure way to get rid of hope: think of Lohgrin.

Holding her breath, grinding her teeth together, Althea made her fingers move away from the pearl. She felt the emptiness immediately—like the ache that came with a broken tooth: close to her mind and heart, so horrible that she didn't feel anything at all. Her hope was gone. She let her fingers come back to the pearl. Like a broken tooth, she hurt less when the raw nerve was shielded by flesh. Like a broken tooth, she could not be healed.

And yet she had healed a little. When she left Hawksnest, she had no thoughts of her own. At Rosignel, she had the thoughts of a flower, turning her face to the sun. Lohgrin's necklace held her in thrall, but she had not been aware of the necklace. Now, she was herself, not enthralled, merely imprisoned in a cramped corner of her former self. She imagined a tiny Althea hunched at the top of the spiral stairway in a slender dark spire. Lohgrin commanded all the rest of her castle, but he'd never noticed this one little place. If he did, then she'd run to the top and throw herself over the edge.

Her fingers froze on the pearl. Was it tingly? Was *he* coming? Althea's inborn magic gave her mastery over a handful of domestic spells and the certain knowledge that Lohgrin was in the pearl. The irregular, satiny pearl was an appropriate symbol for her enthrallment. A mindless water creature had secreted it, layer by painful layer, in a futile effort to protect itself from something that had taken residence in its shell. The pearl got bigger; the creature got smaller. One day there was no room left for it so it died, and Lohgrin took possession of the pearl.

The Inquisitor came and went through the pearl. Althea

didn't know how and didn't want to know how. The pearl would tingle like cat's fur on a dry day, and then he'd come. If she held the pearl very tight, he couldn't come, but if she held the pearl *that* tight, then he knew she was blocking him and that she was not as enthralled as he meant her to be. So she had to be careful, and let him come through sometimes. Althea worried about what would happen when he came for her and she felt his touch in the flesh, not in the pearl. Worry was as dangerous as hope, and much more difficult to purge.

Althea put herself back in her ears, listening for the conversation, almost—but not quite—hoping that they were ready to start back to Hawksnest. There was no conversation—only the sounds she recognized as Darrel's footsteps.

"Thea, we need your help."

Moving carefully, lest she accidentally release the pearl, Althea eased her feet to the ground. Obedience was like listening; something she did very well unless she willed otherwise.

"No, Thea. I want to talk to you, and I want you to answer me."

Althea turned to face the boy. Darrel hadn't so much grown in the last four months as changed, although he had grown quite a bit. She didn't look down when she looked at him anymore; soon she'd be looking up as she did with most men and a good many women. The changes were mostly in Darrel's face and eyes, which had become hard, dark, and intense. When he stared at her, and told her what to do, it was like facing her brother. No, it was worse. Balthan was impetuous; he could be distracted. Darrel was like the Inquisitor: he had a purpose.

She wanted to run away, but that was more activity than she could fabricate in her tiny refuge.

"Thea?" Darrel held out his hand, she pressed hers against her thigh. "Thea—can you hear me? Are you listening to me?"

She nodded. Gestures were easier than words. Words had

to be selected, weighed, and put in order; gestures simply happened. Words formed beneath the pearl. She was certain *he* could hear them. Althea didn't speak except by accident or mistake.

"Tell me you can hear me. Tell·me in words."

Althea raised her chin until her neck was stretched and gaunt. Darrel came so close to the compelling timbre of Mother's Voice. It didn't necessarily mean he had magic. Almost anyone could conjure up Mother's Voice, even Jordan or Drum, who were both head-blind. If Darrel were going to have magic, he should have shown it long before he turned thirteen. Her own magic was nothing compared to her brother's, but it had always been a part of her, as Balthan's had always been a very noticeable part of him. Squirt never showed an aptitude for anything but trouble and escape—or had they all misread the signs?

"Thea. *Where is my brother? Where is Jordan?*"

She cried at the heavens—a thin, high-pitched warble through sealed lips. The pearl tingled beneath her fingers. It turned hot, then unbearably heavy, pulling her toward the ground. Darrel caught her before she lost her balance, before her hand moved from the pearl.

Darrel knew he'd done something extraordinary. His ears rang with the sound of his own voice. His tongue was thick and glued to the roof of his mouth. He felt drained, as if someone had knocked the bung out of his barrel.

"Thea, where's your brother? Where is Balthan?" His own voice again, and doubly ineffective because Drum had come running over and scooped Althea up like a kitten. She was deadweight, except for her hands, both of which were clenched over the pearl.

"You said you weren't going to hurt her!" the farrier snarled.

Whatever he'd done before, he had to do it again, and quickly before Drum whisked Althea back to the wagon.

"Where is the Inquisitor? Where is Lohgrin? Your be-trothed?"

She was limp in Drum's arms one moment, and thrashing the next. He couldn't hold on to her. She tumbled to the ground, blood coloring her lips. She bit them as her hand came away from the pearl.

You may tell them, my dear.

The words tore through Althea's mind like a storm, like the black storm. He'd never announced himself before. He stole into her thoughts, spying on her friends, on her, hiding in the shadows much as she hid from him. But he was close now, and no longer felt the need for caution.

"He knows where we are. He's coming for us. He's coming for the wagon. For me."

The pearl pressed on Althea's throat, choking her. She flattened herself against the ground, but she could not make herself thin enough. She could not disappear; she could not climb to the top of her spire or leap into oblivion. She saw what he saw: the sunlit forest, the ground in front of him as he walked unerringly toward her. She remembered what he remembered: her brother, worn and weary, as still as a statue with a sword clutched in his hands. Jordan moving slowly through a dirty mist. If Dench didn't slip his sword between Jordan's ribs, Ivo surely would.

Tell them, my dear. Tell them.

The Inquisitor allowed Althea to choose her own words. He was an artist in subtle cruelty, a master of self-inflicted tortures. He savored her helplessness; his smile cast a harsh light into all her hiding places.

"Balthan and Jordan—Three days ago—In a cave—Ivo and Dench—He—They're *dead*!"

"No-o-o-oo!" Darrel emptied himself into a scream of rage and denial.

Words continued to pour from Althea's mouth. Once she began describing the images Lohgrin held before her, it

seemed she would never stop. Her words were truthful, as
she saw the truth: the Inquisitor's truth unfolding in her
mind. Jordan and Balthan had a cavern for a tomb. Lohgrin
had the sandalwood box, and he was coming for Althea
and the wagon that her companions had so thoughtfully
provided.

Darrel bared his teeth and shook his fists at the cloudless
sky, then he threw himself on Althea.

"No-o-o-oo!"

He struck her, because her voice had destroyed his world,
because the Inquisitor was somewhere inside her, making
her say these horrible things. Althea would not defend herself, but Drum did. The farrier grabbed Darrel by the scruff
of the neck and hurled him at the wagon. The youth rolled
and lay still. He'd had the wind knocked out of him, but
that didn't help. Nothing could hurt as much as losing his
brother. He couldn't scream loud enough to vent his anguish. He didn't try. He wanted the world to end, but it
wouldn't acknowledge his loss. The sky was a beautiful
blue. The birds sang; the squirrels played. Fugatore tore a
mouthful of grass and wildflowers from the ground.

Fugatore didn't know. Fugatore didn't care. It was more
than Darrel could endure. He got himself to the wagon. He
tore the rope loose. He ran at the horse, waving his arms
and screaming. Fugatore raised his flower-fringed head and
blinked. Darrel threw grass, he threw dirt. His fingers closed
around a rock; he threw that, striking Fugatore high on the
shoulder. The Valorian reared and thrashed with his front
hooves. Darrel heaved another stone at the horse's belly.
Darrel threw one last stone before Fugatore swerved and
vanished into the trees. As soon as Fugatore was gone, as
soon as Darrel was alone, the tears began.

The sky remained blue; the birds and squirrels went elsewhere. Seanna would have gone elsewhere herself. This
wasn't her grief. None of these people were tightly woven

into her life. Drum and Althea had each other, they certainly didn't need her. But the boy was all by himself, and she couldn't hear his grief without sharing it. She felt awkward and clumsy until she touched him, then instinct guided her. Seanna held Darrel tightly in her arms. He cried for both of them.

Darrel ran out of tears. He was numb. He leaned against Seanna, a stranger in his own body. He stepped away from her. Nothing had changed; nothing was the same. Trembling, he opened himself to another onslaught of grief, but it didn't come. For the moment Darrel was beyond its reach.

"We'd best be moving," Drum said to Seanna. "From what Althea says, he's on foot. We might be able to stay ahead of him."

The teamster pushed her hair behind her ears. She was surprised to find her face was wet. "Aye—that sounds good to me." She started toward the wagon, and noticed that Althea wasn't in sight. "Where did she—?"

"I've put her in the wagon," Drum assured her quickly. "The shock was too much for her. She's half-asleep, half in her own world someplace. It's probably just as well."

Seanna nodded. "You covered that pearl?"

Drum nodded, and Seanna started for the front of the wagon. Willie hadn't moved from his place on the right side of the wagon-shaft and Tom grazed contentedly, waiting for his turn.

"Where are we going?" Darrel asked. His voice was deep and raw, barely recognizable. "We're not leaving, are we? You're not thinking of heading *back*."

The farrier wouldn't lie, the teamster didn't think she had to. "If we get moving quickly, we'll be able to stay ahead of him. Althea said he's on foot. He must have lost his horses somehow. It's a little advantage; we've got to take it."

Darrel hesitated a moment, asking himself if he could leave, if he could turn tail and run from Lohgrin. The answer resounded from every fiber of his body.

"Ironhawk!"

He could not run away, he must attack. His eyes fixed on Tom. Carried by a determination that owed nothing to conscious thought, Darrel ran past Seanna and Drum, past the wagon where his precious sword lay in its scabbard, and past Willie, straight at Tom.

"Stop! Come back here!" Seanna was some twenty paces behind when she started running after him. "Don't you *dare*!"

The teamster needed luck—luck to make Darrel trip, or miss his vault, or keep Tom from bolting. Darrel had always been unconscionably lucky. He didn't trip; he landed cleanly on the big horse's back; and when Tom tossed his head, the halter rope smacked firmly into the youth's hand. Darrel seized a handful of mane and slammed his heels against Tom's flanks.

"Ironhawk!"

Bobbintom did not so much obey as bolt, but the result was the same. He sank back on his massive hindquarters, then surged forward. A man could have kept pace with him for his first steps, but he gathered speed with each heavy stride. He followed the cart track; he always followed a road when there was one, but the nuisance on his back was hauling his head away from the track, so he went where he could see—toward the crest of a big hill.

Seanna chased them until Tom broke into a canter, then she stood and swore at them until she heard bells behind her and realized that Willie, half in and half out of his harness, was trying to follow his teammate. She ran back to the wagon and attacked Willie's harness with unconcealed fury.

"You're not going after them," Drum said from a safe distance.

"Damn straight I'm going after them."

She got a blanket from beneath the bench and her whip from beside it. She shortened Willie's reins with a wad of knots and stuffed the blanket under what was left of his harness. She was about to climb onto his back when Drum tried to stop her.

"You know what's out there."

"Aye—I know where he's headed."

"Seanna, he's trying to get himself killed."

"Not with my Tom he's not." She settled on Willie's back. It was an unfamiliar experience for both of them. "I'll be back as soon as I've got Tom."

"Good luck."

"To Hythloth with luck." She tapped Willie with the whip-stock and called to him as she would from the bench. He gave her a sidelong baleful stare and started down the cartway. Seanna let him build up some speed, then she veered him up the slope after Tom and Darrel.

Jordan leaned low over his horse's neck, barely avoiding a tree branch. He held one set of reins in his right hand, and a lead rope in the other. They'd gone a few steps farther down the poor excuse for a trail when he heard Balthan shout as the branch struck him. Jordan glanced over his shoulder.

"No harm done!"

Jordan took Balthan at his word. The ground had leveled; he picked up the pace. Balthan had enough warning to get his right hand wrapped around the pommel. Like Jordan, he had reins in his right hand and rope in his left. Between him and Jordan, seven Hawksnest horses were tied to the rope. They'd spent a day and a half getting out of the cave, and the better part of another day rounding the beasts up.

He'd objected that they were wasting time. Jordan pointed out that the Inquisitor didn't have Ivo and Dench taking care of him anymore. Lohgrin left both sets of gear—his own and that belonging to Jordan and Balthan—undisturbed in the cave mouth. He was traveling on foot. Jordan insisted the Inquisitor's lead was time, not distance, and that they'd catch him long before he got out of Spiritwood. Balthan had been skeptical, but he knew better than to complain—then, before dawn this morning, he woke up with the short hairs on his neck and arms pulled straight up. He roused Jordan. They were ready to move as soon as they saw the cloud.

Balthan would manage to stay in the saddle no matter what breakneck pace Jordan set. If he'd been in the lead, they'd be moving faster, but Jordan knew when to run the horses and when to walk them cool. They'd intersected the storm's path a few miles back, and after tracking Lohgrin by dead reckoning since leaving the cave, they were at last on his trail. Every time the trees opened a bit, Balthan expected to see their quarry. He kept checking his sack and his sword to make certain they were still secured to the saddle with him.

They were.

Jordan reined his horse to a clean stop. He waved the magician forward. Balthan worked his way around the horse line without dropping the rope or getting hopelessly tangled. He was getting better at this, but it took his complete concentration. He didn't see the narrow-eyed wolf grin on Jordan's face until they were abreast.

"Feast your eyes on that—" Jordan pointed through the trees.

Balthan leaned forward, squinting—he suspected that Jordan was farsighted, or else he was nearsighted—but there was something moving out there and with a little imagination he could believe it was an Inquisitor. "Is it him?"

Jordan's lips parted, his teeth were showing as he nodded. "It's him, all right. Come on." He heeled his horse back into the trees.

The magician blocked his way. "Aren't we going to run him down?"

"He'd hear us coming. He'd have time to use magic. I'm not taking chances. We'll get him while he sleeps, if not before."

Privately, Balthan thought the Inquisitor would be a more formidable opponent after dark, but there were many hours of sunlight left. He was willing to give Jordan's notions a chance for a while longer—although he found the idea of thundering across a meadow and trampling Lohgrin with a herd of horses as he tried to outrun them coldly satisfying—and said so.

"It takes a lot to make a horse run down a man. They'd rather veer around. It'd be more dangerous for us than him," Jordan countered. "I wish I'd remembered a bow. That'd take care of everything. He'd never know what hit him."

"I want him to know. I want him to see death coming for him."

Jordan nodded and chuckled to the horses to get them moving again. Balthan took his accustomed place at the end of the line. He allowed himself to think of the future, of bringing the scribe's sandalwood box to Annon in Britain City, and taking his place in the Resistance. Maybe he'd even get his Third Circle—

The Inquisitor picked his way along the banks of the stream that ran through the valley. If Jordan had been willing to risk magic, Lohgrin gave them ample opportunity for attack. The trek had taken its toll, as Jordan suspected it would. He wasn't moving fast and was resting often. Just about anytime, though, that Jordan found himself getting impatient, the Inquisitor would fuss with a glowing box. As soon as Jordan saw that glow, he'd find his patience fully restored.

Then the Inquisitor crossed the stream and started up the far side of the valley.

"Damn!" Jordan waved Balthan forward. "He's going someplace."

"Now or never, Jordan."

"Where could he be going? There's nothing there. Maybe he just feels exposed and wants to get back under cover."

"You had it right the first time. Whatever it is, we can't take chances. We can't wait. It's time to bring him down."

Jordan checked his scabbard. He didn't suggest digging out the mail shirts. Since they'd left the cave, he'd let them rust. Armor wasn't going to protect them from Lohgrin. He worked his way along the lead rope, freeing the seven extra horses.

"We'll drive them ahead of us. I'll try to cut him down. You come up behind me and take him if I don't—Balthan?"

The magician hadn't heard a word he'd said. He was half out of the saddle, squinting down the valley. Jordan followed Balthan's line of sight, and his jaw dropped. There was a horse loping through the meadow on the far side of the stream—and not just any horse, but an achingly familiar grey Valorian horse.

"Fugatore . . ." Jordan rubbed his eyes. The stallion was still there when he opened them.

Lohgrin was surprised, too. He stopped, retreated, and then began a panicked dash for the trees along the opposite crest.

"By the Eight, the Three, and the One—" Jordan's voice was awed and worshipful.

Balthan couldn't see, he kicked his horse forward, Jordan didn't try to stop him.

The Inquisitor had gotten himself halfway to cover, only to find himself trapped and doomed. Another horse burst into the valley directly in front of him. This second horse had a rider and that rider was unmistakably and unaccountably Squirt. Leaving the extra horses to fend for themselves, Jordan slapped his horse on the hindquarters and raced after Balthan.

"Is that what I think it is?" the magician called.

"None other."

A third horse rose on the crest and began the descent. Jordan needed a moment to recognize Seanna, and realize that she and Darrel were riding the wagon team. He couldn't begin to imagine the circumstances that created the drama unfolding on the other side of the stream. He only hoped that he and Balthan wouldn't be too late to join it.

Darrel had seen Fugatore at the same time he saw the Inquisitor. He hadn't seen his brother and couldn't see him now that Tom had achieved a bone-rattling gallop. The youth still held the halter rope, but it was useless. The huge horse was going where he wanted to go. At the moment that was straight at the Inquisitor, and that was fine with Darrel who, if the truth were ever known, was fully occupied staying on the horse. He knew that an ordinary horse would veer, but Tom wasn't an ordinary horse. Darrel wasn't certain that Bobbintom could stop, much less turn, before he ran himself to exhaustion.

Bobbintom did veer, but not because of the terrified man running in front of him with his black robes flapping like the wings of a flightless chicken. Tom veered because he heard the crack of a whip on his side, and that always meant he was supposed to veer away from the sound. Darrel heard Seanna wailing as Willie thundered by, but he didn't dare look back to see what she was doing. He did glance between Tom's ears to see more horses on the far side of the stream. He thought of the churls, and hoped that Tom wouldn't run out before he ran them down.

Seanna had her feet hooked in the girth of Willie's harness. She put the reins in her teeth and knotted her left hand as deeply as she could into his mane. She leaned against his neck to get all the length and power she could from the whip, herding Lohgrin, keeping him in front of Willie.

The Inquisitor made his last mistake: he looked back over

his shoulder. Seanna's whip caught him in the face. He went down screaming. Willie went over him. The screaming stopped.

Darrel heard the silence just before Tom entered the stream. It gladdened his heart: now for the churls.

"Ironhawk!"

He wished he had his sword. He'd lop Dench's ugly blond head—

That blond head, still intact, and now well behind Darrel's shoulder hadn't belonged to Dench. And the clumsy oaf trying to get out of Tom's way wasn't Ivo.

"Whoa! Whoa, Tom! Bobbintom—WHOA!"

Twenty-Three
ɤɤɤɤɤ

One by one the survivors gathered around Lohgrin's corpse. The Inquisitor's chest had been crushed, his spine broken, but he had died when Willie's iron-shod hooves bashed his skull—or so Balthan said as he rummaged the black robes for the precious sandalwood box. He was the only one willing to handle the body, and even blanched and bounded away when dozens of live black beetles swarmed out of a black sleeve. There were two boxes tied to Lohgrin's belt. Balthan removed the one bearing the familiar codex sigil of Virtue; he left the other undisturbed.

"He saw his death coming, but he didn't suffer."

Virtue and vengeance had been served. Balthan closed the Inquisitor's remaining eye and spread a handful of grass over the ruin of his face.

"Do you mean to just leave him here?" Seanna asked awkwardly. Teamsters were always on the move and, among Britannia's citizens, more likely to die alone. Not surprisingly, they had a high respect for burial rites. The Inquisitor had been an enemy while he lived, but in death the crimes of his spirit did not attach to his corpse. All the same, Seanna was not eager to haul his remains in her

285

wagon. "Shouldn't we tie him over a horse and haul him back to Hawksnest?"

That idea brought argument from the Hawson brothers, but Balthan interceded before matters got out of hand.

"We'll make a pyre and immolate him. By the time the wraith finds him, there won't be anything it can do except scatter the ashes."

"And follow us," Jordan added.

"Only if it believes we've got the scroll. I think I can fool it."

Glances were exchanged all around; finally Jordan nodded. "It's worth a try. It takes a lot of wood, you know, to turn flesh to ash. Have you thought of that?"

The magician had. "If I can make enough natural fire to burn through that other sandalwood box, I think the rest will take care of itself."

Darrel wanted to know: "Why don't you just set fire to the box?"

"Because I want to be a mile and an hour away when it explodes."

No one felt foolhardy enough to disagree. Jordan and Darrel offered to collect as much wood as Balthan thought he'd need. Seanna chose to take her team back to the wagon where Drum and Althea waited in ignorance. She said she'd harness the horses and try to backtrack more than the suggested mile from the meadow. Darrel would show his brother and Balthan the way.

"Don't worry about us," Jordan assured her. "We'll catch up by sundown."

Gathering wood for the pyre and rounding up the loose horses were done at the same time and both tasks were completed together. Jordan put one of the saddles the churls had stolen onto Fugatore's back and then put the stallion through his paces while Balthan arranged the pyre, stick by twig. The Valorian was stubborn and willful, but no match for his rider, and neither of them were as hard to satisfy as Balthan. Jordan and Fugatore were charging smoothly from one end of the meadow to the other, dispatching imaginary enemies, while the magician was still arranging the bottom layer of the pyre.

Darrel sat in the grass near Balthan but watching his brother. He hugged his knees and grinned. The dream had come true, after all: the Inquisitor was dead and Jordan was riding Fugatore. He wasn't thinking about Balthan at all when he caught a flash of light in the tail of his eye. Balthan was dragging the corpse onto the bed of greenwood and dried grass. But that didn't account for the flash. Darrel wandered over.

"Need help?"

"Grab his ankles and lift."

The youth was reluctant, but lifting the Inquisitor and swinging him onto the wood was no different from swinging bales of hay off the back of a wagon. He laughed at himself for being nervous, then looked directly at Balthan.

"What made the light?"

"What light?" the magician countered as he went on arranging wood and kindling.

"The light I saw a moment ago. The light between you and . . . the corpse."

"You're imagining things. Hand me that stick by your foot."

Darrel reached for the wood. It was about as long as his forearm and nicely balanced. Suddenly he felt reckless, he raised it to shoulder height. "You'd best *tell me about the light*, or I'll tell Jordan."

He hadn't been certain he could find that funny, commanding voice again, and when he did he knew he'd made a serious mistake. Balthan stiffened as he knelt over the corpse. If the magician had been a cat, the fur on his back would be standing on end. As it was, when his head began

to turn, Darrel expected Balthan's eyes to glow. They
didn't, but that didn't make it any easier to endure the
magician's scrutiny.

"You don't have to tell me about the light, if you don't
want to."

Balthan got to his feet, still silent, still staring. Jordan
and Fugatore were charging headlong down the meadow,
away from the pyre.

"What light anyway? It probably was my imagination. It
was my imagination, now that I think of it."

Balthan snared the youth's chin and held it steady while
he turned his head and peeked through the tail of his eye,
as he'd done back in the Hawksnest yard when he'd first
seen the Inquisitor.

"Not quite," he said slowly. "Not quite yet, but close."
He let go. "You don't quite know what you've done, do
you? You feel a little light-headed. Maybe your ears are
ringing just a bit. But you don't truly know, do you?"

Darrel retreated as he nodded his head. As soon as he
cleared the corpse he meant to throw himself to the ground
and roll out of danger. He forgot that Balthan was another
one who relied on quickness and agility rather than strength.
The magician latched on to Darrel's earlobe and twisted it
cruelly until Darrel was on his knees, staring at the sky.

"It's called Mother's Voice," Balthan explained calmly
to the gape-mouthed youth. "It's the simplest of spells.
Mothers, obviously, use it with their children, almost anyone can utter it if the stakes are high enough. You're no
one's mother, and I don't think you meant to raise the
stakes"—the youth used the little latitude he had to shake
his head: no he had not meant to raise the stakes, or otherwise offend his foster-brother—"I think it's safe to assume
that somewhere in your dung-filled skull, there hides a spark
of magic. A very small spark. A good sneeze might shoot
it out your nose"—he pinched and twisted until Darrel
yelped—"I warn you, Squirt, magicians don't hurl magic

at other magicians unless they're ready for war. You try
Mother's Voice on me again and you'll wish you'd never
been born.''

Balthan let go and Darrel collapsed in the grass, cupping
his hand over his throbbing ear. He'd heard everything the
magician had to say, but he hadn't heard it quite the way
Balthan meant it.

"I'm a *magician*! A magician like you and Annon!"

"Anabarces forfend! Annon is an ocean; I'm a lake
—you're spit in the wind."

"But I'm something!"

"Oh, aye—you're something. Go tell Jordan I'm just
about finished." Balthan knelt again and appeared completely preoccupied stuffing old, dried grass into the Inquisitor's sleeves.

Darrel got up. His earlobe felt like it had been punctured.
He retreated another step, fully cognizant that he had not
gotten a satisfactory answer to his original question. He
decided against asking it again. Jordan and Fugatore were
galloping up the meadow now; he ran out to intercept them.
Jordan noticed his brother's red and swollen ear, but he
could think of a dozen easy reasons why Balthan would
manhandle Darrel; none of them, of course, came close to
the truth. Jordan studied Balthan's handiwork.

"It took you this long to throw some twigs over him like
that?"

"The wraiths might practice necromancy. Some parts
must be burnt beyond recognition before the explosion. A
few sparks now and we'll be ready to go."

The magician began to twist a few stalks of the last
season's tall grass into a taper. He'd snapped a flame onto
the tip when they heard a woman's voice shouting their
names. Althea's head appeared over the hill crest, followed
by Drum who was leading one of Seanna's horses.

"Wait!"

Balthan dropped the taper and ground the flame beneath

his heel. His relief on seeing his sister alert and healthy was
lost within his annoyance at seeing her in the meadow.
"Thea, there's no reason for you to be here—"

Drum lifted her to the ground. The neck of her gown was
loose; it was apparent that the necklace was gone. "I wanted
to see for myself," she said, striding forward until she saw
the ruin Willie's hooves had made of Lohgrin's face. Her
hand rose to her throat, but she did not look away. "Seanna
said you're going to burn him."

The magician put his arm around his sister and tried,
unsuccessfully, to guide her back to the horse. "It's all over.
He's dead. You can put him out of your mind forever."

"Burn this with him." She poured the pearl and chain
into Balthan's hand.

He wasn't prepared for the weight and dropped it. There
was no magic in her voice, but it captured Balthan's attention just the same. He looked at her, and looked at Drum
looming protectively behind her, and got a foretaste of the
resistance he'd encounter if he tried to force his sister onto
any path she did not freely choose. Althea plucked the
cursed jewelry out of the grass and carried it to the Inquisitor's pyre. She held it above her head, then let it fall. It
struck his neck. She was satisfied and turned around. She
walked past Balthan, and Jordan, to Drum who lifted her
up again.

"Now I can forget about him."

"I warned you," Jordan whispered as Drum led the horse
toward the hillcrest. "She's going to do what she wants,
and what she wants is Drum."

"More's the pity," Balthan added. "It's changed her."

He made another taper. This time there were no interrup-
tions. When there were tongues of flame everywhere that
he wanted them, he climbed onto his horse. They caught up
with Drum and Althea and reached the wagon not long
before an explosion shook the air. They turned in time to
see a translucent sphere rise above the ridge. It shimmered a

moment, then disappeared. Moments later a second, louder explosion rumbled through the camp.

Althea smiled and, without saying a word, began preparing dinner.

More than two weeks had passed since Jordan and Balthan set off for Spiritwood. The fields of Hawksnest ripened under the midsummer sun. Field-workers hacked at the piles of brick-hard mud, filling in the flood trenches. Scaffolding continued to obscure the villa silhouette, but there were places where it had been removed and the freshly limed walls sparkled in the afternoon light. If one were careful where one looked, one might believe that Hawksnest was whole again, but, of course, it was not.

A solitary figure stood watch in the guard-porch as the sun passed overhead. His thoughts were far removed from his duties. He did not see the dust plume in the northwest until he could also discern the procession creating it: a red-and-gold teamster's wagon and a string of horses. He had a strong suspicion but waited until his sun-shielding hands framed a tall grey horse and its yellow-haired rider. Then he grabbed the mallet and struck the tocsin with all his might.

"A wagon! A red-and-gold teamster's wagon! And horses, and riders!" The guard malleted the bronze without mercy. His ears rang and he could not hear the words he shouted again and again: "Jordan! He's coming home! They're coming home! They're *all* coming home!"

The procession did not, however, climb the hill to Hawksnest, but went instead to Rosignel where the welcome would be smaller but more predictable. Messengers were dispatched from each villa. They met out of sight in the woods where they exchanged significant details and eliminated the unnecessary surprises before continuing to their respective destinations. Jordan, Balthan, and Darrel would attend a banquet in the cup hall at Hawksnest after sunset; Drum,

Althea, and Seanna—each for their own private reasons—would not.

Word of the celebration spread like fire through Hawksnest villa. In the kitchen the head cook scolded her drudges
and sent them scurrying into the pantries for sweets and
savories. In the upper rooms, Lady Barbara cried as she had
not allowed herself to cry while her sons were gone. Then
she dried her eyes. She selected a gown of the finest white
linen from her wardrobe and ordered her finest jewels
brought up from the treasure room. She also ordered the
furnace lit beneath the hypocaust and a huge bouquet harvested from her precious rose bushes. While the water was
heating, she went across the courtyard to the library. A tray
bearing the remnants of a picked-over meal sat outside the
locked door. Her lord husband had not left the room since
he entered it. His anguish was both real and great, but it
was not quite enough to make him starve. Lady Barbara did
not approve, she knocked loudly on the locked door.

"My lord! Your sons have returned." She hammered
twice more. "The Inquisitor is dead and they have found
some sort of box that will tell us what has happened to Lord
British. It is time to make yourself presentable and put an
end to this!" She walked away without waiting for his
response.

Erwald Lord Ironhawk lowered his hand from the draped
window overlooking the yard between the villa and the gate.
He had made up his mind before his wife came pounding.
He'd had two weeks to ponder and reflect, to read the Avatar's commentaries on Virtue, and to recover from the debili-
tation of Lohgrin's presence. He had not made up his mind
about his foster-son. Balthan Wanderson had gotten himself
mixed up in something much larger than himself, whether
as a pawn or a power, Erwald couldn't, wouldn't guess. He
was more confident about his natural sons. His efforts to
protect Jordan from his blood inheritance had failed, the berserkerang had been awakened. Perhaps he'd been foolish to

think strict education and discipline could bring the boy safely across the threshold to manhood—but a father had to try. The Avatar understood, and Jordan had survived the awakening, or so it seemed. Erwald would rescind his decision to keep Jordan at home, unnominated for his Virtue Quest, for another seven years. He could start this autumn, after the semi-annual Conclave, at the Shrine of Justice.

In his mind's eye, Erwald watched the smile appear on his son's face as he knelt down and offered his grateful thanks and appreciation.

As for the other son, Darrel—Perhaps something could still be salvaged there, although it was, again, of lesser importance now that Jordan was restored. If the boy simply showed an aptitude for something other than mess and mischief . . . But that could wait.

Lord Ironhawk left the library for the private room where his armiger and other attendants awaited him. He called for his most sumptuous garb: a formal dalmatic of black velvet with gold brocade, high boots of shiny dragonskin, the gem-studded medallion that enumerated his virtues, and the heavy, braided gold chain from which it was hung.

Tonight at sunset Erwald Lord Ironhawk would acknowledge that his eldest son was a man. He wished to look the part.

Preparations were being made at Rosignel, though they were necessarily on a smaller scale. Hugh came down from Hawksnest with a wagonload of necessities. He and Ventar waged war on Jordan's appearance. What little assistance Balthan needed he got from his sister. Darrel would be presentable if he were clean. Toward that end, he was last in the bath barrel and was still damp when the horses were brought up from the stable.

Althea set Balthan's floppy hat on his head and tamed the feathers as best she could.

"Your mind's still set?" Balthan asked. His voice didn't rise; he already knew the answer.

"I'm very happy with my decisions." She stood on her toes to kiss his cheek. "Drum and I will be very happy. I don't want magic. I don't want the peerage for myself or as a husband. I've had excitement and adventure—and I didn't like it. I want a garden and children. I don't care if my face and hands get wrinkled. I want a simple life, and Drum offers me that."

Balthan tried to look happy for her, but his smile was painfully forced. "If it's what you want," he said after an awkward moment in which he'd tried to embrace his little sister. She didn't belong to him anymore. If she belonged to anyone it was herself, or Drum, if that's what she chose, but it wasn't him. "I'll tell Ironhawk."

Fugatore had been brushed until his coat looked like pattern steel. His hooves had been oiled and there were ribbons in his mane and tail that would have matched Jordan's dalmatic—if Jordan had consented to wear formal clothing, which he hadn't. *I don't have to make myself grand just to tell my father that I'm leaving for Britain City in the morning.* Hugh and Ventar noted that Ironhawk had lost his title in his son's eyes, and didn't waste too much time arguing with Jordan about his clothes.

The Hawksnest tocsin began clanging almost as soon as they left Rosignel; it set their pace and brought them through the foregate single-file: Jordan, Balthan, and Darrel. The household, led by Lady Barbara and Lord Erwald, waited at the top of the granite steps in the yard as they had exactly a month earlier. The similarities ended there. Jordan met his father's stare as soon as they came through the gate and held it until the tocsin was quiet and he dismounted. Lord Ironhawk extended his arms, but Jordan stopped short of the steps.

"The Inquisitor, Lohgrin, is dead," he began without titles or other polite phrases. "There may be others, but for now the virtue of our family and estate is restored."

Lord Ironhawk explained to his assembled household that

Jordan's reserve must stem from his understanding that where filial responsibility was concerned, the end did not justify the means. Jordan had acted without permission from start to finish; it was right that he be apprehensive at his homecoming. Ironhawk explained all this to his household without noticing that Jordan was becoming stiffer with each word. He was not looking at his son when he said that the disobedience was forgiven and forgotten. Erwald paused to make it clear that he was not rewarding disobedience; nonetheless, he'd become convinced that it was time for Jordan to begin his Quest for Virtue. He had already had the parchment written up requesting the first mantra, the mantra of Justice, and would personally take them to Trinsic that midnight, after the moon gate opened.

Once again Erwald Lord Ironhawk extended his hands to his eldest son, fully expecting what he had seen earlier with his mind's eye to be played out on the steps before the entire household.

Jordan did not oblige. If it had not been for his mother and a few others who looked equally distraught, he would have marched back to Fugatore and ridden back to Rosignel. But for Lady Barbara's sake he came forward, although he would not kneel.

"I will not be able to accept your most-kind offer. The Inquisitor went to Spiritwood to find, and destroy, proof that Lord British did not simply disappear: he was overcome by evil wraiths. I cannot stop anyone else from going on a Virtue Quest while Lord British is imprisoned, but I know what it's like to be held prisoner. Tomorrow morning the three of us intend to start for Britain City. There are people there—magicians and Companions—waiting for us to join them. The only quest I'm interested in is the one to free Lord British. I won't be back until he is."

Ironhawk's arms fell slowly to his sides. "Your Virtue Quest—that's all you ever talked about. Going on your quest, becoming a peer in your own right." He studied the son who had become a stranger. ''What about Hawks-nest—?''

''Hawksnest is my home. There is nothing I want more than to live here and become its lord. But I've seen what happens when evil comes to a place that's not prepared for it. I would rather fight evil in its home than in mine.''

Jordan folded his arms in front of him. He didn't look around, but he'd heard Balthan and Darrel dismount while he and his father were speaking to each other. They stood together: mismatched, unlikely companions, but with them behind him, Jordan was ready for anything his father might say or do.

But Ironhawk did nothing. One didn't have to know what a dragon was thinking to know it was dangerous—and the silent, motionless trio facing him looked as dangerous and implacable as any dragon. If they wanted to go to Britain City—they could leave now as easily as in the morning, without his help or blessing. He was still Lord of Hawksnest, and they recognized that implicitly by staying at the bottom of the steps. He could stand and wait until they recognized it out loud.

Lady Barbara watched the standoff evolve. In time her husband and her eldest son might realize how much alike they were; in the meantime the household was getting restless and the food in the cup hall was being served to flies. She came midway down the steps and took them both in hand.

''Lord British can be saved tomorrow. Tonight we are all together and we *will* celebrate.''